THE ROAD
TO VINEGAR HILL

Harry McHugh

MERCIER PRESS

IRISH AMERICAN BOOK COMPANY (IABC)
Boulder, Colorado

The Arts Council
An Chomhairle Ealaíon

First published in 1989
by W H Allen, London
Published in 1998 by Mercier Press
PO Box 5 5 French Church Street Cork
Tel: (021) 275040; Fax: (021) 274969
e.mail: books@mercier.ie
16 Hume Street Dublin 2
Tel: (01) 661 5299; Fax: (01) 661 8583
e.mail: books@marino.ie

Trade enquiries to CMD Distribution
55A Spruce Avenue
Stillorgan Industrial Park
Blackrock County Dublin
Tel: (01) 294 2556; Fax: (01) 294 2564

© Harry McHugh, 1989
10 9 8 7 6 5 4 3 2 1
ISBN 1 85635 207 2
A CIP record for this title is available
from the British Library

Printed in Ireland by e-print Limited
105 Lagan Road Glasnevin Dublin 11
e.mail: books@e print.ie

Published in the US and Canada by
the Irish American Book Company,
6309 Monarch Park Place, Niwot,
Colorado, 80503
Tel: (303) 530-1352, (800) 452-7115
Fax: (303) 530-4488, (800) 401-9705

THE ROAD
TO VINEGAR HILL

Also by Harry McHugh

BITTER HARVEST

*To Angela, Nuala and
Terry*

Ireland in the 1790s

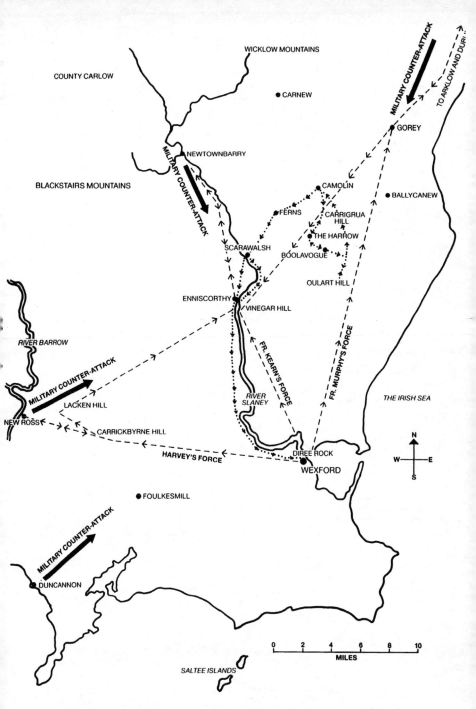

Wexford and the surrounding area in 1798

ONE

'Whilst not wishing to alarm you unduly,' said the Dean of Studies, 'Father Superior wishes me to inform you that we are all in imminent danger.'

He paused and stroked his thin, high-bridged nose between pinched fingers as he studied the students assembled in the refectory. Satisfied that he had their attention, he continued. 'Our beloved King Louis has been forced to fly from Paris. The mobs are hunting him everywhere.'

His audience gasped.

'Father Superior and the Professors agree that the mobs may attack this college at any moment. Therefore, we shall divide the clerical students between us and make our way in small parties to a House in the Low Countries. The lay students must leave within the hour and return to their homes, employing the utmost circumspection to avoid contact with the armed bands which are roaming the countryside. Any who are in difficulty may see me in my study. May God bless and protect you all!'

He hurried from the dais. The excitedly chattering students streamed from the refectory.

Except one. Conal O'Carran sat staring at the dais.

The Senior Prefect saw him. 'Budge yourself, boy!' Then, as Conal made no move, 'Do you hear me, boy? Hurry!'

Conal stared stupidly at him.

1

The Prefect, anxious to make his own arrangements, yet conscious of his duties, gripped his arm and pulled. 'What ails you? Did you not hear that we must hurry!'

'I don't know where to go.'

'You don't know . . . You are a lay student. You must go home.'

'Where is my home?'

The Prefect gasped. 'Where is . . ? Come, boy. You must see the Dean at once.'

Conal allowed himself to be rushed away, along the echoing stone corridors, up the winding stair and into the Dean's tower room.

The Dean clapped his hands with irritation. 'Haste!' he said. 'There is not time for delay.'

'Your pardon, Father,' said the Prefect. 'The boy, O'Carran, is in difficulty. I leave him with you.' And he fled.

'Quickly, boy! What difficulty?'

'I don't know where my home is, Father.' Tears leaped to his eyes and shamed him. He rubbed furiously with his knuckles.

'Tears, boy, tears! Are you a girl? What age are you?'

'Sixteen, Father.'

'And still lacking fortitude. For shame! Where do your parents live?'

All the nights that he had lain in the darkness longing for the father, mother and family he could not remember! He put his hands to his throat, but uselessly. Sobs burst from him.

'At such a time!' cried the Dean indignantly. He clapped his hands. 'Cease, boy! Cease, I command you!' He shook Conal's shoulder. 'Tell me about yourself. Quickly!'

But Conal was incapable of speech.

With sudden decision, 'Come! Father Superior. We must see Father Superior!'

Once again Conal was rushed; downstairs, along corridors, upstairs.

In the midst of the wild disorder of servants hastily packing boxes and trunks, Father Superior sat reading his

2

Office with imperturbable concentration. The Dean had to speak twice before he gained the old priest's attention.

'Your pardon for disturbing you, Father Superior. There is a difficulty. The boy, Conal O'Carran...'

The old man peered at them over thick, square-framed spectacles. 'Did we not agree, Father, that the boys should go. Surely any matter of discipline...'

'No, Father Superior. It is not a question of that. I assure you I am quite capable... No matter. There is urgency. The boy tells me that he does not know where his parents live. I cannot conceive...'

'What is your name, my son?' asked the old priest.

Conal blushed. Being addressed by this remote, almost mythical person tied his tongue.

'His name is Conal O'Carran, Father Superior,' said the Dean. 'I would suppose him to be Irish. Not French, certainly. I cannot obtain any sensible answers from him. At a time when speed is so essential and emotion least desirable...'

'O'Carran,' said Father Superior. 'O'Carran. Yes. I do believe... Patience, Father. The mob has not yet arrived.' And, with a twinkle, 'And martyrdom is an end vouchsafed only to the most worthy. O'Carran. How long have you been with us, my son?'

Conal was surprised to hear his own voice. 'For as long as I can remember, Your Reverence.'

'Aaah! Memory returns to me. Long before you came to us, Dean. A little boy, scarcely more than a babe, brought to us from Ireland by an ailing priest, a Father... No, the name has gone. No matter. He died within days. A fever. May the Blessings of God be on him now! But there was something... Ah yes. The fees paid by some advocate. And an address...'

He stood with surprising agility. 'Peace, my sons, peace!' he called to the bustling servants. 'No more, I beg of you for one small moment...'

They stood still, clutching books, papers, bundles. The Dean almost danced in agitation as he watched the old man calmly examining the room.

3

At last, 'The armoire!' said the old man. 'My sons, have you yet emptied the armoire?'

'Yes, Father Superior,' said one man. 'All the books and papers are most carefully packed in this box. I, myself, have done this.'

'I regret that your work must be undone, my son. Will you please unpack it.'

'Father Superior!' cried the Dean. 'With the utmost respect, I must object. Every moment is...'

'Is one step nearer to the tomb, my son,' said the old man soothingly. 'You and I have fewer steps left to us than this boy. Let us attempt to help him.'

A space was cleared on the table and the contents of the box piled on to it.

Father Superior surveyed them. 'Now, where?' he mused. He patted his lips with his fingertips. 'Something there was which would help me to remember. Ah, a book. Yes, a History of Ireland. Find that book.'

Everybody searched in fumbling haste, the servants merely adding to the confusion because they could not read. Conal found the book.

'Excellent, my son. That book holds a slip of paper.'

Conal found it inside the cover and read aloud, 'Brigadier Jacques O'Carran, rue Garridier, 27 bis, Paris.'

'Excellent!' exclaimed the old priest with delight. 'Your problem is solved. God go with you, my son.' He sat down and continued his Office.

The road to Paris was a mire of dirty snow and mud. A keen east wind drove half-frozen rain across a landscape apparently empty of all life except the wet, mud-plastered figure of Conal, as with his small bundle, he slopped, head-down, towards the distant capital. The few francs the Dean had given him might pay for food and lodging, but not for transport.

At first he simply trudged on in the direction they had pointed in when he left the College. His mind was empty. Life had always been the College routine, a rule as unquestionable as the seasons, leading to no known destination. It had been broken only by a few friendships

4

and by the private longing for those special, unknown people whom all others seemed to have, called Family. There were no females at the College and the word Mother meant a person indefinable but desirable, the nagging of a thought or an emotion just beyond memory, the consciousness of loss and lack.

Only when he had left the known vicinity of the College did he slowly begin to realise that routine was gone forever. Ahead lay mystery and a person named Brigadier Jacques O'Carran.

He passed through a village – a huddle of drab hovels. He could smell the smoke of fires, but did not see the inhabitants, did not know that they saw him – a wet, muddy vagrant, not worth the trouble of robbing.

On into the desolate, flat countryside along the ever-stretching ruts. The further he travelled the more bedraggled he became, and the safer because of it.

Afterwards, his memory was only of mud, rain and cold, of misery increased occasionally by the chill spattering from a passing coach or carriage, lessened occasionally by the coarse food and warm fire of some wayside tavern on whose straw he spent the night.

More people appeared, but he spoke only when necessary and was seldom addressed. He was merely one amongst the anonymous thousands tramping the roads of France from misery to misery. Occasionally soldiers appeared, usually self-appointed, their only uniform a few tatters of tricolour – dour, suspicious half-brigands, assuredly to be avoided. There were many of them at the gates of Paris, but they were looking for more profitable prey than a woebegone boy.

Paris meant scintillating light, gaiety, shops crammed with the riches of the world, all the wonders of art and learning. So he had always understood. The reality was drabness, filthy streets, boarded shops, furtive people and an atmosphere of depression, doubt and foreboding. Few people could even stop, much less answer his questions.

Suddenly he was caught up in a crowd all hurrying in

5

the same direction. There was gaiety and excitement in the air now, an atmosphere of holiday, smiling faces, chattering voices. This was much more in keeping with the reputed Paris and Conal went happily. The people were rough, dirty, ill-clad and, as the crowd thickened, sickeningly smelly. But by that time the press was too great to escape. Accent and patois made the chatter incomprehensible, but obviously they were on their way to an entertainment.

They spilled out to join the hundreds already gathered in a large square. Invisible forces compacted them into a solid mass around a large platform in the centre. Because of his height Conal was able to see clearly. On the platform was a peculiar erection like the framework of a high, narrow doorway. Several soldiers stood on the platform and many more surrounded it. From amongst these a woman in tattered finery was thrust on to the platform. The crowd screamed at her and flung stones and filth, despite the protesting bellows of the soldiers who received more of the missiles than the woman.

She was forced to her knees between the uprights and her head was thrust forward and clamped in position. Her face, dirty, tear-streaked and terror-filled, was thrust out towards Conal. Her mouth was open and she appeared to be screaming, although nothing could be heard above the wild shouts of the mob. Filled with unreasoning fear he struggled to get hrough the crowds. The woman needed help. Could nobody see her agony!

There was a flash.

He stared, unable to understand, deafened by the shrieks of the mob. A soldier stooped, then held aloft . . . What, in God's name, was that horror dangling from his bloody fist?

He swayed, fought his rebelling stomach, twisted madly and fought to escape. He was unaware of the people he wrestled and punched and of those who struck and clawed at him. At last he was free, out of the square, in an alley blessedly empty. He fell against a wall and vomited, shook and wept and vomited.

TWO

Elizabeth Street was one of the quieter, middle-class Dublin streets. Roadway and pavement were soundly and cleanly cobbled, with not even a wind-blown paper to mar them. A row of limes stood in each pavement as stiffly straight and meticulously placed as guardsmen. In the summer they shaded drawing-room windows, protecting curtains, carpets, furniture and ladies' complexions against the ravages of sunlight. Now, in March, their branches were black lace fluttering against the slate sky of late afternoon.

Each trim house, solid, double-fronted and approached by a flight of steps, gleamed with its shining windows, varnished paintwork and winking brass.

On the railings of number 24, a small brass plate discreetly advertised:

Select Academy
for the
Daughters of Gentlemen
Jeremiah Standish, Esq

Through the glass of a third-storey window, a girl's face could be seen from time to time peering anxiously into the street. Each time it reappeared it was more anxious than before. At last the girl flung up the window and protruded first her head, then her shoulders and finally as much of herself as she safely could. Quite forgetting that she wore only chemise and petticoats and oblivious of the cold March wind, she searched the empty street.

As she turned her head again, she saw, through the window of a house opposite, a snuffy old gentleman with his wig knocked awry in the excitement of trying to put on his spectacles. She stuck out her tongue at him, laughed at her own impudence, pulled in her head and slammed down the window.

Nuala Grogan was sixteen and this was her last day at the Academy. She had passed, more or less successfully, through the courses which custom and Jeremiah Standish, Esq considered to be essential equipment to arm a young lady when she went out into the drawing-rooms of the world to do battle for the most eligible of the available bachelors.

She turned and scowled at the trunk which she had been packing. On her bed was a heap of clothes – drab, durable, schoolgirl clothes. She stared at them in anger and frustration. Then, becoming aware of the chill, she shivered. Groaning, she fumbled amongst the heap and dragged out the dress which she had discarded forever only a few minutes before. She held it out at arms' length and viewed it with loathing. Discarding it had meant the end of school, the end of childhood, of stupid rules. To replace it, there should have been a choice of fashionable gowns – the beginning of Life, real, exciting Life, full of rapturous, undefined adventure. More immediate had been the prospect of appearing as a lady of the world before her drab schoolfellows.

Another shiver argued that the dress had at least one desirable quality and she struggled into it, tousling her hair as she did so. On the chest of drawers was a small, rippled mirror in which she examined her wavering reflection. She felt an odd satisfaction that her disordered appearance accorded with her feelings and she grimaced to make it more so.

'Oh, I'm so miserable, so disappointed,' she told herself. 'That hateful dressmaker! She promised!'

Her lower lip pushed tremulously forward, she blinked, then the tears spilled and she sobbed into an inadequate handkerchief.

She stopped in sudden horror at the thought that at any minute the other girls would be back from the dancing class and, instead of finding the young lady of fashion, as she had boasted, would see not only her usual drab self, but tears too. What pleasure that would give them! Nuala Grogan, known for her self-confidence and determination, the envy of them all, the girl who would conquer the ballrooms of Ireland, of England, even of Europe. For she would travel and see and experience everything. They all knew that. She had told them often enough. And that she meant to come back to Ireland and marry a fabulously rich, wonderfully handsome man with great estates. And she would keep a great court like an ancient Irish queen, thronged with nobles and ladies, minstrels, bards, huntsmen, men-at-arms, wolf-hounds, stables full of magnificent horses. And Life would be music, gaiety, excitement...

And her eyes were red and slightly swollen. To be seen like that! Hastily she dipped her hands into the jug, shivering at the coldness of the water, and dabbed her eyes. When she had dried them, she went again to the mirror and quickly combed her dark-brown hair.

'I must be calm. No. I must be angry. That's it! Angry! That dressmaker. It's all her fault. They know dressmakers are undependable.'

She examined her angry self, hoping it was sufficient armour, but doubting it. And the doubt brought the sting of tears again. Quickly she blinked them back. Perhaps even yet...

She ran to the window and peered out, but drew back as she saw Mrs Standish stump up the street behind a demure crocodile of girls.

A few moments later footsteps and tongues clattered up the stairs. The door was flung open and a plump, red-haired girl rushed panting into the room, then stopped abruptly.

'Oooh!' she cried, round-eyed. 'You haven't...'

'Don't say it!' cried Nuala. 'Don't dare say it, Sophie Watson!'

'But I... Nuala! Why? Oh!' She burst into tears and flopped on to her bed, her fat shoulders heaving.

'Oh, Sophie, for goodness sake. It's bad enough that the

9

– the damned dressmaker...'

Sophie sat up with a shriek. 'Nuala Grogan!' Fat hands pressed fat bosoms. 'You said a bad word!' She was delightedly shocked.

'Pooh! Damned, damned and... triple-damned dressmaker. There!' She twirled round the room. 'I'm grown up now. I can say what I like.'

Sophie wailed again.

'Sophie, for goodness sake. What is it now?'

'You're leaving me. I'll be all alone.'

Nuala sat and hugged her. 'Fiddlesticks! The place is full of girls.'

'But nobody like you, Nuala. That's what Monsieur Armand said, too, at the dancing class. Oh!' She sat up abruptly, eyes round with excitement, hands fluttering. 'Imagine, Nuala! Madame la Marquise! You know how Monsieur Armand is forever talking about Madame la Marquise this and Madame la Marquise that. Well, there is a real Marquise. Well, I mean there was. Because... Oh, it's too dreadful!'

'What is?'

'Oh, Nuala. The poor lady. They've – chopped – off – her head! Isn't that dreadful?'

'Who did?'

'Those dreadful people in Paris, with that awful big chopper machine. Poor Monsieur Armand. He was so sad. And Mrs Standish said, let it be a lesson to us because the Irish people would chop off the heads of all the ladies and gentlemen if we let them.'

'Which Irish people? You're Irish and I'm Irish.'

'I mean the Irish Irish, silly. We're English Irish. Anyway, Mrs Standish said we mustn't let them chop off our heads.'

'Stuff and nonsense! The common people here are not like the French. They're just dirty, dull and stupid, and they smell disgustingly.' She wrinkled her nose and shivered her shoulders. 'Anyway, nothing exciting ever happens here. I only wish it would.'

She jumped up and danced about, clapping her hands.

10

'No more school. I'm going home. No more school. No more...' She stopped, her eyes flashing. 'That dressmaker!' She clapped her fists together. 'When papa comes tomorrow, he shall drive straight to her and the coachman shall whip her and lash her and...'

There was a loud knock. Sophie sprang up and both flicked tidying hands over themselves.

'Come in!' Nuala called.

They sighed in relief when they saw Annie, the new maid, distinguished by raw, red face and hands.

'The missus says... Oh, God save us, no. I was near to making a hames of it again.'

She squeezed her eyes shut in concentration. 'Mr Standish presents his – er – com... something or other to yourself, I mean to Miss Grogan, and he wants to see you. No, he doesn't either. He says, er, well, whatever it was, sure, 'tis the same thing, isn't it? In the...' She opened her eyes with a bewildered look. 'Well, sure, I dunno. Herself says if 'tis before five o'clock 'tis the study, but after that 'tis the withdrawing-room. God, didn't I remember that well! But, sure I can't tell the time.' She finished with a wail of anguish.

The girls were by this time rolling on the beds, helpless with laughter.

'Ah, for the love of God, yous're no help to a poor girl at all!'

Nuala sat up and wiped her eyes. 'All right, Annie. Tell him I'll be down directly.'

A few moments later she went downstairs to find Annie standing apprehensively outside the study-cum-drawing-room.

Annie whispered, 'I remembered something I forgot, but thanks be to God, they don't know.' She thumped the door as if trying to smash it down, then opened it just wide enough to poke her head through. 'Here she is, missus... er... ma'am, I mean.' Then, meeting Mrs Standish's cold eye, 'Oh God, I forgot again.'

With an air of one determined to do the right thing, she flung open the door with such force that it crashed

11

against the wall and announced, 'Miss Grogan, sir and ma'am.' Then she relaxed and, with a wide grin, asked, 'Did I do it right that time?'

Mrs Standish raised patience-seeking eyes heavenward. Nuala tapped the girl on the shoulder. She, only then realising that she was blocking the doorway, scrambled to one side and raced off to the kitchen.

Mrs Standish, a large, angular woman, was sitting bolt upright beside a small fire, holding a frame with a small piece of embroidery in it. A long-departed pupil had left this behind and Mrs Standish, although never adding a stitch, used it to impress visitors with her industry and artistic ability.

Mr Standish was small and slight, in such contrast to his wife that, when they walked out together, rude boys shouted, 'Three ha'pence!' after them. He had a way of standing with his hands behind his back and his meagre chest pouted, and when he was about to speak he would rise on his toes, looking like a bantam-cock about to crow. On this occasion he was also standing on a small footstool behind the table.

'Aha, aha!' Miss Grogan, a chair!' He gestured grandiosely and Nuala sat.

'This is an occasion both sad and pleasant, my dear.'

'Oh, sad, 'Miah, sad,' his wife sniffed.

'Yes, yes,' he cut in, barely concealing his annoyance at being interrupted. 'But pleasant to think that the tender seedling which we have so assiduously nurtured will now be presented to the world as a newly-opened flower, carrying beauty and fragrance wherever it may go.' (This was plagiarised from the *Private Schools Journal*).

'You stand on the very threshold of life, Miss Grogan. Tomorrow you will step forth to meet the world. For this momentous day, Standish's Academy has equipped you well, as I hope you will tell those of your acquaintance with young daughters. I am confident that the world will greet you and welcome your many accomplishments.'

He paused, cleared his throat unnecessarily and asked, 'Is that not so, Miss Grogan?'

12

Nuala completely failed to understand the question.

Seeing this, he said, 'What I mean is that you will mingle with Society, the Best Society? There will be entertainment in your home? Your dear father is a wealthy landowner, is he not?'

'Yes, I suppose he is,' said Nuala, still puzzled. 'I have never thought about it.'

'Good, good, good!' He beamed with obvious relief. 'I am sure he has much to attend to on his estates – a most busy man, to be sure. Absent-mindedness would therefore be quite understandable.'

Nuala, feeling very stupid, shook her head. 'I'm sorry, Mr Standish, I don't understand.'

'Of course not, Miss Grogan. Why should you? Nothing at all to concern you. Just the small matter of fees for the past three terms. I have written several times, but, as you say, your father is a very busy man. However, when he comes in the morning...'

He was obviously worried.

Nuala felt heat in her face and cold in her back, and she was filled with a vague foreboding. She assumed annoyance to hide everything else and stood haughtily. 'I shall remind my papa in the morning, Mr Standish,' she said, with what she hoped was the correct tone of cold dignity.

'Of course, of course,' he said hastily. 'These small matters of business, Miss Grogan. Purely a question of keeping the books correct.'

THREE

The imposing front door of 27 rue Garridier stood open to what had obviously been a beautiful hallway, now splattered and littered. On the left, presumably the concierge's room, the door hung upon one hinge. In the room were dirt, human excreta, broken bottles, a smashed chair crouching in the corner and an air of uneasy brooding.

From above came wild singing and shouting which grew louder as Conal climbed. Through the actual door he could hear raucous male voices and shrill, half-hysterical female voices gabbling, singing and shouting, to the accompaniment of the clink and crash of glass, staggering footsteps, bumping furniture. And laughter rising above all. Laughter without humour, threaded with uncertainty and fear.

He stood in indecision, afraid to knock, afraid that somebody would come suddenly from the room, afraid to go without knowing, afraid of the streets outside. At last he forced himself to knock; but it was a tap that could not possibly penetrate that pandemonium. He knocked again, much louder than he had intended.

It was as if Death had struck. A deep, thick silence oozed breathlessly from the room. After a long pause the door was slowly opened. Eyes glared at him.

A uniformed man pushed a bold-eyed girl from his lap and leaped to his feet. He was large, red-faced, with shining black hair and fiercely curling moustaches. The fierceness was in his eyes also as he advanced, so that Conal shrank back.

'Stand still, boy!' The command, like the crack of a whip, held Conal rigid.

'And who, in the devil's name, might you be?'

Conal swallowed, licked his dry lips and strove to speak.

'Answer! Who sent you here?'

Conal shook his head. 'Nobody,' he croaked. 'I came ... That is to say I am seeking ... Brigadier Jacques O'Carran, if it please you, sir.'

'Sir, sir!' roared the man. 'What the hell kind of title is that to use! Citizen, boy. Citizen! A title fit for any man.' He turned to the room and shouted, 'What say you, my friends?'

They yelled their indignant approval.

14

The man swung round again. 'Your name, boy. Quickly!'

'Sir, that is to say, citizen, my name is O'Carran. Conal O'Carran.'

The fierceness changed to surprise, then to anxiety. 'Conal O'Carran!' he shouted and he leaped and embraced him. But as he gripped him he whispered urgently. 'Say nothing about me or about yourself. Deny nothing I say.'

He whirled round to the crowd, smiling broadly. 'Citizens all, give welcome to my young cousin, Conal O'Carran, who is newcome from Ireland to join the glorious Revolution!'

Relief swept through the room like a breeze through the desert. Fears and doubts were veiled and clamour returned. He was surrounded and welcomed boisterously.

The bold-eyed girl squirmed through to him. Hands on hips, she eyed him saucily. 'He is a handsome one, this, Citizen Soldier. Tiens! He is big and strong; and will be bigger and stronger yet. Such black curls! And the eyes, so blue, so marvellously blue!'

She grabbed his hair with both hands, pulled down his head and kissed him full on the lips. Conal's deep blush and wide-eyed amazement brought laughter from them all.

Then he was hauled to the table and given a mug of wine to drink to the new, the glorious France. He drank and his mug was refilled. Again he drank, and again, and again. It was impossible to empty the mug, impossible to speak or to do anything but grin and drink. Numbness spread over his face, sight became blurred, voices were . . .

'Rouse up! D'ye hear me. Rouse up!'

Through his stupor Conal became vaguely aware of being shaken, pummelled, slapped; but there was no pain, no real sensation. Then a torrent of cold water sluiced his head and chest. Gasping, he opened his eyes; and shut them immediately against the stab of the light. There was a thudding ache behind his forehead, his mouth was

15

rough and dry, his tongue thick and leathery.

'Drink this.'

Through cautiously opened lids he saw a wavering glass. He shook his head and immediately groaned with the pain of it.

'Forgive me, sir,' he mumbled. 'I am very ill.'

'Ill!' A roar of laughter almost split his skull. 'You've got a bellyful of bad wine, imbecile. Drink!'

In spite of the appalling smell and worse taste, Conal drank. His gorge rose and he jerked upright. A bowl appeared magically just where it was needed. He sank back again, weak but relieved.

'Here. Clean yourself.' A cloth fell across his face. Gratefully he dried his hair and face.

'Now this.'

The towel was whisked away and a cup of hot black coffee was thrust into his trembling hands. He gulped and felt life and awareness slowly seeping back.

He looked up. The man, no longer fierce, but grinning at him, was straddling a chair. He thrust out his hand and said, 'Welcome, cousin.'

Conal took his hand and, at this first touch of kinship, tears sprang to his eyes. 'Are we truly cousins?'

He shrugged. 'The same name, a certain likeness . . . Evidently my father, may the good God give him rest, thought it so.'

'Can you tell me then who I am, my parents, where they live?'

His cousin stared at him in amazement. 'You don't know these things?'

Conal shook his head and swallowed a rising sob. 'I know no other life than that of the college. There they could tell me only that I had been brought by a sick priest who died before he could tell them anything but my name. I remember him vaguely, and a ship and a storm. Before that only a . . . How can I describe it? A feeling of the loss of . . . of everything.' The tears would not be held back. He covered his face with his hands, shamed by his unmanly behaviour.

But the hands which took his and drew them from his face were warm and sympathetic. 'Come, lad. If I can help you, I will. Why did you come here?'

When Conal had explained, he said, 'First, then, I am Captain Jacques O'Carran. My father was the Brigadier. They murdered him in ninety-one.' He drew in his breath sharply and clenched his fists. 'God, to lay my hands on the butchers!' His expression changed immediately to anxiety. 'And that is something. There is danger here. I was a soldier of King Louis. I do not know if I am suspect. Those who were here last night – not all are to be trusted. I intended leaving Paris today. But now...' He laughed, partly from frustration, partly from ironic amusement. 'Now I have a family unexpectedly. What am I to do with you?'

'All I want is that you should tell me how to find my family.'

'But I know nothing, save that my grandfather came from Ireland. There was trouble of some kind, about estates, I think. My father was still a boy when his father died. There has been no connection with Ireland... Ah, but wait. My father spoke of the O'Carrans of Duncarran. That will be the name of the place. Oh, and more – it is in the north of Ireland. And... yes, it cannot be far from Belfast, because I recall my father saying that it was from there my grandfather sailed. But more...' He shrugged and shook his head.

'I shall go there and find my family.'

'Ah, wait, wait, lad. How long has it been? Eleven, twelve years? And nothing in all that time. Who knows what has happened?'

'But I must go. I must!'

'Believe me, Conal, I have great sympathy for you, but it would be madness, I think. Far better for you to stay with me. No matter who rules France, they will need soldiers and young men of education to train as officers. I will make sure that you get that training.' He jumped up. 'So, my young cousin, quickly. We must be off.'

Conal stood and said diffidently, 'Please do not think

17

me ungrateful, but I cannot go with you. All my life I have dreamed of finding my family. I could never remain contented here without at least knowing what has happened to them.'

'But wisdom, Conal, wisdom,' said the Captain. Then he gave a roar of laughter. 'I sound exactly as my father did when speaking to me.' He raised his arms and let them fall in resignation. 'If you must, then you must. Come, I can at least help you safely on your way.'

The crunch and creak and rattle of the stage-coach which had brought Conal from Belfast died away and left him in dripping silence. He stood in a grey, twenty-yard circle of misty rain which encompassed the rutted road ahead and behind, and wild hillsides clothed in tough grass, sodden bracken and gorse. On his right a shallow, muddy, rock-strewn stream wound down the hillside. This, the coachman had said, was the road to Duncarran. It was the place he had asked for, though God alone knew why anybody would want to go there. It was the only place of that name, and he couldn't hold the coach all day.

He examined the streaming track dubiously. His family surely lived in a large house, perhaps even a castle. But there was nothing to be gained but added wetness by standing in the penetrating rain. The nearest habitation was a long way behind and an unknown distance ahead. Perhaps, by climbing the track, he could at least find shelter and information.

As he climbed the way became steeper and rougher, pitted with muddy holes, scarred with outcroppings of sharp rock. Water poured down it, penetrating his boots and squelching coldly between his toes. Mud spattered him to the thighs.

He stopped frequently to look about, but all he could see was rain-swept wilderness, so that at last he became convinced that he had been misdirected and was about to turn back when he glimpsed a slight movement. He stared, then moved a little nearer and realised that he was looking at a man who stood in what at first seemed to be

18

the mouth of a cave.

'Good day,' he said.

There was no reply, so he walked a little closer, but warily. He saw then that the man was standing in the doorway of a hovel built into the side of the hill so as to be almost part of it – the walls appearing as low, steep banks, the weed-grown thatch of turf merging into the wilderness.

The man's stooped posture disguised his considerable height. His face was long, thin and sunken-cheeked. He wore a ragged tailcoat, equally ragged shirt and breeches, and nothing else.

'Let you come in out of that, for God's sake,' said the man, and he disappeared into the dark interior.

Conal walked cautiously to the opening. There was no door and no windows. He peered in. A turf fire burned in the centre of the floor with a number of boulders set around it. Although the air was thick with smoke which the hole in the earth failed to disperse, he could examine the small space. A heap of bracken and heather lay in one corner with a few ragged coverings. In another corner were a pile of turf and a small heap of potatoes. Beside the fire was a three-legged iron pot and a bottle with a broken neck. He could see nothing else.

The man stood at the far side of the fire and watched him with sardonic amusement. 'My house does not please your honour.'

Conal blushed. 'Pardon me. It is simply that I . . .'

The man looked puzzled. 'You have an odd accent. Where are you from?'

'From France.'

The man's face lit with joy. 'From France!' he shouted as he almost ran to the doorway and pulled Conal in. 'Think of that, now. From the land of Liberty itself! Sit down, sit down there and get yourself warmed and dried off.' He pushed Conal down on to one of the boulders. 'Well, now,' he said, as he sat on another, 'didn't this turn out a great day after all. Tell me all.'

'I don't understand. Tell you what?'

'Of the Revolution, of course. Of the destruction of the damned landlords. Of the freedom of the people. Of all the joy that must be abroad in that blessed land. Of what brings you from it to this God-forgotten country. Aye, that first of all.'

'I am seeking a place called Duncarran.'

'Duncarran! Sure that's just up the hill a piece. But what, in the name of God, would you be wanting in that midden?'

'I am looking for my home.'

The man stared in amazement. 'Your home? Did you not say you were a Frenchman?'

He listened to Conal's explanation with a pitying expression, slowly shaking his head. There was silence, then he said, 'Well, you poor misfortunate devil. To think of you leaving the glories of France and travelling all that long, hard way for nothing. God help you, lad, you've neither home nor family here.'

'Then where? Please tell me. Is there another place of the same name?'

'I'll tell you what I can. I don't know all the ins and outs of it, because I'm only living in this place myself these past couple of years. But the way I've heard it, the O'Carrans were a great family in these parts in the long ago. They had great lands and they lived in the castle which was called Duncarran. It's just an old ruin now in the Besant Park below. But the way people tell it, the last of the family died out some ten or a dozen years back. A time of famine it was, I think, with the cholera after it that killed many of the people. What is certain is that there's nobody of the name of O'Carran living in these parts now.'

Through all the misery of the college there had been the hope that he would find again the warmth he had lost; now he stared at desolation.

After a long silence he said, 'But the lands. There must be lands belonging to me.'

'God help your ignorance. Did they teach you nothing of the history of Ireland in that fine French college? Well then, I'm a schoolmaster myself. What do you think of

20

that! My name is Michael Canahan and this palatial place is my home and my school.'

Conal thought that the man was either a liar or mad. 'A school must have . . .' he began.

'A school must have a teacher!' said Canahan with fierce pride. 'A teacher is a treasury of knowledge. And I am that. I have travelled the country and studied long and hard, even with the great schoolmasters of Munster. And my scholars get from me all that you got in your fine French college. Oh, maybe not the Philosophy and Theology, if you ever got that far, but the Irish with all its poetry and history, Latin, Greek, Mathematics, Geography, aye and even the English tongue, God blast it! Oh, a great centre of learning I have here!' He laughed bitterly. 'And what fine rewards there are in it for the schoolmaster. This snug house, these fine clothes, a few potatoes to eat, and the constant risk of imprisonment if I'm caught teaching my school. Because the Irish must be kept ignorant, dirty, landless, downtrodden and hungry. The English law says so; and the English sword is always ready to enforce the English law. And that's the beginning of your Irish education, Conal O'Carran.'

Conal stood up uneasily. The man's passion, the wild gleam in his eyes, made him sure that he was mad, and that he had best get out of this place. 'Er, thank you for the warmth and shelter, sir,' he said. 'I will walk on to Duncarran.'

'And what are you thinking to find there? A city? A tidy little town? For God's sake, what they call Duncarran now is eight or ten hovels squatting round a muck-heap. I have told you, you have no home there or anywhere. Any lands the O'Carrans had were stolen by the English long ago and their home smashed to ruins. One of Cromwell's lackeys named Besant got the most of the land around here. He built himself a great house away below there in what they call the Besant Park, with a big wall round it. But there's been nobody living there for years. Like so many more of the blasted landlords, the Besants are over in England, living high off the hog on the rents they get

21

from Ireland.'

'Who lives in the house?'

'Nobody. The place lies empty. There's cattle and sheep grazing in the park, but that's all.'

'Then that is where I shall go. The land and anything on it rightfully belongs to me. I shall live in the house and I shall go to the courts and demand my rights.'

'Have you not listened to me at all? The courts are English. They say the lands belong to the Besants. You go anywhere near them and you'll end up either in gaol or transported as a slave to the Indies. Get it into your head, you have no lands, no home, no rights, not even the right to be alive! That's what it means to be Irish in this enlightened age!'

'But I am not a peasant,' said Conal indignantly. 'I am an educated man.'

'Aye, maybe. And that's another thing. When your father sent you to France to be educated, he broke the law, so you dare not ever tell anybody in authority about your education.'

'But what am I to do? Where can I go?'

'Well, first off, you'd best sit down again.'

Conal hesitated.

'For the love of God, what else can you do? You've no place at all to go, unless it's back to France.'

Conal stared blankly at him, blinded by the realisation that there was literally no place for him in the whole world. He sank slowly on to the stone.

'France!' he said, and he shuddered. 'You think it a joyful land. It's nothing but fear and hate and bloodshed and misery. I wouldn't go back, even if I had the money; and I have none.'

Canahan eyed him in silence for a few moments, then said, 'There could be a way for you to get back your lands.'

Conal's head jerked up in sudden hope.

'What are you, a Frenchman or an Irishman?'

'I am Irish, of course.'

'Oh, by blood, by birth. But could you live as an Irishman is forced to live these days – in hardship and poverty and oppression?'

'What has that to do with me regaining my lands?'

'Everything!' Canahan spat the word. 'What real right have you to Irish land if you are not truly an Irishman? To prove that you are, you would need to live like one. So I'll make you an offer. I've to go away from here from time to time. Where and why is no matter to you at the present. But it leaves my scholars without a teacher and they fall back in their studies. My offer is that you live here with me and help with the school. But, before you answer, let me tell you that you'll get no pay and little food beyond potatoes and maybe a sup of buttermilk and an odd bit of oatcake. No fine clothes, no better roof over you than this. If you can live like that, then maybe you'll be ready for me to tell you.'

Conal jumped up in anger. 'You're playing games with me!'

'Oh, no game, boy. No game at all. And no great things to come just from wishing. You'll need to face up to it. You thought you'd only to come back, after years away, to pick up wealth with no bother at all. Now, when you find that there's no crock of gold at the end of the rainbow, you think you've met hardship. Well, let me tell you, you've yet to meet true hardship. When you do, and when you can face up to it and live with it, then maybe you'll be ready for me to tell you what you want to know. So, there's for you. My offer still holds. What's your answer?'

Conal clenched his fists and stared about in helpless bewilderment. He saw a dirty, ragged, barefoot peasant and the squalor in which he lived.

'You don't understand,' he said. 'After years of hope ... To come to this!' His face twisted with disgust. He shuddered. 'I couldn't. I won't.'

'Then you may go to hell for all I care!'

Conal shrank back from the venom. Then frustration and anger rose in him. To be spoken to thus by a tattered misery of a man!

'And to hell with you too!' he shouted.

He ran from the cabin. Forgetting to stoop, he banged his head against the low lintel. As he scrambled back down the track, tears of pain mingled with tears of disappointment for the world of promise which had crumbled to nothingness.

FOUR

Although her father was not due until noon, Nuala was ready long before that time. Her trunk stood by the hall door. She had sat on it for a few minutes, then stood and paced the hall. Then, although she knew it was unnecessary, she had climbed the stairs to search her room for anything forgotten. And whilst she was there, there had been no harm in looking out of the window to see if the dressmaker were coming. Then downstairs again to find that the hands of the clock had scarcely moved.

All around the life of the Academy went on: the muffled buzz of lessons, the plinking of a spinet, a sudden agonised cry of 'No, ladies, no!' from Mr Standish, and the overriding sounds from Annie in the kitchen, where she was either singing a tender-love song or being horribly done to death. Nuala felt as if she were nowhere, suspended between school and the world.

Frequently she opened the door and searched the street. If the dressmaker came, she intended changing immediately and going out to parade her finery in the bright, blowy morning. But as time crept on it became more and more difficult to cling to hope. Disappointment urged tears, but angry pride forbade them.

Just before twelve the whole school assembled,

giggling and chattering, to see her off. Her friends surrounded her and reminded her for the hundredth time that they would be friends all their lives, they would write to each other regularly, meet in Dublin during the season, attend each other's weddings and the many subsequent christenings and, presumably, finish by burying each other. The other older girls, whilst envying Nuala's coming freedom, whispered loud comments on the absence of the vaunted finery. Her friends, greatly shocked, echoed these unkind comments to Nuala, just in case she hadn't heard them. And in between, to ensure that everybody appreciated their importance in the proceedings, they continually embraced and kissed her and topped their enjoyment with orgies of tears.

In the background huddled a covey of threadbare teachers. In the foreground, facing the door, stood Mr and Mrs Standish. Annie stood clutching the doorknob, proudly conscious of her supreme importance and ready to wrench the door off its hinges.

Nuala smiled until her face ached and thought them all a pack of tiresome fools.

Promptly at twelve sounded the clatter and rattle of a coach on the cobbles. A pause, during which Annie quivered with anticipation. A loud rapping of the knocker.

'Open!' crowed Mr Standish, and the door was flung back with a crash.

A poorly-dressed footman stood on the step. In the street stood a heavy, old coach and four from whose window a fat, red face peered anxiously. The footman ran back to open the door and Mr Aloysius Grogan hopped out, nimbly enough for all his stoutness, waddled across the pavement, up the steps and into the hall. A performance watched with great interest by the whole assembly.

Standish stepped forward, hand outstretched. 'This is an honour, sir, which the Academy appreciates deeply.'

Grogan snatched the hand, then flung it away. 'Yes, yes. Charmed. Great hurry. Where's m'daughter?'

25

He peered at the mass of young femininity. Nuala moved, but Standish waved her back and took Grogan by the arm.

'First a little refreshment, sir. This way, if you please.'

'Great hurry,' said Grogan, allowing himself to be drawn. 'Perhaps one small glass. An occasion. Appreciate that. But must be off.'

Standish led him into the study and closed the door carefully. Pouring something vaguely vinous from a decanter, he offered it and a plate of seed-cake.

Grogan's eyes bulged at the cake. 'Good God; I mean – er – wine alone, I think. Your health, sir.' The liquid vanished in a gulp, followed by a grimace which decried Standish's cellar. 'Now, must be off, Mr, er –'

'There is just one small matter, Mr Grogan, which I am sure has escaped your memory.'

'Eh, eh? What's that?' Grogan glared down at him.

'The, er, well, the question of fees for the past –' He jumped back from the roar which erupted from Grogan.

'Money, is it! Dunning me, are you, begad! Well, I'm damned! Damn if I ain't!' An even greater roar, this time of laughter, burst from him. 'Send a bill, schoolmarm. Send a bill along with the rest of the tradesmen!'

Flinging open the door he waddled out into the hall. 'Where's my Nuala?' he shouted.

She moved towards him, but he waved her to the front door.

'Say all your g'byes, m'dear. Fowler! Trunk aboard? Good, good, good. Lively now, girl. Get all the kissing and weeping done. Must be off.'

Nuala was surrounded, kissed and wept upon, but almost immediately she was plucked from the throng and hurried towards the door.

Standish, in a last, despairing effort, rushed forward but was swamped by the tide of weeping, tittering, chattering girls which surged out into the street after Nuala and her father.

Nuala, too bewildered to make any protest, was not so much assisted as thrown into the coach, and her father was just climbing in after her when the coachman called, 'Bums, sir!'

Grogan whirled to face a seedy-looking individual who was approaching with one hand held behind his back.

'Mr Aloysius Grogan, sir?' he asked. Then he gaped in fright at the mouth of the big pistol which Grogan had whipped out.

Grogan jumped into the coach, shouting, 'Drive on, Tim!' and away they went, whip cracking, sparks flying from the wheels as they battered the cobbles, the coach swaying dangerously.

Nuala threw an astonished glance at her father, then jumped up to kneel on the seat and peer through the back window. The whole Academy and many of the neighbours were staring after them, and at the same time trying to listen to the conversation between Standish, wringing anguished hands, and the seedy-looking man.

When they turned the corner, she turned to her father. He was lolling back, mopping his face with a large crimson handkerchief.

'Dished 'em!' he exulted. 'Double-dished 'em!'

'Papa!' she said sharply. 'Who was that man?'

'Fowler, m'dear. Footman. Thundering idiot, but does as he's told.'

'You know quite well I mean the other man, the one you threatened.'

'Hoity, toity, miss! Save that tone for your husband.'

'I am disgraced!' she cried angrily. 'I have a right to know.'

'Watch your tongue, young lady. Want none of y'tantrums.'

Nuala played a trump card. 'Mama will be furious when I tell her.'

That deflated him. With an agonised expression, he begged, 'Oh, Lord, now, m'dear. No need to upset your dear mama. She don't have to be told.'

Nuala was about to answer when she noticed the street they were in. 'Stop, Tim, stop!' she shouted. 'We're going the wrong way.'

27

But Tim could not hear.

'Papa, tell him to stop. We must visit the dressmaker. The wretched creature did not deliver my new clothes.' At the same time she leaned out of the window and called, 'Tim, stop!'

The coach began to slow, but Grogan poked his head out of the other window and shouted, 'Pay no attention. Drive on!'

'But this is not the way to the dressmaker's.'

'It's the quickest way out of this damned town, and we're taking it.'

'But, papa, you simply do not understand. I need lots of new clothes and bonnets and shoes and boots and, oh, all sorts of things. We must turn back.'

'Sit down, girl. We're not going back.'

'But why, why, why?' she wailed, drumming her heels on the floor. 'I cannot possibly go home looking like this. I haven't a decent rag to my back.'

'Hogs, dogs and divils!' His roar shocked her into silence. He waggled a fat finger in her face. 'No more tantrums!' He sat back, breathing heavily.

She began to sob.

'Roaring hobs of hell! Can't a man get away from weeping women? Oh, dammit to hell, you've got to know sooner or later, I suppose. The woman didn't deliver, 'cause she thought she wouldn't be paid. And she wouldn't. I've no money.'

'But you could send it to her.'

'Don't you understand plain English, girl! I'm stony. Got no money.'

'Then why don't you get some?'

'Why don't I . . . What, in the name of Jupiter, are you . . . Where would I get money?'

'Well, I suppose, from wherever one does get money.'

'What'd they teach you in that school? Where the blazes d'you think money comes from?'

She shrugged. 'Well, I know gentlefolk have money, and common folk don't, so they're poor. But we're gentlefolk, so we must have money.' She was triumphantly sure of her logic.

He gaped at her, shaking his head in amazement, unable to speak for a moment. Then, 'I knew it. I knew it. I knew it! Told your mama. Listen? Not she. Now, expensive education, and you know nothing. Nothing!'

With her face flaming with anger, she began, 'Ladies are not supposed...'

'Quiet!' he roared. 'Listen. Learn something. Not alone don't I have money, I owe it. Everywhere.' He pointed a quivering finger at her. 'Feller outside school. Trying to serve a writ. On me! Begad, that was a close one.'

She stared with complete incomprehension. 'What is a writ?'

'For debt. They'd have clapped me in the Marshalsea. The debtors' prison. Me!'

Looking both puzzled and horrified, she said, 'I just don't understand. I have always thought we were gentlefolk and rich.'

'Rich! Me? Rich! Entertaining, keeping a decent cellar, big house, servants, horses, paying for your education. Away flies the cash. How the devil do they expect a gentleman to live these days?'

'Well, where do people get money?'

'From their land, of course.'

Triumph again: 'Then why don't you get it from your land?'

'Oooh!' he groaned, clutching his head.

'I am truly trying to understand. This is very serious for me. My whole life is in ruins!' She wept again.

He fumbled in his pocket, pulled out a flask and took a gulp of brandy. Then, after expelling a long breath, he put away the flask and turned to her with exaggerated patience.

'I don't own the land. Not a scrap of it. Sir Julius Besant owns it; and he employs poor devils like me to collect his rents. Now d'you understand?'

'Then why don't you get some land of your own?'

'Hellfire, girl. Land costs money.'

'It's all most confusing. If you can only get money from

29

having land, and you must have money to get land...
How did Sir Julius Besant get the money to buy land in
the first place?'

'Didn't. Lucky dog. Inherited it from his father.'

'But somebody...'

'Oh, Gawd! Are we going to have this all the way
home? If you must know, the first Besant took the land
from the Irish who had it before.'

'You mean he stole it?' she asked, horrified.

'For God's sake, girl! Don't say things like that. Don't
ever repeat it. Not to anyone. Enough for you to know
that I'm flat, up to m'ears in debt. So forget all your fancy
notions. We're poor – dog, dirty poor!'

He pulled out the flask and took another, longer drink.
Thus anaesthetised, he settled back with a handkerchief
over his face and was soon snoring.

The old coach rumbled on. The discomfort of the worn,
lumpy and musty upholstery, the constant sway and
lurch on the sagging springs, the bumping of the wheels
in and out of ruts and potholes, and the growing chill and
damp all added to her misery.

Vaguely, through the dirty window, she was aware
that they had left the city. Impressive stone walls lined
the road, protecting the estates of the wealthy. These
gradually gave way to open fields with cattle grazing the
sparse spring grass. Here and there, crouching on tiny
patches by the roadside, were small, windowless mud
cabins with smoke seeping through holes in the thatches.
From some, white-faced spindly children, barefoot and
clad in tatters, emerged and tried to run alongside, claws
beseeching halfpence.

But beggars were so common that they had no
meaning for her. They clattered through a wretched
village where many of these beggarlings waved, cried and
implored. Their very numbers forced her to look at them,
to see them; and she realised that she was seeing poverty.
She shrank from the window. Then the odd thought
came that to these children she represented wealth. Her
despised clothes were far removed from their tatters. For

30

a moment she was comforted that the old, rattletrap coach shielded her from their misery. But then came an appalling thought. Her father had said they were poor. Did that mean that she would soon be forced to exist as they did? To be reduced to rags, hunger and filth in a stinking hovel?

So frightening was the thought that she turned to her father for reassurance. She shook him to try to waken him, but got only grunts and snuffles as he heaved his fat into a more comfortable position.

She stared again through the window and saw only a deepening atmosphere of poverty, misery, decay and brooding sadness, like that of a garret where some forgotten hero is dying of senility and neglect. The ruin of a round-tower standing on a hill beside the broken arches of a cannon-shattered abbey might have been a tombstone. And the epitaph: The Glory Has Departed.

The weather changed after they lunched at an inn. The sky clouded and rain hid the countryside. The windows misted and showed only water-drops, forever forming, hesitating, then wriggling to join others in erratic streams. Having only the choice between watching these, or listening to her father's snores, whilst being constantly battered by the lurching coach, Nuala sank deeper into misery.

In the late afternoon Grogan woke abruptly on the top note of a prodigious snore and returned to reality with grunts, coughs, mouthings and hawkings in his throat. He trumpeted into his handkerchief, then pulled out his flask.

'Still here, eh, m'dear,' he grunted. Then, after a long drink, 'Aah! That's better.'

He pulled out a large watch and peered at it with eyes screwed almost to extinction in his fat cheeks. 'H'm. Thought it was later than that.'

He pulled down the window, letting in a cold, wet blast, and called, 'Fowler! Damn you. Where are you man? Fowler!'

The footman came riding alongside, dripping rain from

every corner of his face and frame.

'Ride on to Mr Rowley's place,' Grogan ordered. 'My compliments and I'd like to beg hospitality for the night. Tell him to expect us about six. Off you go, man!'

The urging was quite unnecessary. Fowler kicked his horse and battered off into the wet gloom.

Grogan slammed the window. 'Brrr! Miserable weather, m'dear. No matter. Won't be long getting to Rowley's. Fine house. Stayed there last night. Excellent claret. Brandy very good too. Oh, and wonderful table.' He smacked his lips.

The prospect of warmth, comfort and food cheered Nuala a little, but she made no reply. The feared reality of poverty had faded, become almost dream-like in the numbed state of her mind after the hours of worry, monotony and discomfort.

Some time after dusk had fallen on what promised to be a stormy night, the coach stopped before a pair of large gates. There came the sound of voices, then Fowler opened the door and cold, wet wind rushed in. The dim carriage lights revealed his saturated wretchedness.

'What the devil's wrong?' Grogan demanded.

'She won't open the gate, sir.'

'Who the blazes is *she*?'

'The old bitch... beg pardon, Miss. The old woman at the lodge. She's as deaf as a post, and she says there's nobody at home.'

'Still the blasted idiot, Fowler! Can't do the smallest thing right. Clear to hell out of my way!'

With some difficulty in the cramped interior, Grogan bundled himself into a cloak. Helped by Fowler, he clambered down to the streaming road, bowing his head as the full sweep of rain caught him. He splashed across to the gates. Inside was a small lodge in the lighted doorway of which stood a beshawled old woman.

'Hi, you, woman!' he shouted.

'All gone away! Nobody at home!' she screamed.

'Open these blasted gates, you old fool!'

'Nobody at home!'

'I'm Mr Grogan. Mr Aloysius Grogan of Ballyna!'

'All gone away!'

He coaxed and cajoled, shouted and raved, shook the gates, offered bribes, cursed the weather and the woman, shouted for Rowley. But still he received the same parrot-like answer, until at last even he realised that she was simply repeating what she had been told to say.

'Blast you, Rowley!' he shouted. 'I'll call you out for this!'

He waded back to the coach. 'Duffin!'

'Sir?' came a cry of suffering from the bundle on the box.

'Drive straight home!'

'Ah, God, Mr Grogan, sir. Will you just look at the weather that's in it. And the blackness of the night. Sure I can't see the road under the horses' hoofs, sir.'

'Did you hear me, Duffin?' Grogan yelled.

'I did, of course, your honour. But, in the name of God, sir. The danger of it. And Brian O'Sullivan has been out on this road some of these nights.'

'Then by God, I hope he tries to stop us. I'll blast him to tatters. Drive, man, and drive fast!'

He climbed back into the coach and flung off his sopping cloak.

'You cannot possibly mean that we are to travel all night,' Nuala wailed.

'You can cease your whining, chit! God, if ever a man was tormented!' He gulped at his flask, which he had replenished at every stop. 'Blast their eyes! Think I'm done, do they? I'll show 'em.'

FIVE

Conal stumbled down the track, tears and the rain in his face almost blinding him. His clothes were saturated and muddy. His feet squelched in cold wetness and ached from constant impact with sharp rocks. He went without conscious thought of direction, fleeing from Canahan and Duncarran, from disappointment, from nothingness.

Water streamed under his feet. He slipped on a muddy slope, lost his footing, fell backwards and slid bodily for several yards. He lay then with the rain beating down on him and cold, muddy water sluicing down his back, in the uttermost depths of misery. He was so wet and cold that it seemed further wet and cold could make no difference. Indeed there was a perverse satisfaction in being as low bodily as he was mentally. It was of not the least concern to anybody in the world that he was as exposed to the elements as any rock or bush. If he lay there and died, nobody would know or care. There was simply nothing, nobody, nowhere. In the past, nursing some wrong in a hidden corner or under his blankets, there had always been the consolation that it could not last, that one day he would return to people who would love and care. That hope was utterly destroyed. Conal O'Carran was no more than a twig at the mercy of a stream in spate.

At the same time as this thought came, he slipped again. He struggled involuntarily against it, turned on all fours and scrambled to his feet. It was easier to move than to stand still, so he went on down the track in the fading daylight.

When he reached the road he hesitated. To his left it led back and back with Paris at the end of it. And then? Drabness, blood, horror and all-pervading dread were inextricably associated in his mind with the name of the city. There was warmth in the thought of his cousin. But to become a mercenary. To fight. For what? He had never been eager to fight anybody, not even those school bullies who had forced it on him and invariably beaten him. Even then he had felt no real enmity. They had been merely part of the general misery.

He thought, 'One fights one's enemies.' And at once he thought of Canahan. *There* was somebody he would delight in fighting and beating. But there were others. Those who had robbed his family and him of their rightful possessions. It was them he should fight. But who were they? Where were they?

There was no answer, yet he turned right and splashed down the darkening road.

The hillside on his right gradually lowered until it reached road level; and there he found the great wall. Massively built of stone blocks, it stood eight feet high, reaching inwards across the land, stretching ahead down the road. Behind it stood huge trees whose bare branches stretched over the road, swaying against a sky still darkened by rain-clouds, but faintly lightened by a sliver of moon.

A gust shook the branches, showering him with chilly drops. He looked up angrily to curse the tree, then stopped at the thought: 'This is the Besant Park. This tree is rightfully mine – every branch, twig and leaf of it. And all the trees and every blade of grass and every grain of soil for miles around. It was to this I should have come home. Yet a thieving usurper has parcelled up my lands and can live in luxury on the rents from them. He has cut off an immense tract here and built a wall round it. Hundreds of acres of my good land imprisoned and left to rot!'

He fumbled at the rough surface, found a handhold, a foothold, scrambled up and reached an overhanging branch which helped him to the top. He dropped into sodden undergrowth on the other side.

Everywhere about him were great trees, their tops sweeping the fitful moonlight, their feet hidden in a tangled mass of dripping undergrowth. He forced his way through the matted growth until at last he emerged into billowing parkland. Here was a riot of tough grass, thistles and gorse. Good land, where corn should have stood thick and golden in the harvest time, left as a playground for rabbits and foxes.

As he walked on, he saw in the distance the glisten of moonlight on the wet roofs of a great house. He came to a wild shrubbery, a madhouse for evergreens, which surrounded what had once been lawns and gardens. He fought his way against branches which whipped and caught and slimed his face with their wet leaves and emerged on to a great expanse of overgrown lawn which swept up to the terrace on which the enormous pile stood.

Like an unruly beard on the face of a man long sick, the weeds flourished riotously on the once-smooth turf of the lawn, swarmed the steps, the balustrades and the leprous statuary and, squirming through the cracks in the flagstones, covered the terrace in a rank mat.

He was looking up at one end of the house: a great cliff of smooth stone soaring to four storeys, patterned with shutters bleached bone-white. Moving to the left, he came to the front. A wide gravel drive, after winding from the road through the woods and park, had once swept to the foot of the thirty-yard-wide flight of steps; but it was smothered now. There was a massive front door through which a coach could have passed with ease and, on either side of it, window after blank, shuttered window, and rows and tiers of windows above them. And the colossal pile stank of slow death.

The maddening thought was that it had been built with money which was rightly his. So little did the usurper think of his victims that he could rob them, squander a great part of his loot in building this enormous house, then leave it like a rotting tomb.

It stood in utter silence – cold, aloof, contemptuous, mocking him.

'You damned tyrant!' he shouted.

And back came the mocking echo. Then silence – blank,

sphinx-like silence.

Had he possessed the power, he would have blasted the place to the winds in an instant. But there it stood – secure, impregnable, despising his weakness, as the Bastille had stood above the people of Paris.

But the Bastille had been stormed and smashed, its gates flung wide and all its hollowness exposed. This was no invulnerable fortress either. He ran and foolishly threw himself against the impervious bulk of the front door. The shock sobered him. The greatest might could be made to yield to subtlety. Moving swiftly along the terrace, he tried shutter after shutter, working along the front, down the side and through an archway into the stable-yard. There he found a small window, shutterless, broken and easily opened.

Climbing through, he found himself in almost total darkness, but cautious groping revealed that he was in a small pantry and he found a door facing the window. This led him into a black passage. With hands scraping the walls, he moved cautiously along. There were many doors, but those which were unlocked opened only on to blackness. He came to a passage at right angles. A few yards along this he stumbled up three steps, fell against a door which swung before him and stumbled out into a vast hall.

Faint, watery moonlight filtering through the dirty fanlight and cracks in the shutters revealed a great tiled space with an immense staircase sweeping from its centre halfway to the first floor, then dividing into two upsweeping curves to a balcony.

The place echoed to the clacking of his heels on the tiles. He opened a door and passed into a vast emptiness – a salon so long and so high that he could see neither the far end nor the ceiling. Through the cracks in the many shutters fingers of weak moonlight revealed the silent vacancy.

A pistol jabbed into his back. His heart jerked painfully.

'Sweetly now, my bucko. Turn and go back the way you came.'

His heart was thumping and seemed to fill his throat, making him struggle for breath. As he slowly turned, the man turned with him, prodding him with the pistol. Crossing the hall, Conal thought of the dark passage ahead; hope of escape! But a light appeared behind him from an unshuttered lantern.

'Step sweetly now, cully. Be tricksy and I'll blast your backbone through your belly.'

They went on, turned right at the cross-passage and stopped at a door.

'Open it!'

Conal was thrust into a small room aglow with the light and heat of a blazing fire. A large, black riding-cloak covered the window. On the floor in front of the fire was a heap of straw and beside it two bottles and some bread and meat on a handkerchief.

'Turn now, cully!'

His captor was a young man of medium height, but powerfully built, very wide and thick in the shoulders. He wore his flaming red hair in a pigtail, tied with a black ribbon. His face was coarse and fleshy, his eyes shone with what could have been merriment or cruelty. His dress, though crumpled and muddy, was dandified. He stood, legs astride, toying with a long-barrelled pistol as he examined Conal.

'Well now, here's a quare-looking young cockerel. What brings you sneaking into my house?'

The worst effects of Conal's fright had worn off and the cosiness of the room comforted him.

'Speak up, blast your eyes!'

The rasping voice made Conal start and, oddly, reminded him of school and so roused resentment. He spoke in bravado and without thought: 'It is not your house, but mine by right!'

The man stared, then laughed. 'Your house! I beg your honour's pardon, your young lordship.' He rubbed his jaw with the pistol barrel as he eyed Conal from top to toe. 'Begod, you're a sorry-looking lad. Were you rolling in a ditch or what?' His tone changed abruptly to a rasp.

'Get over into that corner. I'll listen while I eat.'

Conal backed into the corner. The man sat on the straw, put the pistol within easy reach and began to eat. 'Right,' he said, through a mouthful of bread and meat, 'Talk!'

Conal had not eaten since early morning, and, although he had been increasingly aware of hunger, his other worries had predominated. Now the sight of food was torture.

'You have enough food for two. Give me some and I'll tell you my story.'

The man's mouth gaped, displaying half-chewed food. Then he began to chuckle and almost choked. He grabbed a bottle, swigged and swallowed. 'Stap me guts! You've still a squawk left in you, then.' He laughed. 'Well, a man's the better for a touch of boldness. Eat away then, cully. But no tricks!'

Conal was still eating, feeling vigour swelling in him from the warmth and food, when the man finished and wiped his mouth with the back of his hand. He lit the stub of a clay pipe and lolled back, puffing contentedly.

When he had finished everything, Conal told his story.

'So,' the man said, 'you're running away. Like a frightened little doxie, you're running away and not knowing even where you're running!'

Conal was indignant. 'I am not running away. I don't know . . .' His voice tailed away and he spread his hands helplessly.

'You don't know what to do.'

Conal nodded weakly.

'Well, I'm no kin of lords or titles. Not that I know of, that is. My dam was Moll Sullivan of Stoneybatter and she 'gat me in the way of business. At the age of five I was kicked into a Dublin gutter to live or starve as pleased me. I can neither read nor write. But there's many in Ireland know Brian O'Sullivan and have cause to know. I'll wager my breeches' seat there's scarce a gent in the four kingdoms set out on a journey without wondering will he meet with me and be the poorer for it. Whilst the rest whine and starve, I fight. These poxy squires and landlords rob the poor, and I rob them. Maybe the nubbing cheat'll get me in the end of all; but begod they'll pay me plenty and give me a merry life before I'm done. They'll not make O'Sullivan run!'

'I was not running! I tell you, I didn't know what to do. I still don't know what I shall do.'

'You don't? And you the lad with all the fine learning and the respected name before the people. Well then, let me tell you this. If 'twas me, I'd say to myself, "Here are my people being robbed, starved and tortured by a pack of bloodsucking bastards. They've stolen the lands from me and them, murdered the one half of them and put laws on the rest the way they're worse than slaves. 'Tis a thing to make the devils of Hell feel shame, and 'tis past time something was done about it!" And, by bloody boots, I'd up then and rouse the people behind me and I'd not rest 'til every one of Cromwell's bastards was dead or driven from Ireland.'

Conal was fascinated. 'How would you go about it?'

'How? You ask me that! You're lately from France and you ask me that! Blister me! You must have been a bloody poor scholar.'

He spat in disgust and struggled to his feet, then paused. 'Maybe 'twas little of use they taught you. Here then is something I learned as a chiseller scarce high enough to snatch a spud from a cart. A man is born into this world with two legs to stand on, two arms to fight with, a bit of something in his skull to think with, and damn the thing else. If he can't or won't use those to get what he wants, then he'd best lie down and die. And be damned to him!'

He stuck the pistol into his belt, threw the cloak round his shoulders, paused and listened. Rain was driving loudly against the shutters.

'That's a Hell-sent night; but there's work to be done, please God.'

He paused at the door and grimaced. 'If you're ever wanting a general for your army, remember Brian

40

O'Sullivan.' Then he was gone.

Conal woke cold and stiff. The fire was out and pale morning light seeped into the room. Through a crack in the shutter he peered at the chill morning. The rain had stopped, but there was wetness everywhere. He saw with surprise that the land he had thought wasted actually supported a large number of cattle. A half-formulated plan for staying in the house had to be revised.

He opened the window and shutters, climbed out into the damp cold and crept away. When he reached the shrubbery, he felt relief and was immediately self-scornful for sneaking through his own land afraid of some early cowherd.

He thought of O'Sullivan's words: 'Two legs to stand on, two arms to fight with, a bit of something in his skull...' O'Sullivan would be in no doubt what to do next. His cousin was another who would act without hesitation. There was a similarity between the two men – an emanation of power, a contempt for circumstances, a complete confidence in themselves which was as much a part of them as their limbs. Hatefully, the thought came that Canahan, too, had force and power. 'Which was why you ran from him!' He could almost hear O'Sullivan's contempt.

When he came to the wall he climbed it and dropped into the road. A short distance away, towards Duncarran, large gate-piers obviously guarded the entrance. In front was a strip of fenced pasture with bog stretching away beyond it; to the right the wall stretched away to a bend in the road.

Which way? Away from Duncarran, that was sure. Why? 'Becase you're afraid of meeting Canahan,' came the reply. But he comforted himself that he needed food and help and that there must be a town in the opposite direction where he could find both. He set off towards the bend in the road.

As he rounded it, he saw, almost a hundred yards away, two slide-cars blocking the way. The horses munched the wayside grass. The drivers stopped their chat and, to his embarrassment, watched his approach in silence.

He had covered no more than half the distance when there came the thudding of hoofs and loud shouts: 'Clear the road! Clear the road! Way for Mr Grogan!' It was Fowler.

The drivers hastily tugged at their reins, but before the slow animals could respond Fowler was on them.

He had ridden all night, his clothes were sodden, he was cold, hungry and tired and he had been the constant victim of Grogan's bad temper. If the coach were hindered, he would be blamed. Bu this anxiety was exceeded by the prospect of venting his ill-humour. He charged, lashing with his crop at men and horses. This caused greater confusion. One man attempted to reason with him, but he was past reason. Shouting, almost screaming with frustration, he lashed at the man, drove his horse against him and knocked him into the ditch.

Conal watched in astonishment and shock. His first reaction was to remain apart, but when he saw the man knocked into the ditch and in danger of being trampled, he ran forward to help. Fowler, however, saw Conal as another victim and lashed at him. It was only a glancing blow on his shoulder, but it stung. It was the culmination of all his disappointment and misery, and Fowler the personification. He dodged under the next swing, grabbed Fowler's arm and pulled. The result was quite unexpected by both. Fowler, caught off balance, was flung sprawling on to the road. The ease of it delighted Conal. Without thought or hesitation he flung himself on the prostrate footman and fought for possession of the crop. He felt real pleasure as Fowler struggled, inviting his punches, and it seemed so easy to tear the crop from the frantic fingers. Pressing his palm against the man's face, he pushed himself to his feet. Then he lashed the squirming body. Fowler's screams, terrified and pain-filled, were like soothing music.

The carters were cheering wildly at first, but then the man who had been knocked into the ditch tried to stop Conal. But he was deaf and brushed aside the hand which

42

hindered his pleasure. The interference was, however, enough to enable Fowler to scramble to his feet. He rushed at Conal, who saw only a hated face apparently gliding slowly, inviting towards him. He dropped the crop, swung his arm and felt his fist smash delightfully into the face. Fowler was knocked into the muddy ditch.

At that moment the coach arrived and Grogan's purple face jutted from the window.

'What in hell's wrong now? Clear the road, you blasted louts, or I'll set a whip to your backsides!'

The men pulled frantically at their horses. Conal, still trembling with excitement, waited. Fowler, bedraggled and muddy, crawled from the ditch and Grogan's eyes stood out like knobs.

'Screaming devils of Hell! What've you been up to, you bloody idiot?'

'That fellow attacked me, Mr Grogan, sir,' whined Fowler.

Conal strode to the coach and made a slight bow. 'I presume this fellow is your servant, sir. Permit me to inform you that he made a vicious attack on all of us, and for that reason I found it necessary to thrash him.'

Grogan's face became so suffused that it seemed as if the blood must spurt through the skin. He flung open the door, barely missing Conal, and lurched down to the road.

'I'll have the hide ripped from your back for this, you blackguard!'

Conal's face flamed. He swung his arm, but was stopped by a cry from the coach.

Nuala was standing in the doorway, her hands pressed against her mouth. Her face was pale and strained after her restless night, her eyes wide with fear. Conal stared, conscious of womanhood for the first time in his life. Forgetting everything but the necessity of reassuring her, he bowed.

'Your servant, Miss. My humblest apologies that you have been forced to witness a scene of such ugliness. I beg you to believe that it was not of my seeking.'

The fear left her eyes. She stared down, first in surprise, then with interest. A moment ago he had seemed wild and dangerous. Now she saw a young man, very untidy and mud-spattered, but very handsome, with curling black hair and very blue eyes; a young man who was obviously, and very pleasantly, hers to command. She saw and enjoyed his frank admiration. Suddenly aware of the situation again, she blushed; then screamed in fear, 'No, papa, no!'

'Get away from there, you dog!'

Conal whirled to find himself menaced by a cocked pistol in Grogan's shaking hand.

'Get away from that coach!' yelled Grogan frenziedly.

Nuala jumped down and stood between them.

'Papa, please, papa!' she begged, her hand on his raised arm. Then she turned to Conal: 'Oh, go, please go before something dreadful happens!'

Conal was trying to still his trembling knees, the temptation to run checked only by the certainty that he would be shot if he did. Hoping desperately that he appeared dignified to her, he bowed. 'Very well, Miss. Once again my humble apologies to *you*.' He walked away, trying to hold up his head in spite of the involuntary cringing of his back from the expected bullet.

'By Jupiter, you'll pay for this!'

Grogan's yell gave him hope that the pistol had been put away.

SIX

When they were back in the coach, Grogan turned angrily to Nuala. 'Fitted you better to've stayed in the coach. Nice behaviour for a young girl – interfering in a brawl.'

44

'I was afraid you would shoot him.'

'In Hell's name, what else would a man do when attacked by a murderous lout?'

'He didn't attack you.'

'Dammit, don't argue with me, chit!' His roar made the horses jump in their harness. 'Did they teach you no better manners for all I paid 'em? You saw the lout raise his fist to me. You heard what Fowler said.'

'Fowler attacked them first.'

'Well, I'm damned. Damn, if I ain't!' He flung hat and wig on to the opposite seat and clawed his bristles in fury.

Nuala stared and then began to giggle.

'What now?' he gasped.

'I have never seen a gentleman without his wig,' she said, still giggling. 'You do look droll.'

Grogan fell back, closed his eyes, clenched his fists and gasped for air and patience. Then he sat up, deliberately calm.

'Right. Right. Stuck in that school, you know nothing of the world. Then listen to me. Get it stuck in your silly little mind. Those same people you're snivelling about'd be happy as Larry slitting our throats! Happened in France already. Millions of 'em against a handful of us. Taught from their cradles to hate us. Let 'em get out of hand and – massacre! Every last one of us. So, drive 'em down. Drive 'em down and keep 'em down!'

Her automatic impulse to reply was quelled by renewed consciousness of cold, weariness and hunger and she sank back listlessly.

After a time they branched to the right and climbed a slight rise to their drive entrance, marked by two stone pillars, each topped by an irregular lump – the weathered remains of a local mason's conception of lions. The gates, long fallen, lay rusting amongst nettles. The weed-grown drive wriggled in a shallow S through ragged shrubbery and emerged between scrubby lawns at the front door.

If a dozen blind apprentices had come from unfinished Babel and, starting without plans and from different points, had begun to build, they would have produced something like Ballyna House. It was a sprawling, up and down, asymmetrical, unstyled accident. There was an abundance of windows, many bricked-in, odd in shape and size, appearing not to have been painted since they lost their first coats and so warped and shrunken as to have left cracks and gaps to make whistles for the wind. The many broken panes had been stuffed with paper and old rags, and the few remaining were coated in grime.

Twenty or thirty ragged and dirty men, women and children clustered round the step – the beggars who were to be found at every large house, haunting the kitchen doors and fighting with the dogs for the scraps. The dogs were there too, all sizes, breeds and mixtures running in and around the crowd, barking in discordant excitement. The chorus yelled sycophantic welcomes when the coach arrived. Jostling, pushing and pulling they fought for places near the coach in the hope of pence.

The butler, barefoot and wearing a ragged and ill-assorted livery, hurried down the steps, accompanied by three tattered footmen. These carried staves with which they hacked a passage to the coach-door which Grogan was vainly trying to open by pushing at it and thumping any head which came within reach. At last the footmen managed to get it open. Grogan hopped out, snatched one of the staves and charged the mob, whose members fled nimbly out of range, enjoying the diversion.

'Get to Hell out of this, you stinking scum, before I set the dogs after you!' he yelled.

As the dogs were equally enjoying the game, this caused great amusement; and Grogan, realising this, flung the stick at them.

In the meantime, Nuala alighted and went straight to her room.

Grogan thumped the butler. 'Get in, man. Get in. Claret, you fool, and plenty of it.'

''Tis ready for you, sir,' whined the butler, running ahead of him.

Grogan stumped into the morning-room, dingy and overcrowded with battered furniture, but blessed with a blazing log fire. He threw off his hat and overcoat and lowered himself with a groan into an armchair before the fire.

'Felix! Where in hell are you, man?' Then, as the butler sidled in, 'Damn you for a fool. Pour out!'

The butler poured a generous glass of mulled claret from a jug which stood steaming on the hearth. Grogan received it reverently, raised it slowly, savouring the fragrant steam, took two or three sips, swallowed a deep draught, then said, 'Aah!' He thrust out his booted legs. 'Pull 'em off!'

Felix tugged off the muddy boots and substituted violently embroidered slippers which had been warming.

Grogan drank again, stretched his legs to the blaze and wriggled his toes. 'Tell the kitchen to hurry. Ham, eggs, beefsteak, coffee. Plenty of everything. Piping hot! Fetch pens, ink and paper and that fool, Fowler.'

Like an anxious ghost, Felix flickered from the room and, after a few moments, reappeared in the same fashion with the writing materials.

'The meal will be with you any minute now, sir.'

'Where's Fowler?'

'Well, sure, he's ... er ... he asks you to excuse him, sir. He's in his bed, complaining that he's very ill, sir.'

Grogan laughed, a deep, almost contented rumble emanating from his claret-comforted belly. 'Tell the poor, sick man – three minutes, else I'll be there to kick him from his bloody sick-bed!'

He emptied his glass, refilled it and struggled from the chair. He sat at the table where Felix had set out the materials, picked up a quill and, without bothering to test its point, dashed off, with many flourishes and blots:

Ballyna House
March 179-

To the Rt Honnbl Sir Maxwell Leering JP

Honnerd and Dear Sir Maxwell
   My respectfull Complements and my Dear Wife as

well to you and yr grately honnered Lady Mother and addressing you as Madjustrate I beg leave to tell you that there is Murder & Bloodshed & Villany rampent in our Peacefull Co. to wit in the person of a most fritefull lowt he made a vicious attak on my footman Fowler, the bearer of this presence and a blasted fool but onely doing his lawfull duty and an attemt to strike me with my young and innersent daughter Nuala just new from school in Dublin who I hope to have the honour to meet you soon looking on.

Trusting confidentially in you to arrest and punish this Rascal and with my best respexts and my Dear Wife to you and Your Honnerd Lady Mother

I have the honner to be Sir

Yr Most Humble Servant Sir

Aloysius Grogan

Fowler and breakfast arrived together, the footman looking as miserable as a wet cat and coughing hopefully. He was chased off with the letter and Grogan was just beginning his meal when his wife sailed in like a man o' war surging to the attack.

Georgina Grogan had been blonde and pretty in her youth, but her features were blurred now by sagging flesh under her eyes, around her mouth and about her jaw-line and neck. Heavily applied cosmetics served only to emphasise the coarsened skin.

'You monster!' she greeted him. 'You outrageous monster! Cease, cease, cease!' She flapped both hands at him to stop his opening mouth. 'Do not, I pray you, make matters worse by attempting to excuse your monstrous behaviour. My baby! My poor, dear Nuala! Come home in rags! Like any beggar child!' Breath shot from her nostrils in what, if she had not been a lady, could only have been called a snort.

Grogan took advantage of it to mutter, 'Now, now, Georgina, m'dear.'

'Don't you Georgina me, sir! Don't you dear me, sir! Don't dare, you, you ... How can I express! Bailiffs at the doors, at the very doors of the Academy. In full sight. One can imagine the letters those girls will send home. The shame of it!'

She inhaled deeply and again he tried to defend himself. 'Think o' me. Might've been dragged off to the Marshalsea.'

'Precisely! The wonder is you didn't insist upon it to make our disgrace complete. And to insult Mr Rowley. The poor, dear gentleman. To think of you being turned from his gate in that fashion. Aloysius!' she exclaimed in a rising scream. 'To what dreadful state have you brought us? Why did I ever leave my dear parents? Why did I not go long ago to my dear brother?'

Her loud wail of anguish as she flung herself on to a sofa prevented her from hearing Aloysius mutter, 'Because he was too blasted miserly to have you.'

SEVEN

Conal walked away from the coach, striving to appear dignified, though fearful of a bullet. Confidence grew with distance, then leaped as he heard the coach move off. He looked back to see it disappearing round the corner. The carters were staring after him, but he walked on.

He was filled with new and exciting emotions. Primarily there was astonishment and pride that he had defeated Fowler. At the College there had been occasional pummels, but nothing like this. He had actually defeated a grown man. He rubbed his sore knuckles and laughed with pleasure at the memory of the punch he had given.

49

He congratulated himself that he had acted as a man should act, as Brian O'Sullivan would have acted.

Mixed with this were thoughts of the girl. At the College there had been no females, not even as servants. They had been rarely seen, and then only at a distance. He could not recall ever having spoken to one. The girl in the Captain's apartment had been the first in his experience. He blushed as he remembered the smell and touch of her – a memory which he had recalled many times since with a mixture of excitement, pleasure and guilt. But the girl he had just met was quite different. He could not define the difference except that whilst the French girl had excited him, she had also frightened, even repelled him; whereas this girl had excited him in a way which was happy and hopeful. With surprise he realised that hitherto 'people' had meant males. Now the word, and indeed life itself, had acquired a new and delightful dimension.

He heard hoofs behind him and he turned to see one carter disappearing round the corner and the other running towards him, holding the head of his trotting horse with the slide-car bouncing behind it.

'Run!' the man shouted. 'Get off the road!'

Conal stood and stared.

'They'll be after us,' the man panted as he came up. 'Run, for God's sake!'

'Who'll be after us?'

'The constables. Leering's men. Grogan will report you and there'll be men on horses hunting us.'

Conal's previous confidence now began to wane, but he objected, 'I have no cause to run.'

'No cause! Oh, God! And you after beating a landlord's man. They'll skin you for that, if they get you. And they'll have me for destroying their lovely road with a slide-car.' He grabbed Conal's arm. 'For the love of God, run!'

Against his will, but infected by the man's fear, Conal ran with him.

The great wall stretched endlessly on their right; on the left a vastness of empty bog. They ran on, the man glancing fearfully back from time to time. At last they reached the place where the wall turned and ran up the hillside.

The man stopped.'We'll go up here now. Lift the back of the car to hide the tracks.'

The car, consisting only of two long shafts with cross-pieces, was easily lifted across the verge and a little way up the hill. The man found a dead branch of furze and ran back to brush the road. Then he was back. They climbed quickly, helping the horse by lifting the car over the roughest places. Suddenly rain sheeted down and the man stopped and grinned. 'Isn't that a God-sent drop of rain! There'll not be the leastest trace of us now, so we can both be on our ways at our dead ease.'

He held out his hand. ''Twas a chancy thing you did back there, but here's the thanks of Micky McCann for it.'

Conal shook his hand. 'My name is Conal O'Carran.'

'Where are you heading?'

Conal shrugged. 'I don't know. I am looking for people with the same name as myself. Do you know of any?'

Micky shook his head. 'It was a great name in these parts once, so I'm told, but there are none left that I know of. I'll tell you this, though. The man you'd need to talk to is Aidan MacShane. I do believe he'd some connection with them.'

'Will you take me to him?'

'I will, of course, if that is what you want; but, d'ye know, your best course would be to leg it out of this while you've the chance.'

'I must meet this man, MacShane. Please!'

'Well, Aidan is a hard man; but if you must...'

They were still some twenty yards from the low, mud-walled cabin when a man stooped out of the doorway. He was tall, thin, black-bearded, black-haired, gaunt and hollow-cheeked.

'What brings you here, McCann?' he shouted.

'Ah, well, Aidan,' said McCann nervously, 'the way it is, d'ye see, the young fellow here is after beating the bejasus

51

out of Grogan's man on the road below. And, d'ye see...'

The man was walking towards them. 'Then he'd best get to hell and gone out of this; and you with him.'

He stopped suddenly and stared at Conal, then he turned to McCann. 'Leave him here and take yourself off. And say nothing. You hear me!'

McCann nodded, grabbed his horse and hurried away.

MacShane beckoned to Conal. 'Come you with me.'

As they neared the door, he called, 'Mother! Come out here to me.'

An old woman, barefoot and in a ragged dress, came out.

'Tell me who you see, mother,' said MacShane.

She shuffled nearer and peered short-sightedly at Conal. 'Mother of Mercy!' she whispered.

'Hold on now!' MacShane warned. 'Who are you, young fellow?'

'My name is Conal O'Carran.'

'From where?'

'Lately from France.'

The old woman put her hand to her face and wept.

'Do you know me?' asked Conal eagerly.

MacShane gripped Conal's shoulder. 'Know you, lad! Why wouldn't I know you, and you the living image of your father, God rest him! I'm your uncle; and she's your grandmother – your mother's mother.'

The story flashed round the countryside. The descendant of the O'Carrans, who were great chieftains in the old days, was home again. He had come from France – the place where the people had risen and rid themselves of the landlords forever. He had come to help them to do the same here, and he had started by walloping Fowler, Grogan's man, and by defying Grogan himself, even in the face of a loaded pistol. He meant to take back all the O'Carran lands and see that every man got a good farm of land. All would have sound houses, good food in their bellies, clothes to their backs and shoes to their feet. And they couldn't wait to get to MacShane's house to hear more.

But MacShane met them with anger, refused them a sight of the hero, sent them back home and warned them of Conal's danger if Leering should discover where he was.

In the late afternoon, however, Larry Dolan came down from his poteen-still in the mountain wilderness. He was a squat block of a man with scarcely any neck to support his spherical head, and with a round face, merry eyes, button nose and full, fleshy mouth, all topped with red bristles.

MacShane went out to meet him. 'Thanks be to God you've come, Larry. You've heard about the young fellow, I suppose?'

Larry laughed. 'The Messiah, you mean. Sure they're likely talking in Dublin at this very moment about the mighty young warrior who is come to rid Ireland of the English forever.'

'Ah, will you, for God's sake, give over your joking. My brain is addled wondering where I'm to hide him. Like a good man, will you go and fetch Michael Canahan, till I see would he have any idea what to do.'

'Had you forgot that Michael has gone ...' He looked round cautiously.

MacShane slapped his forehead. 'Oh, God, aye! What the hell am I to do?'

'Well, let me have a sight of the young hero, anyway.'

'I don't want him seeing or talking to anybody.'

'Oh, very well, so,' said Larry airily. 'But I did think that between our two selves and Michael Canahan there was what you might call a special relationship.'

'Ah, for God's sake, Larry, will you see it my way. He's just a lad, not yet seventeen years of age; and my own sister's child. Not alone does he not know of the way things are here, but he is puffed up with the idea that he has only to call to have a great army marching behind him to win back the O'Carran lands. I don't want him talking to anybody until I've had the chance to drive some sense into him.'

'Do you know that you could be wrong?'

'How the hell could that be?'

'The way the people are talking, maybe they would follow him. Did it not strike you that they need a leader? And that we need the same thing?'

'A young lad, for God's sake.'

'Think about it, Aidan. Just think about it; and then, when Canahan comes back, we'll have a talk.'

EIGHT

Sir Julius Besant had never seen his Irish possessions and had no desire to see them. A gentleman could not be expected to travel to, much less to live in, such a barbarous place as Ireland. Society demanded (and Society was very demanding) that a gentleman should have chambers in London, a country place in the Home Counties, a house in Bath, another in Brighton and still another, in normal times, in Paris. The money to pay for these and for clothes, wine, horses, gambling, mistresses and all the other social necessities was simply there at call. His legal people had tried to explain, when he inherited, that there were persons in Ireland whose duty it was to collect monies for him; but it had all been very tiresome and unnecessary of comprehension.

What an appalling nuisance then when one's lawyers droned endlessly about unpaid bills and lack of money to meet them. One realised, of course, that there had been a run of bad luck at the tables and at the races, that the chit Margaretta had wildly extravagant tastes and... oh, there were dozens of reasons. But absolutely no cause for a gentleman to be annoyed by vulgar discussions of money. Particularly when the answer was so obvious. If there were not enough money, the persons responsible must produce more.

So those whose duty it was to administer the estates received letters telling them of the increased amount which would be required from them. Whilst being coldly polite, the letters also inferred that, should they find their duties too difficult, there were many aspirants ready to take their places.

Sir Maxwell Leering owned several hundred acres, was steward for most of the 30,000 acres owned by Sir Julius and overseer of the bailiffs who were responsible for the rest. Apart from the profits of his stewardship, he also held the proxy for the nomination to a seat in the Dublin Parliament which Sir Julius owned. Since a Member of Parliament had many ways of enriching himself, he had elected himself to the seat.

The tone of the letter from London, which implied his absolute subservience, infuriated him. There was no way he could retaliate, but he could reassure himself of the position he held locally. The bailiffs, including Grogan, received summoning letters.

The London letters had frightened them. Indeed, Aloysius was terrified. But letters from vague people in faraway London were lightsome things compared with the chilling menace of Maxwell Leering who was there present and who could reduce them to immediate beggary.

In a very few words he destroyed all their vague plans for the usual hedging and procrastination, and he sent them away filled with dread and a most unusual sense of urgency.

Grogan scurried with the rest to get as far and as quickly as possible from that cold menace; but his heart stopped when Leering said, 'Grogan. Remain!'

As soon as the others had gone, Leering said, 'I understand that you are actually in debt to our patron, Mr Grogan.'

Aloysius mumbled something about temporary financial difficulties, but Leering cut straight into him.

'On the due date you will bring me all monies outstanding. All! In addition to the increased rents required of you. We understand each other, do we not?'

Red-faced, Grogan muttered, 'We do, Sir Maxwell. Indeed. Yes.'

'Then I will bid you good day.'

The amounts which Leering had ordered would be more than was required in London, and Leering would pocket the difference. That was understood, though never mentioned, by everybody concerned. It was now up to the bailiffs to get more from the lands than they would have to pay.

A few farmed some of the land themselves; but this was considered ungentlemanly, and most leased it in small lots, varying from twenty to forty acres, almost invariably to Protestant farmers. The poorest parts, in lots of an acre or less, were let to Catholic cottiers. Grogan leased all of his to Lucius Biggen.

Biggen was the third son of a Devonshire farmer, who, after his father's death, had found himself a virtual slave to his eldest brother. Four years previously, he had been recommended to Grogan and he had been overjoyed to take a lease on the land without questioning the punitive rent he was asked to pay.

He was a bachelor, a Wesleyan and English – three excellent reasons for ensuring that he would live in isolation, hated automatically by the peasantry and barely patronised by the minor gentry. His only satisfaction was in gradually improving the productivity of the land. Now, just as it seemed that he might begin to make a small profit, Grogan sent for him and called upon him to pay more than he could foresee the land producing.

He protested, pointing out that there was an agreement about the rental. Grogan offered a fig for an agreement made in different times, hinted that the assistance of his friend, Sir Maxwell Leering, MP, JP, was readily available for the annulment of any agreement, and assured him that there were 'a thousand bare-arsed farmer's sons' who would fight to take over the lease.

'On the due date,' said Aloysius, 'you will bring me the amount stated. We understand each other, do we not?'

'Yes, Mr Grogan,' said Biggen miserably.

'Then I will bid you good day.'

Biggen farmed as much of the land as he could, except for ten acres leased to MacShane and the poorest parts to cottiers.

All over Ireland the system was the same. It was the small farmers and the cottiers who had to find the money.

The cottiers were the Catholic, native Irish whose families had originally owned the land. Their leases, of less than one acre, were of only six months' duration. On these plots they erected tiny, turf-thatched mud cabins and grew potatoes, kept a few fowl, perhaps a pig, or, in exceptional cases, a cow. Their rents were very high, and were increased if they made any improvement, such as building an outhouse for the pig, so that the pig lived with the family as a consequence. In addition, they had to pay County Cess, Hearth Tax, Vestry Cess and Tithes to the Church of Ireland vicar. They hoped to pay by working for the farmer, but, as he only called upon them when he had no other choice, and as the pay was low, they were almost always forced to make up the difference in cash or kind. To lose a fowl or a pig in this way was very serious; but to lose even a part of the potatoes upon which they and their families depended for their very lives was a tragedy. Yet complete catastrophe lay in the inability to pay the rent. That meant eviction and starvation.

There were many homeless; and it was nobody's concern whether they lived or died. There was constant poaching, and thieving of vegetables, fowl and even sheep and cattle which neither imprisonment, deportation nor even the death penalty could quell.

To the native Irish, people like Leering, Grogan and Biggen were robbers and interlopers. There were numerous Irish secret societies which avenged wrongs by burning crops and barns, breaking down fences, maiming cattle and occasionally murdering landlords and bailiffs.

Biggen knew the danger he ran, but he had no alternative but to raise the rents of his cottiers and reduce the wages.

NINE

Georgina Grogan should have been accustomed to disappointment. Her life had been a succession of unfulfilled promises. She was born in London, and her family lived just outside the fringe of society. Her father, Emmanuel Portis, just lacked the position in the Civil Service which would have placed them at least in the outer suburbs of Society. But they were always almost on the point of crossing the invisible divide. The Ladies' Academy to which she was sent, the best her parents could afford, and which they hoped would enable her to meet the daughters of Society, proved to contain only girls whose parents' aspirations equalled her own. There were suburban tea-parties, soirées, card-parties, dances, even balls, attended assiduously and expensively because there was always the possibility that acquaintance would be made with one of those mythical people who held the magic key. But always the people met were as anxiously seeking as they.

Then dear, clever papa had secured elevation. True, the post was in Dublin and Dublin society was not Society; but neither was it the wilderness and it could be a step, perhaps *the* step. But the post, though impressively titled, proved to require papa's presence in Athlone, then in

Cork, then in Belfast; and they were further from Mecca than ever. The one hope: marriage to a wealthy landowner, was pursued decorously, then keenly, then anxiously and at last frantically. They were not alone in this field. There were other mamas, other daughters, with more astute minds, better and sharper weapons, much more ruthlessness than the Portis ladies. Prize after prize was carried off without their being able to get within reach.

Then, a stroke of incredible luck. A riding accident almost at the gates of their house, and young Mr Aloysius Grogan was carried in with a broken leg. Miles away from his estates (vaguely to the south) to which he had been returning, what more natural than that they should have kept him until he recovered? What better nurse than the gay and sprightly Georgina? What more willing and exultant patient than Aloysius, who had been scouring the countryside on a similar quest to their own? What romance! What flutterings from mama at the sight of the dear, young couple. What joy at the announcement. What happy preparations. What gaiety at the wedding. What cheers and tears as the young couple left in their carriage for the journey to their country estate. What tears and tantrums from Georgina on seeing Ballyna House and meeting a snuffy, drink-sodden and obviously poverty-stricken father-in-law! And what groans from Aloysius when he realised that five golden guineas was not a token, but the whole of the dowry!

The ineffective Portis couple had also produced a son, evangelistically named Mark, from a tacit understanding that he would one day take Holy Orders. That belief persisted long after Mark had made it plain that he was not prepared to take orders of any kind from anyone, least of all his parents. He did, however, take instruction, wherever and whenever he could get it, in the lethal use of swords and pistols. Before he was twenty, he had left home. In less than three months, he had fought and won his first duel – his carefully chosen victim being the heir to a fair patrimony whom he had winged with such delicacy, and over whom he expressed such concern as to enable them to become firm friends afterwards. A series of further duels with members of the clubs to which he now secured entry made most others hesitate before questioning his extraordinary luck at cards. Attempted enquiries by the law into one duel at which, permitting himself the luxury of disliking and becoming annoyed with his opponent, he had carelessly but thoroughly killed him, made it necessary to close mouths at some expense. After that he had departed to Wexford and the lands which the deceased had wagered and lost.

The news had come to Georgina that her brother was now landed and wealthy. She wrote immediately to say how very pleased she would be to bring his three-year-old niece to visit him. There was no reply. She wrote again, in case her letter had gone astray. Still no reply. A year later, she wrote again and this time she received the reply:

My Dearest Sister,

If I should ever have need of you I shall send for you, though I fear that if the time should ever come you will be far too feeble for any journey longer than the one from your hovel to the graveyard.

Your most affectionate brother,

Mark

On Nuala's return home, Georgina, who had been well aware of their poverty, but had lacked the urge to do anything about it, now faced three facts. One, that Aloysius would continue to hide from reality behind a jug of claret. Two, that her daughter had become a beautiful young woman. Three, that in experience she was far better equipped for the hunt than her mother had been.

Clothes were indispensable, but, in the absence of

money, seemed to present an insoluble problem. Like a fairy godmother, Miss Emmeline Prouty appeared. After long exile and apprenticeship at a Dublin fashion-house, she had returned to Newtownarchibald to care for her ageing parents, to build up a dress-making business amongst the ladies of the county and, hopefully, to marry Jonathan Dawson, Master Tailor.

To Miss Prouty's delight, a distinguished lady of the county appeared as her first potential customer. This lady, she learned, had just recovered from a long and mysterious illness, during which her wardrobe had fallen far behind the fashion. Even now she was in too weak a state to undertake the long, tiring journey to the Dublin houses. Yet clothes she must have now that she was to take part in the social life of the county again. There was also her daughter, newly returned from school (there were hints of exclusive English and Continental establishments) who required clothes also.

Mrs Grogan was delighted to have found so close at hand so clever a person as Miss Prouty. Miss Prouty was delighted that Mrs Grogan was delighted. An appointment was made for choosing and measuring. In her maidenly bed that night Miss Prouty found great difficulty in picturing Mr Dawson's dashing moustachios because her mind was so busy totting up her potential profits.

After nearly three weeks of what Nuala called 'the screaming boredom' of home, during which she spoke to nobody but her parents and the servants, refusing to go out in case anybody of importance should see her in her dowdy school-clothes, she swung to the heights of delight when her mother announced the discovery of Miss Prouty. There followed hours and days in the pleasures of planning, studying styles and patterns and materials and colours and shades and matchings and contrasts; the thrilling agonies of deciding between this and that or perhaps the other; the constant excited chatter; the final choosing; the long discussions on the way home and at home, with the heart-stopping fears of wrong choices and the wonderings was it too late to change. Then the waiting and wondering and agonising because every choice had assuredly been wrong, every garment would be ludicrously unbecoming. The fittings and the sickening certainty that all these peculiar pieces of material could only be assembled into unwearable reach-me-downs. And again the waiting, endlessly. At last (and, 'Thanks be to God!' said Tim Duffin, the long-suffering coachman) the multitudes of carefully wrapped parcels were delivered, laid on the beds and opened with bated breath like Aladdin's caves, with Ohs! and Ahs! and Just look at this! The tryings on, the posturings and squintings into mirrors from impossibly gymnastic angles, the mutual admiration, the callings for appreciation from gasping maids and even from Aloysius in spite of his blankly unappreciative grunts. Miss Prouty's enormous bill and subsequent, increasingly hysterical reminders were used to light his pipe.

At long last, Miss Nuala Grogan of Ballyna House, young lady of fashion, potential toast of the county, belle of the Dublin balls, breaker of hearts, rode out on her magnificent mount (a sad and scrubby hack in reality), clad in a full-skirted, emerald-green riding habit, white lace foaming at her throat, a tiny emerald-green, white-scarfed topper perched jauntily on her red-ribbon-tied chestnut tresses. A butterfly, newly emerged from the chrysalis, spreading her gorgeous wings for the admiration of the world.

The day was dull, the rough road, muddy and pool-patched, stretched empty ahead. Not a soul in all the countryside to appreciate the new-born beauty. There should have been some gay-thronged, nearby mansion to which she could have ridden, oh, so casually, just happened to be passing, at which she would have been surrounded by a host of rich, dashing, handsome, fiercely competing young gentlemen, arousing the envy, but also the loving admiration of all the quite presentable young ladies. But she and her mama had not yet gone calling; and when they did it would be to a succession of drab, run-down houses like their own, inhabited by dull, gossiping old women, guzzling, red-faced, grunting old men, a few silly, giggling young women, and oafish, potato-faced louts of young men – a very few even of these. She had met them all before when she was a child, oh, years ago, well, nearly a year, at a Christmas Party at the Barclays'.

Then who was to admire her? What was the use of her finery? Where could she go to show it off? She laughed bitterly (admiring her grown-up cynicism), then tears pricked her eyes at the sadness of her position. Followed immediately by annoyance at herself for the childishness of tears, and also annoyance at the stupid, unappreciative, empty world.

The horse clopped on through the mud and pools. Dark clouds rolled over the damp landscape. Nothing to be seen but brown, rotting ferns, wet furze, black, leafless bushes, rough hillside and stretching bog. Nobody on the road ahead. Nobody on the land. She was the last person on earth. Her debut was a complete failure and the obvious course was to go back home. To what?

Then she met Conal O'Carran again.

TEN

On the night of Canahan's return, Dolan and MacShane visited him.

Dolan had brought a jar of poteen and, after pouring for them, he asked, 'Now, Michael, what excitements from the big world?'

Canahan eyed him sourly. 'It's a thing I wonder about you, Larry Dolan, if this movement is no more than diversion for you.'

'And if it was, what of it? Did you ever find me lagging when there was work to be done?'

'Ah, for God's sake, give over, the pair of you!' said MacShane. 'You're like a couple of dogs forever snapping at each other. I'm after a long day's work, and I'm giving you a lump of my sleeping time. Give us the news, Michael, man, whatever it is.'

Canahan hesitated, staring into the turf fire, obviously still annoyed; but he took a drink, shook his shoulders and began to talk. 'I've been thinking and thinking all the long road back and I've yet to decide is the news good or bad or what. It's true, what we heard. There's a big number of merchants in Belfast, and in Dublin too, they say, are backing this lawyer, Wolfe Tone, in what they call the Society of United Irishmen. He holds that if all Irishmen were united, no matter what their class or creed, then we could get a Parliament which would give justice to all.'

MacShane stood abruptly. 'Parliament! Blather! I'm going to my bed.'

'You wanted me to tell you,' said Canahan sharply, 'but you'll not stay to listen.'

'What more is there to hear? Parliament, for God's sake! A bunch of landlords passing laws to hold on to their thieveries and get more.'

'Ah, sit down, Aidan, and have another sup,' said Dolan. 'Hear the man out, anyhow.'

Grumbling, MacShane sat and accepted the drink.

'Well, now,' said Canahan, 'I should have no need to say it, but I've no more faith in landlords and their Parliament than you have. But there are a few things to remember. The merchants have money, they're against the landlords and they want to get their own men into the Parliament. Then again, your man, Tone, has the French ideas of Brotherhood, Freedom and Equality; and, by damn, I'm with him in those!'

'I'm with the French in one thing, anyway,' said Dolan. 'Cut the head off every landlord and take back the land.'

'Will you hold your whisht till I'm done,' said Canahan.

'I was at a meeting – Catholics and Presbyterians both were at it. The way it was put to us, we're as bad off as each other. All came from a branch of some society or other, and it was put to us that we'd do far better altogether in the United Irishmen.

'Now I'd a talk afterwards with a few from both sides, and none of them rich merchants; and what came out of the talk was that the way the United Irishmen started need not be the way it will finish. Think of that, the pair of you. Supposing they do get men in their thousands and then they get the back of the hand from the Parliament, as they will... What then?'

'Begod,' said Dolan, 'I'm beginning to like the tune.'

'I said blather before,' said MacShane, 'and I say it again. Men in their thousands, moryah! We've the devil's own job getting half a dozen together in the Whiteboys when there's work to be done.'

'True enough,' said Canahan, 'but we're just who we are. If men came from the outside with lawyers, merchants and money behind them, the local men would listen, I think.'

'I wonder, would they,' said MacShane.

'Aidan, you're forgetting something,' said Dolan. 'There's young O'Carran. You'll not have heard of him, Michael.' He told of the beating of Fowler and the reaction of the people.

'Ach, I've told you already,' said MacShane. 'He's nothing but a lad with a head full of dreams.'

'Aye, and he's put the dreams into the heads of the people,' said Larry Dolan. 'With the three of us behind him and the help of the men from Belfast, we could have every man in the Barony. Aren't they begging him to lead them!'

'I dunno,' said MacShane, wagging his head slowly. 'I dunno. D'ye see, there's something else about him. He's been brought up in the fine French college to think of himself as a gentleman. Now he hasn't said one word, mind, but I'm telling you this, he hasn't taken kindly to the rough life we've to lead. And I wonder does he see

65

himself now as one with the people?'

They finally decided that he should send Conal to talk with Canahan, and then MacShane went home.

When he had gone, Canahan told Dolan of the visit he had already had from Conal.

Larry laughed. 'Well, begod! And never a word out of him about that.'

Canahan paused, took a drink and eyed Dolan. 'It's well known, I suppose,' he said slowly, 'that MacShane has the lad in his house?'

'Sure every dog in the county knows it.'

'And does MacShane think to keep him hid for the rest of his life?'

Dolan laughed. 'Don't you just think you're the foxy devil?'

'Now what d'you mean by that?'

'Could it possibly be, I wonder, that you're thinking that maybe the word would get to Leering's men, and that a touch of Leering's justice would convince the lad to do what you want?'

Canahan shrugged. 'Well, supposing I had thought that, would I be wrong?'

Dolan laughed again. 'Now how the hell could the schoolmaster be wrong?'

ELEVEN

The Personage was of the highest nobility. This most definitely did not mean that he was inspired by the lofty ideals of King Arthur's knights of old. He owed it all to his ancestors. One of them, a very ambitious individual, had managed to catch King James I of England at a moment when the monarch was not dallying with his pretty boys and had secured authorisation to take an army across to the north of Ireland with the stated purpose of taking the land away from the native Irish and adding it to the king's possessions. James signed a warrant without reading it and thereby handed over vast portions of Irish territory to the Personage's ancestor. He, having raised money from men who foresaw the prospect of large profits, gathered an army far better armed and equipped than anything the Irish could muster and succeeded in taking over the whole of the north of Ireland for his Great and Glorious Majesty. In doing so, he slaughtered large numbers of Irish and drove the remainder into the wilder, less valuable parts of the country, replacing them with the speculators and with people gathered from the poor of Scotland and England to do the work. His Majesty also rewarded his unselfish loyalty with an imposing title.

His successors used their riches to gain greater titles, so that the Personage ranked with the highest in Britain – a man of enormous wealth and power, a man to be treated with the greatest deference, a man whose name was never used lightly.

Now the Personage was worried. It was all the fault of those blasted Presbyterians and their stubborn insistence on practising their own religion, instead of flocking obediently every Sunday to the parish church where they would have learned to be contented tenants, properly respectful to those whom Providence had placed in lawful authority over them, and where there would have been none of these cursed liberal ideas about rights and equality. His father and a few others had been too generous. Instead of lashing it out of them or sending them off in irons to the Indies, they had allowed them to go to the Americas, there to spawn and spread their pernicious ideas. With the result that the damned Colonists had had the impudence to declare themselves independent of the Crown to which they owed not only their allegiance, but their very existence. Worse, they had actually taken up arms against the forces of the Crown.

And worst of all, they had had the damned effrontery to win.

Then the disease had spread to France, with even worse results – King and nobility all swept away, almost overnight, by gangs of filthy ragamuffins. Now, the disease had returned to Ireland. This could mean calamity. Immediate action was essential.

Sir Maxwell Leering was not easily impressed, but nothing had ever happened to him to equal an invitation to take lunch with the Personage. He and his fellow-magistrates went like pilgrims to a shrine.

They were met by a charming young gentleman who introduced himself as Mr Robert Stewart, private secretary to the Personage. He had distressing news for them. Only a few hours earlier, the Personage had become indisposed. Nothing of any gravity, fortunately, but his medical advisers had insisted upon rest and quiet. Most distressed that he was unable to be with his distinguished guests on this most important occasion, he begged them to accept his apologies and to permit his secretary to act in his stead.

What he had actually said was: 'Bobby, you'll handle this bunch of bog-trotters. I'll certainly not share a trough with 'em. You know what's wanted. Butter 'em up, and, if that don't work with any of 'em, then spend money. But, mark me, you'll account for every farthing. Oh, and remember the warning we got about that slippery fellow, Leering.'

When the excellent meal was over and he judged the guests to be sufficiently mellowed, Mr Stewart rose.

The Personage had invited them because their positions were of such importance that it was no exaggeration to say that the future of the country lay in their hands.

They were aware of the appalling events which had taken place in France; but were they aware that Ireland was menaced by the same evil ideas? They were being spread at this very moment by a group known as the Society of United Irishmen. This had been started by a group of Presbyterian merchants in Belfast and was being organised by a Dublin lawyer named Theobald Wolfe Tone. The avowed aim was to rally all the native Irish, in other words the mob, behind them. This was a threat to their positions, to their property, indeed to their very lives.

The Personage, then, and all who held dear the future of their country, the Crown which assured the continuing possession of their privileges, and the Established Church which was their surety of salvation, called on them to use the utmost of their powers to stamp out this evil in its infancy. The Personage asked them, indeed he besought them whilst appreciating the sacrifices he was asking of them, to remain in their own districts so that they could deal immediately with even the slightest hint of the evil.

The Personage hoped they would visit him again from time to time so that they could review progress; and assured them that those who unselfishly served their country in its hour of need would not go unrewarded.

Finally, should any gentleman anticipate difficulty in complying, would he kindly remain and see Mr Stewart in private – with a strong hint that it was hoped none would remain.

There was a moment's awkward pause, none wishing to leave before the others, all wishing to remain and plead their particular (monetary) difficulties without the rest knowing. Leering stood and went to their host.

'My humblest service to the Personage, Mr Stewart. My gratitude and appreciation of his hospitality and my hopes for his speedy recovery,' he said in a loud, clear voice. Then, in a low whisper, as he bowed and shook hands, 'Tomorrow at eleven?'

Mr Stewart gave the faintest signal of agreement, the smallest hint of a smile, which broadened as all the others hurried to take their leave.

The following morning, in the privacy of Mr Stewart's study, the price was agreed to compensate Maxwell Leering for remaining at home instead of occupying his very profitable Parliamentary seat. Between gentlemen, of course, no mention was made of the fact that Leering would lease the seat to somebody else and gain considerably by the transaction.

TWELVE

Conal felt like a released prisoner as he strode down the hillside. He scarcely noticed the dull, cold dampness of the day as he breathed deeply to rid his lungs of the smoke and smells of the cabin.

His uncle had given him a message from Michael Canahan inviting him to have a talk about his future. He had thought it over and decided to go. How could he, a leader of the people, be afraid of a miserable school-master!

He came out from a sunken, bush-sheltered boreen on to the road, and there, undecided whether to go on or go home, was Nuala Grogan. Against the brown and russet of the countryside, she made a picture of striking loveliness.

Although startled by his sudden appearance, she saw that she had found the admiration she sought. He stood speechless, unthinking, staring, enjoying.

But the stare went on so long that she blushed, then was annoyed because a young lady of fashion only blushes deliberately. This prompted her to pertness, but she checked herself, because it was unfair and because of the warm, satisfying admiration which shone in his eyes. And because his eyes were blue, friendly and pleasantly disturbing. And because he was, well, not exactly handsome, but his face was, well, his features seemed to match, to fall exactly into place and to be altogether just as they should be and, somehow, familiar.

The horse stamped and snorted. Conal woke and realised with embarrassment that he had been staring for a long time. He blushed. His hands seemed to swell to huge, useless, dangling appendages. His feet gained a life of their own and refused to stay still. His lips, tongue and jaw would not obey the prompting to speak, whilst his numb mind produced no coherent thought for him to utter. He had often suffered from shyness, but this was a combination of paralysis and St Vitus' Dance; and, to compound his discomfort, he was quite sure the girl must think him an utter fool.

Nuala recognised him as the fierce young man who had beaten Fowler. Momentary fear was swept aside by his obvious shyness, to be replaced by the very pleasant awareness of her power over him. She smiled.

To Conal it was as if, like a diamond suddenly lit, a greater beauty flashed into being. It was also as if he had been sandbagged.

'Good afternoon, Mr – er – Oh, dear, I don't know your name.'

Conal was enjoying the music of her voice. Meaning barely filtered through. 'Conal,' he said.

The horse snorted, drowning his voice. It lowered its head, then flung it upwards. Automatically, he took hold of its cheek-strap and shouted, 'My name is Conal O'Carran.'

Quite unaware of what he was doing, he began to lead the horse.

She made no objection, indeed, scarcely noticed. His accent intrigued her and she asked him about it. And he told her. He asked about herself. And she told him. Along the road they went, oblivious to the bleak countryside and the louring clouds, chatting like old friends.

Conal could never have said later how long it was before the rain swooped on them. 'You'll get wet!' he cried anxiously.

'I'll get wet!' she shrieked, aware of the danger to her new clothes. 'Goodbye!'

71

She slapped the horse into a trot, her head down to the driving rain. She was more than a hundred yards away before she remembered him and turned to wave. She saw, standing in the rainy road, a bedraggled peasant.

Conal, unconscious and uncaring of his wetness, saw a fairy princess. He watched until she disappeared, then wandered dreamily back to MacShane's, completely forgetting his intended visit to Canahan.

THIRTEEN

Three mornings later two petty constables arrived to arrest Conal. He was alone in the cabin. When he objected, they clubbed him insensible, put fetters on him and carried him out to their cart. He was still unconscious when he arrived at Leering's house. On one side of the rear yard was a long, low building which was used as the local courthouse. They carried him into it, chained him to a ring in the wall and left him.

Leering was out hunting and when he returned he brought back to luncheon several gentlemen, most of whom, including Grogan, were interested in the cases to be tried.

Conal regained vague consciousness after lying for more than an hour on the cold floor. For some time he lay feeling very ill, suffering great pain in his head and striving to remember what had happened. After a time he became aware that a partly heard, repeated noise was a voice saying, 'Get up, lad. Get up from the floor, lad. You'll be better if you get up from the floor.'

He raised his head slowly. At a constantly varying distance was a wavering shape. Sometimes it was vaguely like a man, but it flowed and blurred. The effort of trying to identify it increased the pain in his head. He closed his eyes, laid his head again on the floor and sank back into peaceful blackness.

It was just after three o'clock when Sir Maxwell Leering and his guests entered the courtroom, preceded by the clerk and several assistants to the constables who were guarding the prisoners.

Leering walked slowly down the room, mounted the dais, stood behind the table, surveyed the room in silence, then settled into his chair. Below him was a table and chair for the clerk. In the centre of the room was a small, railed enclosure for the accused. On either side of this were the seats for the spectators. Along the back wall were the prisoners chained to their rings.

Although forty years of age, Leering was a bachelor. This was partly because no lady whom he had yet met would have been of sufficient use for his advancement, partly because the women he met always appeared, after short use, to be either stupid or scheming, but mainly because his mother, a widow, to whom he was devoted, ruthlessly routed any woman who appeared to become too attractive to her son. He had often rid himself of no-longer-wanted women by showing them attentions in his mother's presence.

He was tall and thin. Chin, nose and forehead were prominent, lean and harshly strong, in contrast to his mouth which, when he forgot to control it, fell into wet slackness. To men he emanated a disdainful coldness; for many women he had the hypnotic attraction a snake is said to have for a rabbit. For both there was the attraction of his power and money.

As Leering's eyes traversed the room from prisoners to constables and guests, there was no change in his expression of distaste. Then he took from the table a penknife with which he began, very carefully, to pare a nail.

'I intend to conduct the day's business as expeditiously as possible. The prisoners will do well to note that the

73

court will deal severely with any time-wasting. Clerk, call the first case!'

The clerk rose, turned and bowed obsequiously to Leering, who ignored the courtesy, and called, 'Patrick O'Neill!'

An old man was thrust into the dock. He was charged with stealing timber. He had found the bough of a tree on the road and was dragging it home when he was arrested. His attempt at explaining that he thought the bough to belong to nobody were silenced by a blow from a constable. He was fined five shillings, but, as he could not pay, he was sent to gaol for a month.

The clerk then called, 'Denis Gorman, Liam McKenna, Michael McKenna,' and three young men were hustled into the dock.

One of the guests, a Mr Hamilton Vesey, stood up. 'Sir Maxwell, these are the three blackguards I spoke of. I beg as a favour that an example should be made of them. Five of my cattle were incurably lamed by them and had to be shot. A hundred yards of fencing was destroyed, and I feel very strongly...'

'Mr Vesey!' Leering's voice slashed like a sabre across the whining monologue. Vesey gasped. 'You may safely leave the conduct of justice to me, as the Crown has deigned to do.'

Vesey, slow to understand, looked round at his fellows for enlightenment; but not even an answering look was forthcoming. The man beside him tugged surreptitiously at his coat-tails and he sat abruptly.

Leering placed his elbows carefully on the table, folded his hands together and very deliberately rested his chin on them. He eyed the prisoners. There was silence for a moment into which his words fell like icicles.

'You three will be committed in custody to await the next Assizes; when, I assure you, you will be punished with far greater severity than lies in my power to award. The least you can hope for is transportation to the Indies, but my personal recommendation to their Lordships will be that you should be hanged.'

'No!' They shouted together. 'We're innocent. We were never near the place. I swear to God we're innocent!'

But they were dragged away and out of the court.

'Let there be no more of these unseemly disturbances,' said Leering. 'Next case!'

'Malachy Coyle!' called the clerk.

Coyle, obviously better off than the rest of the prisoners, brushed aside the escorting constables and stepped into the dock. 'Your honour,' he began.

'Silence!' Leering's voice lashed him.

'Mr Brownlow, your case I believe. Kindly give the facts so that we may save the time of questioning.'

Warren Brownlow, a small landowner, stood up importantly. 'Thank you, Sir Maxwell. Most grateful for your courtesy, sir, and only too willing to assist the course of justice. I have said many a time, and my friends will bear me out . . .'

'The facts, Mr Brownlow!'

Brownlow reddened. 'Well, your honour, the facts, well, as I told you at luncheon . . . The facts are . . . well, as I told you then. You see . . .'

Leering looked and spoke to the prisoner and at the same time flapped his hand downward at Brownlow in a command to be seated. Brownlow, completely confused, sat down. Slowly he came to a conclusion. He turned to the man beside him and muttered, 'Damn, Willard, I think Leering insulted me.'

'He did,' Willard whispered. 'You're surely not thinking of doing anything about it.'

Brownlow blinked at him. 'But I . . . Damn, I ought . . .'

'Don't even think of it,' hissed Willard. 'He'd fillet you in a trice, and well you know it.'

In the meantime, Leering was addressing the prisoner. 'I understand you have a horse?'

'Correct, your honour, quite correct. And a grand beast . . .'

'Spare me the coper's talk. Mr Brownlow offered you five pounds for the beast, I understand?'

'Indeed he did, your honour. For an animal worth

75

twenty-five or thirty pounds in anyone's money.'

'You are not here to sell me the horse, fellow. Are you a Roman Catholic?'

'I am, of course, your honour; but what ...'

'The law, fellow, expressly states that a Roman Catholic may not own a horse of greater value than five pounds; and that you may not refuse an offer of that amount from a Protestant.'

'But, sure, your honour, that's only one of them old Penal Laws.'

'Don't bicker with me, fellow, or I'll see that you get a taste of the baton. But since you have raised the subject, and for the edification of you and your like, be informed that the age of a law has no bearing on its efficacy. The Penal Laws were passed for the excellent purposes of ensuring that the Rule of Law of a Protestant King and a Protestant Parliament would obtain in this papist-ridden country. And I thank God for those laws, which I and my fellow magistrates will ensure are enacted.'

He turned to the spectators. 'Mr Brownlow, I presume you have five pounds?'

Brownlow flushed, hesitated, looked at Willard who stared studiously forward, then slowly stood. 'Why, yes, Sir Maxwell.'

'Give the fellow his money and send your groom for the horse.'

Brownlow counted five sovereigns into the hand of a constable who thrust them into the unwilling hand of the prisoner, whom he then pulled from the dock.

'Put back that fellow. I have not yet dismissed him.'

Coyle was still staring bitterly at the money as he was pushed back.

'The case is not yet closed,' said Leering. 'You have broken the law and must be punished. Fined one pound!'

Coyle stared in amazement. 'Fined!' he said incredulously. 'What kind of blasted justice ...'

He did not see Leering's nod to the constable, but the baton cracking his skull effectively silenced him.

Leering dealt even more summarily with the next few

cases. One of his own tenants had been evicted but had gone on living in his cabin. His plea that he had nowhere else to live was answered with the assurance that he could spend the next three months in gaol. Five men from Tanrego were committed, without questioning, to the Assizes. They were accused of driving off cattle and leaving them many miles away – a common type of protest against the increase of grazing land which deprived men of employment.

At the beginning of the proceedings Conal had been hauled to his feet and propped against the wall. Although conscious, he was unaware of what was happening. There was a slow, dull, throbbing pain in his head which marred both sight and hearing. Two men were required to drag him across into the dock. It was a vague relief to him that he could lean on the high rail.

Leering examined him, tapping the table, then asked, 'Is the fellow intoxicated? Stand up straight, man!'

One of the constables pushed Conal to a more upright posture and held him there.

'The last case, I believe, clerk?' said Leering.

'Yes, Sir Maxwell.'

'And a very interesting one at this particular time. Mr Grogan, I presume this is the lout of whom you spoke?'

'That's the blackguard. I leave him to you, Sir Maxwell.'

'You may do so with all confidence. What is your name, fellow?'

Conal was not even aware of Leering, much less of the question.

'Ah, a surly rogue, are you! Who is this fellow, clerk?'

'His name is Kieran, or something such, Sir Maxwell. These Irish names...'

'Quite, quite! Barbaric, I agree. No matter. Gentlemen, we have here the type of rascal who is becoming far too common – the big, overgrown lout who is given to attacking those weaker than himself; the type which, unchecked, produces our footpads and highwaymen. Worse still, this is the type which, in France, forms the murderous mobs.

'You, fellow, had the audacity to interfere with Mr Grogan's footman in the performance of his duties. Not only that, but you dragged him from his horse and assaulted him most grievously, causing injuries from which, I understand, the poor fellow has not yet recovered. To compound your crime, you insulted and even threatened Mr Grogan in the presence of his daughter.

'It is quite obvious to this court that, unless severe action is taken at once, you will degenerate into one of our worst criminal types . . .'

Conal was dimly aware of being in a strange place, of a voice speaking unintelligibly. If only the pain would stop throbbing in his head, he could perhaps understand what was happening.

'The sentence of this court is that you shall receive thirty lashes, the sentence to be carried out immediately. Take him out.'

He was pulled from the dock and was aware of hands on him. He struggled weakly and they twisted his arms behind his back. The different pain increased his awareness. He was being forced along. By whom? Why? He tried again to struggle, but was too weak. 'What?' he tried to ask.

'Line up these other rascals in the yard where they will benefit from the example,' Leering ordered.

Conal was grateful for the fresh air which seemed to lighten the thick pain in his head. He realised that it was fresh air, that he was being forcibly held, that there were many people about; but it was all dreamlike. Flitting in the recesses of thought was the idea that shortly he would waken in his cot in the college.

But he was being manhandled. Somebody was tearing at his shirt. Cold air struck his torso. It was no dream. He was being forced across the yard towards a peculiar timber erection. Immediately he was back in the square in Paris.

'No!' he shouted. 'The poor woman!'

He tried to dig his feet into the cobbles, but they

dragged him. His struggles grew wilder and it took three men to tie him, struggling and shouting, to the triangle, his hands stretched high, legs wide apart, the broad, white back naked to the lash.

A constable, stripped to the waist, stepped forward trailing the thongs of the whip.

He looked up at his hands. His head was still not quite clear. He was puzzled because the frame to which he was tied was different from the one he remembered. There was no gleaming blade above. In this position they could not ... He fought against the rebellion of his stomach. He tried to struggle, but, stretched as he was, with his weight dragging on the biting cords, there was nothing he could do.

Meanwhile, the constable drew back the whip, rising on his toes and judging the distance to that broad, white target. He leaned back, then, breath whistling through clenched teeth, he slashed. Clearly sounded the rush of thongs and the smack as they hit and bit.

Conal screamed and leaped, shaking even the strong triangle. Never had he felt, nor even dreamed such pain – all the worse because he could not understand what was happening.

'Oh, God!' he shouted. 'What is it? Help! God, help!'

The weals ran in purple diagonals from hip to shoulder, clear against the white, quivering skin. The body sagged as far as was possible given the cords.

Swish! Smack! Again the agonised scream, the leaping, shaking, quivering body. The torment was worse than the first; and, even more horrible, was the knowledge that it would happen again any second.

Six times the constable laid on the lash, trying always to break virgin skin. Then, crossing to the other side, he used the whip back-handed, laying the weals in grid-iron fashion. Each time the lash was laid on now, blood spurted. It ran down Conal's back, spattered the triangle and sprayed from the back-drawn whip.

He was in torment. His back was one tortured wound. His body shook so much with nervous shock that the triangle rattled continuously. He had bitten his lips and his tongue, his throat was burning dry from repeated screaming, tears, sweat and mucus covered his face. Yet over and above all was shame that he had befouled himself. After the next blow he felt no more.

The constable signalled to a man who came forward with a bucket of water. He was about to throw the water, when the constable stopped him, stooped and slurped from the bucket. A nod and the water sluiced over the tortured body. But Conal returned only briefly to the edge of consciousness and fell back again at the next stroke. The slack body accepted the lashes, only the nerves responding.

The twenty-ninth stroke was just being delivered when Nuala cantered gaily into the yard. She pulled up her horse, looked round at the assembly, then at the bloody object hanging from the triangle. She screamed and fell from the horse in a faint.

'Who the devil is this chit?' demanded Leering angrily.

'Hem, m'daughter, Sir Maxwell,' said Grogan, as he trotted across to where a constable was raising her head from the dirty cobbles.

Leering was much nearer to her. 'Is she always so inopportune?' he asked.

He glanced contemptuously at her as she lay in the constable's arms. Then he looked again. Her hat had fallen off, her hair lay in thick, glossy brown tresses over the man's arm, her face was pale, her delicately blue eyelids and her softly-curving lips trembled. She was altogether too attractive to be held in the arms of an unappreciative lout.

'Stand aside, you!'

He knelt and took her in his arms. He lifted her, his face a mask disguising the thrill of her warm softness. Holding her, so still and helpless, he felt pleasantly strong and protective, as he had never felt towards any female.

'Come, Grogan. We shall take her into the house.'

'What about the prisoner, Sir Maxwell?' asked the constable.

Leering turned with Nuala in his arms and viewed the bloody wreck contemptuously.

'Complete the punishment and release him.'

He turned and strode into the house, absorbed in his delightful burden.

FOURTEEN

The weather on the days following Nuala's meeting with Conal had been too bad for her to go riding or for Georgina to risk damage to their new clothes by going calling. It was long after her father had left that she learned that he had gone hunting. Not, she knew, that she would have been allowed to go; but, had she known, she thought, she could at least have ridden with her father to the meet. Just possibly there might have been somebody there... somebody, well, other than the local louts. Somebody... surely there had to be somebody, somewhere, some time. And he would be – well, exciting, different, romantic... A soldier, perhaps – gallant and dashing. Or an explorer. Yes, an explorer – just returned from far-away, glamorous places, and he would be planning an even more exotic journey; but, for all his courage and strength and daring and self-reliance, he would want a sympathetic companion. And the dream went on to courtship, parties and balls with all the gay, important and titled people who would know him, and...

'And your mammy says will you come at once to your dinner, Miss Nuala.'

Nuala looked round vaguely from the window-seat in her bedroom from which she had been staring blankly through the dirty pane. Bridie O'Hara, one of the maids, fifteen years old and all blushes and puppy-fat, had obviously been speaking to her.

'What?'

'Ah, God, miss. Sure she'll have me hide if you don't come this minute. Amn't I after telling you three times already.'

Nuala thrust forward her head at the girl and widened her eyes in mock terror. 'Oooh!' She jumped up and seized her by the shoulders and swung her round and round. 'Oh, Bridie, Bridie, Bridie O'Hara! This is such a dull place. A dismal place. A – dirty place. A – a – a damned dirty place!'

Bridie was horrified. 'Miss Nuala! That's bad. 'Tis a sin, a mortal sin, so 'tis!'

'Well, I don't care. I simply don't care. But don't tell mama, will you?'

'Sure, don't you know I won't,' said Bridie indignantly. 'Besides, wouldn't it be a sin too for me ... Ah, I wonder would it, though, if 'twas only the way I was saying what someone else said. And, sure,' she blushed and giggled, 'I'd love to say it.'

'Bridie!'

'Ah, I wouldn't tell, so I wouldn't. But you're a terrible girl, Miss Nuala, and will you come, for the love of God, and eat your dinner before the missus has me kilt entirely.'

So, to sit in the freezing dining-room, because that was genteel, whilst the warm kitchen was not. To eat, or rather to pretend to eat, lukewarm and rapidly congealing boiled fat bacon and soapy potatoes. To listen to mama's unending empty chatter. To think that miles away, somewhere, there was a great wide world of excitement and enjoyment, thronged with gay, laughing people who neither knew nor cared that Nuala Grogan, who could outshine them all if given the chance, was buried in a rubbish-dump called Ballyna House.

She sifted from her mother's chatter that her father would be eating at Leering's house with the other gentlemen. Slowly the idea came that nobody could object if she just happened to be riding in the vicinity and thought to call and accompany her father home. At least somebody, some men, would see her in her new riding-habit.

So, having said nothing to her mother, she had ridden off. So she trotted into the stableyard. And stamped on her mind forever was the picture: the group of gentry, the line of wretched prisoners, the sweating constable, and that pitiful, horrible wreck hanging from the triangle like meat from a butcher's hook.

Leering's mother had appeared, as if by magic, as soon as he stepped into the house with Nuala in his arms.

'In the sitting-room, Maxwell. On the couch, if you please. Now, away with you. Both of you. This is no place for gentlemen. Nor for young, unescorted ladies, if the truth be told. Away, please!'

Leering put his hand on Grogan's shoulder and urged him out. 'We tread on dangerous ground, Aloysius.'

And Aloysius' heart gave a great jump of delight.

Nuala wakened to the sharp cut of smelling-salts. She pushed them away and, still hazy, sat up. The picture leaped clearly into her mind. 'Oh!' she groaned and put her hands to her eyes, trying to erase the horror.

'Look at me, girl!'

The voice had the undeniable authority of a pistol shot. Nuala jerked up her head and stared at Lady Leering. She was a tiny woman, stiffly upright, in clothes as rigid and black as ebony; her face was long, white, keen-featured, lined and as hard as carved ivory.

'Don't ever come to this house again unless by invitation and escorted! Elizabeth!'

A maid – a long, thin imitation of her mistress – moved from the shadows.

'Escort this young person out!'

Still queasy and trembling, but feeling above all as if she had passed through a shower of ice, Nuala was scarcely conscious of being led. Nor was she fully aware of the gentle care with which Leering helped her into his

83

carriage and wrapped her in a luxurious fur rug, though the softness and warmth were like a blessing to her chilled and sickened body.

Their horses in charge of a groom, who trotted behind, she and her father were driven home. They went in silence, because she was too numb and sickened to speak, whilst her father's mind was awhirl with wonderful plans.

When they arrived, Nuala came suddenly alive, jumped from the carriage and fled to her room, where she locked the door, threw herself on her bed and wept.

Aloysius stamped into the hall, leaving the expectant coachman and groom without their expectations, and flung off his hat and coat.

'Felix!' he yelled. 'Felix, where the hell are you, man!'

Like a cringing genie, the butler materialised and in a few moments Aloysius was settled, slippered and clareted by the fire. After one great gulp, he rubbed his protuberant belly and grunted in appreciation.

'And now, Felix, m'lad,' he said jovially, 'my compliments to Mrs Grogan and will she favour me with a few moments of pleasant conversation.'

When she appeared, 'Aha! There y'are, Georgina, m'love. Settle yourself in the warmth of the fire, m'dear. Begad, a fire's a great thing on a cold, damp evening.'

'Aloysius,' she said as she crossed the room, 'there is something strange afoot. And whenever I find you jovial, I tremble to think what terrible things are about to happen to us.'

'Tremble! Tush!' He laughed comfortably, fondly.

'Oh, you laugh! But what has happened to my poor, dear baby? I saw you both arrive in Sir Maxwell's carriage, but when I went to her room she had the door locked and would not answer. She was crying. I know it. So I demand to be told what calamity you have brought on us now.'

'Dammit all, woman, will you listen?'

'Don't dare speak –'

'Good news!' he shouted.

84

'Good news?' she asked doubtfully.

'The best news ever! Now, will you sit down quietly and listen to me?'

'But why is Nuala crying?'

'Ah, bellyache and tantrums.'

'Aloysius, you disgusting –'

'Listen, woman!'

She sat bolt upright, folded her hands precisely and pursed her lips, far from believing, disapproving, but quiet.

Aloysius, not quite daring to show his grin, deliberately poured another glass of claret, sipped it, then settled himself more comfortably.

'Georgina, m'love, want you to know that've been worried. Very, very worried. Nearly buried in debt. Couldn't permit it to go on. Said to m'self, "Something's got to be done." But what? Where can a gentleman get money when his income ain't even enough to keep a roof over himself and his loved ones? Thought and thought till m'head ached. Then today – Poof! – Leering gave me the answer. Not directly, y'understand. Just something he said. But I pounced on it right away. Trust me.'

He paused, took another drink and peered over the glass at her, to find her regarding him with the expression of a school-teacher listening to a weak excuse. He leaned forward. 'How would you like to be the wife of a Member of Parliament?' And he lay back and chuckled triumphantly.

'Aloysius,' she said doubtfully, 'are you playing games with me?'

'If I am, it's a great game. Played in Dublin with all the nobs. I mean it, Georgina. By Gad, I mean it!'

He certainly had her interest now. She was half out of her chair, bent towards him. 'Tell me . . .' she began. Then she flung herself back into the chair and exclaimed, 'Oh, how foolish I am to allow myself to be deceived by you yet again!'

He flung the glass, still half-full of claret, into the fire – an absolutely unthinkable thing for him to do – and bounced to his feet. 'So, you don't believe me, heh, woman? No faith in y'husband, heh?'

She was impressed, in spite of her misgivings. 'Very well, then, tell me.'

'Don't know if I should, now. Hard thing for a man to find's own wife mistrusts'm.'

'Oh, fiddle-faddle! You're bursting to tell me.'

His underlying high spirits bubbled over in another chuckle. 'Leering lunched with the Personage t'other day ...' Georgina's eyes lit at the name '... and had a long, very important discussion. All very secret, y'understand. Matters of State. 'Nough said. But, as a result, Leering's not taking up his seat in Parliament at next session. In any case, Government'll break any day. Be an election. Anyhow, important thing's he's offering seat to rent – private arrangements to be made with the man he chooses.

'Woman, d'ye know what it'd mean? Thousands to be made just from selling the vote. Get on the right side of the right people an' there's sinecures by the hundred, all nice, fat salaries for doin' nothin'. An' there's the Pensions List. Man makes himself useful to the right people, gets a pension from a grateful country. An' Leering knows all the right people. Introductions go with the seat.'

Georgina was looking at him as if he had suddenly been transformed into the Good Fairy. 'Oh, Aloysius! It would be wonderful. To live in Dublin! To meet the aristocracy! Perhaps even to be invited to Dublin Castle!'

She lay back with shining eyes as she saw her heart's desire within reach at last. And Aloysius smirked complacently. Then her face hardened and she jerked upright.

'But why should he let the seat to you? Where would you get the money? Many others will want it.'

'Aha!' He grinned. 'Now listen to this.' And he told her what had happened.

'You mean to tell me,' she said, 'that Maxwell Leering actually carried her into the house, knowing that his mother was there?'

'He was smitten, m'dear. Banged, stung, shot! Knocked head over heels! If you'd seen how he fussed over settling her in the carriage!'

'Well, that is amazing. Maxwell Leering! But I still don't understand...'

'Obvious, ain't it? Nuala plays up to him an' the seat's mine.'

She lay back and thought, then, 'Do you intend her to marry him?'

He shrugged. 'Good catch. Can't see how she could do better. But so long's she keeps him dazed until he lets me have the seat...'

'Well, I don't know. He is so very much older. And then, one does not wish to be coarse, but, well, the things that are said about him and women...'

He flushed. 'Bah! Few servant girls. Silly women. Nothing at all. He wouldn't dream of treating Nuala as anything but a lady. Dammit, woman, don't talk like that. Y'know I'm deuced fond of the girl. Wish her all happiness. I'd cut Leering's liver out at the mere suggestion.' He emptied his glass at a gulp and wiped his red face.

Georgina considered again. 'You may be right. Maxwell Leering is a cautious man, and at an age when settling down may well appeal to him. But... his mother!'

He shuddered. 'That blasted corpse! I know, I know. But if he makes up his mind, he'll manage her. No, everything depends on Nuala.'

'And what if she refuses?'

'Refuses!' he repeated incredulously. 'She's m'daughter. She'll damn well do as she's told. Blast everything! Georgina, woman, think what it'd mean to us. Put it to the girl.' He waggled his hand. 'Life in Dublin with the nobs. Y'know. Dress it up. An' don't forget, it's this or the Marshalsea for me. You tell her that!'

FIFTEEN

News of Conal's arrest had sped round the countryside. Unseen by Leering and his guests, many men waited behind walls and hedges. When it was over, they were able to speak to the released prisoners and heard what had happened. Then Aidan MacShane and Larry Dolan drove a cart into the yard.

Conal lay unconscious on the dirty cobbles. The constables were sluicing down the triangle and the cobbles. Red water ran in the gutter.

James Anstruther, the man who had carried out the whipping and whose bare torso still bore splashes of Conal's blood, hefted a broom and demanded, 'Who gave you permission to come in here?'

Larry hopped down from the cart, put on an expression of mock stupidity and said, 'Sure, we were sent by some men outside. About forty of them, I'd say. All friends of the lad there. Will I give them a shout, the way you can question them?'

The constables looked at each other. Then, 'Get him out of here!' said Anstruther.

'We will, sir. We will indeed, sir,' said Larry with mock subservience.

He and Aidan lifted Conal carefully and placed him, face down, on the straw in the cart.

Then Larry said, 'Before we go, sir, I think 'tis my patriotic duty to tell you that some of those fellows out there are not the leastest bit respectful to men of your high standing. Believe me, your honours, there's those amongst them who'd think nothing of calling on you one of these dark nights. And d'ye know, they're the wild sort of fellows who'd think nothing of doing to you what was done to the lad there. And, sure, fine bred gentry the likes of yourselves might not be able to stand up to such rough treatment the way a coarse Irishman would.' He knuckled his eyebrow at them. 'Mr James Anstruther and Mr William Jacoby, I'll bid you a very good night.'

Leading the horse slowly, they left the yard.

Larry turned at the gate and called, 'You will take care and you going home these dark nights, won't you, your honours!'

Conal's grandmother took over the nursing. She and MacShane's wife stripped him and washed him. Old Kattie MacShane had some reputation as a 'wise woman'. She prepared a great poultice of boiled herbs which she laid on his back and she sat by him throughout the night.

He was completely unconscious for two days, and then spent the best part of a week alternating between writhing delirium and a dead stillness. His grandmother was there always, sleeping only in occasional dozes, waking always when he began to babble, taking every opportunity to slip water or a portion of half-liquid potato and milk into his barely responsive mouth. She cleaned and bathed him. And she prayed.

Slowly the great wound dried and scabbed. Every few hours she covered his whole back with a salve she had made. By this time the delirium had left him, but he was still half-dazed and, although there was less pain, the slightest movement cracked the scabs and caused agony. Constantly lying on his face became acutely uncomfortable. His body ached to turn and often, when he had at last managed to get to sleep, he begun to turn involuntarily and woke immediately to excruciating pain.

For a long time all thought was concentrated on his body, on the avoidance of greater pain. Although he knew somebody was caring for him, he could not see who it was, could hear only a voice crooning comfortingly, simply making noises which conveyed the desire to comfort. One day, however, when she came to feed him, a sudden burst of appetite caused him to turn his head. He found that he could do so against the stiffness and with only slight pain. He saw her face – plain, even ugly, with wisps of white hair sprouting from the chin, very wrinkled and not too clean; but her eyes were deep, clear blue and filled with such tenderness that he wept. With difficulty, he reached out and took her hand – rough, bony, gnarled with rheumatism, but warm and wonderfully comforting.

She stroked his head. 'Thanks be to God, you're on the mend now.'

But after he had eaten well and settled in some contentment to sleep the really bad time began. His mind was clear, though much was vague or missing. He remembered the visit of the constables, the struggle and blackness. Everything between that and the triangle was like a swirling mist which varied between complete obscurity and uncertain awareness. Clear memory began with the first sight of the triangle, but it was mixed now, as it had been then, with that frightful scene in Paris. Vivid was the terrible shock of the lash – still so agonising in memory that his flesh cringed from the remembered expectation of agony cutting into unbearable agony. Then nothing until the slow emergence to pain, sickness, discomfort and weakness. And now, overwhelming everything, was the feeling of utter shame from the knowledge that a power, contemptuous and invincible, had used a barbaric punishment to torture and mutilate not only his body but his mind and his very dignity as a human being. Here, in his own country, of which he had dreamed for so long, to which he had returned with such optimistic joy, where he had hoped to find the loving warmth of a family, he had been degraded to a level below the animals.

The ever-present knowledge of his bodily weakness compared with the indifferent omnipotence of his enemies made him weep; and his tears confirmed his own helplessness. But self-pity fed anger and hatred and bred dreams of revenge. These dreams were comforting, so he encouraged them until they occupied almost all his waking thoughts, and they became plans, constantly changed. The wilder they became, the more comfort, even a kind of happiness, they brought him. But they were daydreams. When he slept, his enemies were all-powerful again. He raced endless, dark miles pursued by a red, roaring head, and a gigantic figure flailing at him with a monstrous whip whose lashes were gleaming knives. And always, as he almost escaped, the way was blocked by something formless, the greatest dread of all, a thing which was an icy, menacing voice.

So he slept badly and was glad to wake and wash his mind with thoughts of revenge. He welcomed every small sign of increasing strength because it seemed to lessen by ever so little the power of his enemies and brought nearer the time when he could actively seek revenge. The method was still far from clear, but the essentials were the torture, mutilation and death of Fowler, Grogan, the man with the whip and the owner of that voice.

One day the priest, Father O'Reilly, visited him.

'Thanks be to God you're back with us,' he said. 'I was here several times. Did you know I gave you the last rites? Indeed I did, you were so far gone. But I can see you're on the mend now. God and His Blessed Mother be thanked for it; and not forgetting Kattie MacShane.'

Conal merely muttered a greeting.

'You've plenty of time to yourself, there on your bed day and night. Time for thinking, and for praying, too, I hope.'

Conal flashed a look at him and the priest shook his head. 'Ah, God help you, lad, there's a terrible bitterness in you.'

'Haven't I cause!'

'Well, 'tis human, of course. I can understand it, aye, and sympathise; but, as a priest, I've to help fight human weakness. And there's no doubt of that, Conal: a weakness it is. Ah, but you don't need me to tell you that. I'm sure the good fathers in the College instructed you well. All I would say is: don't let the Devil have his way entirely.'

He laughed and looked at Conal, hoping for some sign that he had reached him; but there was none. He sighed

91

and stood up. 'I'll remember you in my Mass, as I have every day since it happened you.'

The reply was automatic, lifeless: 'Thank you, Father.'

On a sudden impulse the priest said, 'You're a fine, handsome young fellow, when you're at yourself, that is. Tell me this: did you never meet any young girl who made you think of her a second time?'

In spite of himself, the answer was in Conal's eyes. The priest laughed. 'Thank God! For a time there you had me thinking human nature was changing. Goodbye, now, Conal. Say an odd prayer for me.'

This was the first time he had thought of Nuala Grogan. No, that was not quite true. He had refused to think about her. He had deliberately buried the memory of his happiness as he had talked to her. Now he was annoyed that the priest had forced him to think of her. His mind rebelled against holding, simultaneously, pleasant thoughts of her and murderous thoughts about her father. But from then on he was never able to think of Grogan without thinking of Nuala.

Father O'Reilly had caused a further complication. The voices of long-gone preachers and teachers insisted upon being heard with arguments against any form of revenge.

After that he slept even less. Against the background of pain, weakness and mortification, lust for vengeance fought a constant battle against Nuala and Charity. Though he grew stronger and could lie more comfortably, it was often late into the night before he could sleep; and when he did, he was tormented by wild dreams.

One nightmare took over from all the rest and haunted him nightly. He was the operator of an apparatus such as he had seen in Paris. Enormous soldiers held his enemies close by. He spoke to an immense crowd of the evil which had been done to him and they wept for him. He explained what the apparatus would do to his enemies, and the crowd laughed and cheered. Slowly and deliberately, to prolong his pleasure, he turned to choose his first victim; but, when he looked at them, though they were alive, their torsos ended smoothly at the shoulders.

The crowd, also seeing this, shouted their angry disappointment, screamed that they wanted blood, and they pointed behind him, shouting, 'Her! Her!' He turned and saw the woman who had been executed in Paris strapped to the apparatus. When he hesitated, they shouted, 'Her or you! Her or you!' and began to advance on him menacingly. A voice whispered to him, 'You are more important than she; and she is already dead.' He recognised the voice of Temptation, knew that he should resist it, but pretended that it was not really he who set the machine in motion. That terrible knife flashed... And, dangling from the soldier's bloody fist, was Nuala's lovely head.

He would awaken in a sweating panic to find slow relief in the realisation that it had been only a dream. But, as night approached again, he fought against sleep, exhausting himself physically and mentally, delaying his recovery.

He had many visitors and he welcomed them all. No matter what they talked about they hindered thought. They were angry at the injustice he had suffered, and they told stories of other victims who had exacted highly coloured, fully detailed vengeance. It surprised him that the most lurid stories came from the meekest men. He mentioned it to Larry Dolan.

'Ach, talkers!' he said. 'The curse of Ireland. Pay them no heed. Leave off thinking until you're strong and well, then we'll talk about payment for wrongs done. Just lie there and take your ease and get plenty of sleep into you.'

Conal told him he had difficulty in sleeping, without saying why.

'Isn't it well, then, I brought you a drop of good medicine.' He produced a jar of poteen. 'Get a good slug of that into you and you'll sleep like a babby in his mother's arms.'

It worked. Night after night of deep blankness. The only trouble was that the 'slugs' had to be larger after a few nights, and increasingly large. Then he would wake with his head throbbing, his mouth dry and foul-tasting and his stomach revolting at the very thought of food.

Kattie MacShane, gentle nurse turned tyrant, shouted and even screamed at him to give up the poteen which, she said, was undoing all her good work. But even the ill-effects were preferable to the nightmare, and he continued to drink until the jar was empty. He lay awake that night, afraid of sleep.

The next day Michael Canahan visited him for the first time. After the first greetings, not very cordial on either side, he said, 'I'd say you're past the worst of it. Can you get up from that bed?'

Without replying, Conal began to struggle upright. He was angry with his own weakness and he persisted. With sweat streaming down his face, he got to his knees. From there to his feet required more effort than he had ever given to anything in his life. But he managed it, swayed and fell flat again.

Canahan made no move to help him. All he said was, ''Twill be easier next time.'

'How the hell would you know?'

'This way!' Canahan pulled off his coat and shirt and showed his bare back – a mass of rough puckers and scars. 'Twice it happened me.'

'But why?'

'For no more reason than it happened you. And we're not the only men in Ireland to bear these marks. But I want you to listen. The last time we met I promised I'd tell you how you could get back your lands.'

Canahan spoke of the United Irishmen and, even though he sometimes forgot that he was not in front of his class, Conal was interested.

'Would they help me to get my rights?'

Canahan hesitated. 'Well, the first thing they'd need to do when they'd taken the land from the landlords would be to decide who should own it.'

'So the true owners would come into their own again.'

'Everyone would come into their own again. Now, I want you to think of this. The people here look to you as their leader. Here's your chance to lead them into a branch of the United Irishmen. I'll come and talk again when you're up and well.'

That night he slept deeply and dreamlessly.

SIXTEEN

Georgina warned her husband not to discuss the events
of the day with Nuala. In fact he was to avoid her for the
next two or three days; and for a start, he was to leave the
drawing-room and keep out of the way. He grumbled
that it was the only comfortable room in the house, that
he was snug in his chair and wished to remain there until
supper.

She shrugged. 'As you wish, my love. If you prefer a
seat here to a seat in Dublin, I should be less than a dutiful
wife to gainsay you.'

'What? Now wait, Georgina. Don't understand you at
all.'

'Of course you don't, my love. How could a man
understand that it is impossible for a mother to speak
confidentially to her daughter whilst he is present? What
would a man understand about a young girl?'

'But, dammit, Georgina, she's up in her room.'

'She is. And she is probably still weeping. But after a
time she will tire of weeping. She may even fall asleep for
a short time. Then she will feel hungry and will creep
downstairs.' Her tone of soft reasonableness changed
abruptly to derision. 'And if she catches one glimpse of
you she'll run back again, and I shall lose the opportunity
of speaking to her at the one time above all when she is
most likely to be prepared to listen!'

'Tell you what'll do, then –' he began.

She almost leaped from the chair and stood over him,

and Aloysius met a Georgina he had never known existed. 'You stupid, lazy creature!' She stood, her arms akimbo, quivering with anger and determination. 'Since the day I first met you I have had to suffer your vain promises, your idleness, your drunkenness and a host of other failings which have brought us to the verge of beggary. Now we have the opportunity not alone to solve our money problems, but for me to get at last some of the things I have longed for and deserved all my life. Left to you, it would be just one more opportunity lost, and, in a matter of months, you would be in gaol and Nuala and I would be homeless and starving.'

He tried to interject.

'Quiet, you stupid man!' she hissed. 'Understand me well. I will play the submissive wife no longer. I intend that we shall go to Dublin; and I shall allow nothing to stand in the way of that. Nothing and nobody! Least of all you. Two things alone you are to keep in mind: you are to become a Member of Parliament; and to achieve it, you will do exactly what I say. Now, without any further argument, you will go to your room, and you will remain there until morning.'

Stupefied, he got up from the chair and went to the door. There he turned and opened his mouth.

'Aloysius!' she warned.

'I'm hungry!'

'A tray will be sent up to you.'

He nodded, paused to look in amazement at her, shook his head, sighed and left.

As predicted, Nuala peeped round the door about half an hour later.

'My baby!' Georgina crooned, with open arms, and Nuala ran to her.

'Now tell mama what has upset her chicken.'

Nuala saw again the dreadful, bloody thing hanging from the triangle. 'Oh, it was horrible, mama!' She shuddered and hid her face in her mother's shoulder.

Georgina patted her. 'There, there, baby. It's all over now; and we must ensure that you are not frightened in that way again. You must try to forget it.'

'But I can't!' Nuala wailed. 'I keep seeing it in my mind, and I know I shall have bad dreams about it. Why did they do it, mama?'

'Why did who do what?'

'Why did papa and the others punish the man like that?'

Georgina shrugged. 'Goodness, child, how should I know? But, now, you were rather naughty to go there at all. It was men's business, my dear; and ladies do not interfere in that. You may be sure they had the very best of reasons. I must confess I know little of these matters; but I do understand the necessity for guarding ourselves against these people.'

'Which people?'

'Why, the common people, of course. You must understand, my dear, that they hate us, and are always a danger to us. I am sure you have heard of the dreadful things the common people have been doing in France. These people would be just as horrible if men like your papa and dear Sir Maxwell did not protect us from them. The man you saw had probably committed some terrible crime and was being justly punished for it.'

'But why should they hate us?'

'Because we are different. Not the same class. Not even the same sort of people. We are... well, it is rather difficult to explain, but there are ladies and gentlemen and there are common people, and they're quite different. And then, remember, these people are Papists.'

'Does that make them very different?'

'Of course it does! Goodness, they adore images and they lock up young girls in convents for shocking purposes. And they hate the King and would kill him if they could and put a Papist King in his place, and then they'd burn us all at the stake. But why are we bothering our heads about these things? They are matters for men to deal with. We have far more interesting things to talk about.'

She gave Nuala a great squeeze and, in an excited tone, she said, 'And we are going to talk about them now. Go and sit over there, my dear, and prepare yourself for some delightful news.'

Nuala, catching the excitement, stood up. 'What is it?'

Georgina raised a playfully admonitory finger, then pointed with it. 'Over there, young lady. Sit down and listen carefully.'

Nuala sat on the edge of the chair. 'Oh, mama, please don't tease me.'

Georgina laughed. 'Patience, my chicken, patience! Tell me, how would you like to live in a fine house in Dublin? Meet all the best people there? Join in all the fun and excitement? Be a part of the gay world of real ladies and gentlemen?'

Nuala's eyes seemed to grow larger and shine brighter with every word. 'Is it true, mama?'

Georgina smiled. 'It could be. It might very well be. And, if everything goes well, it will be.'

'Oh, mama! When? Tell me, when? And where shall we live? Shall we have a fine new carriage, and liveried servants, and lovely clothes, and ... Oh, when, mama, when?'

Georgina explained about the seat in Parliament and their absolute dependence on Leering's favour.

'So you see, my dear, we must all do our best to persuade dear Sir Maxwell to let your father have the seat.'

'I don't like his mother.'

'But you don't know her.'

Nuala had not intended ever revealing what had taken place between her and the old lady, but she was forced to tell it now.

'Oh dear!' said her mother. 'How very unfortunate. I must think what is best to do. You must understand that Sir Maxwell is devoted to his dear mother and he would not like it if we had offended her or even displeased her. We must please him in every way, mustn't we?'

'If you say so, mama.' She shrugged indifferently. 'I am sure I have no wish to displease him.'

'But, chicken, that is not enough. We must do things to

98

please him.'

Nuala was puzzled. 'What things?'

Her mother laughed. 'What a darling little innocent you are! It will be much more difficult for me than for you.'

Nuala was more puzzled than ever. 'I simply do not understand, mama.' She shook her head. 'I don't.'

Her mother laughed again, very merrily. She leaned forward and spoke very deliberately. 'You are a lovely young lady. A very lovely young lady, I am proud to say. Not all young ladies are beautiful. Now men, bless them, all admire youth and beauty. I am sure Sir Maxwell admires you, the dear man.'

'But he has only seen me once, and that was, well...' She shivered.

'Next time he sees you,' said her mother hastily, 'it will be quite different. Now what you must remember is that it gives a gentleman great pleasure to be in the company of a beautiful young lady. Providing, of course, she is pleasant and agreeable, willing to listen to him, to encourage him to talk about himself and to admire him.'

'Do you mean to say that if I behave like that he will let us go to Dublin?'

'Exactly so, chicken.'

'Well, I don't see anything difficult in that,' said Nuala slowly. Then, with sudden realisation, 'If that is all...' She jumped to her feet, reached with both hands, pulled her mother up and danced her round the room, singing, 'We're going to Dublin, to Dublin, to Dublin! We'll sing and we'll dance and we'll... Oh, mama!'

During the night Georgina thought over the matter of Lady Leering and the following morning she ordered the carriage and sent for Nuala. She told her that they were going visiting, but refused to say where until they were on their way. Then she said that they were going to visit Lady Leering, stressed that all their plans depended on it and instructed Nuala in how she was to behave.

When they arrived, they were kept waiting some time

before being ushered by the maid-servant into the Presence.

Georgina gave Lady Leering no time for speech. She curtsied, as did Nuala behind her, and said, 'My dear Lady Leering, having heard with the utmost disgust of the atrocious behaviour of my daughter yesterday, I have brought her here at the earliest possible moment to make what amends she may.' She turned her head. 'Step forward, miss, and say what you have to say!'

Nuala, with eyes demurely downcast, took two paces forward, curtsied again and in a very low voice said, 'I most sincerely apologise for my bold behaviour, Lady Leering, and I beg that you will forgive me.'

Before Lady Leering could answer, Georgina said, 'And may I add the apologies of a mother who had mistakenly thought she had reared her daughter to practise the niceties of social behaviour. Our apologies, furthermore, for disturbing your ladyship.' They both curtsied again and Georgina said, 'Thank you, your ladyship. Good morning.'

She turned to Nuala. 'Go now, miss!' They made to leave the room.

'One moment!' The words were as much a command as an invitation. Georgina turned, her head inclined obsequiously. Nuala stopped with her hand on the doorknob. She felt a sudden, desperate longing to be out of this room, away from this cold, old woman; and at the same time she felt a dissatisfaction with herself.

'Courtesy, madam, demands courtesy,' said Lady Leering. 'And, young lady, courtesy begets courtesy. It is, unfortunately so rare in these times and particularly so in this place, that I should be failing myself if I were not to acknowledge it. I am appreciative, madam, of the thought which brought you here; and, may I say, I consider you acted in the strictest correctness.'

'Your ladyship is too kind,' said Georgina with another curtsy.

The old lady tinkled a little bell. 'You will stay and take a dish of tea with me.' Again it was more command than invitation.

Nuala would long remember the half hour she spent perched on the edge of a hard chair in the background, sipping a cup of unwanted tea and feeling like a deliberately discarded exhibit, whilst her mother and Lady Leering discussed the dreadful decline of good manners amongst people, and particularly young people, in the circles which were supposed to represent polite society. As the time dragged endlessly on and the old voice peck-peck-pecked at the cold stillness of the room, she felt that all laughter and gaiety, all the exhilaration of life had been killed for ever and that she, unwillingly allied to these two alien creatures, was being forced to share the joyless celebration of the murder they had committed.

'How old are you?'

She jumped, rattling the cup and saucer.

'Nuala! Really! Daydreaming, I do declare! Her ladyship wishes to know how old you are.'

Nuala blushed. 'I beg your pardon. I am – er – I am seventeen, your ladyship.'

'A child, a mere child.' Something peculiar happened to the old lady's mouth, as if a twisted crack had appeared in the ivory, and Nuala realised that it was supposed to be a smile.

Georgina rose and gracefully placed her cup and saucer in exactly the correct position in exactly the correct place. 'Your ladyship has been over-indulgent with two penitents; and we, I fear, have trespassed on your kindness.'

In the carriage, Nuala waited until they were clear of the house, then expelled her breath with a whoosh, bounced two or three times on the seat, flung her arms above her head, snatched off her bonnet, flung it on to the opposite seat and exclaimed, 'What a horrible, horrible old woman!'

Georgina laughed, preening herself. 'We did excellently well, my chicken. Excellently well. Except for the fact that we did not see Sir Maxwell, I think we may very well congratulate ourselves.'

Nuala sank back into the corner, closed her eyes and felt a faint, unaccountable nausea.

SEVENTEEN

Leering had set out early that morning to visit Mr ~~Stewart, the secretary.~~

~~Stewart was not surprised when his visitor was~~ announced, though he pretended to be so. He was elaborately courteous in his greetings.

But Leering cut in abruptly. 'Sir, you and I can, I believe, dispense with subterfuge, for I am convinced that our aims are similar and that we can be of mutual assistance.'

Stewart smiled noncommittally, but, by the merest suggestion of leaning an ear, invited Leering to continue.

'May I take it that we cannot be overheard?'

Stewart spread his hands and smiled reassuringly. (After all, Leering could not possibly know that a secretary would have his own secretary whose standing orders were to press his ear to the keyhole and scribble notes of all conversations such as this.)

'Very well, then,' said Leering. 'I will be blunt. I seek advancement, as do you.'

There was an expression of hurt in the eyes of young Mr Stewart, the faithful servant who lived solely to be of service irrespective of reward.

'Come, sir,' said Leering, 'do me the courtesy of not underestimating my intelligence.'

Stewart laughed.

'I have, I am quite sure, the answer to all our worries.' He explained. There existed the Peep O' Day Boys and a few smaller groups, composed mainly of the lower orders amongst the members of the Established Church. These came together when threatened by the activities of the native Irish and other disaffected groups such as the Presbyterians. He had begun strengthening his local group of Peep O' Day Boys, but their weaknesses were that membership was almost entirely composed of small farmers and servants, and that they acted only sporadically and ineffectively. What was needed was a new organisation for high and low; the upper classes to lead and the lower to obey. Such an organisation could not only combat the menace of the United Irishmen, but could succeed in a task long uncompleted: the driving out from the Province of Ulster of all the native Irish. In Cromwellian times the order to the Irish had been 'To Hell or Connaught'. That cry could be raised again; and this time it would be followed resolutely.

He could organise such a society; but, in order to do so, he would require first the assistance of Mr Stewart, then the support and actual membership of the Personage, as a figurehead, of course. From that would come the support and membership of every person of standing in the Province and, later, in the country.

Given that leadership, the common men would flock to the society. It would be constantly stressed to them that their interests lay in direct and active opposition to the native Irish and their supporters, and that the only permanent safeguard would be the ridding of the Province of all disaffected elements. This body of men, well-armed and completely committed, would be available to the leadership at all times.

Stewart had listened with interest. At this point he held up his hand. 'One moment, sir, I beg you.' He went through a small door and returned carrying a snuff-box which he had just taken from his pocket. He did not tell Leering that he had sent his secretary on a spurious errand. 'Do you snuff, sir?'

The two then discussed the important question of how, having organised this society and earned the gratitude of the Personage and the entire Establishment, they would ensure that gratitude would be expressed in tangible form.

'So, my dear Maxwell,' said Stewart eventually, 'I think the first step would be an invitation to you and Lady Leering to the next social event of importance to be held here. Leave that to me.'

'No, Robert, I would not wish my mother to be present.'

'Your mother? I had meant . . .' With some concern, 'Do I understand you are not married?'

'That is so.'

Stewart pursed his lips. 'Oh! Oh, dear!' His look was a fresh examination of Maxwell Leering. 'I should not have thought . . . Hem! Believe me, m'dear fellow, I have a mind as broad as . . .' He spread his arms to show no limitation. 'But the Personage . . . Great stickler for the moralities, y'know . . .'

Leering flushed with embarrassment and anger. 'Great God! Are you implying that I'm a . . . Dammit, I'm a man, sir! And I'm ready at any time to defend . . .'

'No more, no more, no more!' Stewart took him by the shoulders and shook him gently. 'A terrible mistake on my part. I most humbly beg your forgiveness. My anxiety to secure the support of my master, you understand? Please tell me that you forgive me.'

They parted allies.

EIGHTEEN

The following morning Ballyna House was honoured with a visit from Sir Maxwell Leering. He had come, he said, to enquire after the health of Miss Grogan following her distressing collapse at his house. He begged forgiveness for his delay in calling, but yesterday it had been his duty to attend on the Personage. He also wished to thank them for their visit to his dear mama, who had expressed to him her pleasure in their visit. (Actually she had described Georgina as 'a dowdy, poor creature' and Nuala as 'a pretty child, inclined to pertness'.)

Nuala was impressed. She thought him quite handsome in a worldly-worn way, very well-dressed; and his air of the great world, the ease with which he mentioned being on friendly terms with the Personage were to her like a glimpse through a palace window.

Georgina expressed her delight only with difficulty. She wanted to hug herself in congratulation.

Both ladies were charming to him and he wished to bathe awhile in their charm, particularly in the fresh charm of this most desirable young lady. But Aloysius was present, had been present when Leering arrived, and could scarcely have been ordered from the room, much though Georgina wished to do it. Deaf and blind to his wife's hints and glances, he flapped obesely in his concern to have his guest comfortably seated, pressed claret and snuff on him and monopolised the conversation, driving it along the dull road of local topics. Leering cut short his visit, but only after a vague arrangement that he would call to take Nuala riding.

Aloysius, having escorted his visitor to the door, returned, glowing with pride in his success as a host, to the drawing-room from which Nuala had been sent.

'You stupid, bumbling idiot!' his wife greeted him. He looked as if she had slammed him on the head with a hammer. 'You ruined it! The entire visit. You ruined it! And after all I said to you. Did you think, you zany, that he came to see you? He came to see Nuala! And you gave him no opportunity with your stupid talk of Barclay's gout and of horse liniment and... Oh, what a fool I married!'

And she swept out of the room.

*

At the time of mentioning the possibility of taking Nuala riding, Leering had thought that perhaps a week or two should pass before making definite arrangements, but it was only three days later that a servant arrived with a letter to Mrs Grogan requesting that Sir Maxwell Leering should be permitted the pleasure of her daughter's company on the following day. The return note graciously gave a mother's consent.

Nuala was excited by the prospect of getting away from her dull surroundings and flattered that a gentleman of the world should seek her company, so she greeted him with an enthusiasm which heightened his pleasure in seeing her again. He was extravagant in his compliments on the attractiveness of her riding-habit, gallantly helped her to mount and rode off with her in such a state of exhilaration that he was quite unaware of the stares of servants and beggars, of the self-congratulatory smile of Georgina as she stood at the front door, or of the delighted grin on the fat face which peered from a bedroom window.

They had ridden for fully five minutes before he became aware that he was experiencing happiness.

They rode up into the hills and down into pretty, lake-patched valleys and eventually to the summit of a great hill which was crowned with a large, circular, roofless building of stone.

'How odd,' she said. 'What is it, Sir Maxwell?'

'An old palace or fortress, so they say – the Irish, I mean.'

'It looks ancient.'

He laughed. 'It does, I suppose. But these Irish are much given to exaggeration when speaking of their past. They would have us believe that they were not always the half-savages they are today. According to them, everything was wonderful "in the old days". All the women were beautiful, all the men tall, handsome and enormously strong. They had great kings, who kept court in such places as this. All nonsense, of course. But look, the view is very pleasant.'

106

Away below them on one side a sea lough stretched far to where it curved behind the enclosing mountains. On the other sides the brown of the hills was patched with the greens of valleys and fields and woodlands changing from blue to purple in the distance.

She turned to him and said, 'Is it not truly beautiful!'

He stared deliberately into her eyes. 'I find the view quite enchanting.'

His admiration and desire were plain and she was flattered and excited. Yet she felt an unaccountable fear. She was conscious of her inexperience, her inability to cope with his strength and self-certainty. The sudden horrifying thought came to her that he was viewing her as he might examine a horse which he was thinking of buying, and that he could acquire her as easily as the horse. In confusion she blushed and hung her head – presenting to him an even more delightful picture.

He laughed. 'Come, my dear. I shall show you the Irish as they really are, and then a building far finer than this ruin.'

She looked up and he smiled at her and she blamed herself for being a foolish little ninny. If the girls at school could only see her now, dressed in her beautiful habit and being squired by this important man whom she had the power to attract! And, realising that she was not powerless, she smiled brilliantly at him and exulted at the effect.

'Which way?' she asked.

He pointed down a smooth slope of turf.

'I'll race you!' she challenged and spurred her horse into a gallop.

Her hack was no match for his thoroughbred, but he gallantly allowed her to lead until she reined in and called to him, 'You cheated. You are not truly trying.'

He laughed as he came up to her. 'You deserve a far better mount, my dear. Perhaps, one of these days, you will accept one from me.'

She could read the desire in his eyes again, and again she exulted. He was rich, the potential source of many desirable things. But she spoke with deliberate lightness. 'Lah, sir! Whatever would dear mama say!'

'Oh, I should ask her, of course. And, if she agreed, what then?'

'Why then, sir,' she said, wide-eyed, 'what could I do but obey mama's wishes?'

He laughed with delight in her, then said, 'Come, let me show you as I promised.'

He led the way up a long hill and paused on the crest and pointed away down. The hillside below them was rough with rock, gorse, bracken and heather. Near the bottom was the great wall surrounding woodland, shrubbery, parkland and lawns with the house, enormous even from this distance, set in the midst of it.

'Oh, the Besant House,' she said. 'I have never seen it before.'

'Yes,' he said, 'the Besant House. The property of our lord and master, Sir Julius Besant, who lives in England and has never seen the place.'

She was surprised by the bitterness of his tone and she looked at him and saw, as well as bitterness, the desire for ownership.

He led the way by a rough path which gradually grew steeper. After a time he stopped and said, 'It would be better, I think, if we dismounted and led the horses for a little way.'

She was relieved because her nag had already stumbled several times. They went on foot, in single file, down a narrow gully. This eventually opened out and he waited for her. She found herself staring down into a bowl in the hillside in the centre of which a dozen crude hovels squatted in disorder round an open space. The rough windowless mud walls and the wild, weed-grown thatches gave the huts the appearance of scabrous, hairy beggars crouching round a filthy marketplace. The open space was littered with muddy offal in which pigs, poultry, dogs and cats rooted for titbits, whilst numerous half-naked children played shrilly amongst them. An atmosphere of poverty and misery lay over the place like the miasma over a swamp.

She wrinkled her nose in disgust. 'What is that dreadful place?'

'There, my dear, you see the Irish who claim such noble ancestry. They call it Duncarran.'

'Why do they live in such..? Ugh!'

'Because they are barbarians, my dear, lacking all culture, all sensitivity. But come, we will ride quickly through.'

They mounted and had ridden down a little way when there was a wild scurrying amongst the children and they disappeared into the cabins. When they rode through there was neither sight nor sound of human life; yet she was very conscious that many eyes were watching them. She held her breath against the stench and closed her eyes against the squalor; but she could not close her mind against the fear of poverty. It was like a living presence menacing her.

When she could no longer hold her breath, she expelled it audibly and opened her eyes. They were clear of the place and she breathed the pure air gratefully. Much nearer now, she could see the Besant Park like a beautiful oasis. Below it was the road and beyond that fields and bog stretching away to the purple of distant hills and the far misty lift of the mountains. The lovely view seemed to wash her eyes, yet her mind still saw the dreadful place behind her, lying like an ulcer on Beauty's cheek.

She shivered. She felt his hand on her arm and she turned to him. His voice was full of concern. 'My dear, how can I apologise sufficiently for subjecting you to such a disgusting sight. I was utterly thoughtless.'

For a moment his touch brought comfort; then, unaccountably, she wanted to snatch her arm away. One thing only prevented her, and that was the memory that he stood between her and Poverty; and Poverty was the festering sore behind her. So she sat, eyes closed, inwardly shrinking from his touch, yet welcoming the fact that he could shield her and excited that she could command his strength.

109

She opened her eyes and smiled at him. 'I was being very silly,' she said.

Half an hour later, having traversed nearly a mile of drive, they arrived at the house. Leering produced a large key and, with effort, using both hands, he unlocked the front door. It creaked and groaned as he pushed it inwards.

She smelt dampness and decay as she peered into the dimness of the hall and only his hand on her elbow persuaded her to enter. He led her across the echoing emptiness to a door in the right wall, which he opened, and they passed into a vastness faintly lit by the odd fingers of daylight which pierced the cracks in the shutters. The air was musty and dank. She shivered.

'This is the ballroom, my dear.'

'It feels as if it is haunted.'

'Not at all. There was much gaiety here once. And there could be again. A thorough airing and cleaning and repainting and this would truly be a fitting place to house a gentleman.' He looked at her. 'And his lady.'

She had a horrifying vision of herself locked in this mausoleum with him forever. Shivering inwardly, she forced a tremulous smile. 'Whatever it might be, sir, it is now cold and drear; and I grow weary. I should like to go home now.'

Dutifully he escorted her home, talking lightly all the way of the places he had visited, the people he had met – of the great world of her dreams.

She was glad to reach home again; yet, no sooner had he gone, than she was chiding herself for her stupid fears.

The following Sunday morning Georgina escorted her family to church. There were three of them – Mrs Georgina Grogan, Miss Nuala Grogan and a fat, red-faced man, believed to be the husband and father, a very quiet, self-effacing fellow. It was some time since any of them had attended church. Georgina had carefully avoided exposing her shabbiness to their neighbours. Now, however, she and Nuala were dressed as finely as any and, as for the third member of the party, well, nobody noticed him anyway.

It was a pleasant late-April morning with warm sunshine and an expanse of shower-washed blue sky lightly flecked with cloud. The clamour of the birds proclaimed the joy of the morning. Trees and bushes were clad in new green. And all was obviously designed as a background to show off the beauty of the ladies in their finery and the elegance of the gentlemen.

When the service was over the congregation gathered in the church yard for the important business of seeing and being seen. Leering and his mother had waited, as usual, in their pew until the congregation had assembled outside. They then emerged, gave hands and platitudes to the curate, then paraded the pathway, Leering coldly hat-raising, his mama icily nodding as they received their due from the assembly.

He almost passed Nuala as deliberately unseen as the rest, but she caught his eye, smiled and curtsied. Then, half-feeling that she had smiled deliberately, a touch of shame made her blush. Leering, however, misinterpreted the blush and his heart gave a sudden, very pleasant kick. He stopped and there were polite murmurs exchanged, even by a slightly thawed Lady Leering who expressed to Georgina her approval of the Christian religion and its beneficial effects on The Young. A fat red-faced nonentity in the background raised his hat and bowed six times.

The pause was momentary. Lady Leering had to be settled in her carriage by her attentive son. But the nonentity, to his complete confusion, found his hand being shaken by no less a person that Sir Maxwell Leering. That shaking was a prelude to the kissing of Georgina's hand, followed by the slightly more pro-longed, slightly more fervent kissing of Nuala's hand.

Maxwell had, naturally, told his dear mama that the Personage had expressed willingness to promote his advancement but had intimated that the acquisition of a wife was a first essential.

111

Leering called two days later to bring the Grogans' invitations to the Hunt Ball, which had always previously been delivered by a groom. He stayed and took tea with the ladies. Mr Grogan, he learned, was indisposed. Nothing serious, but confined to his room. For an hour he balanced the cup from which he had taken one sip and talked to Nuala, who sat beside him on the sofa, whilst Mrs Grogan was busily engaged with her sewing on the other side of the room where the light was better.

In the fortnight before the ball he took Nuala riding three times.

At last came the Hunt Ball – *the* social event of the year. The courtroom had been cleared except for the dais, which, draped with bunting and festooned with plants and flowers, held the musicians. Curtains and tapestries hid the white-washed walls and so the prisoners' rings. Alcoves had been contrived with wooden frames decorated with bunting and sprays of blossom, all set around with shrubs and banks of spring flowers. The floor, sanded for days then polished for more days, richly reflected the soft light of hundreds of candles set in glittering chandeliers borrowed from the house. At the end opposite the dais a long table was laid with a huge punch-bowl as the centrepiece of a multitude of other drinks, dishes of sweetmeats and a profusion of fruit in scintillating cut glass bowls.

Leering, dressed in the black silk coat, waistcoat and breeches, black buckled shoes, frothy white cravat and cuffs and small, well-powdered wig, which was becoming the fashionable evening-wear for gentlemen, stood at the door with his mother to welcome the guests. If she had changed her dress for the festivities, it was unnoticeable. She was there to do her duty and she was very obviously and grimly doing it.

Every room in the house was brilliantly lit and the curtains had been left open so that the light streamed out on to the drive and lawns. Lanterns were set at frequent intervals along the drive and the front steps. Footmen opened carriage doors and helped the guests to alight.

Ostlers took charge of the horses of the mounted gentlemen. Inside, maids and footmen led the way to cloakrooms and from there by decorated passages to the ballroom.

Georgina planned and managed that they should be amongst the last to arrive and secretly congratulated herself when she saw Leering's expression change to delight when he saw Nuala.

She was vividly beautiful in a gown of deep red velvet. The full skirt flowed out in sweeping folds from her slim waist; above, it clung to her soft curves and showed to perfection her white, delicately rounded shoulders. Her eyes, taking darker colour from her gown, were deep and limpid and they shone with happiness and excitement. Her first ball!

Any other guests were left to arrive ungreeted. Leering was taking no risks that his prize would be claimed by any of the unattached young gentlemen. He led her straight into the dance. She, whilst appreciating his elegance, his importance and what he could mean to her and her family, was conscious only of the brightness of the scene, the gaiety, the music and the rhythm and flow of the dance. All she wanted was that life would go on like this.

Leering, seeing her happiness, thought it entirely due to him. He felt his youth return, saw the achievement of his plans being doubly satisfying because of being shared with this delightful girl. And the many attempts by other men to claim her for a dance, the envy in their eyes, their bitterness when he froze them away, the hard eyes of many of the other women, all convinced him that Nuala was the essential partner for him.

He was aware and heedless of the fact that they were being constantly watched by almost everybody in the hall. The old ladies, out of Lady Leering's hearing, had much to discuss in the fact that he, a most eligible bachelor for twenty years, had been hooked at last; and they looked at Georgina with new respect. The younger men who had tried to dance with Nuala were growling together their disgust that 'an old man like him' should be claiming the attentions of a young girl. There was much discussion about whether they had been insulted and whether or not they should demand satisfaction.

This was finally heard by Barclay, who burst furiously into their midst. 'You stupid young idiots! Cease this talk of duels immediately. There is not one of you who could stand up to Maxwell Leering with either swords or pistols. Dammit all, don't you know he'd killed more than one man before he was the age of any of you.' And Barclay joined the older men to discuss the forthcoming elections.

None of this interfered with enjoyment. Great quantities of liquor were consumed, openly by the gentlemen, secretly behind fans and in the shelter of alcoves by the ladies. The younger people, forgetting their host and his constant partner, concentrated on enjoying themselves.

The music and the sounds of laughter and gay chatter floated out on the night air to where, in the shadows, the ragged descendants of those who had once owned this land listened and looked at the brilliant gaiety of this alien world. And there were those amongst them who recalled that Versailles had been like this only a short time before.

Supper, the high-spot of the evening, occupied nearly two hours of solid eating and copious drinking. During it, Leering had Nuala seated beside him, whilst his mother was many yards away, hidden behind mounds of food and decorations, at the other end of the table. Nuala was intoxicated enough by the gay atmosphere, by the extravagance of the compliments paid to her by so many young men, by their obvious admiration and their jealousy, by Leering's charm and masterfulness and his cool command of everything and everybody contrasted with his deference to her. Two slowly-sipped glasses of sweet wine elevated her to fairyland. Maxwell, as he had begged her to call him, was the Fairy Prince and the assembly were his courtiers. She laughed and chattered, frequently with an accentuating touch on his sleeve and even on his hand, but unaware of his transports when she did so. He ignored all outside attempts to claim his attention and it was as if he sat with her inside an enchanted glass wall.

But he was still conscious of duty to be done. Towards the end of the meal, catching many with full mouths, he rose and tapped his glass. As by magic, the noise stopped.

'My friends and neighbours, may I say first what happiness it gives to my dear mama' – bowing to her – 'and myself to see you all so obviously enjoying our hospitality. I know you do not wish to hear long speeches. Many of you are ready to settle down to cards, and we younger ones are anxious to return to the dancing. There is, however, an announcement which I wish to make. Duties of the highest national importance and urgency will claim my attention and energies for some time to come. I am not at liberty to specify what those duties are. Suffice it to say that I take them up, and gladly do I do so, at the express request of a Personage who shall be nameless. That being so, I must vacate my Parliamentary seat. In those circumstances, I must, as a duty, nominate my successor.'

He raised his glass. 'Ladies and gentlemen, I ask you to rise and drink the health of your new Member of Parliament, my dear friend, Mr Aloysius Grogan.'

NINETEEN

With the aid of a stick, walking very slowly, Conal reached the corner where the boreen from MacShane's cabin entered the road. Although it was only a quarter of a mile, he had had to stop many times to rest and had often been tempted to go back. But ever since Canahan's last visit he had been determined to overcome his weakness. His first great achievement had been getting from his bed to a stool by the fire, and that had not been until two days after the visit. For a week that and the return journey had been enough to exhaust him. Then, when the weather became warm, he had managed to get outside the cabin and rest there for an hour or two. From that he graduated to walking ten or a dozen paces out and back, then increasing the number of paces day by day. Gradually he grew stronger and became more confident. Scores of paces grew to a hundred and then to hundreds, until, having achieved five hundred paces the previous day, the warm sunshine, the urge to get away completely from the boredom of the cabin and, above, all, annoyance at the slowness of his progress and the desire to be completely active when Canahan called next forced him onward until, triumphant, but completely spent, he reached the corner.

There was a pleasant grassy bank beside the road on which the sun shone warmly. With a groan, part pain, part satisfaction, he lowered himself on to it. Then, very carefully because he was still stiff and sore, he lay back and closed his eyes.

He was very thin. His gaunt face was doubly pale because of the illness and long confinement. He felt utterly exhausted and knew that he would have to rest for a long time before he could begin the return journey.

The warmth of the sun, the scent of flowers and grasses, the murmur of insects and the mourning of a wood-pigeon lulled him and he dozed – not quite asleep, but relaxed and feeling his weakness being supported and comforted. It was pleasant, but he longed to be strong and active again. His constant dependence upon others was a worry which increased daily. But what worried him more was that his mind and his will were as listless as his body.

Along the road Sir Maxwell Leering rode in company with Miss Nuala Grogan. Their horses jogged easily and they chatted in complete enjoyment of each other's

116

company and of the beautiful morning in their world full of promise.

Leering happened to glance down. 'Look at that idle fellow, my dear,' he said, with a contemptuous laugh. 'Can you wonder that there is so much poverty in the country?'

Nuala, glancing across him, saw only a sleeping figure. 'Mama would say, "Come day, go day, God send Sunday,"' she said and she laughed companionably as they rode on.

'The man's voice! Something familiar about the man's voice!'

It required a painful effort to sit upright. He looked after them and recognised Nuala, but the man was a stranger. He suddenly realised the meaning of the man's words, and as he did so he heard Nuala's voice and her clear laugh.

'Whisht, Conal! Are they gone?'

He looked round to see Fergie, MacShane's ten-year-old son.

He nodded. 'They're gone.'

Fergie advanced to the corner and peeped round. 'They could come back. You'd best come home with me, Conal. Grannie sent me to fetch you.'

'Who was that man?'

Fergie stared. 'Do you not know him? Sure, that's Leering, the bloody magistrate. Ah, now, you'll not tell my mammy I said "bloody", sure she'd skin the hide offa me. But that's what all the men calls him. And the woman is old fat Grogan's daughter. Bridie O'Hara was telling my mammy the two of them are going to be married and he old enough to be her father. Isn't that a disgrace of the world?'

To have his weakness so callously mocked by the very man whose cruelty had been the cause of it! And to have that mockery echoed by the lovely girl he so much admired! He had felt degraded before, but now it was as if, as he tried so painfully to crawl up from the depths, he had been kicked further down. He wanted to feel again the hatred and desire for revenge which had nourished him in the early days of his illness, and wanted to feel it too against that heartless girl; but he was cheated even of that satisfaction. He felt so drained in mind and body that he could control neither.

A minute later Fergie was racing up the boreen shouting, 'Conal's dead! Come quick, Conal's dead!'

TWENTY

Leering's ride with Nuala had been quite unexpected. He had been away for some time organising support for his plans, Robert Stewart having advised that the Personage should be presented with the names of as many supporters as possible to prove the viability of the scheme. Having visited all his more influential acquaintances, it had occurred to him that old Barnabas Taylor, a wealthy neighbour, was very well connected, so he had returned home to visit him and ask for introductions. Whilst intending to stay as short a time as possible, he could not deny himself the pleasure of seeing Nuala again.

He was highly pleased at the delight with which she greeted him, not knowing that she was living in such a state of excitement that she was showing her happiness to the whole world. As he was the originator of her happiness, she was truly pleased to see him. Besides, it was a lovely day and she welcomed the change to get away from the gloomy house. Throughout the ride she chattered and laughed at anything or nothing; and she practised being the young lady of fashion.

At Georgina's dictation Aloysius had written to his

creditors telling them that he was taking a Parliamentary seat and requesting time to settle his debts. As she had guessed, they, having to choose between throwing him into a debtors' prison with little likelihood of getting their money, or waiting for a Member of Parliament to make his fortune, chose the latter. All knew that a seat in Parliament was as good as a key to the Treasury.

Relief from worry reawakened Aloysius' self-confidence. Only the day before Nuala's ride, he had come home to announce that he had signed a commitment to take over the lease of a fine, furnished house in Dublin.

'Where d'you think, m'dears? Where d'you think, eh? Marlborough Square, no less. Right among the nobs.'

'Aloysius!' exclaimed Georgina. 'That will be far too expensive. We will never be able to afford it.'

'Tush, woman!'

'Don't tush me, Aloysius Grogan.'

'Sorry, m'dear. Quite carried away. Excitement, y'know. But listen to me. Must have a good address, must we not?'

'Well, yes, that is important, I grant you. But Marlborough Square!'

'Who'd pay us any attention if we lived in some back alley? But Marlborough Square! We've arrived already. Dammit, there's a title in every other house in the Square. Neighbours. Invite 'em. Poof! We're in Society an' nothing's too good for us.'

'But the cost!'

'All fixed. Small deposit in a month or two. The rest later. Perhaps a bit later than they think. But give me a month or two in Dublin and there won't be a thing to worry about.'

She wanted to continue her objections, to re-establish her command. But Marlborough Square! She appreciated as well as he the social advantages of such an address. Indeed, if ever she had been asked to sum up her aspirations, she would have said, 'A house in Marlborough Square.' And now she was to be mistress of a house there, already beautifully furnished, with servants, real, trained servants to obey her every order.

When Nuala heard that the house actually had its own ballroom, she needed to know nothing more about it. It could have lacked kitchens and bedrooms and she would still have been in favour of it.

TWENTY-ONE

Kattie MacShane declared that the only cure for the 'fever' which had stricken Conal was a bran poultice.

But where was bran to be obtained? Neither MacShane nor his neighbours, nor anybody they knew had bran. It could be bought in the town, but who could afford the time to go or the money to pay for it? The word went round: bran was urgently needed for The O'Carran.

Bridie O'Hara heard about it when she called at the cabin to ask after Conal. She had seen him several times and each time she was even more convinced that he was the most beautiful human being she had ever seen. Not that she would ever have told this to anybody, except Maire McCann. But then, Maire was her very best friend; and besides Maire agreed with her that he was beautiful, although she wasn't sure that they weren't committing a bad sin talking that way about him. Had he not been all his life at some class of a school for making boys into priests; and didn't that make him, well, perhaps not a priest exactly, but near enough for it not to be quite right? Although she hadn't admitted it, that had frightened Bridie a little and she had made up her mind to ask Father O'Reilly about it in Confession. Well, not exactly made up her mind, because she knew she would never dare talk that way to a priest. But she had thought of asking the priest, and didn't that sort of make it all right for her to go on thinking about Conal? And, anyway, he was beautiful!

But when she saw the wasted figure with the unhealthy flushed face writhing on the bed, babbling nonsense, she was greatly shocked and frightened. It became obvious to her that she was probably the only one who could get bran to save his life, and that she must overcome her fears and try to get it.

Thinking it over on her way back to Ballyna House, she decided that she would need to be very subtle. The first essential was to find Miss Nuala in a good mood; and that was no problem at all these days, God knows, and she bubbling like a pot with excitement over going to Dublin.

The next essential was to find Miss Nuala alone and no chance of interruption, and, God knows, that was not easy, for she could not rest easy in one place for more than a couple of minutes. Then there was the missus forever skating through the house calling for Nuala to listen to some new plan she'd just thought of. And there was a continual coming and going of visitors these days because of the way himself had become a very important man and they all wanting him to do things for them when he went up to Dublin.

But, God be praised, the chance came early, for Miss Nuala called her to help take all the clothes out of the wardrobes and let her have a look at them to see were they fit to take to the city. And none of them were. Would you believe that now? And practically every stitch new-made only weeks ago. It was bad luck that this put Miss Nuala a bit out of herself, but, with care, the job could be done.

'Isn't that Mrs Avery the kindest woman,' said Bridie, 'the way she does be going about visiting the sick people amongst the Protestants.'

'What on earth are you talking about, Bridie? And who on earth is Mrs Avery?'

'Sure she's the wife of the man, the reverend gentleman, I mean, who does be at the Protestant church

121

at Dunshee. Oh, a great heart she has, and the only pity that 'tis Protestants only she visits, and besides she's no bran, or at the least I'd think she had none. Or do you think maybe she has, and if she had would she let me have a couple of fistfuls of it?'

Nuala stared at her. 'Bridie O'Hara, I do declare there are times when I wonder if you have taken leave of your senses. You talk and talk and talk, but there's no meaning to any of it. Now, will you start with a big breath and then tell me whatever it is you are trying to tell me.'

'Sure, 'tis nothing at all, Miss Nuala, only ... well, the way it is, d'you see ...' She stopped, twisted her fingers almost into knots in anxious thought, failed to find a solution and burst into tears. Gasping through the tears, she said, 'Oh, aren't I the terrible girl, Miss Nuala, and I know I shouldn't be crying the way I am, but I can't help it, he's so beautiful, when he's at himself, that is, but he's that badly, if you could only see him 'twould crack your heart with pity, and Kattie says a bran poultice is the one thing he needs to break the fever, and, God forbid, he might die. D'you think he will, Miss Nuala? Ah, say he won't!'

'Bridie, Bridie, Bridie! You forgot to take the deep breath. Take it now.'

Bridie's plump bosom rose obediently and voluminously and her rosy face grew a deeper red.

'Out!' Nuala ordered.

'Poof! Dear God, I thought I'd burst.'

'Now. Short answers only. Who is ill?'

'Oh, Miss, I didn't mean to tell you, Miss.'

'Who is ill?'

'Conal O'Carran, Miss.'

Nuala remembered the day he had walked beside her horse. There was pleasure in the company, and, for some strange reason, a tinge of sadness and regret.

'What is wrong with him?'

Bridie was confused. 'Ah, well now, Miss Nuala, sure don't you know well what's wrong with him; or at the least what was wrong with him; but this now is from the other, or so Kattie says, and she's a wise woman.'

'How would I know what is wrong with him?'

'Ah, well now, Miss, you'll not hold it against me, but didn't you see him yourself with your own two eyes when they were after lashing him?'

Nuala had a sudden, sickening vision of the bleeding wretch hanging from the triangle. 'No! Bridie, do you mean it was Conal O'Carran who was whipped that day?'

'It was, of course, Miss. I was certain you knew, and you being there at the time. And then again didn't you see him again only two days ago and you out riding with, well, His Honour. At the least, young Fergie says you saw him and he resting himself at the corner of the boreen. And 'twas just after you passed he had his collapse . . .'

In less than twenty minutes Nuala rode out with a small sack of bran tied to the saddle. As she rode, she strove to understand how her father and Leering could have punished anybody so savagely for so very little, and how they could have stood there and watched it and been unmoved. The picture of that torn and bleeding back kept flashing through her mind, bringing the same horror and nausea; but, what was worse, she now felt that, somehow, she shared the guilt.

She tried to analyse this feeling, hoping to find that it was without cause; but she remembered the contemptuous remark Leering had made about Conal and her own reply and laughter. Then she truly felt guilt, and so much shame that she was tempted to return home. But she rode on, hoping it was an act of moral bravery, yet despising herself because she found comfort in the memory that Bridie had said he was unconscious.

Young Fergie saw her coming and warned the family long before she arrived. For more than fifty yards she had to ride towards the whole family assembled before the door. MacShane, his wife and mother and all the children watched her in absolute silence. Even when she stopped they said nothing. When she smiled there was no reflection. Her greeting brought no response. They were blank and watchful. Resentful and a little frightened by their silent animosity, she hoped that they would change when they knew her errand.

She smiled again stiffly. 'I have brought some bran. I believe you need some.'

'We need nothing, miss,' said MacShane.

'Well, not you yourself, perhaps, but Bridie O'Hara told me you needed bran for Conal O'Carran.'

'Bridie is a foolish girl.'

It was a blank, unaccented statement, inviting no continuation and it left her acutely embarrassed. She realised that, as far as these people were concerned, she was just as much to blame for Conal's condition as were her father and Leering. She wanted to explain herself to them, to tell them that she would never have permitted such savagery if she had known, to apologise for all her class for what had happened and to make clear her wish to do something to make amends. But their blank watchfulness and silent hostility, even down to the youngest child, formed an impassable barrier.

Her horse stamped restlessly and it was as if a spell had been broken. A girl's voice called urgently from inside the cabin. Kattie turned and rushed inside and was back immediately. She went to Nuala. 'I'll take the bran from you, miss, and thank you for it.'

Nuala handed down the sack. 'Is he very ill?'

'He is indeed. He could well die. I must go to him. Thank you again, miss.'

She hurried into the cabin and Nuala was left facing a silent wall of MacShanes. She turned her horse and rode away knowing they were still standing in watchful silence.

When she knew they could no longer see her she allowed the long-threatening tears to spill. But before she could savour the luxury of them, she brushed them angrily from her eyes. How contemptible to feel sorry for herself when that poor young man was in danger of death. Murder! If he died, he would have been murdered by her father and Leering.

Her horse leaped with the unexpected cut of her crop. She raced home and went to the drawing-room where her mother and father were eagerly discussing plans.

She burst straight into their conversation, addressing her father. 'Why did you have that poor young man whipped? He had done nothing to deserve that dreadful punishment. And now he is dreadfully ill, and if he dies you and Maxwell Leering will be no better than savage murderers. I am ashamed of you and of him and of everybody who ill-treats poor people!'

Aloysius goggled at her. For weeks she had been full of happiness, greeting him affectionately every time she saw him, and he had enjoyed being the admired papa. This outburst was so unexpected that for a moment or two he could not take in its meaning. But, by the time he had thought and was rising to the boil, Georgina had hurried to Nuala and whisked her from the room.

'Upstairs, my chicken, upstairs!' she was saying as she hurried her along. 'If anything has upset my baby, mama will discuss it with her and make everything right again. Nothing that a little thought will not cure, nothing at all in the whole, wide world...' She gabbled and gabbled and trotted and trotted and urged and urged until she had Nuala safely in her room.

'Shoo, shoo, girl!' she said to Bridie, who had been waiting for Nuala. 'Away to the kitchen and see what you can do to help. Shoo, now, at once!' And Bridie fled, glad to get away before her mistress found out what part she had played.

'Now tell mama what has upset her darling chicken.'

Nuala suddenly realised that she was being treated as a cantankerous child. 'You told me lies! As if I were a silly child whose mind has to be diverted from –'

'Oh, my dear, how unkind! I don't understand you at all.'

'There! You are doing it again. Mama, I am grown up. I am no longer a child. I told you about the terrible sight I had seen' – she put her hands to her eyes and shuddered – 'when I rode into Maxwell Leering's yard. It was horrible.

Brutal, disgusting and horrible. You said the man must have been a wicked criminal. Well, he wasn't. He was a young man named Conal O'Carran, a very pleasant young man; and what he had done was to beat Fowler after he had attacked two men and their horses with his crop. Fowler deserved it. But papa had him arrested, and Maxwell Leering had him whipped – scourged. That is the correct word – scourged!'

Georgina laughed lightly. 'My dear girl, why are you upsetting yourself? Even if he was whipped, he is only a peasant. One must be severe with them. Everybody knows that.'

Nuala stared at her, and her stare perplexed Georgina. She could not understand why Nuala should be troubled, but she was very concerned lest anything interfere with her plans.

'There, now,' she said. 'Let me darken the room and you can take a rest. You will feel better after it.'

'You don't understand, do you, mama? They lashed his back to raw, bleeding flesh, like a piece of butcher's meat...'

Georgina held up a restraining hand. 'Nuala, please, don't be disgusting.'

'He is a human being! They would not do the like to a dog or a horse. It is they who are disgusting, they and anybody else who agrees with their action. I will never speak to papa or Maxwell Leering again!'

She said this with the utmost determination, yet she was conscious that she was trying to crack that irritating calm.

She succeeded. 'My dear, my dear, what are you saying? If you antagonise Maxwell Leering, all our plans will be ruined.'

'I don't care. He is a horrible beast! I never want to see him again.'

Georgina gripped her by the shoulders, her fingers digging so fiercely that Nuala cried out. 'Now listen to me!' Never before had her mother spoken otherwise than gently to her. She was astonished and frightened by the

126

vicious tone. 'All my life I have been deprived of what is rightly mine. And what I wanted for myself, I wanted for you also. Now, at last, it is coming. I mean to have it. I mean that we shall all have it. That we shall live in decency and comfort and respect. That we shall enjoy the good things of life. If you persist in this silly nonsense, then think what it will mean. Your father will be imprisoned for his debts. This house and everything in it will be taken. You and I will be thrown out. Do you understand that? Thrown out with nothing but the clothes on our backs. Think of that! Where would we go? What would we do? Two homeless beggar-women. That's what we would become.

'Now, my girl, you stay in your room and think of what I have said. You have to choose between Dublin and beggary. Think, think, think, you silly little baggage.'

TWENTY-TWO

As the law forbade the practice of the Catholic religion, the people had neither church nor chapel and Mass was said in a tiny valley tucked away in the hills. Under a rocky overhang, at the innermost end of the valley, a rough stone altar had been built. Father O'Reilly said Mass there every three or four weeks. It was not possible for him to be there oftener because his parish was large and he travelled it continually in secret.

It was a Sunday of high summer. Though it was not long past dawn, there was already strength in the sun. The hills basked in its warmth and gave back their thanks in green, gold and purple, in a rich mingling of scents and an orchestration of humming, buzzing and carolling.

It was a day on which it was great to be alive. Conal, climbing the hills with the MacShane family, going to Mass for the first time in many months, felt like a prisoner released. Every breath he took seemed to add to his growing strength. He was still pale, thin and far from his full strength, yet even anxious Kattie had been forced to admit that he was able for the long walk, that it would probably be good for him to go. And, sure, what harm could come to anybody going to Mass?

To ensure that no harm did come to anybody, watchers were posted on the high points round the valley to guard against constables or soldiers.

In all outward appearance, Conal was improving. He talked with everybody, played with the children along the way, even laughed and generally seemed as much on holiday as everybody else. Only *he* knew the deadly apathy which was within. He no longer felt the fierce anger, hatred and desire for revenge. The ambition to regain his lands, to be a leader to his people – they too were gone. Nothing was left but the certainty that he was a creature of no significance in an uncaring world. The present held only the urgency of regaining his full strength so that he would no longer be a burden to the MacShanes and might be able to repay them for all their loving care. The future held nothing.

Amongst his many visitors, Canahan had been occasionally, but nothing of importance had been said between them. He knew from others that Canahan had tried to form a branch of the United Irishmen but very few would join. That MacShane was a member, he knew, but they never talked about it.

When he had first tried to organise, Canahan had asked MacShane several times about Conal, only to be told that he was still far from well. Then he had given up asking. On one occcasion, after an unsuccessful meeting, Dolan had asked him, 'Do you not think we were fools after all to let Leering get his hands on the young fellow?'

'Don't all the people go to visit him? Aren't they all worried about him?'

'True for you, but what manner of bloody good is that to us when they'll not join us? And what good is O'Carran to us lying there on the bed?'

'Let me give you a few things to be thinking about, Larry Dolan. The leaders of the United Irishmen, be they Catholic or Presbyterian or what, are people with money; and, for all their talk, 'tis their lands or their businesses that concern them. What good will come from that for the likes of you and me? Are you ready to fight to take the lands from the present landlords and give it to others? Let them play with their politics and Parliaments, and let them get the men together as well as they can. When the time comes, the organisation can be taken and put to proper use. In the meantime let Conal O'Carran take his ease. He'll be there when we want him.'

But on this Sunday there were many to mock at Canahan and his United Irishmen. There was a fresh breeze blowing through Ireland. This breeze from the American colonies had wafted ideals of 'Life, Liberty and the Pursuit of Happiness' across the ocean to France, to become 'Liberty, Equality and Fraternity'. Now the breeze was blowing through Ireland and the great word was 'Emancipation'.

The old Parliament in Dublin was ended and shortly there would be a new one composed of just, open-minded men who thrilled with the new ideals. They would bring about this Emancipation. It was a glorious, wonderful thing which would transform Ireland into Utopia. It meant the cutting down of rents, doing away with all tithes and taxes, making all Irishmen free and equal, tearing down the walls of the great estates, uprooting the trees and sharing out the land amongst the landless. Happiness and heart's desire for everybody. At long last Ireland was coming out of the dark days, and long years of golden sunshine lay ahead.

Everybody was talking about it on their way to Mass, as they waited for Mass to begin and as they lolled in the cushiony heather afterwards. Even Conal was stirred by the general enthusiasm and optimism to feel pleasure in the happiness of the people; but he did not think of it as anything which concerned him.

Father O'Reilly had talked about it in his sermon. Of course, being a priest, he looked at it differently and said it meant they would be free to practise their religion, to build a chapel, to educate their children without hindrance, for Catholics to become lawyers and even magistrates and possibly, one day, to have a vote and to hold seats in Parliament. He had asked them to kneel and pray God to give guidance to the law-makers to make it all come true. That set the seal on it. Father O'Reilly had promised Emancipation, so it would come.

A few, MacShane amongst them (Larry Dolan never went to Mass), were doubtful. Canahan was openly derisive.

'I'll believe it when I see you all set set up in your snug little farms! I wonder now what the landlords will be doing? I can just see them cracking their faces with big grins to see you all so happy! Slapping you on the back, with, "Paddy, you're a fine fellow. I love you like my own brother. And if there's anything I have that you want, you've only to ask." Ah, you're a pack of fools, ready as ever to be led astray by fine words!'

But they were not to be so easily robbed of their dreams.

'Ah to hell with you, Michael Canahan, and your United Irishmen along with you.'

'You'd disbelieve the word of your dying mother, so you would!'

'Away with your sour face!'

What were the landlords compared with the Parliament? The Parliament was the Law and the Law could do just what it liked. Here it was a fine, hot summer morning, with the smells of the earth and everything growing, ripening, promising plenty, with the songs of the birds and the humming of the insects all jumbled together with the finest prospect Ireland had ever had! Was it any wonder that a man felt happiness surging up in

130

him like a great tide until he had to jump in the air and whoop?

TWENTY-THREE

The election was held a few weeks later. Never had there been such excitement and enthusiasm. It thrilled through the whole country. Liberty was in the very air, almost a palpable thing, darting everywhere with the brilliance and ecstasy of a humming-bird. New songs sprang into popularity with Emancipation and Liberty as their refrain. The people were like the Israelites nearing the Promised Land. It was there just ahead of them, flowing with milk and honey and they danced towards it, laughing and singing.

Everywhere Parliamentary candidates were cheered as wizards who were going to wave their magic wands to bring about the wonderful transformation; who would pour out happiness like yards of coloured ribbon. Bands played, leading rival candidates round their constituencies as they made their speeches. The people had no votes anyway; but a politician must make speeches, and he must have an audience whose job it is to agree enthusiastically with everything he says, and to cheer loudly so that he may be doubly assured of his own conviction that he is the centre of creation and the fountainhead of all wisdom. And no politician in Ireland at that time lacked assurance of his own omniscience for the people yelled their approbation of every platitude.

The courthouse was gaily decorated for Grogan's election. The gentry arrived in their finest clothes and were cheered by the people, who hadn't bothered to dress up. Then came the High Sheriff in full regalia, looking so imposing in his great coach with its fine horses, gleaming harness and dazzlingly-liveried coachmen, footmen and outriders that nobody could possibly have guessed that he was only a little, pot-bellied man with pimples and bad breath whose wife hen-pecked him. He was met by the ever-popular magistrate, Sir Maxwell Leering, who introduced his dear mother, then the beautiful and radiantly happy daughter of the candidate (and you know he's going to marry her, oh, yes, sometime later in the year, so they say, and God bless them both) and then every member of the local gentry who couldn't be elbowed out of the way as he was conducted to the seat of honour.

Amid resounding cheers and a great blast from the band, the candidate, Mr Aloysius Grogan of Ballyna, accompanied by his charming wife, walked the length of the courtroom. What a fine figure of a man in his beautifully cut clothes! What a champion of liberty!

Sir Maxwell (God bless him!) then made a jolly speech, in which he proposed Mr Grogan as candidate. Everybody laughed and clapped, and the members of the lower classes at the back were so carried away that they stamped their feet, whistled and gave wild yells.

Septimus Grace, the lawyer, looking as if he had just emerged from a shower of snuff, got up and said many long words, strung out in involved and unconnected clauses, which, although he did not actually say so, were taken to mean that he seconded the nomination. If he had dripped pearls of wisdom, he could not have been more enthusiastically applauded.

But when Aloysius got up to say thank you very much, the audience really erupted. He didn't actually speak. There was no need; and he could not have made himself heard anyway. They rose in a body, a couple of feet above the floor it seemed, cheering, laughing, stamping, whistling, yahooing, screaming what a fine fellow he was and what fine people they all were, and by God it was hot, but they had never been so happy in their lives. And Aloysius bowed and bobbed, opened his mouth and said nothing, bowed and bobbed again, grinned, wiped his sweating face and glowed with delight.

Then came the serious business of the election. The Sheriff produced a large parchment scroll, very impressive because it had many large wax seals and ribbons attached to it, and he read what he thought was inscribed on it, making only a few mistakes. It appeared that His Gracious Majesty, King George the Third, busy though he was defending the Faith, and being restrained from eating his bedcovers whilst he was doing it, had found time to give permission for this election; and he said that he didn't mind at all if his lieges went ahead and elected somebody to the Parliament in Dublin. So that made it truly legal and binding, and God save the King!

Then the Sheriff shouted that anybody who had a right to do so should come forward at this time and say whatever it was they had to say. And Leering stepped forward and made a statement and read a paper from Sir Julius Besant, who rightfully owned the seat they were all talking about. The paper said that it was all right for Sir Maxwell to vote for anybody he wanted to vote for, and nobody else had anything to say in the matter, because it was nobody else's business but was strictly between himself and Sir Julius (who was also a liege but too busy to attend to the matter himself) and the paper proved it. So the man he voted for was Aloysius Grogan, Esquire of Ballyna House, aforesaid. The 'aforesaid' made it legal so Aloysius was pronounced duly, properly and in every other way elected; and God help anybody who objected because this was a serious business, although the dignity of the occasion had been slightly spoiled by the rowdy behaviour of the people at the back.

And the people referred to, swollen with pride at receiving the notice of the eminent, yelled their delight, rushed to the platform, grabbed the champion of Liberty and carried him shoulder high in triumphal procession.

*

133

It was the same throughout the country. There was riotous enthusiasm in County Down over the election of Robert Stewart, a fine, handsome young man, a great patriot and undoubtedly a champion of the people, for didn't he ride in his carriage wearing a French cap of Liberty!

But the Belfast people outdid everybody. They enthroned their candidates, Sir Hercules Rowley and Mr O'Neill, in a triumphal car and pulled them through the city, with the Volunteers escorting them and a buxom young lady from the opera (of Scots-Welsh parentage) dressed as Hibernia leading them, with a green wreath in one hand and holding aloft a pole surmounted by a cap of Liberty.

At night the city was brilliantly lit and fires blazed on the surrounding hill-tops, with people dancing joyfully round them. And the Volunteer Light Dragoons met at Bunkers Hill (from which another hill had been named) and there they swore never to lay down their arms until Ireland was free.

TWENTY-FOUR

The Grogans went to Dublin long before the Parliament opened as there was much to be done.

Aloysius was gambling everything. Others had rapidly made fortunes through politics and he meant to join them. Leering had made himself considerably richer by this means and, apart from the £2,000 Aloysius would have to pay him as one year's rent for the seat, there was an understanding that he would also share the profits. To ensure that there would be profits, he had instructed

Aloysius well and had provided him with several letters of introduction. In particular these were to Mr Dominick Coulthurst, MP – an expert guide through Parliament's more profitable mazes; and to Mr Herbert Bayliss, an English official at Dublin Castle, whose chief charge was the care and preparation of State documents, and whose chief skill was the doctoring of those documents to the profit of himself and his allies.

Aloysius had not yet sent his rent monies to Sir Julius Besant, gambling that there would be only indignant letters for a few months, after which he would be able to repay the money. He had also borrowed from Biggen, offering a reduction in rent in exchange for a lump sum. Biggen himself had had to borrow the money in order to be able to pay Grogan, but he had done so gladly, not only because it represented a profit to him, but also because he was hoping that Grogan would fail and that he himself would become bailiff.

The greater part of Aloysius' ready money had gone in paying a deposit on the rental of the house in Marlborough Square. But the occupation of this magnificently furnished mansion, coupled with his seat, ensured almost unlimited credit, for a time. Taking advantage of this, he ran up huge bills with tailors, dressmakers, haberdashers and bootmakers, equipping himself, his wife and daughter extravagantly and fashionably. He acquired a new carriage, gleaming blue and gold with bright crimson wheels and a handsome pair of high-stepping chestnuts to pull it. He stocked his wine-cellar with the prodigality that only a man who is not paying cash can show. He engaged a butler, footmen and grooms, equipping them in distinctive livery, and a chef and maid-servants galore.

In every possible way, he dressed his window to catch the eyes of the world. Those inhabitants of Marlborough Square who were in residence (most were still in pursuit of summer pleasures), curious for all their blue blood, peeped from behind curtains and wondered what Solomon had come to live amongst them. Wondered, but

135

did not seek acquaintance.

And when everything was done and they were completely installed and ready for all that the world might offer, a great silence fell on the house. Day after day no other foot than theirs trod the marble steps to their gleaming front door; no strange hand pulled their shining bell-knob; no cards were left, no invitations received. The clocks, and there were many, from the immense grandfather at the turn of the staircase through the mantel clocks like miniature Greek temples, the marbles, the ormolus, the glass-domed, down to the miniature bedside clocks, ticked the dragging seconds through all the vast, sunlit and silent rooms where boredom dwelt. And not only boredom, but anxiety. It was as if, by some magician's spell, they had become invisible. The whole world moved round them unseeing, unhearing and uncaring.

For Aloysius the days were bad. But the nights! No matter how drink-fortified he was when he retired, inevitably he woke, chilled by his own sweat, to an impenetrable darkness peopled by mock demons who gleefully promised utter ruin.

A morning, like any other morning, of being wakened by his valet and being readied to face the day; of descending the staircase (one simply could not merely walk down that staircase!) in the immense silence, rippled only by the obsequious murmurs of menials; of entering the breakfast-room, bright with sunshine, yet with the atmosphere of a funeral-parlour, with the butler and his footmen as undertaker and mutes to assist in the dignified burial of all hope.

But, in front of his place, a silver salver. And on the salver, sheer white, red-sealed, a letter!

To hell with what the servants thought! He snatched it, ripped it open – and all the bells rang, the bands played, the whole world danced and sang and beckoned with welcoming hands to Aloysius Grogan to come and join them.

Mr Dominick Coulthurst MP had the honour to inform

136

Mr Aloysius Grogan, MP that he was now in residence and eagerly invited Mr Grogan to luncheon.

The Sleeping Beauty had been kissed. The spell was broken. The house and all its inhabitants sprang to instant and eager life. The wicked demons, their evil schemes baffled, slunk away.

Magnificently dressed in sky-blue coat, white nankeen breeches, gleaming gold-tasselled Hessians, one of the smart new high-crowned hats and carrying a gold-mounted sword-stick, Aloysius was driven to his appointment. Coachman in maroon and gold coat, white breeches, top boots and cockaded hat, two footmen standing behind, similarly uniformed, but with tricorn hats on their powdered wigs; the sleek coats of the chestnuts challenging the leathers for beauty of polish; the jingling metal sparkling in the autumn sunshine – there was not a smarter turn-out of master, men and equipage in all Dublin.

The route led out of the square, centred with smooth, tree-shaded turf, into Cavendish Row, which sloped steeply into Drogheda Street. Down one side of this was an enclosed Mall with great forest trees from which russet leaves sailed to cover the cobbles so thickly as to deaden the clatter of horses and carriage, laying a carpet of gold almost to the banks of the river Liffey. Across Carlisle Bridge the wheels rolled and hoofs drummed. Down-river a multitude of vessels clustered at the quays – a leafless forest of masts, laced with thin cordage, patterned the blue-gold of the autumnal sky; and the snowy gulls floated, swooped, soared and cried freedom and the joy it was to be alive.

Up Westmoreland Street where the House of Parliament stood imposingly on the right, appearing to be earnestly consulting its learned neighbour, Trinity College, across the way; but probably complaining of the acrid stench which oozed down from the cavalry barracks in Kildare Street; and so into St Stephens Green with its expanse of grass, trees and shaded walks – a delight by day, a haunt of footpads by night.

Meanwhile the house in Marlborough Square had returned to its tick-accentuated quiet in which Nuala and her mother waited, almost without breathing, for the return of Aladdin from the Magic Cave.

It was late afternoon when the carriage returned and the butler admitted Success, Optimism and Excitement in the exquisitely dressed, well-fed and better-wined person of Aloysius Grogan, Esquire, MP. In spite of the fact that the house and the servants were absolutely opposed to displays of any form of emotion, wife and daughter, having shocked the staircase by actually racing down it, captured him in the hall before he had even been relieved of hat and stick and demanded to be told everything. Everything required the remainder of the day to be thoroughly told, retold, supposed about, questioned, redefined, exclaimed over and used as a foundation for a city of continually altering dream castles.

The following day an undistinguished hackney carriage stopped outside the house, then drove away. If there had been a person with very keen vision standing close by, and if he had been focusing with the utmost concentration on the pavement, steps and front door, he might have had a vague impression that a tenuous shape had whisked from the carriage, up the steps and into the house. But the impression would have been so fleeting that he would have dismissed it as a trick of the light. Even Aloysius, summoned to the library to greet a visitor, had to search very carefully before he discerned a greyness. A wisp of gossamer touched his hand. Slowly there emerged from the vacant air the small shape of a man – a grey man: grey-haired, grey-faced, grey-suited, grey-stockinged, grey-shod. And a grey voice whispered that Mr Herbert Bayliss was pleased to make his acquaintance.

It was known officially that Mr Bayliss was employed in Dublin Castle. His name appeared in the Civil Service List. But his colleagues would have honestly denied that any such person worked amongst them. If he did, where was he? Where was his office? When did he come? When did he go?

There was no emotion of any kind in the thoughts which passed from Mr Bayliss to Mr Grogan. There would be little communication between them in the future, apart from an occasional manifestation; but distinctly in the quietness Aloysius heard the chink of pure gold.

That evening Mr and Mrs Coulthurst brought several impressionable and impressed friends to dine, and from then the merry-go-round whirled endlessly, musically, gaily and profitably.

It was very difficult for the conscience of Miss Nuala Grogan to make itself heard above the hurdy-gurdy jangle; but one early afternoon, having risen and breakfasted very late, and having a headache (a most unusual and unwelcome ailment for her) and having no engagement until the evening; having, in fact, nothing at all to do for the first time in weeks, she became aware of an uncomfortable mental stirring. She tried vainly to stifle the memory of a tortured body and of a pleasant young man who might be dead now for all she knew. 'Or care, miss,' said Conscience. 'Oh, how easily you excused inaction with thoughts that Emancipation would solve all the problems of such unfortunates as Conal O'Carran! How logical it seemed that you should say nothing to Maxwell Leering or to your papa, because papa himself would be a Member of Parliament dedicated to the improvement of the lives of the people! And never a thought about it since!'

Conscience could not be placated by sitting in that luxury. Action of some positive kind was required. But what? Well, what if she went to see how Emancipation was progressing?

She slipped out and took a hackney carriage from the rank in Cavendish Row. When she reached the House of Parliament she was escorted to the gallery by a dazzled usher. She sat and sought to be impressed by the assembled wisdom and integrity below. But, judging by the sparsely filled benches, much of these desirable qualities was taking the afternoon off; and most of what was present was relaxing. Surely not actually sleeping!

A little man in an old-fashioned, full-bottomed wig was droning unintelligibly, pausing frequently to shovel snuff into capacious nostrils. Nobody appeared to be listening.

Nuala was amazed, disgusted and very disappointed. She herself had been inactive, she freely confessed, but there was little she could actually do, and she could truthfully say that she had been very busy, well, at least, she had been doing many things. But these were the people whose duty it was. Where were the golden-tongued, soul-stirring orators? The men who could change the whole course of history with a few ringing phrases? Surely not amongst those lolling bodies. She felt exactly as when a play, excitedly anticipated, proved boring.

Presently the speaker sat down. A murmur as of the wind through a drift of dead leaves passed through the assembly. Another man rose and said something quickly in a high-pitched voice. Immediately a dozen were on their feet shouting, each apparently against all the others. A hammer rapped them to order. They sank back to lethargy, lulled by another droner.

She forced herself to remain for a full hour, but she did not understand one word of what was said. She might just as well have been in a dormitory trying to interpret the snores. When she left, she was able to tell Conscience that she had tried, really tried. And Conscience could not think of an objection.

That evening they dined with the Coulthursts. As soon as they arrived Dominick Coulthurst drew Aloysius to one side, excusing himself to anybody within hearing: 'Matters of State, y'know. Important Matters of State.'

The first world-shaking matter was that Lord X had remote estates badly served with roads. A private financial agreement had been reached with Lord X by which he would get his road. It was simply a matter of having a Bill passed in Parliament for the building of a road from town A to village B. Once the Bill was passed, a little financial persuasion would convince the surveyor that the best route was past Lord X's front gate, even though this would add some twelve miles to the length of the road. A lesser financial arrangement with the foreman would also ensure that a mile of private drive would be remade. A number of votes would have to be bought or swapped to ensure the passage of the Bill, but it would still leave a considerable profit.

That piece of everyday business out of the way, there was a much more interesting matter to be discussed. The Honourable Sebastian Strickland, an extremely well-connected English gentleman, had just arrived in Dublin to take up a position on the Viceroy's staff. As was customary, he had been provided with a confidential list of Important People in Dublin Society; and to this a ghostly hand had added the names of Coulthurst and Grogan. The Honourable Sebastian was to be one of the guests at dinner.

'Tremendously influential, m'dear fellow, and very susceptible to the ladies.' A nod, the whisper of a wink.

Aloysius went immediately to Georgina.

'Fellow named Strickland coming tonight,' he muttered. 'English aristocracy. Cousin to lords, dukes, everybody. The Castle, even the Palace. Soft spot for the girls. Right?'

Georgina went to Nuala.

'My dear, the most exciting news! How would you like to be presented at Court in London?'

Would a starving man care to attend a banquet?

'Be nice to Strickland!'

At that moment Strickland was announced and Coulthurst pranced to meet him. Sebastian was a man nearing forty, but aping twenty. His laugh, which sounded continually, was, he thought, boyish, but was actually irritatingly high-pitched. His dress was foppish. His face, long, narrow with a receding chin and small, high-bridged nose, was painted, powdered and patched. From this artistry bulged a pair of dull, fish-grey eyes. A jewelled sword made a plaything for his left hand, whilst his right flourished a highly scented lace handkerchief. A slight difficulty in the pronunciation of the letter 'r' completed his adopted charms.

All the guests were led up to meet him and were acknowledged with polite boredom until Nuala was presented. It was as if life had suddenly come to a doll. Even the fish-eyes sparkled.

Coulthurst's enquiry if he would be kind enough to escort Miss Grogan in to dinner produced flourishes of lace, low bows and extravagant expressions of ecstasy such as Nuala had never before witnessed. She was highly flattered, particularly as she was aware of the envious looks of the other ladies. An amusing oddity of a man became immediately a most charming, gallant gentleman. She placed two fingers on his proffered arm and paraded to the dinner-table like a princess before her courtiers.

'Intwoductions, dear young lady, are always so huwwied, one has gweat difficulty wecollecting names. Miss Hogan, I think Mr – er – our host said.'

Nuala overcame the desire to giggle at the sudden change to oddity and corrected him. The smile, which was all that remained of the giggle, completed the winning of Sebastian.

'Ah, Miss Gwogan. But natuwally there is another name.'

She told him.

'Nuala! How unusual, as befits a most unusual young lady. It becomes you vastly. It expwesses your bwown beauty.'

During the dinner Nuala was introduced to the art of the graceful compliment – an art singularly lacking in what Sebastian called 'wuwal Iweland'. She was also introduced to conversation as she had never known it, and she found herself taking part in it effortlessly, even attempting to match his wit with sallies of her own. She gradually realised, too, that the odd, foppish exterior disguised a man. He was educated, well-read, much-travelled and knowledgeable about the arts. He had soldiered and adventured, matters lightly passed over. Altogether, she found him fascinating, and dinner passed unnoticed, as did also the many side glances from her table-mates who received the barest politenesses from her companion.

Strickland dined with the Grogans. The Grogans joined Strickland in his box at the play. Strickland joined the Grogans for a morning drive in Phoenix Park where it was the fashion to take the air, to see and be seen. And Strickland was seen by his cousin, Lady Rockfield. The Grogans attended Lady Rockfield's soirée, met Lady Rockfield's friends. Presto! They were inside the magic circle.

Each fine morning they drove out along the North Circular Road, which the Duchess of Rutland had recently made fashionable, and through Phoenix Park. In the afternoon they rested for a time, then went visiting, shopping or were visited. In the evening they were undressed and redressed. Then, in carriage or sedan chairs, they went to dine, to the play, to the Rotunda for the music, to play cards, to attend fantastic parties, to dance, to gossip, to play. And to laugh and flirt and to exult: 'I am the prettiest girl here tonight!' How wonderful to be surrounded by handsome, admiring young men who smile and compliment and, excitingly, turn on each other looks of cold antagonism. And then to be claimed by dear Sebastian, who could dismiss them all with a hard-eyed glance. (Could it really be true, as it was whispered, that there had been early morning meetings in the misty park?)

So time flowed pleasantly towards Christmas. The goose laid its golden eggs. Living was expensive, of course. One spent or lost at cards, at dice, at the races. But the goose would continue to lay. A rich, aristocratic son-in-law was a distinct possibility. There was neither time nor need for worry.

TWENTY-FIVE

Conal waded thigh-deep in a river pool hauling out the flax which had been steeping for five days. He threw it on to the bank where the children spread it in swathes to dry. MacShane had a good crop this year. A fortnight earlier he had worked with the whole family pulling the flax, binding it into sheaves and stacking it. It was hard work for everybody, but particularly for him as he had not yet fully recovered. But there was great satisfaction because the exercise in the fine weather helped his recovery, because he felt a share in the family's delight in what promised to be a rewarding crop, but mostly because he felt that he was partly repaying the debt he owed to them.

Being amongst the constantly chattering children, anxiously watching to see that none of the younger ones fell into the river, ensuring that the older ones got on with the spreading and resisted the temptation to belt each other with the wet sheaves (which they did anyway whenever his back was turned), constantly bending and hauling the heavy, wet, stinking stuff, feeling the hard pull on his muscles and the tiredness spreading through him as the day wore on so that evening found him barely able to keep his eyes open long enough to eat the evening meal before falling into a deep, dreamless sleep: all this was satisfaction and comfort. Whilst he was working, conscience no longer accused him of being an expense and burden on MacShane. Most comforting of all, but not admitted, there was no time to think. The work was there to be done, constantly demanding his attention. What had happened, what would happen, what might happen were all considerations which could be left. Contentment was a weary body and a blank mind.

'God bless the work!'

144

He slowly unbent and looked up at Father O'Reilly smiling at him, the children clustered round, fighting to hold his hands.

'Shoo! Shoo, the whole tribe of you!' shouted the priest. 'On with the spreading now whilst I have a word or two with Conal.'

Conal waded to the bank. 'Good day to you, Father.'

'And a very good day to you, Conal. I am glad to see you strong and well again.' He looked into Conal's eyes and saw that the cure was still incomplete, but decided to ignore it. 'You have been in my thoughts and in my prayers many times in these past months.'

'Thank you, Father.'

The priest waved a deprecatory hand. 'Ach, no thanks are due to a man for doing what he is supposed to do. But what brought me was this. A week or two back I'd to go and see the bishop. He has great hopes of Emancipation. I don't know did you ever hear of a Mr Edmund Burke? You didn't. Well, he is Irish, not a Catholic, but a very liberal-minded man, and a highly respected politician in the English Parliament. He's heart and soul in favour of Emancipation and he has recently sent his son across here to tell us that the Prime Minister, Mr Pitt, and the entire English Government is in favour of Emancipation and urges the Irish Parliament to bring it about as soon as possible.

'Now the bishop is a far-seeing man and he is already making plans for when it is here. One of the things he told me was that it will become possible for Catholics to be lawyers, and Catholic lawyers could do a power of good for the people. He wants to find young men with enough education to take up the profession and is willing to help them as far as he is able. Now I thought of you at once and here I am to ask you what you think of the idea?'

Conal sat down, was silent for a moment or two, then said, 'Will you excuse me if I sit down, Father?'

The priest laughed. ''Twould seem I knocked you down.'

Conal looked up, not understanding and not wishing to

145

know. 'I am very tired, Father. You will understand that I am not yet accustomed to the work. It is good to be able to do it. The MacShanes have been very good to me. It's little enough I can do for them.' His tone was flat and lifeless. Speaking was an excuse for not thinking, not making decisions, not answering.

The priest understood. 'I will leave you to think about it. No hurry at all. Goodbye now, Conal.'

Conal did not hear him, was not aware when he went. The rhythm of work, of existence itself, had been disturbed. Into his comfortably blank mind this new idea had been uncomfortably planted. He wanted to reject it, to regain numb comfort, but his mind seized on it as a starving man seizes food. The idea held hope for a future, possibility of repayment for the hurt which had been done to him, even (and he struggled hardest against this) the thought that a lawyer could aspire to equality with Nuala Grogan.

Living with the MacShanes and seeing the happiness they had as an integrated family, in spite of poverty and hardship, each one secure in the certainty of loving and being loved, made him daily conscious of all that he had always lacked, and emphasised his aloneness. Oh, they all, and particularly his grandmother, cared for him and worried about him; but he was not one of them and never could be. Nor did he wish to be. But he longed for what they had.

But hope was a deceiver who had betrayed him before, and so hope was to be resisted.

The children, avoiding this sudden stranger who sat staring and unreachable on the river bank, played more and more wildly until one fell over Conal and roused him. They stood silent and he became aware of their stares and the reason for them. He blushed, then jumped up, shouted to them in mock gaiety, and in a few moments all were back at work again.

In the following days, working hard at the flax – pounding the dried stuff and cloving it to separate the flax from the tow – he achieved, almost in spite of himself, a greater contentment. The sight of the flax being changed magically into threads by the spinning-wheel operated by Kattie or Mrs MacShane gave him great satisfaction. The threads were then warped on the warping tree before being sent to the weaver with the tow for woof. He helped to take it there, saw it set up on the loom by Alex Kilgour, the weaver, and then watched as if witnessing a miracle as it became cloth. When this was brought home, soaked in a mixture of wood-ash and water, washed and laid out in the sun, it lost its dirty yellowness and became pure, white linen. Then he was filled with the pride of achievement. He appreciated for the first time the longing that the people had for land, so that their work – the very life in their bodies – could be transmuted into something of true value. Then he felt 'land hunger'. Previously he had wanted the land because he had been robbed of it. Now he saw land as the major essential of existence. The law had been used to rob him, but now there was the possibility that he could use the law to regain it.

Emancipation was the key.

From then on he worked harder than ever. The work became easier. His full strength returned. His body filled out, grew and rippled with health. Yet still he merely existed. He spoke, played with the children, laughed, sang even and he worked until even MacShane begged him to stop; but always he was apart, as if true life was something for which he had yet to qualify.

After gathering potatoes one morning with his grandmother, they stopped at midday and ate cold, boiled potatoes and water. As soon as he had finished he got up again.

'Will you, for God's sake, give yourself and myself a minute or two to get the breath back in us,' she begged.

He looked at her in surprise. 'You rest. I'll get on with the work.'

'You'll sit down again and listen to me!' She said it with such force that he sat again. 'All this live-long morning I've had not a solitary word from you. Now you mind me,

I'm still your nurse, for, begod, big and strong as you are, you're still far from right. Oh the body is fine and strong, but there is something else ailing you. Are you listening to me?'

He laughed, because he felt it was expected. 'How can I help but listen?'

She seized his hand tightly. 'Look at me, boy! Look into my eyes, the way I can see into yours.'

Although embarrassed, he did so.

She stared at him. 'Nothing!' she said. 'Empty. Do you know what I'm talking about, Conal?'

He flushed and looked away.

'Indeed you do. You go through every day doing the things which come to your hand, eating when it is time to eat, sleeping when it is time to sleep, making noises with your mouth when somebody speaks to you. But 'tis all a show. There is no real life in you. Conal!' The abrupt sharpness jerked him to attention. 'Even now you pay me no heed. Did you hear one word of what I said to you?'

'Ah, gran,' he said listlessly, 'leave me be.'

'Leave you be what? A clod? A half man? Can you see nothing in life? Is there no hope in you?'

He shrugged. 'Maybe. I don't know. I'm afraid to hope.'

'Dear God! Afraid to hope is afraid to live, and if you're that you'd best be dead and done with it.'

'I've thought that too.' Even as he said it, he remembered what Brian O'Sullivan had said to him: 'Two legs to stand on, two arms to fight with, a bit of something in his skull...' The whipping would have made O'Sullivan more determined than ever.

Kattie had been watching him. 'You're maybe not as far gone as you thought. But that aside, let me ask you something has been in my head this long time. Do you know that when you were deep down ill I was desperate to get bran for poultices and the bran was brought by the young Grogan girl. Tell me, why would she do a thing like that?'

Conal blushed, was embarrassed and annoyed by his blushes and blushed all the more.

148

'Twas that daft ha'porth, Bridie O'Hara, told her you were ill. I wonder now she didn't just give the bran to Bridie to bring. A young lady the likes of her with servants to do her bidding. Very worried about you she was, too. Why would that be, d'you think?'

Conal fought harder and even more unsuccessfully against the blushes. He shrugged and said with affected nonchalance, 'How would I know that?'

'Well, then, tell me this,' said Kattie with great innocence, 'you being a young man and seeing these things different from an old woman the likes of me, would you say she was a good-looking girl?'

A vision of Nuala in her green riding-habit flashed into Conal's mind.

Kattie laughed. 'There's things an old woman can cure, but there's other things only a young woman can cure.'

'Ah, what are you talking about, gran? She is a young lady of position, daughter of a Member of Parliament and a Protestant. I am a – nothing.'

'You are The O'Carran of Duncarran!' she stated vehemently. 'Don't ever forget it. Your people were ruling wide and rich lands when some of those who are lording it now were begging crusts from the tinkers.'

Conal leaned back on his elbows, then slowly sank supine, staring sightlessly at the sailing clouds, but seeing possibilities.

TWENTY-SIX

At first the people had expected to hear that Emancipation was an accomplished fact as soon as the new Parliament met. Every source of news was eagerly tapped. Wandering beggars, tinkers, packmen, musicians, ballad-singers, dancing-masters, stage-coach drivers – all who came from the outside world, were asked for news. But there was no news.

They knew the law was notoriously slow, however, and conceded that such a wonder could not really be expected to come about overnight. Then, too, many of the MPs were landowners and were sure to offer resistance, no matter how futile. In the meantime there was great temptation to sit and talk and dream of the wonders to come and to forget about rents and tithes and taxes and the coming winter.

Several men had their carts and horses commandeered by the soldiers for use in the French wars. It was no concern of the soldiers that they were depriving the men of their livelihood, nor that the carts and horses were far too decrepit to survive the long journey. As long as they could mark their lists Horses – 1, Carts – 1, duty was satisfied. They gave receipts which, they said, could be taken to the magistrates for compensation. They omitted to say when this compensation would be paid; and the men, after many futile attempts to see the magistrates, were forced to give up their receipts to wipe off a few shillings of their debts.

Biggen borrowed a couple of armed constables to help him collect his rents. Those who were unable to pay in cash were forced to pay with anything they had, even the precious potatoes which were their food for the year to come, and nobody was evicted. Even though his announcement of an increase in rents for the next half year came as a shock, the optimists called out, 'Make the most of it, Biggen. There'll be no more rents.'

Then the great news came that the son of Edmund Burke had come to Ireland proclaiming that the entire English Government from Mr Pitt down was in favour of Emancipation and ordered the Irish Parliament to bring it into being at once. Even the pessimists could not argue against that.

The name of Wolfe Tone[1] was heard more frequently. The Society of United Irishmen was growing rapidly, it seemed, and becoming more powerful with increasing numbers. They were working for Emancipation too. But, in spite of Michael Canahan's appeals, recruiting was slow. The common argument was: 'Sure, if they've all those thousands already, they've no need of me.' But Canahan knew that the opposition was to himself. He approached Conal again.

'What would I be wanted to do if I did join?' Conal asked.

'Get the other men to join.'

'And after? What would they all do?'

'Don't you see it gives the leaders the power of great numbers!'

'Since they've no votes, I can't see what use they would be; and it does seem that Emancipation will come without any help from us. If they'd some definite plan, now, I might give thought to joining.'

'You mean that?'

'I do.'

Canahan's long, calculating look made Conal feel strangely uneasy. 'I'll hold you to that one of these days,' said Canahan.

Next day came the wonderful news. The Catholic Bishops, gentry and merchants had joined with Mr Burke and with Wolfe Tone and the United Irishmen to urge the Government to hurry through the necessary laws. And they were also going to gather their whole might at a Convention in Athlone, where they would draw up a

1   At that time news travelled slowly and reached the peasants only by word of mouth and heavily tainted by rumour. Rightly or wrongly, to the people, Wolf Tone became synonymous with the United Irishmen. To this day he is regarded as the father of republicanism and a commemoration ceremony is held annually at his grave.

petition to King George stating all the wrongs of Ireland and pleading for their removal. Mr Pitt, who was himself very anxious to curb the landlords who were ruining Ireland, would urge the king to accept it. Surely, then, any hesitation by the Irish Government would be swept aside.

TWENTY-SEVEN

Georgina Grogan was very worried. They were surrounded by crowds of supremely eligible bachelors. It was her obvious duty to secure the best of them for Nuala. She remembered Leering momentarily then dismissed him as no more than a friend; and, besides, he could not match even the poorest of these. Competition from other mothers with marriageable daughters was in the natural order of things. But other mothers had their daughters as very willing allies. Nuala was not only uncooperative, she was actually in opposition. This young gentleman was too fat, that had a very silly laugh, the other was ugly or had bad breath or was a poor dancer or was dull or stupid or could talk only about horses or – 'Oh, I just dislike him. He's...' A distasteful shrug. 'Besides,' and away she went in the latest dance steps, 'I don't even wish to think of marriage yet. There's too much fun. Why should I tie myself down to one of these – ugh! And become all fat and dowdy with a horde of sticky, smelly, slobbering babies! Anyway,' arms flung wide, 'there're dozens and dozens to choose from. Pooh to all of them! I'll choose when I'm ready.'

And it was true, they did pursue her. There was scarcely a minute of any day when there wasn't at least one of them calling at the house. And she treated them abominably: teasing them, playing practical jokes on them, promising them and breaking her promises, setting one against another, flirting with all and refusing to take any seriously. Yet, it seemed, the more outrageously she behaved, the more they flocked round her.

Not all were truly eligible. Dublin was full of younger sons seeking fortune through marriage, and Georgina had them all carefully categorised. But many were listed as Eminently Eligible, and at the head of this list was still the Honourable Sebastian Strickland.

Georgina still held vivid memories of the days when she and her mama had hunted, when the vaguest scent of a quarry had been enough to send them chasing in full cry. Now the abundance of game bewildered her. Her instinct was to bag the nearest available before all got away. Nuala's disdainful treatment of them terrified her. Nightly she lay awake reviewing Nuala's behaviour of the day, dreading that the new day would show all prospects vanished. Daily she would rise determined 'to bring Nuala to her senses' only to find her less manageable than before and the young men flocking as eagerly as ever.

The Parliamentary session finished at the end of November. One did not remain in Dublin for Christmas. One went home to the country and invited relations and friends. Georgina would dearly have liked to invite the Honourable Sebastian, but Ballyna House would have revealed too much of the truth. His announcement that he was going to England, with hints of Christmas festivities in ducal castles, was a relief from embarrassment but there was the worry that he might be captured by some scheming English mama. All in all, though, she comforted herself that a few weeks in the dullness of the country might make Nuala more amenable when they returned to Dublin.

Felix had driven the other servants to prepare the house. They had swept, scoured and scrubbed until he was satisfied that the house was fitting to receive a celebrated Member of Parliament and his fashionable wife and daughter.

They arrived in the early evening after a grey, streaming, cold day. A multitude of candles filled the place with a soft glow and immense log fires blazed in every fireplace.

'Ugh!' exclaimed Nuala as she walked in. 'What a dreadful, filthy hovel!'

That night she went to bed hours earlier than she had done for many weeks and she slept well into the following morning. She woke to a dull, drizzly day. The window showed grey skies, sodden grass, bare, dripping trees, and admitted cold, damp draughts. She dressed quickly and hurried downstairs. Fires were blazing ineffectually against the cold of the draughty rooms. She saw worn and faded carpets, curtains ragged where they existed at all, chipped and broken furniture with tattered upholstery: squalor! Marlborough Square was a fairy tale once heard.

Georgina greeted her. 'Did mama's chicken sleep well?'

'Mama. This dreadful house! Must we live in it now?'

Georgina was pleased. 'Why, of course we must, my dear. Where else? The Dublin house is only rented, and your dear papa would need to become very wealthy before we could afford a country house in keeping. As I am continually trying to tell you, my dear, we are very far from being as rich as our friends in Dublin think us. But we do have the opportunity to become rich and we must make the most of our opportunities.'

'You mean that I must sell myself to the highest bidder.'

'Nuala! How dare you! What a truly dreadful thing to say! I do declare that Dublin has not been entirely good for you.'

Nuala shrugged. 'What *do* you mean, then?'

'Well, what I mean is, well, a young lady, any well-bred young lady is expected, indeed expects herself that she will, in the customary way of things . . . One must, after all is said and done, follow the customs of one's class . . . Society, the Church . . . Oh, you know very well what I am talking about, miss, and it ill becomes you to giggle when your mama is speaking to you for your own good. It

154

is a serious matter and one which you should most earnestly consider.'

'Oh, mama!' she exclaimed irritably. 'You have made sure that I would consider it. And I have considered it. And the thought of being tied for life to any of the fops and braggarts I have met horrifies me. Truly. It terrifies and disgusts me.'

Georgina, wisely, said no more. She knew she had no arguments as convincing as Ballyna itself would make.

They had breakfast. Then Nuala stared out of the window at the dismal day. She went up to her bedroom where her window showed a wider view of the same. She examined her wardrobe and saw only the futility of possessing such clothes in such surroundings. She remembered for the first time that she had not seen Bridie O'Hara since her return. She rang the bell and, after an interminable wait, flung open her door intending to march down to the kitchen to berate the servants for not answering. Outside stood a diminutive, bony, ragged and dirty little girl who shrank back in terror.

'Who are you?' Nuala demanded.

Two wide, fearful eyes stared at her, but the only reply was a gulp.

'I won't eat you, girl,' said Nuala, bending down to reassure her.

But the girl shrank back and tears grooved her dirty cheeks.

'Where is Bridie?'

The girl looked wildly round, seeking escape.

Nuala let out her breath in an exasperated 'Whoosh!' and with a wail the little creature whirled and raced down the stairs.

'Ah, don't be minding her at all, Miss Nuala,' said Felix in the kitchen a few minutes later. 'She does be very shy and not used to the ways of the big world. But Bridie now is not able to come to us any longer. Her mother had a bad fall and Bridie has the care of her and the whole family.'

And that was the end of entertainment for the first day. The second day brought the same weather and no entertainment at all.

On the morning of the third day, when she woke, Nuala promised herself, 'If it is not raining today so that at least I can go riding, I shall not complain. Otherwise, I shall scream.' When she looked out the world was damp and grey. It was not raining, but neither was it promising to be dry. After breakfast she convinced herself that it was actually brighter, so she ordered her horse, raced upstairs and changed into her riding habit.

The whole household ran out into the hall in response to her furious scream.

Georgina headed the rush, hands pressed to her tumultuous bosom. 'Goodness gracious, baby, what is wrong?'

'What in God's name...?' stuttered Aloysius, red-faced, bleary-eyed and stertorous.

A babble of enquiry and conjecture came from the crowd of servants and the raggedy hangers-on who had taken advantage of the occasion to rush right through from the back door and see all the beauties of the house.

'This dreadful, dreary place!' exclaimed Nuala. She flung a hand at the outdoors. 'Look, just look!'

Everybody looked and saw nothing unusual.

'Rain!' she yelled. 'Rain, rain, rain!' Then, seeing their incomprehension, 'Oh, what is the use of talking to any of you!' And she ran upstairs, flung herself on the bed and wept her frustration.

Aloysius grumbled about disturbance and tantrums and young girls who would be all the better for having their backsides slapped. But he was told that he didn't know what he was talking about, that he was not to say anything to her and that, if he only knew it, things were going very well.

Lunch was gloomy and silent, apart from the orchestration which always accompanied Aloysius's eating. Nuala picked and poked, pushed away her plate, stood and was about to leave the room when her mother said, 'Nuala! Your papa has not finished eating.'

'Does he ever?' asked Nuala, and she was gone, leaving

Aloysius spluttering a mixture of angry words and half-chewed food.

She raced up the stairs, along the landing and into her room, slamming the door. The whole world and the climate were in conspiracy to make her life miserable.

A thin ray of sunshine touched her bed. She ran to the window. Dampness, drips, but a clearing sky and a glimpse of watery sun. Within minutes she was out of her gown, into a riding-habit and running down the stairs shouting for her horse. As the released prisoner was galloping away from her gaol, Georgina was trying to drive into a mind filled with the conviction that a horse-whip was a sovereign cure for tantrums that things were going very well indeed.

If she had been asked, Nuala would have said that she was riding aimlessly, simply seeking relief from boredom. Yet she had had no hesitation in turning right on leaving the house. Had she been asked if she ever thought of Conal O'Carran, she would have given an attractive, recently cultivated trill of laughter to dismiss the absurdity of the Darling of Dublin sparing a thought for a peasant. Second thoughts might have made her admit that perhaps, to be quite, and admirably truthful, she had had passing thoughts of him when she had visited Parliament. But then her concern, also admirable, had been for Emancipation which could bring such benefits to the peasantry.

But the question would certainly have made her remember, though not admit openly, that many times in the early days when, splendidly dressed and admiring herself in the mirror, she had thought of Conal's full-hearted admiration and had fleetingly but pleasantly imagined how much more he would admire her present brilliance and beauty. And she might have wondered whether her dismissal of the bright young gentlemen of Dublin was caused by her finding them artificial when compared with the reality of Conal.

The road was rough, rutted and marred by many water-filled holes. Her horse, long unexercised, was as anxious as she to expend repressed energy, so that she was barely controlling it as it hammered along. Suddenly she recognised, and admitted to herself, that the turn-off to MacShane's cabin was only yards ahead. Even as she was offering herself the excuse of concern for the health of a young man who had been unjustly punished, she was fighting to slow the horse. When a racing figure erupted from the boreen right under the head of the horse, the result was inevitable.

Conal had been working in the bog up the hillside, packing turf into the panniers slung on a donkey. He had heard the hard-ridden horse and his first thought had been that somebody was bringing urgent news, perhaps even of Emancipation. He had leaped up on a pile of turf and looked down the road. Although she was still some distance away, he had recognised her immediately. Without a second thought he leaped down, raced across the bog and down the boreen.

As he suddenly shot out, the horse, fighting for its head, reared wildly and Nuala was pitched sideways into a clump of sodden growth. He shouted, punched the horse out of his way and leaped to the fallen figure. He dropped to his knees and cradled her in his arms, wild with alarm.

Her hat had fallen off and it seemed desperately important that he should try to raise her shining hair from the wet herbage. At the same time it was necessary to stroke her cheeks and still to cradle her gently. Staring urgently at her closed eyes, he willed them to open whilst he mumbled incoherent expressions of helpless anxiety.

Her eyes fluttered open. 'That was a very stupid thing to do,' she said.

'Oh, thank God!' he exclaimed fervently and he hugged her closer and kissed her.

It was a very clumsy kiss, landing between nostrils and cheek, but it was very thoroughly applied and, combined with the fervour of his hug, it squashed her nose and cut off her breath. She struggled wildly and he raised his head immediately in anxiety.

'I couldn't breathe!' she gasped indignantly.

'Oh, I am sorry.' He was desperately concerned.

She sat up abruptly. 'You kissed me!'

He gaped at her, only then realising that he had in fact kissed her. Realising further that he was actually hugging her, he took away his arms and she, who had been leaning against them, fell back.

'Oh, God, I'm sorry!' he exclaimed, putting out his hands again to lift her. Then he started back in surprise as she suddenly burst out laughing. He stared down at her, not knowing whether to be anxious or to join her merriment.

Abruptly she was serious and she sat up. 'Your back!' she said. She put her hand on his arm and looked with concern into his face. 'Oh, your poor back. Are you better? Are you quite recovered?'

'Ah, it was nothing,' he mumbled, blushing. 'Thank you for the bran. That was very kind.'

'I was very worried about you. It was a terrible thing they did to you.' She shuddered. 'A savage, terrible, unjust thing. Oh, I am so glad you are better. I was so worried...'

They sat and looked at each other.

Cold dampness seeping through his breeches made itself felt. 'You're sitting on the wet grass. Your clothes will be ruined.'

He jumped to his feet, reached down, took her hands and pulled her up, then snatched away his hands in embarrassment.

They became very busy, she switching and brushing her skirt, finding her hat and putting it on, whilst he brought back her horse which had been champing unconcernedly close by.

But then she looked up at him and asked mischievously, 'Why did you kiss me?'

He shrugged and shuffled, fumbled with the reins, looked at her, then looked away. 'I never kissed anybody in my life before,' he said.

She laughed. 'That was quite obvious. You didn't do it very well.'

'Oh, I suppose you are well used to being kissed,' he grumbled.

She reddened with indignation. 'Indeed I am not! If you imagine that I am the sort of girl...'

'Ah, no, please,' he begged. 'I did not mean that. Truly I did not. But you being so lovely and so...' He gestured impotently to express his fervent admiration. 'There must be hundreds of elegant young men...'

'Oh, them!' She dismissed them contemptuously.

Giving great thought to the matter, he said, 'I am not sorry I kissed you. Well, I am sorry for the way I did it; but what I mean is...' He was staring down at her very earnestly and suddenly realised that she was regarding him with amused interest.

'I'll tell you this,' he said with a rush. 'You're in great danger of being kissed again.'

She threw up her hands in mock horror. 'Save me from suffocation!' But she was grabbed, her hands brushed aside and her face was thoroughly, smackingly kissed all over. She found herself not minding it, indeed rather liking it. Visions of Mrs Standish, echoes of her incomprehensible lectures, of vague, longwinded warnings by her mama! She pushed against his chest. He pulled away his red face, breathing heavily, but still kept his hands on her shoulders.

'You shouldn't be doing that,' she said severely. 'Anyway, I don't think you're doing it properly.'

'Well, I told you, I have never done it before. I don't know anything about girls. You are really the first girl I have ever met. Well, there was one in Paris...' He blushed as he suddenly remembered.

'So you flirted with a French girl!' she said indignantly.

'Ah, no, I didn't at all: that wasn't how it was. She, well...' He told her how it happened. 'Believe me, I was completely astonished. I think she was not a well-brought up girl. They were terrible times...'

He went on to tell her about his life in France and she told him of her school experiences. He told her of his dreams of Ireland and the bitter disappointment of his return; but he also told her of his hopes to become a lawyer. And she told him of Dublin and its gaiety and even of the pursuing young men – which made him angry, not with her, but with them for their impertinence. And time passed unnoticed.

Suddenly it was almost dark.

'Dear God, MacShane will think I've fallen into a bog-hole.'

'And my parents will be thinking the same,' she said with a laugh. 'I must go home. Goodbye, Conal.' She held out her hand, suddenly shy.

He took it in both of his. 'Whatever has happened to me today, Nuala ... well, I don't know what has happened to us. I'll need to think about it. But this I do know, I feel as if I have just been born, as if I never knew life until now. I feel...' He dropped her hand and raised his clenched fists to the darkening skies seeking words. But no more would come. He dropped his arms and looked at her, and saw Miss Nuala Grogan of Ballyna.

'Oh, God,' he groaned. 'You're far and away beyond me. What am I thinking of? Goodbye and God go with you, Nuala.' He raced away up the boreen where he grabbed the donkey's head, smacked it and ran off beside the trotting beast.

Nuala, impelled to call after him, held back the cry, seeing a peasant hauling a load of turf. Yet she watched until he disappeared and, as she rode homewards, she was unsure whether to sing or cry.

Georgina was puzzled. Nuala had returned late from her ride, had gone to her room without a word and had not appeared until the following morning. When she did, all rebelliousness had gone; and so had her usual alternative mood of gaiety. She was quiet and preoccupied. Questions had to be asked several times before they were answered in a flat, uninterested tone. Attempted discussions of the coming Christmas entertainments in the district were killed with monosyllabic answers given merely for politeness. And this was the most puzzling thing of all.

Nuala was very polite not only to her parents but even to the servants.

Yet whilst she appeared outwardly calm, Nuala's mind was actually in a turmoil. She had been longing for an end to the dreariness of Ballyna and a return to Dublin, and one half of her still wanted that. But there was now another half which saw the life of Dublin as an empty, tinsel show, as empty of true satisfaction as a child's dream of a diet of nothing but sugar-stick. So there was a constant struggle between Miss Nuala Grogan of Dublin society and Nuala who had found in Conal somebody vividly real, as familiar to her as her very hands, belonging to her as they did, as essential to her as they were. But neither would accept the other. To Nuala, Miss Grogan of Dublin was an empty-headed doll. To Miss Grogan Conal was a ragged, futureless peasant.

She went visiting with her mother whenever the weather was fine enough, dressed to impress as Georgina was; but her hostesses and their daughters found her very dull company, which comforted them greatly. At other times she went riding to escape from the house and her mother's constant, painfully careful attempts not to introduce contentious topics. And on her rides she wanted, and did not want, to meet Conal; but she did not see him.

He had made a firm decision. He assured himself that it was an irrevocable decision. He would become a lawyer. Only then, when he had a profession, an assured position in the world, would he go to Nuala again. For all his firmness, however, his eyes were forever wandering, searching, and he constantly hoped that perhaps, by chance...

She went riding on the afternoon of Christmas Eve. Still preoccupied with her problems, she paid little attention to route or time until she suddenly realised that it was growing dark and she was far from sure of her way home. She turned back along the rough track she had been following. Before she had ridden a mile it was completely dark under a moonless, overcast sky. She was

162

frightened. The path was so rough that she had to go slowly for fear of a fall. But what frightened her more were the memories of servant-told stories of ghosts and evil fairies. Every looming bush or rock became a heart-stopping meance. She let the reins fall loose, trusting the horse to find his way. He plodded on, seemingly with confidence, but the release of her mind from the concentration of guiding him left it free for all her terrors to enter.

High in the blackness away to her left a bright light appeared. Then another, farther away, another nearer to her right. They could not be from cabins, for cabins had no windows. Then what could they be? The only answer forthcoming was the stories of travellers led to their deaths by strange lights in the night. Trembling, she clutched at the horse's mane. He snorted and stopped abruptly. A tall, black figure stood in the path. She screamed.

'Nuala, Nuala!' He was beside her immediately, hands stretched eagerly to comfort her.

'Conal! Oh, thank God!' She slid, almost fell into his arms and wept against his chest. In the need to comfort and be comforted, hands and lips found an unsuspected and untutored knowledge.

'What, in the name of God, are you doing out riding in the darkness?'

She explained, and, 'Oh, Conal, I was so frightened, first by the dark, then by strange lights and then I thought you were a ghost.'

'But this is Christmas Eve. The lights are the candles the people have set in their doorways to guide the Mother of God to the shelter of their houses.'

'What a lovely thought!'

'And there would be a welcome and shelter for any traveller.'

Remembering her reception at MacShane's, she said, 'Even for the landlord's daughter?'

'The landlord's daughter is not the landlord.'

The barrier rose between them, almost tangible.

'Come, Nuala, I'll guide you home.'

He helped her to mount, then took the rein and led the horse. They went for some distance in silent misery.

At last, following a deep sigh, she asked, 'What are we to do, Conal?' and she leaned down and stroked his hair.

He put up his hand to cover hers and they halted.

'There is nothing we can do. You have your world, far from mine. I will, please God, study and become a lawyer. But that can only be if Emancipation comes.'

'Oh, it will, it will!' she exclaimed; and then she shivered remembering her visit to the dreary Parliament.

Misinterpreting her shiver, he said, 'What a fool I am keeping you here in the cold. Come.'

He started off again, and again there was silence, because there was nothing to be said, yet so much which needed to be said, but could not be said.

They were close to Ballyna before he spoke again. 'I have been thinking and the only thing I can see is that we need, both of us, to think and then to talk. This night week will be the end of the old year, a good time for people to think what they will do in the coming year. If I wait under the big oak in your garden after dark, would you be able to slip out and talk with me?'

Again she put her hand on his head. 'I will. Somehow I will.'

The bobbing lights of lanterns appeared ahead.

'They have come searching for you,' he said. He took her hand and kissed it. 'A week from tonight. God keep you, Nuala.' And he was gone into the darkness.

TWENTY-EIGHT

Maxwell Leering had worked hard, had travelled much, had talked to many people and had met with much success; but when he came to the end of his travels, satisfied as he was, he knew that he had only established a multitude of links between himself and other people. It was true that all were in agreement, that they were aware that there were many others who agreed with them; but the links were tenuous. It was essential to draw in the threads, to bring all the separate units together and to compound them into one single-minded power. To meet a country gentleman in his home, to secure his agreement to ideas which aimed at ensuring his undisturbed enjoyment of his privileges, had presented no difficulty. But to summon the same gentleman from his comfort, to get him to travel many uncomfortable miles simply to attend a meeting at the invitation of an undistinguished country magistrate was impossible.

He had given much thought to the matter, and then, in the acute discomfort of a country inn, as he sat before a miserable, smoky fire and dreamed of warmth and ease before his own blaze with Nuala lovely and loving across from him, the solution appeared ready-made.

Three days later, he and Mr Stewart were with the Personage.

'A wedding!' the Personage shouted. 'I love weddings! Capital, m'dear fellow. An' not before time, you dog. But better late than never, eh, eh? Maybe best of all now, eh?' He gave a throaty chuckle. 'Begad, I envy you. Lovely young bride!' He smacked his lips. 'Delighted, man, delighted. And settle the other business when we have them all together. Congratulate you, indeed I do. Just let Bobby know the date and we'll all be there to kiss the bride.'

He had arrived home two days before Christmas to find, amongst his correspondence, an invitation to a dinner-party at Ballyna House on Christmas Eve. He looked forward to a very happy Christmas.

TWENTY-NINE

Aloysius had made a courtesy call on Leering shortly after returning from Dublin, but had learned that he was away and likely to be away for some time. Georgina, alone, because Nuala had refused to go, had called upon Lady Leering only to be told that she was suffering from a chill and was not receiving visitors. Duty satisfied, neither had thought of them again. The dinner-party to which a great many people were invited was intended to fulfil all their social obligations in the neighbourhood.

Leering arrived late, deliberately. More than ever now he had a position to maintain. He also wished to avoid answering the curiosity of his neighbours about where he had been and what he had been doing. They would all come to heel when he needed them.

Nuala, having arrived home late, still bemused after her meeting with Conal, and rushed into dressing by her mother, was in a state of bewilderment. But Leering thought her radiant and was so much absorbed by his eagerness to talk to her that he did not notice the new Aloysius – a haughty Dublin gentleman who was condescending to hob-nob this evening with a crowd of provincial boobies. He had been drinking before their arrival and had more than kept pace with them since.

They went in to dinner immediately, and Leering offered his arm to Nuala and escorted her in, selected places for them and, ignoring everybody else, talked only to her during the meal. He scarcely ate or drank anything, was unaware of what he talked about. It was enough for him that he could look at her and could admire this most desirable piece of young femininity which would soon be his not only as a seal but as a bonus to mark the success of his work. Nuala, meanwhile, sat numbly, toying with her food and smiling mechanically.

Aloysius had been most annoyed at having his greeting hand touched and dropped by Leering with little more than a faint noise to acknowledge his existence. Georgina had been similarly dismissed and was equally annoyed. Leering's subsequent behaviour, the subject of behind-hand, behind-fan comment by everybody throughout dinner, was even more annoying.

When the ladies had left and the gentlemen got down to the serious business of drinking, Leering sat, not drinking, and ignored them all. He was actually completely preoccupied with his plans and was simply waiting for the opportunity to talk to Aloysius in private. But the others, and particularly Aloysius, felt that they were being deliberately and insultingly ignored. There was much muttering.

Then Leering, suddenly realising the passage of time, called peremptorily, 'Grogan! Surely it is time we joined the ladies.'

Conversation stopped immediately. Aloysius, red-faced and too breathless with anger to get out any words, stood up. The others, taking this as a signal, also stood and began to wander from the room.

Leering, satisfied, said, 'A private word with you first, Grogan!' and sat on, again ignoring everybody but making it very clear that their absence was desired.

The room emptied, the door closed and Aloysius found his voice. The insufferable Maxwell Leering would now learn that he could not treat Mr Aloysius Grogan, MP like a skivvy.

'Leering, I want to protest...'

Leering did not even hear him, was quite unaware of

167

him as anything but a person who was necessary for the furtherance of his plans. He spoke across the other's voice.

'As you know, Grogan, there is an agreement between us regarding your daughter. I wish now to complete the necessary arrangements. I suppose you or your wife have spoken to her about this. I intend to speak to your daughter now. An announcement this evening would suit my plans very well.'

'You... you...' Aloysius spluttered. 'Who the hell do you think –'

Leering became aware of something quite out of accord with the course of events which he had planned. He saw Aloysius for the first time: red-faced, spluttering and highly excited. What ails you, man? Are you ill?'

Aloysius planted two fat fists on the table and leaned forward. 'I am not your bloody lackey!' he yelled. 'How dare you come to my house and... the way you've behaved tonight... everybody talking... m'wife, m'daughter...'

Leering was genuinely puzzled, but also growing angry. 'What are you talking about, man? I am merely following the usual courtesies of speaking first to the father of the young lady I intend to marry.'

'Marry you! Marry you! My daughter will never marry you.'

Leering's face whitened. He stared incredulously at this ridiculous, fat creature who was threatening his plans. But the necessity to succeed curbed his anger.

'Grogan,' he said coldly, 'we have an agreement. Tacit, I agree. But an agreement nevertheless. I am now calling on you to fulfil your half of the bargain. Indeed, I am demanding that you do so. And I urge you to consider the consequences of your failure to do so.'

But drink and anger arising from hurt pride completely blinded Aloysius.

'A fig for consequences. The bargain was for cash. And you've been paid. Now, get out of my house!'

Leering's face was dead, but his eyes were alive, hard

and glinting. He spoke with cold deliberation. 'I could call you out and put a bullet into your skull. But I won't. Not yet. First I will give myself the pleasure of ruining you.'

Aloysius felt a slightly sobering chill. 'What the devil are you talking about?' he blustered. 'Damn, d'you deny me the right to choose a husband for my own daughter!'

Leering continued as if he had said nothing. 'You think you are secure now, that you can do without my help and influence. I'll show you what influence I have.'

He walked deliberately to the door.

'Do your damnedest!' shouted Aloysius. 'See if I care!'

Towards the end of the following week Aloysius rode off after lunch. Nuala and her mother were taking tea in the drawing-room late in the afternoon when the door was flung open and Aloysius stamped in shouting for Felix and claret.

Georgina, so startled that tea slopped into her saucer, exclaimed, 'Aloysius! I declare! Have thought for my nerves!'

Aloysius ignored her and yelled again, 'Felix! Where in hell are you, man?' Then he swung on his wife. 'Leering! That ... that ... I'll kill him! Felix!'

The butler scurried in with a tray holding bottle, jug and glass. 'A minute or two, sir. A minute or two and I'll have it ready for you,' he said as he hurried to the fire. 'I'll have it mulled in a second, sir. Begging your pardon, ma'am and miss.'

'Not ready!' shouted Aloysius. 'Not ready! And why not? Sleeping, I'll be bound, when my back is turned.' He waddled to the fire, grabbed the man by his hair, slapped his face and flung him towards the door. 'Out, clown! Clear to hell out of this!'

Felix fled.

Georgina signalled Nuala to go, but as she rose Aloysius, fighting to regain his breath, jerked, 'Stay!' Then he flung up his hands at his wife as if fighting off her objections. 'Sit and wait!'

He poured claret into the jug, then muttered, 'To hell,'

slopped some into the glass and gulped. He grimaced as the cold liquid ran down his throat, said, 'Bloody idiot!' and set the jug down in the hearth. 'Woman,' he gasped, 'for God's sake redden that poker!'

Georgina, with a great display of patience, pushed the poker into the heart of the fire. 'And now perhaps we may be informed of the reason for this appalling behaviour.'

He snorted and glared at them. 'I'll tell you. I'll tell you, by crackey! Been to Barclay's. Invited. Card party. Men. No doubt about the invitation. No doubt about day or time. What happened? Damn butler says Barclay's not at home. Not at home! Told me that when I could hear the crowd of them talking, laughing. By Gad, I'd've been in there in a trice, but... D'y'know what happened? Dammit, woman, isn't that poker reddened yet?'

Georgina pulled the poker from the fire and plunged it into the jug which Aloysius grabbed and lifted to his head.

'B'Gad, I needed that,' he gasped, wiping his mouth with the back of his hand.

Nuala watched this with distaste. 'Papa! Must you do that?'

He whirled on her, pointing his finger. 'You be quiet, miss. All on account of you, dammit!'

'Nuala!' Georgina warned. 'Now sir, you were about to tell us what happened.'

'Told you, haven't I? Doesn't anybody listen to me in this house? Imagine it. Me! Member of Parliament! Blasted butler shuts door in m'face. In m'face!' He gulped again from the jug.

'But I don't understand,' said Georgina. 'Why did this happen?'

'Obvious. Leering put him up to it. All going to snub me. Thinks he'll down me that way. By Gad, I'll show'm!'

Georgina stood up in exasperation. 'Aloysius!'

He waved her back to her seat, but she insisted. 'Aloysius, explain exactly why Maxwell Leering should do this. You have yet to explain why he went home early from the dinner-party.'

'I have wondered about that,' said Nuala. 'He came

170

straight from the dining-room and left without speaking.'

Aloysius took another drink, and flopped into an armchair. Realising that he had weakened his position, he tried to struggle out of it, but was pinned by his wife's question: 'What did you say to him in the dining-room?'

He looked from one to the other, had recourse again to the jug, only to find it empty, gestured at his wife with it, then flung it into the fire. 'Course! Blame me! Try to do best for m'family.' With a sudden change to maudlin complaint, 'Always loved you, haven't I?'

Georgina spoke with cold firmness. 'Nobody is blaming you for anything. Yet! What did you say to Maxwell Leering?'

Defiantly he replied, 'Told him plain and straight. No use hanging round Nuala. Bothering her.'

'He wasn't bothering me,' said Nuala.

'Course he was. Strickland or one of t'others in Dublin. Much better.'

'I see,' said Georgina.

'Well, I do not see!' exclaimed Nuala angrily.

'Be quiet, dear.'

'I will not be quiet. I am being bandied about like goods on a huckster's stall. Nobody asks me what I want.'

Aloysius gaped at her. 'You mean you want to marry Leering?'

'No, I don't! And I don't want to marry Sebastian Strickland. Nor any of the others.'

'B'Gad, girl, you'll do as you're told!'

'Aloysius!' his wife snapped. 'Calm yourself. And you will both please remember that the servants can hear you.'

'But, dammit, woman, don't you realise –'

'I realise only too well that your quick temper has made great difficulties for us.'

'My temper! Begad, woman . . .'

She jumped to her feet and stood over him. 'Aloysius Grogan, I have had to take charge of affairs before because of your bungling; and I am taking charge now. You will be quiet!'

171

He subsided, grumbling, into his chair. Then, trying to salvage some of his authority, he stood up, went to the fire and inserted the poker; but seeing the shattered remains of the jug in the fire, he pulled out the poker and flung it clattering on the hearth.

Georgina, arms folded, waited for him to finish this performance, then said, 'Now, sit down. Kindly sit down.' She waited until he did so, then turned to Nuala. 'Now I want you to understand quite clearly what has happened. Maxwell Leering has turned against us. He will now do his best to ruin us. He has turned the county against us and he will use his influence in Dublin against us. Remember, he still controls your papa's seat in Parliament; and he has many influential friends. But if we were sure of Sebastian Strickland's friendship, we could defy Leering. His friendship depends upon you.

'You mean it depends upon me marrying him!'

'To put all dissembling aside, yes. He is an excellent match.'

'And my likes or dislikes are not to count. My happiness does not matter?'

'Jumping Jupiter, girl!' Aloysius shouted. 'Will you be happy to see me hauled off to the Marshalsea?'

'Quiet, Aloysius! Nuala, you are old enough and have enough experience now to realise that life is not a game. We cannot always have it as we would wish. You owe this as a duty to us.'

'You are telling me that it is my duty to sell myself to pay my father's debts. Is that it?'

Georgina's face flamed. 'You are insulting, miss! Your debts too. Are you prepared to face ruin? If you don't marry Strickland, then it's outright poverty. Well, which?'

'Oh, stop, stop, stop!' Nuala jumped up in a frenzy. 'I can't bear any more!'

She burst into tears and ran from them. For hours she lay on her bed, trying to think, breaking into tears, fighting against this weakness and trying again to think.

At seven o'clock in the morning her mother woke her

172

to tell her that they were returning to Dublin immediately.

THIRTY

Early on the night of New Year's Eve Conal went to Ballyna House. He crept through the shrubbery to the blackness of the huge oak. There was neither sound nor light from the house. After waiting for half an hour he moved silently round to the back where a light shone from the kitchen. He peeped through the dirty window to see a solitary man-servant eating at the table.

He went back to the oak thinking she might have left a message there; but a thorough search, several times repeated, producing nothing.

New Year's Eve. A night for parties amongst the rich. Her parents must have taken her off to one of the other big houses, giving her no opportunity to leave a message. They would be late returning and she would be unable to leave the house then. But still he waited, comforted merely by being there. At last the cold silent darkness convinced him the waiting was futile. She would come the following night.

MacShane's house was crowded when he got back. There was wonderful news. Mr Pitt, the English Prime Minister, had sent a new Viceroy to Ireland: Lord Fitzwilliam, a marvellous man who had been given the job of chastising the landlords. Before he had been a week in Dublin, he had declared himself wholeheartedly in favour of Emancipation and intended to make certain the Parliament passed it. And to show what sort of man he was and what the landlords could expect he had dismissed John Beresford from his post as Controller of Customs and Excise. It was incredible. 'Brilliant' John Beresford, he was called. Probably the most powerful man in Ireland. A man who had put every relation into some sinecure or other and who had made a vast fortune by selling sinecures to others. Out he had gone, neck and crop!

Fitzwilliam, God bless him! He was the kind of man Ireland needed. He was the boyo would make the landlords dance.

Canahan came late and tried again to tell them that all their ideas were wrong, but nobody would listen. Least of all Conal, who told them what Father O'Reilly had promised about helping him to become a lawyer, and that he would then fight in the courts to regain his lands.

They cheered that. 'So, there's for you, Michael Canahan. No time at all now and every man of us will have his own snug little place.

'And if you catch a wee leprechaun, he'll tell you where to find a crock of gold!' said Canahan bitterly.

The following night Conal went again to Ballyna, but again there was blackness and silence. Even the kitchen was dark. He searched the stables. Coach and horses were gone. He ran back to the oak, searched its trunk, its roots, even its branches far higher than Nuala could have reached. There was no message.

Surely she would not have gone without leaving some explanation! Yet perhaps no explanation was necessary. He had told her to think of the difference between them. What could she have said in a message which would have made it any clearer that she had thought and had chosen!

THIRTY-ONE

At the first opportunity Aloysius called upon Coulthurst and Bayliss, but was told that they had not yet returned from the country. He went anxiously to call upon others. Only a few were in residence, but all greeted him cordially. Gradually others returned, invitations were received, given, accepted. The pace of social life quickened and the Grogans were as popular as ever.

How foolish they had been to worry!

Then, coming home from a dinner party: 'Did you think the Boulters were somewhat cold this evening?'

'Tush! Nonsense!'

The following morning's correspondence: 'Mr and Mrs R greatly regretted, a prior engagement. Sir Peter and Lady A ditto. No invitations.

A call on Bayliss and Coulthurst, known to be back in Dublin: 'Not at home'.

Strickland was back in Dublin. He did not call. There were few young men calling on Nuala. 'The Honourable Sebastian Strickland regretted that due to pressure of duties...' Bayliss and Coulthurst still not at home. No young men called on Nuala.

What relief to be going to a party to which they had been invited weeks before! How frightening to receive icy politeness from everybody, so that they fled back to Marlborough Square and the knowing servants.

A knock on Nuala's bedroom door. Aloysius and Georgina pale and anxious.

'We must talk to you, my dear,' said Georgina.

'No more time for nonsense, miss,' said her father. 'Really serious now. Oh, God!' He fell into a chair with his hands to his face.

'You saw how we were treated tonight, chicken. They have all turned against us. Sebastian Strickland is our only hope.'

'Marry him! For God's sake, marry him!'

'Surely there must be some other way!' Nuala wept desperately.

'No other way! None! I'll get him to dinner if I've to drag'm. Then it's up to you. Oh, God, I must get a drink!' He stumbled from the room.

Nuala lay and wept disconsolately.

Georgina, hovering between escaping and comforting her daughter: 'It's... well... Don't cry, chicken. Your eyes will be red and swollen in the morning. And you must look your best for... You must understand, dear. All girls, I myself... not quite the same perhaps, but... Try to sleep now. The morning...' A long silence. Edging to the door 'Good night, chicken. Sleep well.' The door closed quietly.

She lay unmoving for hours staring at bleakness. Almost every hour of every day since they had left Ballyna she had thought of Conal waiting for her under the oak and going away thinking that she had deserted him. There had been no way of getting a message to him.

The one hope had been Emancipation and she had eagerly followed the news. She had gone several times again to the Parliament and had been rewarded at last when the famous liberal orator, Henry Grattan, confident of the support of Lord Fitzwilliam, had risen to present his Emancipation Bill. The whole house had been hushed, friend and foe under the spell of his magnificent oratory. He had attacked the very foundations of the landlord system, threatening their power, position and wealth, and his irrefutable logic had held them. He had sat down to tremendous applause. A pause. A shaking of shoulders, shuffling of feet, coughing. Then, slowly, the voice of opposition, seeking to make avarice sound virtuous. Halting, growing more confident with muttered agreement, strengthening with the growing realisation of all that was at risk, fired by anger, then bursting out in fiery renunciation. The fight was on!

Fitzwilliam was determined to do what a long line of

Viceroys had failed to do – to solve the troubles of Ireland. He gave Grattan his fullest support. He attacked the landlords, bailiffs and place-seekers. His dismissal of John Beresford struck, he thought, a fatal blow at the opposition.

But Beresford went to England and talked to a few people. William Pitt and his ministers were quietly given their orders; and John Beresford returned to Dublin reinstated in his position without reference to the Viceroy.

Then events moved swiftly. Young Burke was discredited, the British Government stating that he had spoken without their authority. The Irish Parliament rushed through a Bill making it illegal for any body of people but themselves to meet as representatives of the people under any pretext whatsoever, and threatened with imprisonment any who took part in the proposed Convention at Athlone. Grattan's Bill, strongly supported by Fitzwilliam, stood in their way. Suddenly, without explanation, Fitzwilliam was recalled to England. He was driven to the quayside through the city draped in black. Grattan's Bill was flung out of Parliament and Emancipation was dead.

So Nuala crouched on her bed through the long night, seeking vainly for hope.

Aloysius was out all the following day. Georgina and Nuala sat in the silent house waiting for him, not talking, not moving, not even eating. Waiting.

It was after dark when he returned. Georgina met him in the hall, her arms out to him.

'Tomorrow night,' he said. 'He promised to come tomorrow night.'

THIRTY-TWO

The bad news ran through the country like fire through a parched forest and left black despair everywhere. There had been such optimism, so many things to encourage the people to believe that, after centuries of oppression, liberation would come at last. Now they saw how truly powerful the landlords were. Through their relations and friends in England they could even influence the London Government. Now their power was greater than ever. ~~Oppression would not only continue, but increase. The dousing of the light of hope left a darkness deeper than~~ ever.

Fitzwilliam gone as if to his own funeral; Burke shown up as no more than a boastful youth; the liberals and the Catholic body silenced; the United Irishmen declared illegal. Who was there to oppose the landlords?

But the United Irishmen remained. They changed their oath. Before, they had sworn to bring about reform through Parliament. Now they swore to bring about reform. And, having taken their oath, they set to work more vigorously than ever to make their name true. Every Irishman who opposed the landlords must be brought into their society. With this object, agents were sent throughout the country.

THIRTY-THREE

In spite of his conclusion that Nuala had decided against him, Conal had secretly hoped that perhaps, somehow, she would send him some message; and he had clung to the hope that Emancipation would change everything. The bad news was like a death sentence. It ended all his hopes and without hope there was no life.

He was now more conscious than ever of being an increasing burden on MacShane. Canahan had not repeated his offer to help with the school. It seemed to him that his only course was to leave MacShane's and take to the roads; yet he stayed, hoping that he would see Nuala once more before he left forever.

Then word was passed round. There was to be a secret meeting that night in the old Abbey ruins. The message was from Canahan. A man was coming specially from Belfast to tell them how to best the landlords.

Many were uncertain whether to go, disbelieving that anything could now be done and not at all liking the idea of going to the Abbey, reputedly haunted. But they decided that if they all went together at least they would have less fear of ghosts, and they had nothing else to do and might just as well be listening to this magician from Belfast as sitting hopeless beside their firesides.

The ruins stood gaunt in the misty moonlight in a valley across the hills. A lonely, eerie place, fitting background to the wild tales which were told of the ghosts of monks butchered by Cromwell's troops; but an ideal place for a secret meeting.

Beneath the ruins and entered by a narrow, bush-concealed hole was a well-preserved crypt. A large turf fire had been lit in the centre to give both warmth and light, and the men gathered in a large circle around it; many men from miles around and boys, too, only

179

fourteen or fifteen years of age. They all stared to see so many gathered.

A small group stood at one side, Canahan, Larry Dolan, MacShane and a small, dominating little man, red-headed, jerky, continually hopping about and twitching his head like a sparrow.

When there had been a halt in arrivals for several minutes Canahan stepped forward.

'Take a look at the men around you,' he said. 'If there is any man here not known to somebody else, grip and hold him.'

There was confusion as men were grabbed by others from different districts, but soon all were vouched for and there was nervous laughter as they gradually settled down.

Canahan spoke in a hard voice. 'It is not a boys' game. An unknown man would be a spy for the landlords. Our visitor will now speak to you.'

He left the centre of the floor and the little red-headed man took his place. He looked slowly round the circle and it was as if he were a magnet to draw every eye and ear. Then he began to speak in a harsh, high-pitched voice, jerking out the words in quick bursts.

'Understand this! If you are caught here – you'll be gaoled – maybe transported – maybe hanged!' He paused to let this sink in. 'If you tell anything of what happens here tonight – you will be killed. By us!' Again he paused. 'Any man who wants to go home had better do so now.'

Many thought longingly of the safety of their firesides, wondered what trouble they were headed for, but none moved.

'Right! I'm Alexander Montgomery. County organiser for the Society of United Irishmen. The Government says it's illegal. That it's finished. The Government will learn. More of that later.

'Some of us here are Presbyterians. Some are Catholics. A few – other religions. That does not matter. We are all Irishmen. We all suffer from the landlords. Those are the important things.

180

'Emancipation!' He spat the word at them. 'We all dreamed of it. The magic that was to turn Erin into Eden. A farm for every man. Low rents. No tithes. Every man to have a vote. Freedom of religion. An end to the power of the landlords. Like a glimpse of heaven!

'And now Emancipation is dead. Choked before it was born. Stamped into the grave by the landlords.

'Why? Why?

'Who owns the land of Ireland? Well you know. The landlords. What do they do with it? All over Ireland the same will be found. Estates of thousands of acres leased at high rents to bailiffs who send the money to the landlords living in luxury in England. And the bailiffs get the money for their own high-living by squeezing rack-rents from the small farms and cottiers. You and your children starve and go half-naked to provide their fine houses, soft beds, rich dress, wines, lashings of food, carriages, horses, servants, dogs and all the rest that goes to make a fine life for ladies and gentlemen! You pay for it all. And they intend that you will continue to pay. That's why Emancipation was killed. They rule and, as long as they do, you will pay.'

He paused and wiped his lips. There was not a sound in the crypt.

'They say Ireland is a poor country,' he continued. 'Have you any notion of the money that goes out of Ireland every year? More than five million pounds to the absentee landlords. Five million pounds drained from the country every year and nothing in return.

'Tithes! Don't we all love the word! Tithes paid to the Church of Ireland – the Church by Law Established, they call it. Their law, mark you. Tithes amount to more than a million pounds a year. And the most of it goes to men who have never set foot in Ireland. From my own parish of Mountrath five hundred pounds a year is paid out to a man named Dean Scott. Forty years he has been rector and none of us has ever seen him. There is scarcely a parish in Ireland which has the vicar living in it. They're all away in England, living fat off the tithes – some as

181

much as fifteen hundred pounds a year. And then there are the holy bishops who don't live in Ireland either. Some with five, ten, fifteen, even as much as twenty thousand pounds a year.

'And you – poor fools of Irishmen – you would think yourselves rich if you had ten pounds in the year.' Again he paused and wiped his lips.

'But that is not the end of our payments. There's Vestry Cess, hearth-tax, land-tax, road-tax and taxes under other fancy names.

'Most of that money goes to pay fat salaries to men who are called by high-sounding titles in Dublin Castle or the Parliament. To the likes of "Brilliant" John Beresford and all his relations and friends.

'Then there are the pensions. Everybody who was ever anything at all in the Government, and all their relations – all get pensions.

'And not them alone. The English Government have a lot of people they don't dare put on their own Pensions List, so they pay them out of Ireland.'

He ticked them off on his fingers. 'The Duke of St Albans, descended from the illegitimate spawn of Charles II – eight hundred pounds a year. You all know of James II – old Jim Dung! He had a mistress named Catherine Sedley. Her descendants get five thousand pounds a year.

'Nobility, how are ye! Here's more. Evangard Schulenburg. A grand old Irish name, hah! She's Duchess of Kendal and Duchess of Munster. She gets five thousand pounds a year. Her bastard daughter, Lady Walsingham – fifteen hundred pounds a year. The Countess of Darlington – five thousand pounds a year, and her bastard, Lady Howe – five hundred pounds a year. All these ladies kept the present King's grandfather warm in his bed. George II had more of them and the present man over has more again.

'I could go on and on. But do you see the wealth of Ireland draining away? Do you see why you are poor? Do you see what you work and sweat and break your backs for? And do you see that you and your sons and their sons forever will go on in slavery unless you do something about it?

'What can you do?

'Listen to some other simple figures. Landlords and their hangers-on number perhaps twenty thousand. The rest of us – two to three million idiots who let ourselves be bullied and robbed. Think of it! We are more than a hundred to one. Yet we let them treat us like slaves.

'Think of this for a moment: Ireland ruled by Irishmen for the good of Irishmen. All that wealth going into our pockets. Ah, then we might talk of Emancipation indeed!

'What is to prevent it? There is this. The landlords are united. We are not. It's as simple as that.

'But if we were to unite. If all true Irishmen were banded together. Before God, I tell you there is no power in Ireland, nor yet in England, which could prevent us from taking this land for ourselves, from pitching out the breed of leeches and ruling the country for the good of every man in it.'

Abruptly he left the centre of the floor and crossed to Canahan who gave him a pitcher of water, from which he drank.

At first the men were silent, digesting what he had said. Then whispers grew to eager conversation, to loud discussion and argument, to wild excitement. Nobody had ever told them so much, put their position so clearly, given them so clear a picture of hope. When he walked back to the centre of the floor, they hushed immediately.

'Well, there it is. What will you do about it?

'What can you do? Join the United Irishmen. Our leader, Mr Theobald Wolfe Tone, is well-known to you. But there are others – men of power and position. We already have tens of thousands of members. But we want millions. We want all Irishmen united. When we have that, we can take Ireland for our own.

'I'll take no new men tonight. I'll have none join and regret it afterwards. I want you sure. Go home, think about it, talk about it amongst yourselves. One month from tonight I shall be here again. Then, I hope, we'll have you all.

'But remember the warning! Speak to nobody save among yourselves.' He paused, then said in a lighter, almost pleasant tone, 'Else, we'll kill you.'

THIRTY-FOUR

Strickland did not come to dinner. Hour after hour they waited, dreading the growing superciliousness of the butler who came with such anxious deference to enquire if the family were yet ready to dine, to convey the cook's worries and her final message that the meal was now uneatable.

Aloysius returned the following day with the message, transmitted on the door-step, that the Honourable Sebastian had travelled to England on urgent business, that the date of his return was indefinite.

The bills began to arrive, then the letters in decreasing politeness. Then the tradesmen began calling, at first servile, later loud-voiced, demanding, threatening, furiously waving their bills. Aloysius had to take the greatest care before leaving the house. It was only a matter of days before the bailiffs began to gather with carefully palmed writs. Then he did not dare leave the house at all.

One evening they waited long to be called to dinner. They rang for the butler, but he did not come. Georgina went to the kitchen. It was empty of servants. They searched the house. All the servants had gone, except Tim Duffin, the coachman, asleep in his attic nursing the depleted brandy bottle which the butler had given him. And with the servants had gone every portable article of value.

Very early next morning, Aloysius dragged Duffin from his bed and they fled home.

When she wakened on her first morning back at Ballyna House Nuala found it difficult to believe that all the gaiety and luxury were gone forever. Then she was surprised to realise that she had no real regret. It was almost as she had felt as a child when a long-awaited treat failed to equal the anticipation. A feeling that life held only disappointment, yet relief that the waiting was over, that this new experience had nevertheless added something of value to her, or subtracted something valueless.

Very pleasantly came the thought that there was now nothing to stand between Conal and herself. He would surely hear that she was back and would come to see her. For a moment she was filled with eager joy; but it was immediately dampened by the thought that hope brought disappointment.

Something was wrong with her awakening. It was quite a surprise to realise that she was waiting for a maid to appear with her breakfast tray.

She got up. Reality was an empty pitcher on her washstand, a journey through chill, silent dinginess to the kitchen, out to the pump and back to wash in cold water. When she had dressed she went back to the kitchen to find, to her relief, that Tim Duffin had lit the fire and was boiling a kettle. He also produced milk and eggs, and it did not yet occur to her to ask where he had got them. Such things existed. But there was neither bread nor butter, and when she asked and was told that there was none of either she felt the first touch of fear.

She took tea to her father and mother and was shocked to find an almost unrecognisable pair of old people in their bed. The dull hopelessness with which they looked at her made her regret wakening them. She hurried from their room.

Tim Duffin went off and returned with Felix who, to her relief, took charge and even produced a meal.

She saw that the darkness of the house was due to the

closed shutters, and she and Tim went about opening them. Yet it seemed as if no light came in, as if the house were an emptiness of dark and cold. Certainly there was no life. The kitchen and yard which had bustled with servants and beggars were silent places through which Felix drifted ghostlike. In the rest of the house there was the silence of two old and broken people existing from habit. Daily she watched them slipping further into careless senility. They seldom rose before midday, then appeared unwashed and with soiled dressing-gowns bundled over a misassortment of dirty undress.

She tried hard to rouse them with suggestions. They could sell everything available, pay off what debts they could, then go to another part of the country where, ~~perhaps, they could find a means of livelihood. They could appeal to Sir Julius Besant to give them time. They could~~ go to England or even to America, where prospects would be better. But the most she received in reply was a hopeless grunt.

Finally she remembered a vague mention of her mother's brother in Wexford and that he was rich. He, surely, would be their salvation. She had to shake her mother into attention, then old bitterness brought back some life.

'Mark would not give us one penny,' she declared. 'Indeed, it would probably give him pleasure if he knew of our position.'

'But surely your own brother... Unless he is dead?'

'No. We met a Mr Ogle in Dublin. He is from Wexford and told us that Mark lives near Enniscorthy and is a rich and important man.'

'Then surely he can help us.'

Her mother told her of his letter. 'He is cruel, heartless, unnatural. It is hopeless. As well appeal to Maxwell Leering.'

And Nuala even thought about doing that, but she could not overcome the fear and loathing she now had for him.

Through every day of the first week she waited for

Conal to come, hoped for it, yet feared that her leaving of him without a message had been accepted as her answer. But she needed his comfort and advice. The thought of his size and strength gave her hope that he would be able to solve their difficulties. She decided that she would go and find him.

Two hours after she had made this decision she went into the drawing-room to find her mother and father dozing on either side of the fire with the hearth-rug smouldering. Her screams brought Felix and Tim to bundle up the rug and fling it through the window. And she saw, with horror, that her parents watched this without any sign of concern or awareness of the danger they had escaped.

After that she was afraid to leave them for more than a few minutes at a time. When they went to bed she went with them to blow out their candle. She kept the firing out of the drawing-room, taking it in and attending to the fire herself when it was needed.

Yet she watched from the window, hoping for a sight of Conal. Often she would run to the gate to search the road. Then, fearful of some terrible happening, she would run back to the gloomy house to find her parents as she had left them, staring dully into a dying fire.

After more than a week of this she realised that she was simply waiting for catastrophe, that their condition would not improve, that something must be done, and that she must do that something herself. She warned Felix to watch her parents, had Tim saddle her horse and set out to find Conal.

It was a dull day, cold and raining, but after her long confinement the air refreshed her, seeming to clear away the mustiness of the house. There was almost optimism because of her relief at getting away. But the rain grew heavier and, whilst the heavy cloth of her habit protected her at first, it did not prevent the persistent trickles from running down inside her collar.

She saw, here and there, the stooped figures of men, shoulders covered by sacking, working in the fields, and she rode as close to them as she dared. Even though she could not see them clearly she felt sure that Conal was not amongst them, certain that she would recognise him even at a distance and through the rain. She rode on and on. In despair she rode close to one group of men, intending to question them. One said something to his companions and all turned to stare at her with hard, suspicious eyes. She turned away. For two hours she rode, until her clothes were saturated and hung in heavy folds which clung to her chilled body. The more discomfort she felt, the more determined she became to find him. She could not go back to that gloom and melancholy without seeing him.

The only thing left now was the one thing she had been determined not to do: to go to MacShane's. But the rain made it impoosible to see more than twenty yards, and she was unsure of the way. Wet, cold and miserable, she rode on, and so she rode into Duncarran.

The cabins huddled together in the cheerless weather. No people were to be seen at first, but at the sound of her horse they appeared in their doorways and stared. She felt her face burning. She knew she looked bedraggled, wet hair clinging about her face and sodden clothes hanging from her. She felt completely exposed to their suspicious, antagonistic eyes.

Some people ran towards her intending to offer shelter. In terror she whipped her horse and galloped out of the place.

The steepness and roughness of the track forced her to slow the horse and she let him find his own careful way down. She did not see Michael Canahan until the horse stepped in front of him. She gripped her crop, fearing that she was about to be attacked.

'Good day to you, miss. That's a poor day for riding.'

'Good day,' she said hesitantly.

'It cannot be pleasure brings you out. An important errand, perhaps?' In spite of the politeness of words and tone, she sensed an underlying hostility; but she was desperate.

'I am looking for Conal O'Carran.'

'Ah, you'll not find him. He went from here today.'

Dismay brought the despairing words, 'When will he be back?'

'Sure, what would bring him back to this place? Good day, miss.'

He went back into his cabin, leaving her desolate.

The horse moved on. She slumped, utterly dejected, in the saddle, swaying with the movement, remaining in place merely by habit. Her whole world was a gloomy prison which she inhabited with two half-crazed old people.

Long before she reached home she was only half-conscious. When, at last, the horse stopped at the foot of the steps, she remained swaying in her saddle until Tim found her and lifted her down. He carried her into the house, calling anxiously for Felix.

In the drawing-room Aloysius was lolling, melancholy drunk; but Georgina, roused by the anxious mention of her daughter's name, slippered out to the hall. She screamed at the sight of Nuala looking like somebody drowned, then became all fussy motherhood. She had Nuala carried upstairs, where she undressed her, dried and warmed her and put her to bed. She had a fire lit, medicines and liniments brought and applied. And Nuala knew nothing of any of it.

THIRTY-FIVE

Lord Fitzwilliam was succeeded by Lord Camden. In spite of all the efforts of the military, he was greeted with a hail of stones and drove to the Viceroy's lodge through the jeers and hoots of the Dublin crowd.

There was no liberal-minded nonsense about Camden. From the first he set himself on the side of the landlords. To impress on the people that he would not tolerate outbreaks against authority he toured the country in force. He took the earliest opportunity to show his attitude to the United Irishmen. When he was in Naas a man named O'Connor was convicted of administering a secret oath to a soldier of the garrison. Camden ordered O'Connor to be hanged and had his head lopped off and skewered on a pole above the gate of the gaol. The rewards of patriotism were there for everybody to see and smell.

This act banished any lingering hopes the people might have had of obtaining liberty through the law. But, far from being a deterrent, it became very useful propaganda for the United Irishmen. They spoke to increasing audiences, and Irishmen listened and acted.

THIRTY-SIX

Michael Canahan had deliberately misled Nuala. He had heard rumours about her and Conal. To him it meant that Conal was consorting with the enemy; and it had to be stopped.

In fact, Conal had gone to the market to buy two young pigs for Aidan MacShane.

He was convinced that Nuala had decided against him. This, together with his constant worry of being a burden to his uncle and the thoughts and hopes roused by the meeting of the United Irishmen, made a turmoil in his mind. Montgomery had aroused his anger and hatred not so much for the wrongs done to Ireland, but for what he had suffered personally. It was obvious the United Irishmen intended to fight and he felt a tremendous surge of exultation when he thought of being able to use his physical strength to punish those who had caused his misery. Yet he always remembered Paris, the dreadful fear and suspicion and that frightful execution; so that, whilst he longed for Montgomery to return, he feared the consequences.

Having bought the piglets, and being angry with himself because he felt he had done a poor job for MacShane by being bested in the bargain, he drove the cart out of the marketplace intending to go straight back. As he turned into a cross street he heard the agonised screaming of a woman. A cart was coming towards him surrounded by a large crowd. The screams came from the heart of the angrily murmuring crowd.

At the corner of the street a young girl with a tiny baby in her arms was sobbing hysterically. Conal questioned her and she told him, through her tears, that it was her mother who was being whipped at the cart-tail. From the hysterical tangle he gathered that the woman, recently widowed and with a large family to support, had hired herself as a nurse to the children of Major Crawleigh, a local landowner and magistrate. She had been discovered to be pregnant and had been sentenced to four months in prison and a whipping. Though there was no slur on her pregnancy, it was illegal for a woman, knowing herself to be in that condition, to hire herself as a nurse. The baby which the girl was holding had been born in prison. The law, in its mercy, had allowed the mother three months to recover from the birth. She was now receiving her lashing as an example to potential criminals.

By this time the cart and its attendants had reached the end of the street and Conal could see the evildoer. She was stripped to the waist and tied by a long cord round her wrists to the back of the cart. Greater even than her agony was her shame at the exposure of her breasts. It was pitiful to see her trying to cover them with her arms,

191

leaping in a horrible, screaming dance when the lash raked her back, then, with sobs, moans and prayers, trying again to cover her nakedness.

A constable, guarded by three others who held the crowd back with long staves, was slashing the whip across the woman's torn and bleeding back.

'Oh God, oh God, oh God help me!'

Her eyes, filled with agonised pleading, stared from her contorted face right at Conal. He took one step from his own cart to the other, then leaped at the whipper. They fell together, but Conal was up and had dragged him to his feet before the crowd of guards had realised what was happening. He smashed his fist into the man's face and joy rose volcanically as he felt the nose pulp under his knuckles. Then, with a roar, the three guards rushed at him with upraised staves. But a greater roar rose from the crowd as they hurled themselves on the constables.

The woman lay forgotten, unconscious under the cart where her daughter had dragged her, whilst the mob tore at each other in their eagerness to smite the torturers. Conal, quite berserk, oblivious of the blows from his opponent and of the kicking and pushing of the crowd, punched and kicked until the limp body fell, like a half-filled sack, on the cobbles.

He felt his arm gripped and swung round, delighted that he had a new adversary, but found himself looking down into the shrewd face of Alexander Montgomery.

'Come away,' he ordered. 'The soldiers are coming.'

Conal looked for the woman, but the crowd hid both her and the cart. He followed Montgomery through a narrow alley into a series of lanes.

Montgomery leant against a wall and looked at Conal. 'You're Conal O'Carran,' he said. 'Michael Canahan told me about you. He says you've some education. It's a great pity you haven't the sense to go with it.'

Conal's face flamed. 'For a little man, you're very free with your insults!'

Montgomery looked at him, hard-eyed and quite imperturbable. 'Would you hammer me now? That was a stupid thing you did. The woman will still get her whipping. There will be many broken heads and torn backs. And you, yourself, could be on the way to the gallows if I hadn't hauled you away. What good have you done?'

'What else would you expect a man to do in those circumstances?'

'I'd expect him to use his head, not lose it. Oh, you'd great satisfaction beating that constable; as much, I'd say, for your own whipping as for the poor woman's. But others are left behind you to suffer for what you have done. Does that make you feel so fine? When will people learn that there's nothing to be gained by fiddling little outbreaks against the law? They serve only to give the authorities the chance to show greater severity. They effect nothing!'

One moment he was bitter, the next, quite unexpectedly, he laughed. 'However, there's four badly spoiled constables back there, if they're living at all. So you want to fight, do you, young fellow?'

Conal had cooled now. He remembered the consequences of beating Fowler, felt fear and immediately despised himself for it. 'Did you know that I was in France, in Paris?'

'I did.'

'I saw what revolution does to people. It does not bring happiness. It does bring hatred, fear, suspicion and a horrible delight in bloodshed.'

'It does,' said Montgomery equably. 'For some – for the poor and the ignorant who think only of their own suffering. But those who can look forward and who have the ability and determination to build a better future can curb the ignorant by giving them something to work at, to work for.'

'But still it cannot be achieved without bloodshed.'

'What were you doing back there? Could you have stopped the constable by talking to him? Wasn't he just a weapon of the landlords carrying out their continual policy of slavery by the use of terror? Will talking stop the landlords?'

'Talking did not bring Emancipation anyhow.'

'So there's only one answer – the whole people organised and armed. Meet the power of the landlords with greater power and smash them. Then we can build; and to build we need men of education like yourself.' He paused. 'Now, go back and see to your pigs, at least.'

To Conal the way was suddenly clear. Three nights later he led the men by joining the United Irishmen and they all followed him.

When all had taken the oath, Montgomery said, 'You will have noted that some of our long-standing members do not appear to be present. They are on watch outside. Remember to post watchers at every meeting!

'Our motto is, "Unite and be Free". The password, "I know U, I know N, I know I, and so on until United is spelt. Each branch has its own leader. Yours is Michael Canahan, and he will appoint his own lieutenants.

'You all know that there is a law which threatens death to people in groups of four or more found abroad at night. Come and go singly or in pairs and avoid being seen.

'Finally, I will give a piece of news. The French are offering to help oppressed nations who wish to win their liberty. Mr Wolfe Tone is in Paris at this very moment arranging help for Ireland. We will get both arms and soldiers. When they come, we will rise and win our freedom!'

THIRTY-SEVEN

Nuala's illness was a blessing for Georgina. Her previous apathy had been a self-imposed removal from life and its insoluble problems. The necessity to concentrate on nursing obviated the need to think of anything else. She became fussy and managing, continually anxious for Nuala's comfort, searching recipe books for remedies, making new potions and ensuring that Nuala took them, until she discovered others more promising.

But she was fighting more than sickness. Nuala lay completely uncaring, pale and inert, staring at the ceiling with unseeing eyes, or dozing fitfully. Even when the chill was defeated and her mother supported her triumphantly downstairs to sit, well-wrapped, before the fire, she still looked weak and ill. She could not bring herself to eat, to talk or to take interest in anything. Hour after hour she sat staring into the fire, seeing the might-have-been, whilst her father sprawled opposite, dull and fumbling, drooling claret and scattering snuff on his greasy coat.

THIRTY-EIGHT

Conal found the United Irishmen a most satisfying outlet for both physical and mental energy and he slept deeply every night. Canahan gave him the job of recruiting and this meant that he travelled the countryside on foot every day.

One day, from far up the hillside, he looked down at Ballyna House and saw smoke coming from the chimneys. His impulse was to race down there immediately. But if he did and the family were back, he could scarcely walk up to the house in broad daylight. What could he do? What could he say? 'Is Miss Nuala Grogan at home? Mr Conal O'Carran is calling on her!' He could imagine the servants' reply to that. Even if they did not set the dogs on him, even if they took his message to her, what would be her answer? And had she not given her answer already! Yet he had to know if she was there. Surely it was possible for him to find out without her or anybody else seeing him. He would go there after dark.

For the rest of the day he was conscious of acting like an automaton with all whom he met and talked to. On his way back he walked slowly, willing the night to come, yet it was still light when he drew near to Ballyna and he sat down to wait impatiently for darkness.

When, at last, it came, he walked to the gates and slipped inside. He crept through the shrubbery to the big oak. There was a glow from one of the downstairs windows, but no other signs of life. He ran across to the side of the window, slid along the wall and peeped in.

The room was filled with wavering shadows thrown by the flickers of the dying fire. He made out the fat figure of Aloysius sprawled in sleep in an armchair. Another chair had its back towards him and he could see only the edge of a woman's dress.

Nuala had sat there the whole afternoon, staring at the fire and vaguely trying to fight apathy. She knew that there was merely a lull in their misfortunes. The many Dublin creditors must soon find them and absolute disaster would follow. She struggled to appreciate the urgency of their situation and so to arouse herself to plan; but it was so much easier simply to sit whilst nothing happened and lull herself into believing that nothing would happen. Besides, she was still weak and her very weakness urged her to the false comfort of self-pity. None of the miseries were of her making. All that she had wanted was to enjoy life. She had soon recognised the emptiness of Society. Surely she deserved credit for that. She had been ready to give it all up for Conal. But Conal had deserted her. Tears flowed easily. Her already sodden handkerchief was useless. Irritably she thought that she must find a fresh one. That would mean getting up from the comfort of her chair, making the long, cold journey to her room. But the chair was not comfortable. She had been sitting too long. It was stupid to remain there, and tears provided no solution.

She jerked herself upright and thrust herself from the chair. Conal, still not able to see clearly, peered closer. She turned, saw the face at the window and screamed.

Conal, his heart leaping with excitement, overcome by concern for her, rushed to the front door, and was just about to pound on it when it was flung open by Tim Duffin who brandished a large pistol.

'Up with your hands!' yelled Tim. 'Up high, you blackguard!'

Conal raised his hands. 'You don't understand.'

'One wrong move and I pull this trigger.' Tim's shaking voice betrayed a nervousness which Conal feared could make him fire.

The light of a lantern appeared behind Tim. It was Felix.

Tim backed slowly. 'Walk in, slow now.' Conal followed.

Felix raised the lantern. 'Is it bailiffs?'

Tim peered in the dim light. 'Begod, no. 'Tis O'Carran, the young fellow gave Fowler the belting. What brings you here, young fellow?'

Nuala's scream had roused both her father and her mother, who had been in bed. Georgina's tousled, dressing-gowned figure appeared on the stairs as the drawing-room door opened and Nuala and her father appeared.

Nuala, with one ecstatic cry of 'Conal!' rushed into his arms. Unconscious of their audience, they clung frantically to each other, mumbling and kissing with an unappeasable hunger.

Georgina, being furthest away and unable to see clearly, thought Nuala was being attacked. She shrieked and ran down the stairs as fast as her draperies would allow. 'Leave her go, you ruffian! Leave my daughter go! Tim, Felix, Aloysius, stop him!'

Her shrieks penetrated to Nuala and Conal and they parted.

Tim looked helplessly from the couple to Mrs Grogan. Felix muttered something about candles and sidled into the drawing-room past Aloysius who stood gaping and blinking with the effort to understand.

'It is all right, mama,' said Nuala. 'He is a friend of mine.'

She looked at Conal and they both broke into half-hysterical laughter.

Georgina advanced. 'A friend? Do we know him?'

'His name is Conal O'Carran.'

Conal bowed. 'Mrs Grogan.'

'But Nuala! You were kissing him!'

And that set them laughing again whilst Georgina looked on in helpless astonishment.

'It's all right, mama. Really it is. *Everything* will be all right now.' She took her mother's arm and led her to the drawing-room, saying, 'Wait, Conal.'

She was back in his arms in an instant. Felix and Tim came, took one look, shrugged their incomprehension and went to the kitchen. Aloysius and Georgina came to the door and stared at them. *They* saw nobody.

THIRTY-NINE

For several days Conal knew real happiness for the first time. He had the constant, increasingly successful work of organising for the United Irishmen during the day and long hours with Nuala at night.

But when he arrived at the next meeting Canahan took him on one side. 'It has been reported to me that you are consorting with the enemy.'

'That's a lie!'

'You have been seen visiting the Grogan house.'

Conal laughed. 'Oh, is that it.'

'What were you doing there?'

'That's no business of yours.'

'I am your commander. I demand to know why you go to that house.'

Conal suppressed his anger. In a low voice he said, 'I go to see Nuala Grogan.'

Canahan showed no surprise. 'The daughter of the man who had you lashed!'

'She had no hand or part in that.'

'She is still his daughter.'

'Ah, for God's sake, man, if you saw him now – an old man half-mad with fear of the bailiffs and the debtors' prison. He doesn't even recognise me. And he has been cast off by all his own kind. He can do no harm now.'

'You forget that he has done harm in plenty in the past. He'll pay for that, and his family with him.'

Conal's clenched fists quivered at his sides as he whispered, 'As God is my judge, Canahan, if you harm them, I'll kill you!'

'Enough!' Canahan yelled. 'Get back to your place. I order you, as your commander.'

Conal hesitated, then turned with a growl and went.

'I want the attention of every man of you!' Canahan shouted in a voice like a grindstone. 'Think, all of you! Think what it is we mean to do.' His voice slowed and the words dropped like stones. 'We will destroy the whole landlord class. Do you understand what I am saying? We will slaughter every last one of them. We will burn down their houses and rid the country of every last trace of them!'

He paused to gain his breath and composure. 'Henry Grattan, our one friend in the Parliament, walked out of it forever one week ago, because he knew that there was no hope left. The great petition which Mr Burke and the Catholic hierarchy and gentlemen got together in spite of the Parliament was presented to the king. There was no reply. All we have got from England is Camden and his bloody-handed soldiers. They have proved to us that the only way is by force. So, with the help of God, what we could not get for the asking we will take with bullets and pikes.

'There is good news. Wolfe Tone and Lord Edward Fitzgerald have secured the help of the French and they have agreed to send us ships and soldiers. In Dublin, Mr Napper Tandy has organised two battalions of a National Guard, each with a thousand men. They have fine green uniforms with harp buttons with a cap of liberty on them; and they have muskets, pistols and swords. A rich ironmonger has given over his forge and is casting cannon night and day. At this moment shiploads of arms, which the United Irishmen have bought abroad, are being landed on the west coast and distributed through the country.

'But be warned. The Peep O' Day Boys are organising too. They have arms already, and we can expect trouble from them at any time. The Government, too, smelling the trouble that is coming, are enrolling, arming and training Militia to be used against us.

'I have told you that arms are being imported; but don't think you'll be handed a musket tomorrow. There are not yet enough for everybody. We must collect arms of every kind. We will get them from every rich man's house. For the present we need pikes. Our own blacksmiths will make them, but we must supply them with iron and twelve-foot shafts. We start on that work this very night.'

The following night Conal borrowed a horse and cart and went to Ballyna. Having tied the horse to a bush he made his way to the oak and whistled. In a few moments Nuala threw herself breathlessly into his arms, but after one brief kiss he held her off. She sensed his unease immediately.

'What is it, Conal? There is something wrong.'

'It is hard for me to say this. God knows I cannot bear the thought of being parted from you again, but you must go away from here – you and your family.'

She gripped his arms and tried to peer into his face. 'Go away? Where? Why?'

'You are in danger. You must go somewhere, anywhere away from here.'

She clutched him. 'No, Conal, no! I will not leave you again!'

He clasped her fiercely. He had said the necessary, well-rehearsed words, but only now did their full implication strike him. They might never see each other again. For a long time they used kisses and caresses and murmured endearments to hold back reality; but, inevitably, he had to try to make her realise the danger whilst hiding the knowledge of what he had been doing.

Suddenly she cried, 'Conal! I know. It's rebellion! You are planning a rebellion!'

He could make no answer except to repeat that she must go.

'I am right, am I not. There will be killing as there was in France. Conal, you must not take any part in it. You could be killed!' She shook him urgently. Then, with a sudden idea: 'If we must go, then you must come with us.'

'I cannot do that, my love.'

For a long time they argued fruitlessly, but slowly he wore her down. He told her that he had come to collect any arms they had in the house and that the fact of giving them up should be protection enough until they completed their preparations to go far away to her mother's brother in Wexford. There they would surely be safe and he would know where to find her.

Much later, having loaded eight sporting guns, five pistols and a quantity of lead and powder on to the cart, they stood facing each other in the darkness, not touching, yet one in their misery and foreboding.

At last, he said, 'Think of it all this way, Nuala. The way things are now there is no sort of life at all for us. But, with God's help, everything will be changed. Maybe I will get back at least some of my land. Then there would be a life for us.'

She shivered. 'I am frightened,' she said. 'Conal, I am so

dreadfully frightened. I can see no happiness anywhere for us, and, oh...' She threw herself into his arms.

FORTY

There was great rejoicing amongst the men on the following night when they saw the arms, the first which had been collected.

For Canahan's benefit, Conal announced in a loud voice, 'They're a gift from Ballyna House. All they had. Remember that!'

Canahan gave only a hard look in reply.

Some of the men were sent off to the smithy with the old iron which had been collected, whilst the remainder set to work shaping pike staffs. By the end of the week every man had a pike – a fearsome weapon with a three-foot pointed blade equipped with a sharpened hook at the side for cutting a horseman's reins and dragging him from his saddle. There was wild exultation in the crypt when they got these in their fists. God, what a man could do with such a weapon! Who could stand against him! They charged about with them, yelling and whooping, every man a danger to his fellows.

Canahan stormed at them, but it took several minutes to bring them back to sanity and order. He glared at their excited, sweating faces.

'You bloody idiots! You can be heard for miles around. How do we know who is listening out there in the darkness? Fine heroes you'll be if the redcoats creep up and surround the place. With their muskets they could kill every man of us before we got near them.'

There were a few sheepish giggles which he quelled with a glare.

'Pikes are well enough. Indeed, they can be great weapons in the hands of determined men. But we need guns. That will be our next task.

'O'Carran, you think yourself the expert at that job. Pick ten men, go to Barclay's and bring back all that you can find there. But first, blacken your faces so you'll not be known. Take your pikes; but remember we want no trouble at this time. If you can get the arms without being seen, so much the better. If you are seen, avoid bloodshed. We do not want to invite the Dragoons before we are ready for them.'

Two hours later Conal and his ten men stood in the shadow of a group of trees in the grounds of Barclay's house. There had been much self-conscious tittering when they had seen each other's blackened faces, and much excited whispering during the journey, but now they were silent, quivering, half with eagerness, half with fear. An involuntary murmur of, 'Jesus and His Blessed Mother protect us!' did nothing to comfort their nervousness.

'Well, lads,' said Conal, 'here we are.' He was the leader. It was necessary for him to do something, but this was the best he had to offer.

'Aye,' said somebody. 'What do we do now?'

'I'll tell you the truth,' said Conal. 'I don't know. It was easy enough for Canahan to say, "Go to Barclay's and bring back all the arms," but how, in the name of God, are we to get them? Maybe he thought we'd just walk up, knock on the door and ask the butler if he'd kindly bring them out to us.'

There was a nervous guffaw.

Then one man offered in a deprecatory tone, 'Could we not charge in with our pikes, making fierce shouts the way we'd be frightening them?'

'I think,' said Conal, 'the only way is for us to go in quietly through the kitchen. Then we'll get one of the servants to show us where the arms are kept.'

Nobody could think of an alternative, so all agreed. As silently as they could, for the long pikes were very difficult to manage through the trees and bushes, they crept in single file after Conal. He led them to the rear of the house and halted a few yards from the kitchen door. They could hear women's voices and the clatter of dishes.

'Follow close after me, lads,' he whispered.

He ran to the door, opened it suddenly and tried to push in, but was immediately stopped by the pike which he had been holding upright. The others ran into him and there was a tangle of arms and pikes.

In desperation, Conal, still only half-way into the kitchen, hissed at the women, 'Not a sound from you!'

But even as he spoke the jumble of black faces and struggling bodies, looking to the women like an invasion from Hell, brought screams of terror from them. They simply stood, stared in horror and screamed piercingly.

Fear-stricken, the men changed from struggling to get in, to struggling even harder to get away. At the same time there came from the inner house men's shouts and the pounding of running feet.

Conal hesitated for an instant, then, pushing the few remaining men away from him, he ran with the pike slapping and clacking on the branches and threatening to tear out of his hands.

He felt like one of Canahan's smallest pupils offering a very weak excuse for truanting when he reported the affair the following night.

'Great God!' shouted Canahan. 'Eleven armed men terrified out of their skins by the screams of women. What will you do when you've to face the muskets of the redcoats or a charge of Dragoons?'

There were shouts of scornful laughter from the men who had not gone out, and louder protest from those who had. Immediately there was argument which flared into fighting. In spite of Canahan's efforts there was a riot of shouting, struggling men. He had to appeal to Conal and the other lieutenants to help him, but it took nearly ten minutes of concerted, strenuous effort before they secured order.

When all was quiet again, Conal muttered to Canahan,

'You've given us several examples of how not to lead men. Now show us how to do it successfully.'

MacShane pulled him aside. 'Ah, for God's sake, Conal, don't be making bad worse.'

Larry Dolan had watched the fight and now the bickering with great amusement. He stepped forward and called, 'If the men who went out last night would care to come with me, I'll show how to do the job.' He turned with mock deference to Canahan, 'With the General's permission, of course.'

Taking Canahan's angry growl as permission, he said, 'Right, lads. Now for a start leave the bloody toothpicks here. We'll take guns.'

'You will not!' said Canahan. 'The orders are to collect guns, not to use them.'

'I brought all the guns we have,' said Conal, 'and I say we use them.'

Immediately an argument sprang up between himself and Canahan. Dolan calmly ignored them and began distributing guns and ammunition.

Seeing this, Canahan shouted, 'I forbade you do to that, Dolan!'

Larry turned with a loaded pistol in his hand and said, 'So now, I suppose, you'll slap me. Let you two learned gentlemen go on swapping logic. We'll get on with the business of rebellion.' Then, with the slightest lift of the pistol barrel, 'I'm a great man to joke. Sometimes!'

There was no reply; so, after a moment's pause, Dolan said, 'Come on, then, lads.'

Canahan said nothing as they trooped out. Conal hesitated, then ran after them. When he caught up he asked Larry, 'Will you take me with you?'

Dolan paused, then abruptly poked him with the pistol. 'This is the end of talk. Agreed?'

'I do.'

'I hope you do, and I hope the rest of you do, for I'm done with talk.'

He led them to Barclay's, but stopped a short distance from the house.

'Wait here, all of you,' he whispered, 'and make no sound.'

He began to creep away, then returned. 'Maybe some of you did not understand me. Not a man of you is to whisper, cough, or even breathe loudly – else I'll split his skull!'

He was gone again and all stood rigid during the long moments until he returned.

'There are still lights showing,' he whispered. 'We'll wait, and if you've sense you'll do what I do – sleep.'

He lay down in the undergrowth and Conal, who lay beside him, knew that he was soon asleep in spite of the chill night. But neither Conal nor any of the others could match his relaxation.

The slow seconds dragged. Conal thought that surely hours must have passed, but he could not bring himself to waken Dolan. This man he had thought he knew had suddenly become a dangerous stranger, yet one in whom he felt confidence.

Dolan's whisper shocked them all. 'They should all be snug in their beds now. Follow me quietly.'

He led them to the gate where he posted a watcher, along the drive where he posted another, then right round the house, trying windows and posting men as he went. The kitchen window was unfastened and he entered with Conal and three others. He left them in the kitchen and searched the ground-floor until he found the gun-room. It took all of them three trips between there and the kitchen to carry all that they found. He then sent Conal to bring the watchers. Each man was loaded and they left in silence.

It was very late when they reached the crypt and all the others had gone. They were exultant at their success, bursting with self-congratulation and wanting to celebrate, but Dolan stopped them.

'You think you've done wonders. You've done not badly. You'll do better. Get off home to your beds.'

There was some hesitation.

'Now!' he ordered. And they went.

After that, by tacit consent, all administration was left to Canahan, all action was planned and led by Larry Dolan. Using a few new men each time, mixed with those who had been out before, he successfully raided Bent's, Grace's and Halliday's. By that time he had built up a large store of arms, had secured the confidence of the men, but had also roused the countryside.

The pile of guns and pistols greatly impressed the men, but Dolan pointed out that many were old, some even of more danger to the user than to the target, that their supply of ammunition was poor and that they were still far from being equipped to meet soldiery.

All over the country similar acts were taking place. Raids were made on private houses, men were cutting timber and gathering iron for the manufacture of pikes. On a thousand lonely hillsides ragged men were being drilled by starlight. If they were lucky, their drill-sergeants were old men who had served in the English army or navy; if not, they were old members of the Whiteboys or other secret organisations who knew nothing of battles except what they had heard in tales of the old times.

Alarm spread amongst the landowners and their supporters. The Peep O' Day Boys enrolled every active man from the Church of Ireland community. Well armed and mounted, with increasing frequency and in growing numbers, they rode through the countryside at night, beating any peasants they met and raiding and searching for arms.

The gentry bricked up their ground-floor windows, set guards round their houses day and night and ate and slept with arms close at hand.

There were frequent meetings between bands of Peep O' Day Boys and United Irishmen with increasing bloodshed and loss of life.

Canahan tried in vain to stop these skirmishes. The Executive forbade them, urging the men to avoid all trouble until they were fully armed and organised. The men refused to listen. All timidity was gone. There were long-suffered grievances to be avenged, both common and personal, and there were the most recent activities of the Peep O' Day Boys to be avenged.

It was the same all over the country and, where at first action had been confined to the darkness, daylight raids became increasingly frequent. Raids for arms were now made on volunteer arsenals, on police and small military barracks and on parties of revenue officers and soldiers. The secret arms stores grew rapidly.

But the Peep O' Day Boys with the unofficial backing of the law also increased in power. Large bodies of horsemen raided first isolated cabins and then villages. Even when they found no arms they invariably punished the inhabitants and set fire to their cabins.

Each day were were new wrongs to be avenged. The pendulum swung ever more swiftly, mounted ever higher. Men, women, and children were beaten to death, burned to death in their cabins, shot or hung from trees. Horses and cattle were maimed, hayricks, barns, farmhouses and even the houses of the gentry were set on fire, all who refused to give up their arms were piked. In the skirmishes between the United Irishmen and the Peep O' Day boys there was increasing ferocity and it was seldom they retired without leaving dead on either side.

The French Revolutionaries' fashion of wearing their own hair cut short was adopted by the United Irishmen, earning them the nickname of 'Croppies'. They took to wearing green as their symbol, sporting a green ribbon or cockade, a green garment or even a green rag tied round the arm.

Officially the law declared itself against all unrest, no matter who was responsible. To combat it they employed regular soldiers (few enough because of the French wars), the militia – mainly rag, tag and bobtail who enlisted hoping for loot to augment the gratuity, and the police who were usually the servants of the gentry and members of the Peep O' Day Boys. These forces made sporadic raids for arms, but with little success, for the arms were well hidden, and few could be found to inform knowing that certain death from the United Irishmen would follow. Yet, to show proof of their proficiency, they seldom returned from their raids without captives 'arrested on suspicion'. These were brought before the magistrates and it was soon obvious that a Protestant captive was either acquitted or lightly fined whilst a Catholic was sent to serve in the English navy.

This increased the savagery. Individuals amongst the police and the magistrates became targets for attack. Many were stripped naked, placed standing in deep holes filled with thorns and then buried to their necks. In retaliation men were beaten, their limbs broken, their ears sliced off. Savagery fed on savagery until death accompanied by horrible mutilation became the rule.

Larry Dolan's group of raiders had grown in confidence. They became a hardened force which constantly raided and fought. For them, and for Conal with them, it became a way of life. The activities of their opponents spurred them to greater efforts. They made long marches over rough country, usually at night, followed by long waits in ambush, sudden, sharp fights, then more long marches. Sleep and meals were snatched. Days and nights merged and jumbled into weeks in their tired minds. But there was the joy of a man in his own strength, the wild satisfaction of the freedom to destroy the ill-gotten riches of his persecutors; and the exultation over an enemy dead whilst you lived in triumph.

Conal, worried about Nuala, was constantly fearful that she and her family would be attacked. He longed to get her away, but there was always some immediate task, or sheer physical exhaustion or the suspicion of his companions to prevent this.

FORTY-ONE

Terrified by the tales which Tim Duffin brought, Nuala and her family cowered in their house. She had no news of Conal and no means of contacting him. Although the need to take her parents away from danger was obvious to her, she still could not bring herself to go without seeing Conal.

It was quite by accident she overheard Tim Duffin discussing going to Mass the following Sunday. Very early on the Sunday morning she got up and dressed herself in the oldest clothes she could find, ragging them to make herself look like a peasant girl. She left the house, hid along the road until Tim Duffin walked past, then followed him at a distance. After nearly five miles, during which more and more people had appeared on the road, they passed through the village of Ardnabrecan. There was now quite a throng and Nuala searched eagerly.

A group of men appeared from a side alley and she saw Conal amongst them. She called, almost screamed, his name, careless of the people who stared at her.

At that moment there was a great clatter of hoofs and wild shouting and a party of thirty or forty Peep O' Day Boys galloped down the street flourishing cudgels, swords and sabres. They charged into the crowd striking at everybody within range. The people scattered, screaming and shouting. The horsemen galloped over the bridge and away up the road.

Only seconds had passed, but more than twenty bodies lay in the road, Nuala's amongst them.

Conal, in racing towards Nuala, had been struck by the shoulder of a horse and flung aside. But he was only shaken. He thrust away the many helping hands, scrambled to his feet and searched for Nuala. She was being raised by a group of women. His heart stopped at the sight of blood on her unconscious face.

A woman said, 'She is not greatly hurted. A sliding blow is all. The skin is broken but not the bone.'

He bent down and took her from them and carried her to the river. Laying her beside it he scooped water in his hands, bathed her face and washed away the blood from the graze on her temple. She was very pale and still unconscious, but he knew by her breathing that she was not seriously injured. He picked her up and set off back to Ballyna.

Whilst he was still within sight of the people he marched like a man carrying an inanimate burden, but when he knew he could not be seen he rested, leaning against a bank, and looked down at her. She seemed so fragile and defenceless that a wave of protective tenderness surged through him. He hugged her, feeling that he held all life and hope of happiness. But the raw bruise on her temple was a vivid reminder of the fragility of hope. With a groan he settled her weight in his arms and walked on.

FORTY-TWO

The same group of Peep O' Day Boys visited Ballyna House. They hammered on the front door, but Felix refused to open it, so they went round the back. Finding the kitchen door bolted, they smashed it in. Felix, who had raced to the kitchen, was flung aside.

Mr and Mrs Grogan, still in bed, were roused by the noise at the front door. With much befuddled muttering and snuffling, Aloysius scrambled out of bed and shuffled to the window. He was a fat, comic figure in his long nightshirt from under which the empty toes of his bed-socks flopped at each step, and with his tasselled night-cap hanging over one ear. By the time he had reached the window and peered out the men had gone. He looked stupidly from the empty drive to Georgina cowering in the bed, then shook his head slowly and ambled back to the blankets. The bed groaned as he flopped on it, but he was only half-way into it when there was a loud shouting and trampling from the hall below.

This annoyed him. With a half-curse, half-groan he swung his feet out again and made for the bedroom door. Before he reached it there was a pounding up the stairs, the door was flung open and a seeming horde of ruffians poured into the room. They roared with laughter at the sight of Aloysius.

'What the devil d'you mean by this intrusion?' he shouted.

His air of offended dignity only increased their amusement. One with a mock bow said, 'Your pardon, indeed, sir and ma'am, for our trespass into your boudoir. We come by order of the magistrate, to collect all the arms in your house.'

'Get out of here! Get out of here at once. I'll have you horse-whipped. Every man jack!'

'The arms, you old fool. Where are they?'

'Get out, I say!'

Two men grabbed him, rushed him backwards, threw him into the bed and flung the bedclothes over his head.

'Right, lads. Hide and go seek!'

They scattered through the house. Every cupboard and drawer was ransacked, their contents flung to the floor. Aloysius struggled and cursed against his wife's whimpering but effective restraint.

In the midst of the uproar a voice shouted from downstairs, 'Billy! D'ye hear me, Billy! This bloody fellow says the Croppies got them all.' There was the sound of a blow and a cry of pain from Felix.

Feet thumped down the stairs and there was the mutter of voices fading towards the kitchen.

'They're going, Aloysius. Oh, thank God, they're going,' whispered Georgina, releasing her hold on him.

He flung aside the covers and got out of bed. Loud halloos and the trampling of hoofs sounded from the yard, echoed round the house, then faded down the drive and along the road. Aloysius was scrambling into his clothes.

Thee was a light knock on the door. It opened and Felix entered. Blood ran from his nose and from a cut over one swollen eye. 'Oh, sir. Oh, ma'am,' he cried. 'I couldn't stop them.'

Georgina's whimpering became a loud wail at the sight of his injuries. 'We'll be murdered! We'll all be murdered! Oh, Aloysius, what will we do?'

But Aloysius completed his dressing without a word, then he simply said, 'Come!' to the butler and led him from the room.

As he closed the door, Georgina screamed, 'Aloysius! What are you planning to do? Aloysius!'

She scrambled from the bed and hunted for her dressing-gown amidst the litter on the floor; but by the time she had found it, put it on, descended the stairs and searched for her husband, he, with Felix's help, had saddled a horse and was away.

Scorning the road, he galloped across country to Leering's house.

Leering had just returned from church, bringing back several people to lunch. They had just alighted and were chatting on the steps when Aloysius appeared. On seeing him coming Leering asked the ladies to go into the house. He waited with several men.

'Leering!' Aloysius shouted as he approached. 'I want you, Leering!'

He almost fell from the saddle, staggered, recovered with a grab at the stirrup, then swung on the group.

'A gang of your bloody ruffians has just invaded my house!' he shouted as he waddled up the steps. 'How dare you! Damn you, Leering. How dare you!' He gripped Leering's arm. 'Wrecked the place!'

'Take your filthy hand from me!' Leering flung it aside.

Aloysius blazed. 'You blasted...' He slapped Leering's face.

Red finger marks showed clearly across Leering's dead white face.

'There is, of course, only one answer to that. My friends will call upon you.'

Aloysius, quite distracted, shouted, 'No need for fancy formalities. Glad of the chance to shoot you now!'

Leering smiled coldly and ran the tip of his tongue along his lips. 'If two of you gentlemen will escort this person to the south lawn, out of sight and hearing of the house, we can dispose of this matter before lunch.'

There were one or two faint protests which Leering stilled with a look. Aloysius, unescorted, was already on his way to the south lawn.

Ten minutes later they were standing back to back with pistols raised and ready-cocked, whilst the small group of men stood at one side, a mixture of anxiety and excited anticipation. The word was given and the antagonists each measured ten slow paces, turned and faced each other. A handkerchief was dropped. Two shots cracked the silence and Aloysius was dead.

Leering turned casually away as the others ran to the sprawled body. His seconds returned, but before they could speak he said, 'Between the eyes, I think?'

They nodded nervously.

'I thought so.' He raised his voice. 'Come, gentlemen! Lunch is awaiting us.' He turned towards the house.

'But – but, the – er...' A gesture towards the corpse.

Leering waved a disparaging hand. 'The servants will dispose of it.'

FORTY-THREE

Nuala had recovered before they reached the house and insisted that she could walk, but when she tried she was too dizzy and weak and she was glad to be carried again.

Georgina, anxious after the departure of her husband, had gone in search of Nuala and, not finding her, had come to the conclusion that she had been abducted, in spite of Felix's assurances. Standing at the open front door, half-mad with worry, she searched for her husband and daughter. When she saw Nuala being carried she screamed and ran towards them, hair and draperies streaming.

'It's all right!' Conal called and he set Nuala on her feet.

'Oh, thank God, thank God!' She clasped her daughter. 'Nuala, where have you been? What is wrong? Oh! That terrible cut. What happened? I must treat it immediately.'

She rushed Nuala towards the house, then stopped. 'Your papa! Where is he? Have you seen him?'

Conal tried to reassure her as he urged them into the house and settled Nuala on a sofa whilst Georgina fluttered away in search of remedies. She returned with a bowl of hot water and cloths and had just set them down when the grinding of cartwheels sounded on the drive. She ran to the window to see a farm cart stopping at the steps. Two grooms hopped down and pulled something from the back. She screamed and fainted. Conal ran to her, hesitated, glanced through the window, then raced for the front door; but, by the time he had opened it, the cart had gone. The tumbled heap of Aloysius's body lay on the steps.

He ran back to the drawing-room to find Nuala on her knees beside her mother. 'Oh, Conal, what is it?'

'You must take care of her, my love. Don't ask me any questions now. Take care of your mother.'

He carried Georgina to the sofa.

'Now, take care of her, Nuala,' he said urgently. 'And, for God's sake, don't move from the room until I return.'

He ran out again to find Felix staring down in horror at his dead master, sprawled on the steps with a small, blue hole between his eyes. Clutching his head, white faced, Felix rocked. 'Oh my poor master! My poor Mr Grogan!'

At that moment Tim Duffin came panting up the drive. He stopped at the sight of the body. 'Oh, God! Oh God and His Blessed Mother have mercy on us! I was feared something bad had happened when I saw Leering's grooms; but, God save us all, I never thought 'twould be as bad as this.'

'Help me carry him inside,' said Conal.

'God, yes. We can't leave the poor man lying there.'

They lifted the body. 'Lead the way, Conal said to Felix.

'Leering!' said Felix, staring fixedly at the bullet-hole. 'Leering it was did it. With a duelling pistol. The evil man to make poor Mr Grogan fight, knowing well he was the better shot by far.'

'Lead the way, man!' said Conal anxiously. 'Do you want his wife or his daughter to come out and find him like this?'

Like a sleepwalker Felix turned and led the way up to the riotous disorder of the bedroom.

'What in the name of God happened here?' asked Conal, whilst Tim gaped at the body.

Felix raised his hands helplessly and wordlessly.

'For God's sake, man, get a hold on yourself. Lay him here!' They laid the body on a clear space on the floor.

He left them to tidy the room and lay out the body whilst he ran downstairs.

Nuala ran to him. 'What is it, Conal? Tell me.'

He took her in his arms. 'I haven't the full story yet, but I would guess that some gang of blackguards came here and ransacked the house. But that is not the worst of it, because, well, your father...'

'Did they hurt him? Ah, no! I must go to him.'

She tried to leave his arms, but he held her. 'Listen to

216

me. It's worse than you think. Leering shot your father in a duel. He is dead.'

She stared uncomprehendingly, then shook her head. 'Papa was in bed when I left this morning. They were both in bed. So, you see, it can't be true.' Her voice rose suddenly to a scream. 'It's not true, it's not true, it's not true!'

He shook her, then pressed her head to his chest. 'Oh, love, love,' he begged, 'try to be brave. Your mother needs you. Please, Nuala, please!' He hugged her as she shook and sobbed, then lifted her and carried her to a chair.

'I must attend to your mother,' he said.

He found a bottle with a little brandy in it, which he transferred to a dirty glass. Raising Mrs Grogan's head, he trickled a few drops between her teeth. Her lips moved slightly and he gave her a few more drops. She moaned, stirred, her eyelids flickered several times, then she opened her eyes. She stared stupidly at him for a second, then suddenly screamed, 'Aloysius!' and sat up so abruptly that she knocked the glass from his hand.

Nuala was shocked by her mother's scream. Forgetting her own grief, yet seeking comfort as much as offering it, she ran to her mother and they rocked in each other's arms.

Conal left them and went back upstairs. Tim was still tidying the bedroom. The body lay on a sheet on the stripped bed, naked now, and Felix, strangely calm, was washing it tenderly.

Tim rushed at Conal. 'Do ye know what will happen now? The bailiffs will come swooping like carrion crows and they'll take everything, even the master's body.'

'They will not find his body,' Felix stated. 'I will bury him tonight in a place nobody will ever find.'

Conal and Tim exchanged wondering glances.

'How can you bury him?' Conal asked.

'I will bury him!' said Felix with finality.

'Even so,' said Duffin. 'What will come of Mrs Grogan and Miss Nuala when the bailiffs have stripped them of everything?'

217

'Look, Tim,' said Conal, making a sudden decision. 'Go down and put the horses to the coach. They must leave here today – now! You must drive them. Felix and I will take care of the body, and the bailiffs are welcome to what is left.'

'Where the hell am I to drive them?'

'To Wexford. Mrs Grogan has a brother somewhere in that county.'

'Wexford! Do you know what you're saying? 'Tis God knows how many hundreds of miles from this. And in these times!'

'What else, then? Come on, man. You tell me what else!'

Tim scratched his head, turned and looked at the body, sighed and shrugged his shoulders. 'Wexford it is.' He hurried out.

Conal followed him and went to the drawing-room. Nuala and her mother had recovered from the worst of their weeping, but were still locked in sorrow. He pulled over a chair and sat down beside them.

'You must listen to me. Both of you. You must go away from here at once. As soon as news gets out of ... Well, what I mean is, the bailiffs will come and seize everything, even yourselves. So you must prepare to leave – instantly!'

Nuala objected. 'We cannot, Conal. Mama is not well. I, myself, am not well enough to travel. Besides, where can we go?'

'There can be no argument about it, Nuala! he stated. 'You cannot stay, so you must go. It is as simple as that. Tim is preparing the coach and he will drive you to your uncle's house in Wexford.'

'To Mark?' cried Mrs Grogan. 'Impossible! He will not help us.'

'Nuala, Mrs Grogan! There is no time for argument or anything else!' Conal shouted. 'If you arrive on his doorstep, how can he turn you away? Now, for God's sake go and prepare.'

They were so shocked by the violence of his tone that

he was able to rush them upstairs without further protest.

It was nearly three hours, however, before they had everything packed and into the coach. The two ladies, weeping heart-brokenly after seeing Aloysius for the last time, came down to the hall where Conal had been pacing with growing impatience and anxiety.

He helped Mrs Grogan into the coach, then turned to Nuala.

'I may never see you again,' she said. 'Conal, I may never see you again. Why can't mama go alone? Why can't . . .'

He pulled her into his arms, crushing her so that she could say no more.

'I'll come to you, my love. Never doubt that. Somehow . . . When, I don't know.' He kissed her fiercely. Then, 'I'll come!' and he thrust her into the coach and banged the door.

'Take care of them, Tim!' he called.

'With the help of God, I will.'

'Goodbye, my darling,' said Nuala, leaning from the window.

He stretched up and kissed her again. 'God go with you, my love.'

Tim cracked his whip, the coach jerked, the wheels crunched on the weed-grown gravel, the horses stepped out, trotted and the lumbering old vehicle swayed away. Conal followed it, waving to Nuala's fluttering scrap of handkerchief. When he reached the gate the coach was already far down the road. Nuala's tear-stained face and her fluttering scrap of white were fading into the gathering dusk. Then there was just the rutted road. Feeling utterly empty, he turned back to the house.

Aloysius Grogan, Esq, MP lay on the bed, washed, freshly shaved, dressed in a fine suit of royal blue and white, with well-powdered wig and gleaming hessians. In that same outfit he had set out to conquer Dublin.

As soon as it was dark Conal and Felix put him across the back of Nuala's horse and took him a dozen miles across country to a little ruined church overlooking a desolate lough; and they buried him in ground which had been hallowed centuries before Cromwell's iconoclasts desecrated it.

FORTY-FOUR

Mr William Pitt, Prime Minister of England, was a remarkable man. To achieve his position before reaching the age of twenty-five required far more than intelligence, political acumen and wide influence. To hold it for seveteen years at a time when politics differed from piracy only in that the rewards were greater without the risk of seasickness, required a mentality which could have tutored Machiavelli.

He found Irish affairs a considerable nuisance. The Irish Parliament continually annoyed him by passing Bills with which he disagreed and by refusing to pass Bills which he wanted. He solved the problem by appointing men like John Fitzgibbon as Lord Chancellor of Ireland and John Beresford as Controller of Customs and Excise, to ensure that Irish revenues would be directed to buying him the Bills he wanted and to providing him with money and men to fight the French Wars. That the recruits were usually peasants who had made themselves nuisances to the landlords was unimportant.

Buying the votes of the landlords was an expensive business, particularly when money was needed for the wars, so it seemed a good move to send Fitzwilliam as Viceroy to curb the landlords' power. But the old fool had immediately weakened Pitt's control by dismissing Beresford.

That was rectified, of course, by recalling him and

reinstating Beresford; but the problem of the landlords and their damned Parliament remained.

There was unrest in Ireland. A little aggravation of it by the new Viceroy, Camden, could easily bring about a rebellion, when it could be pointed out that the Irish Parliament was incapable of governing and so should be closed and merged with the English Parliament.

FORTY-FIVE

The Rev Mr Jonathan Halliday, curate of Clonleigh, was an earnest, eager, somewhat excitable young man. His vicar, who lived somewhere in England, paid him twenty-five pounds a year to care for the spiritual needs of his parishioners. This pittance, together with a natural diffidence in the presence of ladies, condemned Mr Halliday to a lonely, bachelor existence. However, he was a keen student of the Bible and this occupied most of his lonely hours.

He was very flattered when he was visited by a gentleman who was not only a magistrate and a knight, but was also a friend of a very highly placed Personage. This gentleman discussed the state of unrest of the country and very kindly gave him a pamphlet by an English clergyman which explained how the Book of Revelations was capable of mathematical solution.

After a study of this and a further visit from the gentleman, the terrible truth blazed from the pages of Revelation. The Papists were plotting the extermination of every Protestant in Ireland!

On the following Sunday he preached his finest sermon. Quivering with inspiration, he gave his discovery and his warning to the world through the medium of his parishioners. Their way of deliverance was clear in chapter and verse. To save themselves from extermination, they must exterminate the Catholics.

As God-fearing Christians, his congregation took the lesson to heart. The men armed themselves and went forth to do the work of the Lord.

Their first victims were two men they found digging turf. They beat them to death. They went on and set fire to three cabins, killing an old woman they found in one of them. Next they slaughtered a family of five who were on their way home from Mass.

Augmenting their numbers as they went, they marched to a village called The Diamond where they encountered a large group of Catholics, also returning from Mass, and a minor battle began. From all over the locality men flocked to both sides until nearly five hundred were fighting in the large open space in the village. After two hours the fight was coming to an end through sheer exhaustion when a body of Peep O' Day Boys appeared and swept the Catholics from the field.

The visitors held a celebration amidst the scattered bodies of the dead and wounded. There was much speech-making, particularly from a knighted magistrate who arrived with a group of gentlemen after the fighting had ended, and from these emerged the urgent need for a new organisation to combat the United Irishmen.

The Orange Society was born.

Its growth was so rapid that in a very few weeks it had thousands of members all over Ireland. The Peep O' Day Boys had been menace enough. The new organisation was far worse. It had the leadership of the nobility and the landlords and its members were quickly supplied with arms and horses.

The rumour spread that the Orangemen took an oath: 'In the Awful presence of Almighty God, I do solemnly swear that I will support the King and the present Government; and I do further swear that I will use my utmost exertions to exterminate all the Papists of the

Kingdom of Ireland.'

To Larry Dolan, Conal and the majority of the men, the answer seemed obvious. They must attack before the Orangemen became too strong. But Canahan fought bitterly against this. Orders from Dublin were that they must wait until the French arrived. A fleet was now on its way with soldiers and arms; and they could expect to hear any day that the French had landed. Reluctantly they agreed to wait.

For days the atmosphere was tense with expectation. Then the news came. A French fleet had sailed from Brest to Bantry Bay in the south-west with 14,000 troops. It had actually been within a mile of Irish soil when a fog came down. For four days it had waited in vain for the fog to disperse. Then it returned to France.

Michael Canahan had to bear as much cursing as if he personally had been responsible. He was deposed as leader and Conal was elected as their new leader, Larry Dolan having refused to allow his name to be put forward.

Amongst the landowners who now controlled the Orange Society there was consternation over the narrowly averted threat from the French. The regular army had been depleted by postings to the French wars and the Irish Government was bankrupt, and so unable to equip a regular force of its own. It gladly gave permission to the landowners to raise a force of Yeomanry.

The Orange Society re-named itself the Orange Order. Its members flooded into the Yeomanry and quickly made it so completely Orange that, to the people, Yeos and Orangemen were synonymous. With the full approval of the law, with arms and equipment supplied by their wealthy sponsors, the Orangemen went to work.

The Masters of the different Orange Lodges of the Province of Ulster met in Armagh and issued a statement denying that they had ever taken an oath for the extermination of Catholics. Shortly afterwards the Orangemen in county Armagh descended on the village

223

of Tanrego one night and nailed a notice to every cabin door:

TO HELL OR CONNAUGHT WITH YOU, YOU BLOODY PAPISTS: AND IF YOU ARE NOT GONE IN THREE DAYS WE WILL COME AND DESTROY YOURSELVES AND ALL YOUR PROPERTIES.
WE HATE ALL PAPISTS HERE!

Against the orders of their local leaders, the men of Tanrego decided to fight for their homes. They appealed for help and men flocked in from the surrounding area. On the evening of the third day they sent the women, children and old men into the hills to hide. Armed only with pikes, they waited for the Orangemen.

But the force which came was mounted and was far superior in numbers and arms. Twenty-six out of forty-two men were killed and the cabins, their contents and any animals were destroyed. The Orangemen then scoured the hills and killed everybody they caught. On the following morning little more than a quarter of the population of Tanrego was left alive.

With lamentation they buried their dead, salvaged what they could from the embers and straggled away from Hell towards Connaught.

There were immediate attempts at revenge throughout the North, but these proved worse than useless. The Orangemen had organisation, horses, the finest of equipment and were always in large groups, whilst the United Irishmen were physically incapable of travelling to come together in large numbers, had long since expended their ammunition and could not get more.

The Northern representatives of the United Irishmen went to Dublin and urged the Executive to begin an immediate, country-wide uprising; but this was opposed by the majority, in whose home areas the Orangemen were neither so strong nor so active as they were in the

North. They claimed that they were still unprepared and that they must wait for a second French fleet if they were to have any chance of success. In the meantime, they ordered, there should be no more fighting and all efforts should be concentrated upon the collection of arms. From that time, the Executive lost the support of the men of the North.

But the Orangemen in the North pursued their policy of driving out the Catholics. In one month, in Armagh alone, five thousand people were harried from their homes to wander west and south in search of homes and villages where there were already scores of thousands without.

FORTY-SIX

'What will we do? What, in God's name will we do?'

The cry and scores of variations of it, echoing every emotion from terror to fury, chorused through the milling mass of people in Duncarran. Everybody was there: men, women, children, babes in arms, the old, even the bedridden had been carried because they could not be left unprotected in their cabins. They had flocked in from many miles around, urged by the need for the sense of safety created by numbers and by the faint comfort of being with others faced with the same terrible choice: to leave their homes for ever that day or to stay and be slaughtered. All their lives they had worked and struggled to keep their squalid cabins and their meagre potato-patches because misery and near-starvation were preferable to the certain, slow death of the homeless. Now they had the choice of that slow death for the strong and quick death for the weak, or quick death for all from the muskets and sabres of the Orange Yeomanry.

'What will we do?'

Men shouted or growled it, women wept and wailed it, clutching their babies to their breasts, their children to their skirts. The babies and younger children cried without understanding, echoing their mothers' fear and grief. The weak and the old, timid in the knowledge of their utter dependence, whimpered their helplessness. And threading through were the whispers, mutters and cries to God, His Blessed Mother and to the Saints for miraculous deliverance.

'What, in the Name of God, are we to do?'

Larry Dolan pushed his way through the crowd and poked Conal in the back.

'You're being asked a question,' he growled.

Conal turned, surprise added to worry. 'What question?'

Dolan stretched his face up to Conal's and spoke slowly and deliberately. 'What are they to do?'

'How the hell would I know!'

Dolan grinned sardonically: then, his expression fierce, 'Don't you know why they have all come here?'

Conal gestured with open hands, shook his head and said, 'Well, I suppose...' He shrugged and was silent, but looked his question at Dolan.

Larry snorted contemptuously. 'Begod, there's nothing the equal of education for making a man ignorant.'

Conal flushed. 'Well, you're the wise man, Larry Dolan. Tell me; because it's obvious you're bursting to do just that.'

Dolan stared back, hard-eyed. 'For the whole of their history, in times of trouble, the people of these parts came to Duncarran in the sureness that they would find a strong man with a strong arm to aid and protect them, and with a strong head to advise them. The most of them do not even know it, but they have come here looking for their leader. Will they find him, d'you think?'

Conal looked back at him in misery and uncertainty, then turned slowly and surveyed the assembled suffering. How easy it had been to say that they were his people, that he was their leader. Now they needed a real leader.

In his perplexity he looked again at Dolan, who grinned savagely. 'What ails you? You're foot-loose and fancy-free. Not a soul in the world but your own self to be worrying about. There's not a thing to stop you from walking out of this place with never a backward look.'

He thought with sudden longing of Wexford and Nuala waiting. Then he remembered the highwayman's scornful words: 'So you were running away!' He gave a short laugh at himself, then a longer, defiant, boastful laugh at Dolan. 'Right!' he said, slapping him hard on the shoulder.

He pushed through the crowd shouting, 'Make way. Make way for The O'Carran!'

Jumping up on to a rock beside one of the cabins he bellowed, 'Hear me! Quiet, all of you, and listen to me!'

Those nearest quietened and looked up curiously at him, but those further away had not heard.

'Dolan, MacShane!' he shouted. 'Quieten the rest of them!'

Both men were surprised at the command, but they began to push through the crowd calling for quiet and pointing to Conal. In a few moments all were facing him and pressing forward. Curiosity was on every face and on some even the faint flicker of hope.

Conal looked down on them, then quite unrehearsed came the words, 'I am The O'Carran of Duncarran. In times past, whenever danger threatened, it was to The O'Carran that your forefathers looked for leadership. You ask what you are to do. This is your home. It is my home. We will not be driven from it by the threats of the Orangemen. We stay, and we fight!'

There were anxious mutters from several parts of his audience.

'Think!' he shouted. 'A man is born with nothing but a brain in his skull to think with, two legs to stand on and two arms to fight with. If he will not use those things to get what he wants and to keep what he has, then he'd do

227

better to lie down and die. And be damned to him!'

There were cheers from some, but mutterings of complaint from others.

'The men of Tanrego fought,' shouted one man. 'And we all know what happened to them.'

'Maybe they did not use their brains,' Conal answered. 'Supposing now... Yes. We will not wait for them to surround us. We will ambush them before they ever get here.'

'We'd need guns for that job, O'Carran,' shouted Dolan. 'With them riding fast, we'd need powder and lead.'

That checked Conal. 'You are right, of course,' he said hesitantly.

~~Immediately there was clamour from his opponents~~ ~~and he realised that if they went unchecked they would~~ destroy the command he had established.

'Ah, for God's sake, stop your whining!' he shouted. 'Those of you who will not fight had best run away from here and leave those of us who will. We need ammunition. Then we must get it. And I know where to find it.'

In the early darkness Conal and Dolan stood in the woods behind Leering's house with nearly forty men, many armed with swords and sabres, the rest with pikes. Twenty others had been sent to lie in hiding outside the main gate to guard against surprise. MacShane, with a small group, had been left behind to guard Duncarran.

Impressing on them the need for silence, Conal ordered the men to spread out and make their way through the trees towards the house; but it was dark in the woods and noise was unavoidable. They had not got more than fifty yards when they heard a dog barking ahead of them.

'Damn it to hell!' Dolan grunted.

'Stop. Pass the order to stop!' Conal ordered.

After much hissing and shushing there was silence.

'Larry and I will go ahead. The rest follow a short distance behind, but stop before you come to the edge of the woods. And if you get to that dog, kill it.'

'Sure, 'tis only a poor beast,' came the objection.

Dolan snorted. 'You bloody idiot, whoever you are. Slit its throat before it tears out your own!'

They moved on. The barking sounded nearer, yet it was odd, Conal thought, that it did not come more quickly. Then he guessed the reason.

'Larry, somebody has that dog on a lead.'

'Begod, you're right. Blast the dark! Here, take a hold of my hand and we'll go ahead and find him.'

The hand which Conal gripped felt like a gnarled branch, neither warm nor cold, seeming inanimate, yet emanating strength which he found very comforting. They walked on in silence until Larry gave a slight squeeze at the same moment that Conal saw a vague lightening of the darkness ahead. He gave an answering squeeze and they went on more slowly. He felt a downward tug and he sank to all fours. Slowly they crawled into the greyness of starlight.

The barking sounded from their right, suddenly more urgent. Larry's breath warmed Conal's ear. 'It has our scent.'

Conal saw first the movement of the dog, then, behind it, two shadowy figures. He tapped twice on Larry's arm.

'I see them,' Larry whispered. 'They'll have guns. Wait!'

He felt the ground until he found a stone, then he stood slowly and fitted the stone into a sling. Conal was surprised at the faint whirring. He saw a man stagger, heard his cry, then the dark shape of a huge dog came leaping out of the darkness. He only had time to get up on his knees and raise his sabre when the dog leaped. He thrust towards the blackness in the air above him. With wrist-jarring force the dog struck the point. Its body slid down the length of it and he fell backwards under the weight of stinking fur.

Whilst the dog was still in the air there was the flash and crack of a pistol. Conal struggled from under the limp, foul-smelling body and, with difficulty, pulled out his sabre. There was another flash and crack and something snatched at his sleeve. He did not hear the whirring of Larry's sling-shot, but again a man cried and a pistol cracked.

'Come on,' Larry called. 'They're running away.'

They ran out into the open. Two figures ran twenty yards ahead of them. The men came crashing out of the trees behind.

One of the fleeing men gasped. 'Shoot, Jacoby. Shoot, man!'

'Can't. Dropped it.'

'Constables,' Larry panted. 'The boyos who lashed you.'

The muscles of Conal's back crawled, remembering the lash. Then strength seemed to pour into his legs, air to stream into his lungs. He felt immense, tremendously powerful. He laughed at the pitiful efforts of his victims. So slowly they seemed to move, so rapidly he was overtaking them. He did not know it, but he was swinging the sabre in great sweeps as he ran, and he was yelling and laughing.

'Lash me, would you! Then how do you like that! And that! And that!'

There was an inexplicable hindrance to his movements. There was a continual noise. A voice. Somebody was holding his arms. No, several people. The voices held some sort of meaning. His own name. Of course. It was Dolan's voice. His own men were holding him. Why? He struggled. There was a sharp sting in both his cheeks.

Larry Dolan was standing in front of him. 'Conal! For God's sake, Conal!'

He relaxed, looked in surprise at Larry's concern and asked in a calm voice, 'What ails you?'

'What ails *me*! Leave him go.'

The hands released him.

Remembering, Conal asked, 'Did we get them?'

Larry shook his head in wonder. 'Boys, oh boys, oh boys!' He turned Conal and pointed.

Conal looked curiously at the two untidy heaps. 'They're both dead,' he said in a surprised voice.

'Oh, begod, they are!'

Conal smiled. 'Well, isn't that great. Come on now, and we'll get the arms.'

He walked on towards the house and the rest straggled after, muttering excitedly about what they had seen, staring after Conal with amazement and a tinge of fear.

As they drew near the house they bunched together again, but Larry halted them. 'Conal!' he called softly, then, to one of the men, 'Go and bring that bloody madman back here.'

The man ran, touched Conal nervously and gestured backwards.

'What's wrong now?' Conal asked when he returned.

'There could be other guards,' said Larry. 'We'd best split. If you'll take the one half of the men, I'll take the rest and we'll surround the place. Then I'll meet you and we'll see where we can get in.'

They set off again in two straggling arcs. As they were approaching from the rear the house was partly obscured by the stables and other outbuildings. Posting men every few yards they gradually surrounded the place. Conal and Larry with seven men arrived on the expanse of gravel at the foot of the wide steps which swept up to the front door.

No light. No sound. The lower windows were all bricked up. The upper showed no signs of life. They advanced up the steps. Blinding flashes from the upper windows, ear-splitting crashes of muskets, shouts of pain from three men as they fell.

Conal, Larry and two men raced up to the shelter of the portico and the deeply recessed door. The other two men and all who had been posted at the front raced for the shelter of the nearest bushes. But another volley, following almost immediately after the first, brought down another two men. Shots and cries sounded from the back.

'Surprise!' exclaimed Larry bitterly. 'I wonder who it was got the surprise!' He thumped and kicked the door. 'Like a bloody fortress.'

231

Conal examined it. 'The fanlight,' he said. 'A man could break through there.'

Larry looked up. 'Begod, I think you're right. Heft me up on your shoulders.'

Conal stooped and Larry, with the help of the other two, stood on Conal's shoulders. Slowly, wobbling, Conal raised himself until Larry whispered, 'Hold it there. They're little, leaded panes. I'll need to take them out quietly.'

Conal patted his leg.

'Stop him! Stop that man!'

The sudden shouts made both Conal and Larry turn. 'Hold on!' shouted Larry even as he fell.

The shouts had come from the side of the house and were taken up by others in the bushes. A man on a grey horse appeared racing from the rear. Several men leaped from cover and, in spite of a fusillade from the upper windows which claimed another two, ran to cut him off. But he was too fast for them. He cut across the lawn, gained the drive and disappeared down it.

Larry shouted, 'After him! Shout to the men at the gate to stop him.'

Almost all the men, including those who had been in cover, streamed towards the drive.

'Not all of you, blast it!' Larry screamed. 'The pikemen stay. The pikemen stay!'

About a dozen heard him, hesitated, then returned and went into cover out of musket-range. The rest vanished down the drive shouting wildly.

'Quick, Larry. If that lad gets away we'll have the Yeos down on us.'

Conal lifted him again and suffered from the grinding of his heels until he heard the whisper, 'I have it. Grip my feet and heft me higher.'

The weight went from Conal's shoulders and a moment later there was a light thud as Larry landed on the inside. There was the sound of bolts being withdrawn – middle, top, bottom. Then nothing.

Trembling with anxiety Conal whispered, 'Larry, will

232

you, for God's sake, open the door.'

'Blast it, man, amn't I trying to do just that. The bloody thing's stuck. Push, will you!'

Conal and the other two pushed, but the door remained firm.

'Oh, God, Conal,' came Larry's agonised whisper. 'The bloody thing's locked and no key in it!'

They stared appalled at the door, then Conal whispered urgently, 'Come back out, Larry.'

'Aren't you the great lad for jokes!' came the bitter answer. 'There's no way to climb back up.'

Then there was silence. The three exchanged anxious looks. Light shone through the fanlight. They heard Larry shout something and a great crash of muskets reverberated through the house.

Silence. Then a mocking voice called, 'Would any of the rest of you care to climb through the fanlight?'

'They've murdered poor Larry!' screamed one of the men and he flung himself against the unyielding door.

Conal, dazed and desperate, pulled him away. 'It's no good. No bloody good at all. We've failed.' Then, suddenly remembering, 'Dear God, we must get the men back to Duncarran.'

'What about the lads who've been shot?'

He was in an agony of indecision. They could not leave wounded men to be massacred. Yet to go into the open to pick them up would be stupid. Through it all, he realised with surprise, he had forgotten that Leering was in the house. He had been revenged on the men who had actually whipped him, but the man who had been really responsible was still alive, safe in there, despising his weakness. Surely there must be some way of getting at him. But how? Only through that door. How could they get that door open? The wounded men... Yes.

He gave whispered instructions to the two men, then shouted through the door, 'Blast you to hell, Leering! We'll be back another time.'

The men ran, one to the left, one to the right, keeping close to the shelter of the wall. Even so, men leaned from the windows and fired. Conal, hidden in the shadows a little way from the portico, gave a cry of pretended pain, then crept back to a corner beside the door. He watched the two men break from the ends of the house and speed towards the bushes. There were several shots but both disappeared unhurt. One by one the men who had been hiding in the bushes rose and ran away towards the drive.

The last man stopped out of range and shouted back, 'Run for it, lads. We're all away now.' From several places on the lawn where bodies sprawled came plaintive cries for help. The man hesitated, turned and ran.

From his hiding place Conal counted seven bodies on the lawn. Three near the steps were still, but he thought he could detect faint movement from the others. Indeed, he realised with horror, one was trying to crawl.

Above him a window squealed as it was lifted higher.

'He moved, I tell you,' a voice whispered.

'Ah, you're dreaming, man. But let's put another couple into him.'

Conal clenched his fists in impotent fury. But before the shots came one of the men said quite loudly, 'What?' A pause, then, 'Come and see for yourself. They're miles away by now.'

Then there was silence. Conal risked a peep upwards, but could see nothing. He felt a touch on his leg and looked down to see the prone figure of the first man who had detoured through the trees then, following Conal's instructions, returned to crawl along the front of the house. Others lay behind him and there were more on the other side of the portico.

They waited, minute by minute, in utter silence. Then, with surprising clarity from inside the house, a woman's voice: 'I tell you I will not have that – that thing in my house!'

After a pause a key grated in the lock and the door swung open.

Conal's rush plunged his sabre through the first man and hurled his body back into the hall. The two carrying Larry's corpse dropped it and fumbled for their weapons, but they and another two died immediately on the swords and pikes of the leading invaders.

Lady Leering screamed, then shouted, 'Murder! Get out of my house!'

From upstairs, above the sound of pounding feet, came a shout, 'Watch out for her ladyship!'

'Clear of the stairs, lads!' Conal shouted. All scattered to the sides, Conal pulling Larry's body, whilst a big man scooped up Lady Leering, ignoring her indignant shrieks, ran to a side room with her and thrust her in.

'Stay there now, ma'am,' he said. 'And pray for the souls of the departed.' He slammed the door.

The hall was lit by three candles set in a holder on a small table at the foot of the stairs. The walls were in shadow, but so was the head of the stairs. Conal strained his eyes, but could not see the men above. He could hear them, however: a faint, urgent whispering. He guessed that they were trying to persuade each other to lead a charge down the stairs. He looked round desperately and saw two muskets lying beside the dead bodies. There were pistols in the belts of the other two. He whispered to the men beside him.

His sudden, high-pitched yell shocked the silence. Feet scattered above. One of his own men cried fervently, 'Holy Mother!' But he and three others had already raced across the hall, swept up the weapons and disappeared into the shadows. A shot cracked down the staircase and whined off the tiled floor.

He stared upwards but could see only shadows. To charge up the stairs would be suicidal. To fire would only reveal where they were and invite a volley. They were no better off. Only then did he remember the reason for the whole expedition.

'Search the rooms, lads.'

There was an immediate rush.

From the room into which Lady Leering had been put a pistol cracked. The voice of the man who had put her there sounded in the tone of one chiding a naughty child, 'Now that was not a ladylike thing to do, ma'am. You could have hurted somebody doing the likes of that.'

His voice was overwhelmed by shouts. 'Here! There's a great load of them here!'

Everybody rushed, luckily escaping the scattering of shots from upstairs. A solitary candle lit the room, but it was enough to show that the place was like an arsenal. Muskets, pistols, sporting guns, barrels of powder and bags of bullets were heaped everywhere, with flints, wads, ramrods and powder-horns.

'Every man take two muskets, two pistols and all the ammunition he can carry,' Conal ordered. 'You and you, arm yourselves and run to the gate to bring back the rest of the men.'

A man came to him. 'I am after thinking. Those buckos above. I worked in this place as a boy. There's another stairs goes up from the kitchens.'

Conal slapped the man's shoulder. 'Good man!'

He split the men into two groups, set one to watch the stairs and, with his informant and the rest, crept to the door which led into the servants' quarters, compliment- ing himself that at last he was behaving like a real leader. He was just about to open the door when he was stopped by the thought that leadership required the ability to think ahead. He whispered instructions. His men crouched low. He lay on the floor, then swiftly swung the door. The roar of musketry in the confined place was like a physical blow. The three armed men who had been waiting on the other side of the door fell. One, they found, was dead, the other two badly wounded. They disarmed them all, reloaded, then cautiously made their way to the kitchen.

The narrow staircase climbed for a dozen treads, then bent backwards to that its head was hidden. Faint candlelight shone down it.

Conal pointed upwards in warning. He examined the stairs with care, feeling again that he was acting as a prudent leader. He left two men to watch the stair and took the rest quietly back to the gun-room where he assembled all the men and ordered everybody to load two

236

muskets. The first half he left again in the hall whilst he led the remainder back to the kitchen, stationing them with their muskets aimed at the ceiling where the head of the staircase would reach the landing above. The muskets roared and were echoed by those firing up the main staircase.

Every man dropped his empty musket, snatched a loaded one and raced, front and back, up the stairs. In seconds the remaining five defenders were shot, hacked, trampled. The men leaned exhausted against the walls and watched in amazement as Conal ran frantically about examining the bodies.

'He's not here. Where is he? Leering, blast you, where are you?'

He whirled on the men. 'Search! I want Leering.'

They searched every possible hiding place, but found nobody else.

Conal was enraged with frustration. 'He must be here!'

Then a man said, half-admiringly, 'Ah, the cute devil. He must be the one got away on the horse.'

'Unless the lads at the gate caught him,' said another.

Conal laughed with relief. 'That's it,' he said eagerly. 'That must be it. Come on, lads!'

They ran down the stairs to the hall and met the two messengers coming in from the gate. 'They're gone. All the men were gone when we got there.'

'They can't be gone. Why the hell would they go?' Conal stormed. 'How can we carry all the stuff in there? Did you look for them? You know where they are hiding.'

But the men assured him they had searched.

'Should we not be getting back to Duncarran?' a man asked.

'God, yes!'

Conal snatched the candles and ran, with the light wavering eerily, to the corner where a big grandfather's clock ticked imperturbably. Nearly half past ten. He smashed its complacent face with his musket.

Carrying what arms they could, a pitifully small portion of the whole, they ran out of the house.

'Help!' The weak cry came from the lawn.

'Oh, God!' Conal wailed inwardly. 'The wounded. We can't leave them.'

He stood on the steps, quivering with indecision. Some of the men had run out on to the lawn and returned now carrying two wounded. The rest, they said, were dead.

'Transport!' Conal thought. Relief flooded through him.

In a very few minutes they had assembled a chaise, a dog-cart, a huge coach and five farm carts, all with horses harnessed to them. They loaded the dead, the wounded and all the arms and powder. Then they all climbed up and started down the drive.

A man suddenly whooped and shouted. 'Begod, we beat the bejasus out o' them!'

Everybody laughed. Then a man began to sing and soon all joined in the song which had recently become popular.

> *'Oh, the French are on the sea,'*
> *Says the Shan Van Voght!*
> *'Oh the French are on the sea,'*
> *Says the Shan Van Voght!*
> *'Oh, the French are on the sea,*
> *They'll be here at break of day,*
> *And the Orange will decay,'*
> *Says the Shan Van Voght!*
> *'And the Orange will decay,'*
> *Says the Shan Van Voght!*

They roared it at the top of their voices and were still singing as they turned from the tree-shadowed drive into the road. All were silenced at once and the carts stopped and they all stared. The darkness of the far hillside was dotted with glowing patches; and the sky behind the hill was a great flickering redness. The cabins and Duncarran burning!

They gazed appalled. Then there was an uproar of anguish, anxiety, fear and anger. They called for wives, children, parents, sweethearts. Then, as if by agreement, they turned on Conal and cursed him for taking them from their homes.

He, leading in the chaise, lashed the horses and the vehicle raced up the road. After a moment of wailing indecision and argument the rest followed as fast as they could urge the horses. Even above the pounding of the hoofs and the racket of the vehicles he could hear their cries and curses against him and the Yeos equally.

The two men in the chaise with him had to hang on to avoid being flung into the road as it swung and bounced after the frantically-lashed horses. Conal's wild eyes were fixed on the leaping fires on the hillside and the ever-brightening glow beyond. Unconsciously he was praying in a shouting gabble that the people had been able to escape into the dark, hidden glens.

He topped a rise and saw, away down the road, many tiny points of light which weaved and bobbed like fireflies. He stared at them, then hauled on the reins. The chaise rose on one wheel amid cries of alarm from his passengers, threatened to overturn, then fell again as the horses dug in their hoofs and stopped. Silence.

'The Yeos!' a man whispered. Then his voice erupted in a night-shattering scream, 'The bloody Yeos! I'll slaughter the bastards!'

'Listen to me. For God's sake, listen to me,' Conal begged. 'At the foot of the dip, where the trees are. We can catch them there.' He tugged at a man, almost flung him from the chaise. 'Run back and tell the others what we mean to do. Get them here quickly!'

The man leaped down and ran back. Conal whipped the horses into a swift run down the hill. In the dip small trees and bushes bordered the road. He leaped down, swung the chaise across the road, unharnessed the horses and tied them to it. Faintly he could hear the other vehicles approaching; but he could also hear distant yells and hoofbeats from the road ahead.

The dog-cart arrived first with five men crammed into it, including one of the wounded. Two lifted him out and carried him some distance out on to the bog, whilst Conal and the others unloaded the arms and added the dog-cart to the barricade.

The yells were louder and nearer.

The coach came next, crunching and lurching down the hill. It had just arrived when Conal saw the first of the torches top the far side of the dip. In swift silence he drove the men to take out the arms and the other wounded man. Then one of those he had placed beside the road came to him.

'The powder, Conal. Where's the bloody powder?'

A flood of torches was descending on them, the horsemen yelling and singing.

'Oh, God,' said another man. ''Tis all in the carts.'

They had muskets, bullets, swords, no pikes and no ~~powder, and the muskets were not even loaded.~~

~~The men ran from their hiding places, caution~~ forgotten, screaming for powder. The horsemen heard them and pulled up their horses milling and stamping. Voices shouted questions and curses.

Finding themselves almost helpless to fight, the men cursed Conal again, looked back anxiously to see if the carts were coming, then whipped round to see the torch-lit body of Yeos at the top of the hill.

From the cluster of horsemen an unmistakable voice sounded clearly: 'They've set an ambush at the foot of the hill!'

Conal screamed in helpless frustration, 'Leering!'

There was a moan from the men around him, then a desperate cry from one, 'Dear God, they'll murder us all!'

Leering's voice again: 'Spread out from the road! Circle them!'

The host of torches split as the Yeos rode out on to the bog in two advancing arcs. Conal's men hesitated momentarily then turned and ran. He stood quivering with anger and frustration, staring at the arc of advancing torches, then turned and raced back up the hill to warn the men with the carts. As he panted upwards he cursed his own stupidity for failing to distribute the powder and lead, for not ensuring that his men would be instantly ready to fight. But now, if only he could reach the carts in time, they could still strike back. The Yeos would never think of a second ambush. Everything depended upon his speed. Stupidity again! He should have taken a horse. He stopped and looked back. The torches were still scouring the dark bog. It was surely too late to go back for a horse. Was that cowardice? Then he heard the carts and raced towards them.

They were spread over a hundred yards of road and others were still arriving and questioning whilst he was trying to explain what had happened and what he wanted them to do.

'They'll come up the hill at a walk. They'll not expect another ambush. For God's sake look to your arms!'

But only a few had heard and the late-comers were full of questions and furious because they could not get answers.

Conal charged amongst them, pummelling them, urging them to get arms. A few tried to obey. The gabble of the rest suddenly crystallised into the knowledge that their fellows had been massacred. They had listened to him before, so had the others. They would be fools to trust him now. It only required one man to say, 'I'm away!' and to begin running for the rest to follow.

Once more he found himself alone. Anger at their desertion was tempered by the knowledge that his poor leadership was to blame. But those thoughts were swamped by the sight of the torches converging cautiously on the vehicles in the dip below. If only he had planned better, he could have destroyed every man down there without loss of any of his own. The desire to slaughter them all was a screaming lust in him. And perhaps it could still be done. Here were the carts and a huge amount of powder.

Hastily he began unharnessing the first horse, hampered by the darkness, by the tangle of carts and horses and by continually stopping to look down the hill. The horse would not stand still. He broke a nail on a buckle and cursed. No more sentimental nonsense. If men could die, so could horses. He pulled out a keg of powder and sprinkled a trail of it linking together the piles of kegs which he placed under each cart. Then he led the trail away to a hollow twenty yards off the road.

Lying there he could no longer see the Yeos, but he could discern the glow of their torches, could even hear their voices. He made a small heap of powder which he hoped to ignite with a spark from a musket. It would have to be done at just the right moment. He stood cautiously in an attempt to see them, but, as he did so, he realised that he had no idea how long the light would take to reach the carts. They were still not in sight. He lay again, resolved to set the spark as soon as he saw the first torch.

He heard hoofs and the glow brightened. He gripped the musket. The flint would have to be as close as possible to the powder. Where was the powder? He couldn't see it. He couldn't feel it. There was only one thing to do. The flash of the flint was blinding. There was a Phut! and a line of fire ran across the ground.

He leaped to his feet. The Yeos were nearer. They would surely see the swift run of fire. The blast would probably kill him rather than them. He ran away, his feet catching in tussocks, his back tense with the expectation of explosion. He risked a backward glance, gripped and fell at the same moment as he registered that he could no longer see the running fire. He landed with his head and shoulders in a wet patch. With tears streaming down his face he beat the wet ground with his fists as he cursed his incompetence once more.

So great was his shame that he was tempted to stand and shout to the horsemen so that they would race and punish him for his stupidity. He actually pushed himself up from the prone position and was still in the act of rising when it happened.

The Yeos, who seemed surprisingly far away, were milling round the carts. In the torchlight he saw the horse which he had been trying to unharness rear wildly. It lunged against one of the mounts. Conal saw it clearly – a grey, Leering! The rider shouted as he was almost flung off, clawed at the saddle, and dropped his torch. Redness, then a great flash, a tearing sound, a glimpse of horse and rider blasted into the air, black against orange-red flame, then completely disintegrating in an even greater explosion.

The blast knocked him flat and breathless. He lay listening to things whistling through the air, to the shouting, trampling and screaming of men and horses.

He stood to stare and to exult that he had triumphed at last. Burning pieces of the shattered carts were scattered over a wide area; a confused heap of men, horses and debris lay in the road. Other men and horses were staggering about dazedly. He saw clearly that one of the horses had only three legs, that a man was stupidly trying to fit his severed arm back into its socket. Someone called, 'Sir Maxwell! Where is Sir Maxwell?' Others repeated the cry; but there was no answer.

He turned and ran directly away from the road, but turned after a few hundred yards and made diagonally down towards the dip. When he looked back, torches, far fewer than there had been, were spreading over the bog on both sides of the road. It was obvious that they had no sure idea whether there had been anybody about.

He reached the road and trotted up from the now empty dip towards Duncarran. But he was not half-way up the hill when he remembered the wounded who had been carried out on to the bog. Even though the Orangemen were still at the top of the hill, he forced himself to go out and search, feeling again that it would be no more than justice if he were caught, but also feeling virtuous and gaining some small comfort from it. But he had no idea where the men had been put and he dared not cry out. Searching in the blackness, continually tripping over clumps and low bushes or stumbling into pools, was quite ineffectual. Feeling the sense of desertion, yet trying to comfort himself that any who had been left alive would have called to him, he returned to the road and set out for Duncarran.

Half-way up the track, in the light of a late-risen moon,

he stumbled on the horribly mutilated body of Michael Canahan. The cabin was untouched, had evidently not been seen by the attackers. He gripped the corpse by the hand, intending to drag it inside and found himself holding only the hand. Horror-stricken, he dropped it, staggered away and vomited. His hands were sticky, black in the moonlight. He held them away from his body as he ran up the track to where the stream brawled unconcernedly. He washed his hands over and over, then scooped water over his face and head and finally into his mouth, gulping and gulping its cleanness. At last he stood up, dripping, shaking his head and hands, then rubbing his face and hair.

He walked on until he could look into the hollow at Duncarran. Thick smoke was still rising from the glowing remnants of thatch which outlined the blackened ruins. A few people moved listlessly, searching for anything which could be salvaged. He stood watching them, knowing that he should go to give what help and comfort he could, yet afraid to face them.

'Well, what do you think of it?'

He leaped with fright at the sudden voice, then turned swiftly. Alexander Montgomery stood, hands on hips, staring coolly at him.

'Where did you spring from?' Conal demanded angrily.

'Oh, I came to visit Michael Canahan. He'd sent word for me to come, d'you see, to try to drive some sense into the heads of a few of the madmen round these parts. Well, I've seen Michael, or what the butchers left of him; and I see what's left of the people of Duncarran below there. Now would you tell me just what you and that madman, Dolan, have been at?'

'Larry Dolan is dead, God rest him. Killed by Leering. And fighting is what we've been at. Fighting against the bloody Yeos who've been doing the likes of this!' He gestured at the ruins.

'And you're proud of it, are you?'

'I killed Leering – blasted him to tatters! And there's more of them dead in the same blast, and still more back at Leering's house.'

'Ah, you're too modest. Add in Michael Canahan, thirty or more who lived there below, surely another twenty in the scattered cabins – oh, and how many of your own men? How many came back with you?'

He paused, awaiting an answer, and when none came, 'Do you tell me you slaughtered them all!'

'I did what ... It's easy to talk. D'you think I don't know, that ... Ah, for God's sake, leave me be!' There were tears running down his cheeks.

Montgomery stood silent for a moment or two, then, very quietly, but bitterly, he said, 'Now, maybe, you know the curse of the Irish people – men who can't, or won't think, and who will not take orders from those who can! Am I right?'

Conal stood, head down, and said nothing.

'Blast you, O'Carran, stand up like a man and answer me! Am I right?'

Conal faced him, but with shame. 'You are,' he whispered.

'Well, what do you mean to do now?'

Conal gestured emptily. 'Find the MacShanes ...'

'Their corpses, d'you mean?'

'Ah, no!'

'Ah, yes! So I ask again, what d'you mean to do?'

'I don't know. I hadn't thought.'

'That could well have been your epitaph. Well, there's one thing sure. You can't stay here.'

Conal stared blankly at the truth of what the little man had said.

'There'll be nobody left in this place after tomorrow. No more than there is in Tanrego, Laughlin Bridge, Ardnalucan, nor a score of other places. More than two thousand killed in the last few weeks and over seven thousand driven out. If it goes on, the Orangemen will have the North to themselves, which is what they want.'

He paused and eyed Conal. 'Tell me this. Are you ready to obey orders now?'

Conal nodded.

245

'Do you truly mean that?'

'Great God, man, don't you realise that it will be on my conscience for the rest of my life that if I'd only had more experience, more training, if I had thought and planned...'

'Well, there are those with all the qualities you lack. Will you be guided by them?'

'I will.'

'Right. Then this is what you'll do. Go to Dublin. Find a man named Malachy Murphy. He's a tailor, living in Fiddlers Alley. Give him the password, "A friend in the North sent me to ask is his coat ready." He'll ask, "What colour is the coat?" And you'll answer, "As green as grass."

'When you're sure you have the right man, tell him all that's happening here. He'll give you your further orders. Tell him I said that.'

FORTY-SEVEN

Tim Duffin was cold, tired and worried. Driving an ill-matched team to pull the ramshackle coach at night was no easy job. Nuala had suggested that they should stop somewhere by the wayside, and that he should join her and her mother inside the coach where they were trying to sleep under rugs and blankets; but he had refused, saying that he was not tired, that it would be best for them to drive as far as possible from Ballyna – anything rather than admit that embarrassment would have made him far more uncomfortable inside than he was on the box. He swayed, nodding into a doze in spite of the cold, then jerking awake, peering ahead at the road in the faint light of the flickering lamps and the odd, watery rays of moonlight which glanced through the great, blowing clouds.

They were struggling up a steep hill when a mounted figure levelled a pistol at his head.

'Pull up, else I'll put lead in your skull!'

At the same time, another rider, on the other side, wrenched open the door, thrust in his head and flourished a pistol at Nuala and her mother.

'Hogs, dogs and divils!' he exclaimed in disgust. Withdrawing his head, he called, 'There's the luck of hell, Gameser! A brace of fecking motts dossing in the coach to save the cost of a bed.'

Nuala snatched at the pistol. But she had not reckoned on his strong grip. He leaned in again and knocked her sprawling on the floor.

'Bitch's get!'

Georgina flung herself on him and ripped her nails down his face. With a shout of pain he punched her in the mouth.

'Pox on you, Buckeen!' shouted Gameser. 'What's amiss?'

'They're a pair of battling motts. I'd to souse them in the chops.'

Mrs Grogan and Nuala struggled up. Nuala's cheek was bruised and painful, but her mother's bleeding mouth concerned her more.

'You murderous ruffians,' she raged. 'You'll hang for this!'

He laughed. 'Ah, the nubbing cheat'll rot waiting for me. Give! Purses, rings, jewellery, the lot!'

'You'll get nothing from us!'

'Then, bejasus, 'twill be a pleasure finding them for myself.' He made to enter the coach.

'No, oh no!' Mrs Grogan whimpered. 'Here!' She gave him her purse and began to pull off her rings.

Realising that resistance was hopeless Nuala gave up all she had.

Gameser bent his head to look in through the window.

'Whip it up, Buckeen. I'm near frozen in this plaguey wind.'

Tim leaped, knocked him from the horse and sprawled with him on the road. There was a crack and Tim rolled over, groaning, with a bullet in his stomach. Gameser scrambled to his feet and kicked Tim.

'Pox on you for a fool!'

He remounted and rode round the coach. 'Whip it, Buckeen. The coachie's got a ball in his guts.'

Snatching the remainder, Buckeen slammed the door and the two galloped off into the darkness.

Nuala pulled open the door and jumped down to Tim who was writhing with his hands clasped over the wound from which blood trickled through his fingers.

'Oh, God, Miss Nuala,' he gasped. 'I tried to . . .' His words were choked in a retch.

Nuala stepped back in horror. Her hands fluttered helplessly.

'Mama!' she called. 'Tim is wounded. He is dying. Mama, come and help him!'

But Georgina, dabbing tenderly at her cut mouth, stared with a horror and helplessness to match Nuala's. Her whimpers of pain grew louder, more hysterical.

Nuala, still suffering from pain and shock herself, screamed, 'Mama, you must do something!'

But Georgina's only answer was a scream louder than Nuala's.

Nuala looked again at Tim and immediately covered her eyes. 'Help!' she shrieked. 'Somebody, help!'

But there was no reply except Tim's bubbling moans and the hysterical sobbing of her mother.

'Oh, for God's sake, be quiet, mama!' She gripped her hand and pulled. 'Stop, stop, stop! Come and do something!'

But the attempt to pull her from the small safety of the coach increased Georgina's terror. Nuala left her and ran down the hill, shouting for help until her skirts tripped her and she fell. She lay on the rough, wet road, unmoving, silent, feeling that this was the end of everything. There was no help anywhere.

'Help yourself, you silly goose!'

It was almost as if she had heard a voice, and it came again, 'Get up. You're not hurt, but poor Tim is dying!'

She scrambled to her feet, snivelled once, rubbed her eyes and nose with the back of her hand and walked back.

Her mother was shrieking, 'Nuala! Where are you, Nuala? Don't leave me!'

Nuala, now coldly, numbly calm, walked up to her and slapped her sharply across each cheek, shocking her into silence.

'Now come and help me!' She pulled her, sobbing, from the coach.

'Be quiet! We must get him into the coach. Take his feet and I will take his shoulders.'

Georgina stared in horror at Tim who was now unconscious. Nuala pushed her, forced her hands down to grip the feet. 'Lift!' she commanded. She gripped the shoulders. 'Lift, damn you!' And Georgina lifted like an automaton. They half-carried, half-dragged him to the step.

'Now hold him there!'

She ran round the coach, climbed in and seized him under the armpits. 'Lift!' she cried and she dragged him, with small help from her mother, into the coach and on to the seat, where she made him as comfortable as possible.

Georgina stood stupidly in the road, dabbing automatically at her mouth.

'Get in now, mama. You must hold him on the seat.'

The words had no meaning for Georgina. The coach was now a place made disgusting by the horrible, bleeding body. It was no place for her.

Nuala realised the uselessness of talk. She got out, closed the door, walked round the coach and shouted, urged, pushed and thumped until she had forced her mother on to the opposite seat.

'Take care of him!'

She slammed the door, kilted her petticoats, climbed up to the box and took the reins and whip. She had never before driven anything larger than a pony-cart and it was with trepidation that she shook the reins. To her great relief the horses started and pulled fairly well together. Whilst they were walking to the top of the hill there was no great difficulty, but once there the off-leader began to trot whilst his fellows lagged. This slowed the coach. A pull on the reins halted the three, but set the other dancing. She could not sort out his reins, so she tried whipping his companion who tried to start but was held by the stationary rear pair.

'Oh, blast you all!' she exclaimed and, in her annoyance, she gave the reins a downward slap which started them all off, but out of unison. She heaved back and, obediently, they slowed. When she again shook the reins they took off in fair harmony, but at a pace which set the coach rocking and threatening to pull the reins from her hands. Self-preservation forced her to slacken her grip and gradually they found their own pace, but there was still no complete agreement and the result was a sinuous path from one side of the road to the other. Though this required her to hold on more tightly to her seat than to the reins, and although she knew it must be far from comfortable for the passengers, she could do no better.

Gradually she was able to take her mind from the horses and consider their position. The first necessity was to find a doctor for Tim. But they had no money to pay a doctor. They also needed money for food and for changes of horses. It was impossible for them to continue. She did not know the road and could not manage the team for any great distance. She could see no way to solve their problems, so she told herself it was useless to worry beyond getting the coach to the next inn.

An ostler ran out when he heard the coach approaching – a loutish fellow with spiky red hair and a grinning, foolish face. Luckily, the horses stopped of their own accord. When the ostler saw her on the box he gaped and then began to laugh so loudly that several men appeared in the doorway and joined in the laughter.

Nuala's eyes flashed and she reddened with anger. She

climbed down from the far side, walked round the coach straight to the ostler and gave him a resounding slap in the face, which effectively quietened both him and the group in the doorway.

She strode at them and, sheepishly, they made way for her. Inside, she called imperiously, 'Landlord!' and a round-faced, fat man appeared, making washing motions with his chubby hands.

'Are you the landlord?'

'Denis Daniel Breen, at your service, miss or ma'am.' He beamed and bowed.

'I want a doctor. Send somebody immediately.'

He became aware of her bedraggled appearance.

'Well now, that would be a matter of not a little difficulty. Doctor Portland being the nearest and living not a little distance. That's for one thing. For another thing, it being the time of night it is...'

'Whilst that is being done, have my coachman carried in very carefully and put to bed. He is badly injured.'

'Now, not wishing to –'

She stamped her foot. 'Do as I say, man! At once!'

'Well, now... I suppose... Er, well...' He could not meet her determination and hurried off calling for a man to ride for the doctor.

The gawpers in the doorway shuffled aside as she hurried back to the coach. She opened the door and found Tim unconscious in one corner, his lower half soaked in blood, her mother in a faint in the farthest corner. The ostler, still stupidly rubbing his cheek, stood at one side.

'Come here, you! And you, and you and you,' pointing to the biggest men.

They shambled unwillingly to the coach and looked in. 'Jesus, Mary and Joseph!'

'You two go round to the other side and take his shoulders.' She ordered, directed and bullied them into lifting Tim from the coach and carrying him into the inn.

'Jacks-a-cracky!' exclaimed the innkeeper. 'You can't put him into one of my good beds. 'Twould be the ruination of it.'

'You inhuman creature. Lead the way!'

Grumbling, he led the way to a small bedroom, where a girl who had been preparing the bed promptly fainted.

When they had laid him on the bed, one of the men said, ''Tis a priest that lad needs more than the doctor. I'll fetch Father Hayes in a hurry.'

The other men and the innkeeper, still complaining about his bed, followed him, carrying the maid.

Nuala hurried back to the coach. The cold air blowing through the open doors had revived her mother and she was cowering in the corner, staring horrified at the great patch of blood on the opposite seat. Nuala climbed in and closed the doors.

'Now you must listen to me, mama,' she said firmly. 'You must regain control of yourself. Tim is in bed and they have sent for the doctor and the priest. We must stay at the inn for the night.'

'I will not sleep in that filthy place,' she moaned petulantly.

'Then you may stay in the coach alone all night.'

'Oh, Nuala, what is to become of us? We have nothing and Mark will refuse to have us. I know it. What will we do? Where can we go?'

'We will do as best we can. For the moment we must search our baggage for anything of value.'

They found two rings and four necklaces. They had no great value, but Nuala estimated them to be at least enough to pay their bill at the inn. She took her mother inside and sat her beside a fire.

She found the innkeeper in the taproom talking with the men and it was obvious that they had been discussing her.

'Mr Breen, I wish to speak with you!' She turned back to the parlour and he followed.

'Now, lookat, Miss, I suppose it is. This is a respectable house...'

'You insolent lout! Do you dare to suggest that we are taking away from the doubtful respectability of this wretched place?'

'What I mean –'

'I am not in the least interested in what you mean. We are travellers who had the misfortune to be waylaid by two murderous highwaymen. They robbed us and shot our coachman. Yet all you can talk about is your miserable respectability. Shame on you. Have you no Christian feelings?'

'I'm a poor man,' he said doggedly. 'My feelings don't matter, I suppose, nor do they pay bills. If you've been robbed, who'll pay for the damage to my good bed? That's what I want to know.'

'Mr Mark Portis of Enniscorthy in the County Wexford, who is my uncle, will see to it that you are repaid.'

Even as she said it, Nuala hoped that the certainty was as great as her voice conveyed; and it flashed through her mind at the same time that she had never before spoken to anybody as she had to this man. She was not only surprised by the fact, but also by the realisation that, in spite of her troubles, she was actually enjoying it.

'Wexford's a damn long piece from this!'

'You are an insolent creature. How dare you insinuate that we are trying to cheat you!'

'Oho! What's all this about cheating?'

A tall, thin, stooping old man stood in the doorway. He carried a stout stick under his arm and held a big snuff-box from which he took a hearty pinch.

'Doctor Portland, very much your servant, Miss,' he said, snapping the lid and bowing. 'On my way home from a card game when the fellow met me with the message.'

Nuala introduced herself and her mother and told what had happened.

'Aha! Thieves, rogues and vagabonds abroad in these devilish times. And you're one of 'em, eh, Breen?' He poked his stick into the man's round belly.

'Ooof! No, doctor, sir. I'm ...'

'Only a middling sort of rogue. Hear me, man! A room and supper for the ladies and quick about it!' He thwacked

253

the tight breeches-seat.

'Wait here, m'dear. I'll go and see the patient.'

In less than ten minutes they were eating hungrily. The doctor returned before they had finished.

'Eat on, eat on, ladies. I'll join you in a glass of wine, if I may.'

Nuala watched him anxiously as he slowly poured and sipped the wine.

'What do you want, ladies? Fancy lies or plain truth?'

'The truth, please, doctor,' said Nuala.

He held the glass up to the light and stared through it. 'I left him with the priest, who can do more for him than I can. He won't last the night.'

They wept. Two violent deaths in so short a time.

'Oh!' Georgina moaned. 'What is to become of us?'

'Poor Tim,' said Nuala. 'Is he conscious?'

'He was when I left him. Would you wish to see him?'

'I would like him to know that we had not left him alone.'

'Come, then.'

Tim lay quietly, his face yellow against the pillow. The priest knelt beside him. When he saw her, Tim smiled faintly; but the smile twisted to an agonised distortion of his features. Sweat stood out on his forehead and his breath was hoarse in his throat. Yet through his agony his eyes, gazing at Nuala, were filled with shame and apology.

When the spasm had passed he whispered, 'I was not a good guard for you and your poor mother.'

'Oh, don't, Tim, don't!' She touched his hand lightly. 'You were very, very brave.'

His eyes shone with gratitude.

Blinded as she was by tears, the doctor had to lead her from the room.

Tim died just before dawn. Father Hayes told her that he had been quite peaceful. He said he would make the arrangements for the funeral, but, well, there was the expense of a coffin.

Doctor Portland came to her aid. 'I'll foot any bills, my

dear and send you one big one for the lot,' he said offhandedly.

She thanked the priest and, when he had gone, with sudden decision, she told the doctor their circumstances, even to the fact that they were not sure of a welcome from her uncle.

'But we have a few pieces of jewellery, and these you must take.'

'Pah! What do I want with trinkets? Go on your way and pay me when you can. Surely this uncle of yours cannot be such a blackguard that he would refuse to help his only relations when they are in such need. Don't worry, my dear, you'll pull through all right.'

'But, doctor, we cannot take advantage of your generosity. Yet, there is the matter of somebody to drive the coach. The coach! I have just thought. The coach and horses could be sold. Would it be possible for you to lend us a groom to drive us? Then he could return to you with the coach.'

'Jupiter, girl, you won't owe me as much as that!'

'No matter. It will help to repay your kindness.'

'Pah! Nonsense! You must be more business-like if you are to face the world, my dear. Now this is what we'll do. I'll gladly lend a groom and I'll settle everything here. I'll get rid of the coach and horses when they return and I'll send you the balance. And I'll advance you five guineas from that to help you on your way.'

In the late evening, three days later, they arrived in the town of Enniscorthy. The landlord of the inn at which they enquired stated that he knew of Mr Mark Portis. His expression added that he knew nothing to his advantage, and it was very obvious that he was most curious to know why anybody should wish to visit him. However, he gave directions to the house which, he thought, was about fifteen miles away.

They drove out into the country again, lost their way several times on the little winding roads, received reluctant direction at wayside cabins and eventually drove up a short drive to what they had been told was Mr

Portis' house.

Although no lights or other signs of life were to be seen, and in spite of the objections of the groom who had been instructed to take the utmost care of them, Nuala insisted that their baggage should be unloaded and that the coach should drive away before she rang the bell. She was determined to present her uncle with a *fait accompli*.

Standing on the step in the chill darkness with their baggage round them, they heard the bell jangling discordantly in a seemingly empty house. There came a deep baying from obviously large dogs, the quick scrabble of paws across tiles, then a savage growling, barking and scratching at the other side of the door.

Georgina clutched at Nuala. 'Oh, Nuala, Nuala, let us leave at once. If the door is opened those savage brutes will kill us.'

'You must be calm, mama,' said Nuala, trying to hide her own fear. 'Somebody will send them away.'

Their voices excited the dogs. Bellowing, snarling, slavering, they flung themselves at the door, their bodies thudding against it, their claws seeking to tear down the barrier.

Georgina dragged at her arm and wailed, 'I am terrified. Oh, come away. Come away from this dreadful place!'

But Nuala was more determined than ever. 'We have nowhere to go. There must be servants in the house.' She tugged again at the bell-pull, setting the dogs frantic.

From above them a female voice called, 'Who, in God's name, is that?'

Nuala stepped back and looked up, but could not see anybody.

'Is Mr Portis at home?' she called.

'He's not, then. He's away to dinner with Major Griffiths. Good night!'

'Don't go!' shouted Nuala desperately.

'What is it you want? Can't you hear the way you've upset the dogs?'

'We are relations of Mr Portis and we have travelled a long way to visit him. We will come in and wait for him.'

'Come to visit him! Does he know?'

'No, we had to leave in a hurry.'

'Well, then, take my advice and go back in a hurry. Mr Portis has little liking for visitors.'

Nuala lost her temper. 'Girl, woman or whatever you are! Come down, chain those dogs, then admit us. At once! Otherwise I shall report your behaviour to my uncle, Mr Portis.'

There was no reply, nothing but the noise of the dogs, then they heard the woman's voice in the hall. 'Away with you, you brutes. Into the kitchen!'

The barking died to a grumbling and faded. Then there was a curious slithering sound, which later proved to be made by the woman's bare feet on the tiles. The door opened a crack.

Nuala pushed it wide against hesitant opposition and led her mother into a bare hall lit only by the flickering candle the woman carried. She was barely five feet in height, with a thin body, thin face and greying hair pulled back into a tight knot which seemed to stretch the skin of her face.

'What is your name?' asked Nuala coldly.

'Judy, ma'am,' the woman replied nervously, bobbing a curtsy. 'Judy Boyle, ma'am. And sure 'twas neither harm nor insult I was offering to yourselves, but good advice only.'

'Bring in our baggage.'

As she said this, and realised at the same time how tiny the woman was, she felt ashamed; but she felt she must maintain the superiority she had gained. She and her mother watched in silence until the woman had struggled in with all their luggage.

'When do you expect Mr Portis to return?'

'Lord above, ma'am, I haven't the leastest notion. It could be minutes or hours.'

'Very well. Kindly show us where we can wait in comfort.'

'Well, I don't know about that, ma'am. D'you see...'

'Do as you are told, woman! Can you not understand

that we are both exhausted after a long journey?'

Judy shrugged helplessly, then led them to a door which opened on to a large, high-ceilinged room, filled with tall, dark furniture and with an atmosphere as cold and uninviting as a vault.

'I'll tell the master when he comes back.'

'Where are you going?' asked Nuala sharply.

'Back to the kitchen, ma'am. Mr Portis would skin me if he found me in the best room.'

'Best room! This morgue? And do you mean to leave us without light or fire?'

'Oh, God! I don't know what to do. I need the candle to finish the heap of mending I've yet to do. And the dear Lord knows he'll kill me for letting you into the house.' The woman was shaking with anxiety and fear.

'Listen to me,' said Nuala firmly. 'I will accept full responsibliity. Now go, and bring more candles, light a fire and then prepare a meal for us.'

The woman stared at her in amazement.

'Don't stand there. Go and do as I say. I will explain to my uncle that you were held up in your other work.'

'Ma'am,' said Judy timorously, but determined to make Nuala understand. 'This is the only candle I have. The rest are locked away. His orders are that there are to be no fires lit save in the kitchen for cooking and 'tis long out now. And there's not the leastest scrap of food I can give you. 'Tis all locked away, and himself has the key.'

'Do you mean to tell me...' Nuala could not believe what she had heard.

Georgina gave a low wail. 'I told you, Nuala. I told you what manner of man he is. I told you we would not be welcome here. We must leave now, before he comes back.'

'Mama! Be quiet!' Nuala clenched her fists with determination, yet looked helplessly from her mother to Judy. 'We have nowhere to go. We must stay.'

'But I don't wish to stay. This is a horrible house.'

'That's the true word, miss, begging your pardon. You'd do better any place than this.'

'Don't either of you understand? We are homeless. We have no money and nowhere else in the world to go.'

Judy shook her head slowly. 'You know best, miss. But I'll tell you, you'll get no welcome. Sure, doesn't he keep the dogs to drive people away from here!'

'Judy! Hellfire and damnation, woman, where are you?' the bellow came from the kitchen.

Judy vanished. Nuala and her mother stood, clutching each other's hands in the cold darkness.

Nuala prayed silently for the strength to stand up to him.

Another bellow, 'Oh, have they indeed! Then they may clear out as quick as they came. Here, Fang, Wolf!'

His footsteps rapped across the hall accompanied by the pattering of the dogs. He appeared in the doorway with the candle raised high, the growling beasts on either side.

He was a large, powerfully built man with a small head sitting squatly on his shoulders. His eyes glittered under thick, black eyebrows. His jaws, chin and upper lip, although cleanly shaven, were almost black. His thin nostrils flared above a thin-lipped mouth. With his head thrust forward he examined them in silence for a moment. Then he spoke in a slow, hard voice.

'So my loving sister has come to visit her dear brother. And this, I suppose, is the fruit of your love-match. Say How-de-do to your Uncle Mark, my dear. Then collect your traps and clear to hell out of this. I'll have no pauper relations living off me. Come on. Step lively before I set my pets on you!'

Georgina, who had been cowering away from the dogs, gave a little scream and pulled at Nuala; but she took one step towards him and faced him, trembling inwardly.

'I am sure the County would be most impressed if they were told that you had used dogs to drive away your only relations!'

'Shut your mouth, chit! You are as ill-mannered as could be expected from your getting.'

'I intend to say what I have to say. And if you set those

dogs on us, I'll go straight from here to Major Griffiths and tell him of your treatment. Now understand. My father is dead. We are homeless. We had only two alternatives: to beg on the roads, or to appeal to you.'

'Then I advise you to take to the roads. You will fare better.'

'Shall I tell Major Griffiths what you advise?'

'So you'd blackmail me, you little bitch!'

'Indeed I would!' She laughed suddenly as she realised the truth of what she was going to say. 'As I feel at this moment, and that is quite desperate, I would shoot you to help mama.'

'Well, I'm damned!' He stared in astonishment. 'Five feet of nothing and threatening Mark Portis!' He gave a laugh – short, hard, but not quite humourless. 'D'y know, I do believe we must have a common ancestor – one with more backbone than the rest of my breed.'

He laughed again, paused in thought, kicked one of the dogs and asked it, 'What d'you think?'

Then he walked across to them and stared down. Georgina shrank behind Nuala, but she faced him determinedly.

'So,' he said with a twisted smile. 'No trembles. No feminine vapours. And what about you, sister, dear? Ah, not much backbone there, eh?'

He turned to Nuala again. 'Right, my beloved niece. I'm going to allow you to stay. But, before you overwhelm me with loving gratitude, let me tell you this. You'll work for your keep, and you'll work damned hard, both of you. I am going to break you, my dear. I am going to show you for the first time in your pampered life, just what life is really like. There are too many damned parasites in the world. From now on, there'll be two less.'

He turned and left the room, booting the dogs ahead of him.

Nuala, shaking with sudden weakness, had barely the strength to stagger to a chair. She collapsed on to it, her teeth chattering, her arms clasped tightly about herself as if she were holding in her very life. Even though she was aware that her mother was sprawled on the floor in a paroxysm of sobs, she could do nothing to help her.

Slowly she regained control. She realised that her mother's loud sobs might bring Mark back. That fired her. She must never allow him to know the effect he had had. Still shaky, she stood and bent over her mother.

'Hush, mama, hush!' She gripped her arms and forced her to rise. 'We shall be all right. Hush!'

But she was far from feeling as confident as she tried to sound.

They spent the night in a tiny, damp bed in an attic with such a slope to the ceiling that it was barely possible to stand upright. They were cold, hungry and weary and the discomfort of the narrow, damp, lumpy bed, with insufficient coverings, made restful sleep impossible. They dozed and wakened, dozed and wakened through the long night.

Judy called them at six o'clock. 'Himself said I was to call you at five, when I got up myself; but God knows, I couldn't do that knowing how weary you were. But you must get up now because himself will be up shortly.'

Nuala was sick with fatigue and she ached after the uncomfortable hours, but she was determined to show no weakness to her uncle. Nevertheless she made her mother stay in bed and left her sleeping restlessly when she groped her way downstairs from the cold attic.

She remembered the dogs and knocked cautiously on the kitchen door, which set them barking until Judy quietened them. Then Judy opened the door and took her hand.

'Don't show fear of them, or they'll eat you,' she said, giving small comfort.

The huge beasts stood in the warmth of a fire which filled the large, stone-flagged kitchen with a heartening glow. They grumbled throatily at her.

'Here!' Judy called and they advanced slowly and warily, still rumbling. 'Put out your hand to them and, for God's sake, hold it steady till they get a whiff of you.'

Nuala thought it was the most terrifying thing she had

ever had to do. She closed her eyes and held out her hand, using all her will-power to keep it steady. She heard the growling die and peeped through half-open lids. They sniffed her hand, then looked up at her with big, mournful eyes.

'Why, they're not really savage at all. They're simply ill-treated.'

'Take care. They're savage enough; but when they're used to you about the place they'll not bother.'

'Unless I order them!'

The dogs cowered away.

Mark Portis was standing in the doorway. 'Come!' The dogs slunk to him and crouched at his feet. 'Strangers!' They rose, teeth bared, the hair bristling on their great necks. 'Guard!' They disappeared silently, one to the front door, the other to the back.

'Take a lesson in obedience, my dear niece; and note that if I order them to attack, they will rend anybody I indicate.'

He called them back and dismissed them to a corner of the kitchen.

'I expect and get similar obedience from every member of this household. That includes you and my dear sister. Where is she?'

'I told her to stay in bed.'

'You told her! My orders were that she was to be up at five.'

'Mama has had a very bad time. Less than a week ago –'

'I have no time to listen to your stupid lamentations. You have wished yourselves on me uninvited. I have agreed to permit you to stay. But on my terms. And they are – work and absolute obedience.

'Judy!' he shouted, and she came running from the scullery. 'First, as a reward to you, there'll be no supper tonight. Second, when she and her mother have worked for two hours you may give them something to eat. And if I catch you being soft with them, I'll have the hide off you. You understand me, woman?'

'Yes, sir,' said Judy fearfully.

'Now you. You have three minutes to get that lazy bitch down here. Then I'll be up with the dogs to hunt the pair of you out of this.'

Nuala was seething with anger, but she was quite sure that he meant exactly what he said. She ran upstairs.

Georgina, when she finally understood what Nuala was saying, was terrified. Weeping and groaning she dressed with Nuala's help and hobbled downstairs. The momentary comfort of the fire was completely dispelled by the news that she would have to work before she ate. With a wail of despair she sank on to a settle beside the fire and rocked her misery. Nuala's and Judy's arguments were useless. Then Mark appeared with the dogs and she leapt up with a shriek and fled into the yard.

Stables, sheds and outhouses were set around the yard and in one corner was the dairy where a girl was scouring milk-pails. Judy introduced her as Mag Kinsella. She was an ugly girl with a squat, lumpy figure, pock-marked face and coarse straggling red hair. But the warmth of her grin lightened the gloomy morning.

'Yerra, Judy,' she said, 'you've a face on you the length of a wet week. What ails you, woman, dear?'

Judy merely shrugged and sighed.

'Oh, the big, black fella, is it? Sure he was in here not long since and I gave him a few tales of what the Croppies have been doing to the likes of him. All politeness I was and terrible anxious about the danger he was in. D'ye know 'twas small comfort he got from it.' Her bellowing laugh was so infectious that Nuala joined it, in spite of herself.

'That's the way,' said Mag. 'Don't let that fella get the better of you. After all, God help him, isn't he the miserablest creature alive.'

Judy showed Nuala how to churn, but, hard though she tried, she could not turn the handle fast enough. Judy relieved her and told her and her mother to help Mag with the cleaning of the cream pans. This entailed washing them with near-boiling water, scouring them with sand, rinsing them and setting them out in the open to dry. Georgina's nose wrinkled with disgust as she flapped ineffectually with a hot, sopping cloth held gingerly between thumb and forefinger. Nuala forced herself, rolled up her sleeves and did her best to imitate Mag. Long before they had finished her hands were red and sore.

They then helped Judy to strain the butter, put it into a block and take it and the buttermilk to the cold room. Staggering over the uneven cobbles, slopping the milk over their skirts and feet, gasping for breath and feeling as if their arms were being racked, they thought they had reached the depths of drudgery.

Their next job was to collect the eggs under Mag's supervision. Although they found the smell of the poultry-house nauseating, this work was at least lighter. Then Georgina picked up an egg clotted with bird-lime. She promptly dropped it and stared in horror at her filthy fingers and retched.

'Oh, I can stand no more!' she gasped.

'What ails you?' Mag asked.

Nuala, close to vomiting herself, gestured at her mother's extended hand.

'Oh, the bit of shit, is it?' Mag asked lightly. 'God love you, ma'am, sure that's lucky!' And she rubbed the hand briskly with her apron.

Nuala laughed in spite of her disgust and felt a surge of affection for the cheerful girl and a renewed determination to fight her uncle.

When the eggs had been stored Mag led them to the pig-sties. She opened the gates and chased the pigs out into the yard. The floors of the sties were deep in mud and ordure. She took an implement like a rake, made from a piece of board fixed to a long handle, and began to pull out the foul mixture. The disturbance of it raised such a stench that it drove Nuala and her mother away.

'Ah, come back here!' Mag called. 'You'll need to push it into a pile and the men'll take it to the muck heap.'

And they had to take similar implements and push and pull the stinking stuff away from the sties.

'Don't let it bother you at all,' said Mag cheerfully. 'In a day you'll be well used to it. And, sure, what harm is in it? 'Tis great stuff for spreading on the land. And the pig, now, is surely a great beast. I tasted the meat of one once and 'tis surely the stuff God has on His own table.'

After that Mag took them to an outhouse and had them help her to prepare the pig-swill. This evil-looking mess had then to be scooped into pails and carried, slopping skirts and shoes, to the sties, into which Mag had chased the pigs. Through low, swinging traps it was poured into troughs to the squealing, gobbling animals.

'Ah, you'll both be great after you've a bite in you,' said Mag.

The thought of eating was almost more nauseating than the smells.

'Come on now. Let you swill yourselves under the pump and take a good drink and you'll be all sweet and new.'

Nuala then discovered that water, which had always been a thing to be used copiously and without thought, required labour to produce, particularly from the rusty pump whose cold handle was agony to her maltreated hands. But the first drink did revive them. In spite of the cold and awkwardness they managed to wash hands and faces and ran the water over their skirts and shoes. Even though this left them dripping, it was preferable to the filth.

At last they returned to the warm kitchen.

'There y'are then,' said Judy. 'Sure, 'twasn't too bad now, was it? Sit down at the table and I'll bring you a bite.'

'How can I sit with my skirts wet through?' Georgina wailed. And Nuala, her cold feet squelching in her wet shoes, her sodden skirts clinging to her legs, was tempted to join in.

'You must kilt your skirts and go barefoot as we do,' said Judy. ''Tis the only way you'll work in comfort, and a splash from the pump clears away all the dirt.'

Georgina was horrified. 'Are you suggesting that I should walk barefoot, through mud and filth?'

'Ah, well, take your breakfast.' She emptied on to the bare table a small heap of potatoes boiled in their skins and added two mugs of buttermilk. 'I should not give you the buttermilk by rights, but himself is away on the land and won't miss it.'

They stared. That this should be considered a breakfast! To Nuala it represented a clear statement of the life of hardship which lay ahead.

'This is not breakfast!' stated Georgina indignantly. 'A little bacon or ham, eggs, a few slices of cold beef, bread... The usual things one eats for breakfast.'

'His orders are that you are to eat what we have ourselves.'

Georgina stood up. 'That is enough. I absolutely refuse to be treated in this fashion. Nuala, I will not stay one moment longer in this house!'

Nuala put a restraining hand on her arm. 'Where can we go? Tell me, mama, where can we go?'

'There has to be somewhere better than this.'

'Where?'

Georgina sank on to the wooden form, leaned on the table and wept. Nuala, having no comfort to give beyond stroking her hand, let her cry for a while, then said, 'Try to eat, mama. Even this is better than nothing.'

She picked up a potato, stripped away part of the skin and began to eat. At the first bite she realised that she was hungrier than she had ever been in her life, and that the potato tasted better than anything she could remember. She lost count of the number she ate, and was glad to see her mother eating too.

After breakfast Judy took them to help with the housework. She had to teach them how to make a bed and how to dust and sweep. First their own attic, then the corridor and the stairs leading down to the second floor. And having swept the bare boards they had then to get down on hands and knees and scrub – this having been especially ordered by Portis.

Having then cleaned the second floor corridor, Judy led them into Mark's room. It was furnished with a large

266

four-poster bed with a blue silk canopy, curtains and inlays, a big wardrobe, a dressing-table, a marble-topped washstand, several straight-backed chairs, an easy chair and, what immediately attracted Nuala's attention, a large bog-oak chest which stood at the foot of the bed.

In helping Judy to make the bed, she contrived to push with her knee at the lid of the box. It was securely locked. She was as certain that it contained wealth as if it had been made of glass through which she could see heaps of golden coins. For the first time she felt hope, which she refused to analyse.

There were four other bedrooms on the same floor. The one next to Mark's had only a four-poster bed with canopy, curtains, bedspread and inlays of black silk, a small table and a chair. This room, Judy told them with pride, had been used by the old owners solely for laying out the dead.

'Wouldn't you feel grand and proud,' she said wistfully, 'to be lying in that bed and you dead, and everybody crowded round you, keening and praying for the repose of your soul, and telling all the bestest things they could remember about you!'

Nuala was glad to get out of there.

The other rooms were poorly furnished as guest rooms and were obviously seldom used; but they were luxurious when compared with their attic. There was a key in one of the doors and, on impulse, Nuala took it and then pulled the clothes from the bed and opened the windows.

'Ah, God, what are you doing?' asked Judy fearfully.

'We shall sleep here in future.' She locked the door and pocketed the key.

'God preserve us, himself will be mad angry.'

'He will not get to know.'

All day thoughts of the black box disturbed yet comforted her. Her thoughts were far from clear, apart from the knowledge that they would need money if they were ever to get away, and the certainty that there was money in the box. She refused to consider that the money did not belong to them. Yet, at the same time, she told herself that her mother had some indefinable right to it. Then, too, since they were working for him, he owed them money. She would worry about ownership later. In the meantime the thought of the money was a comfort which she hugged to herself.

At noon more than twenty men straggled in, casting curious glances at Nuala and her mother. They stood around the table in silence for several minutes until Mark entered, and all bowed as he walked through without acknowledgement. Then they sat. From the fireside Judy carried out of the kitchen a tray trailing savoury odours which all sniffed enviously before eating from the huge mound of potatoes on the table.

When the men had gone, the four women sat and rooted for their dinner amongst the litter of skins. Afterwards all the leavings had to be gathered for the pigs and fowl, the table scrubbed, the pots scoured and the kitchen swept. Judy then brought two heaps of dirty clothes – Mark's and the men's. Once more Georgina tasted degradation as she struggled to achieve some semblance of cleanliness in a greasy, smelly shirt.

They limped up to bed that night, sick, aching and bone-weary. They went to the room which Nuala had chosen. She locked the door and, with impeding help from her mother, made the bed. They took off their wet clothes, thought with longing of a hot bath and fell into the bed.

Nuala lay with closed eyes, striving to relax, to let her weariness ooze into the bed. She thought of a few prayers, of Conal, of the doubtful future, of the black box. She sat up abruptly and shook her mother.

'What?' Georgina grumbled.

'Mama. Listen to me! Did grandpapa Portis leave a will?'

Georgina was asleep again. Nuala shook her and even pummelled her, but she had to ask the question several times before her mother vaguely understood.

'Oh, Nuala, let me sleep. I don't know.'

Nuala released her and she was asleep immediately.

In the last moments before she slept herself, Nuala thought, 'It's our money, and we shall have it!'

FORTY-EIGHT

Danger came unexpectedly out of the night as Conal trudged heart-sick and numb with weariness towards distant Dublin. A drumming of hoofs from beyond the next corner, a sudden flare of light. Instinctively he threw himself into the deep ditch. Through the thick growth he watched a body of Dragoons sweep past, the flames of their torches streaming behind them; and by this light he saw, behind eight of the troopers, prisoners bound to the saddles and facing backwards. He glimpsed a pale, boyish face with a dripping gash over one eye. Then they were gone.

He lay listening to the hoofbeats fading away to silence, panting from unconsciously holding his breath, waiting for the thudding of his heart to quieten, yet revelling in the relief which flooded him. Self-contempt jerked him to his feet – contempt that he should be glad that others were prisoners and not he. He stood in the road and stared back the way the troopers had gone. Well-mounted, well-armed, confident, the troopers stressed the impotence of himself and his people. Montgomery was right. They needed vast, well-armed, well-organised and, above all, well-led numbers. The logic of the orders from Dublin was obvious now. He was glad that he was gong to Dublin to meet those leaders.

He walked on, borne up for a time by anticipation; but then weariness dragged at his steps. His bones ached with tiredness, his heavy lids had to be forcibly kept apart, his body yearned to drop and sleep. But he was sufficiently aware to know that he must hide first. He left the road and scrambled up a rough hillside, searching in vain for a place of comfort and warmth, but finding only rocks and scratching bushes. Then he tripped and fell, mercifully into a hollow thickly-grown with springy heather. Its resilience cradled him and he slept immediately.

Chill rain woke him, stiff and still tired, to a grey morning. He staggered, shivering, down to the road and waded it, head-down to the rain, utterly miserable. Dublin was in the immeasurable future. Dreams of a vast Irish army sweeping irresistibly through the land were nonsense. The only real things were hunger, wet, cold, stupidity and helplessness.

The old man standing in the doorway of his cabin had to shout three times before Conal heard. He stopped and gaped stupidly at the man.

'Come in out of that before you're drowned,' the old man called, and Conal went in to the welcome warmth of the fire.

''Tis well for you I saw you,' said the old man. 'These are chancy times for a man with a cropped head to be walking in the full light of day.'

He made Conal strip and dry himself, gave him potatoes to eat and 'a sup of poteen to drive out the damp' and then Conal slept.

When he woke his clothes were dry. He dressed and would have left the cabin but the old man warned him to wait until it was dark. The Yeomanry was very active. Any man with a cropped head, or wearing anything green was a target for them. He gave Conal an old hat, 'To keep the head on your shoulders.'

He told how, on the previous day, the Yeomanry in Drogheda had grabbed a Mr Turner, torn the green stock from his neck and were about to whip him when some of the gentry identified him as a rich local landowner. Then, however, they caught a butcher named Bergan who was wearing a ring with a small shamrock in it. They stripped

him, tied him to his own cart and flogged him through the
town until he was dead.

'So you'd do well to walk tippy-toe and through the
dark, young fellow,' the old man advised.

Conal followed that advice from then on, walking only
at night and spending the days in friendly cabins; and in
every one he heard tales of the ruthlessness of the Yeos.

Throughout the country informers were at work,
scores of arrests were made daily and, since the testimony
of informers was not acceptable in the law-courts, any
who survived the ill-treatment of the Yeos during or
after arrest were sent, without trial, to the English army
or navy.

There were many stories of the Yeos attacking
innocent families, stripping them and driving them naked
along the roads with their whips; of cabins destroyed
when searches for arms had been fruitless, the people
cruelly beaten and often killed; of bodies of Yeos galloping
along the roads taking pot-shots at people working in the
fields and slashing with their sabres at any they
encountered on the road.

And there was counter-activity. Yeos, police, paid
witnesses and informers were found piked or clubbed to
death. A constable was found completely dismembered,
and in the hand which lay on his torso was a note
threatening similar treatment to any who dared to bury
him.

The effects of all this were made vividly clear to Conal
as he journeyed south. Men were being lost to the cause
through being slaughtered, deported to serve in the
English forces, or frightened from the ranks. Arms
collected with the greatest difficulty had been captured.
Meetings of the determined ones who remained were
increasingly difficult to hold, any form of training was
almost impossible. The rebellion was being stifled before
it had even begun. Spurred on by the urgency to report all
these things to the leaders, he travelled as quickly as he
could, and the terror which was loose made him worry
more than ever that Nuala was at risk from both sides.

271

The country straggled imperceptibly into the city and was suddenly lost. He walked street after street with no sense of direction and arrived in an area of brightly lit drinking places, gambling-houses and brothels. The streets were thronged with people who had neither the time nor the patience to answer the questions of a bedraggled peasant. They were an astonishing assortment: brilliantly dressed young men, powdered and patched, strolling in search of entertainment; equally colourful ladies anxious to supply it; soldiers, naval men and sailors from the merchant ships anxious to satisfy anxiety, but with an eye to cost; clerks and shop-men with their belles, parading for vicarious enjoyment of the gaiety of the more free and fortunate; unattached beaux and belles ogling unattached belles and beaux; sedate and comfortable masters of trade escorting plump and sedate spouses for a gentle partaking of the evening air; pot-boys and personages, pimps and pickpockets, parsons and plumbers; and everywhere beggars of every age from the hired baby in the arms of the half-drunken slut; through the parent-tutored tots, the wise and wizened-faced children, the hard-faced older boys and girls, the bitter men and women many exhibiting wooden legs, a single arm, scrofulous necks, bulbous wens, ulcerous faces or limbs, with no differentiation between the genuinely maimed and the disguised or artificially decorated, to the old – seemingly aged beyond possibility – striving to beg yet another hour of life for all its misery.

A fat woman ceased trundling her barrow of fish. Spreading her amplitude over one of the shafts, she lifted a cold-eyed, long-faded mackerel and gnawed toothlessly at the chilly flesh.

'Fiddlers Alley, is it me jew'l!' She spattered Conal with half-chewed fish. 'Why wouldn't I know it and I borned and raised by me sainted mother that's dead and gone these twenty years, may the good God shower the blessings of Heaven on her, in Spenser Street hard by.'

Through the thick, adenoidal accent, marred by too much fish and too few teeth, Conal gained a vague idea of the directions.

'A thousand thanks,' he said. 'And the blessings of God on you.'

'Ah, no thanks needed at all. And now you'll be buying some of my lovely fish, plucked straight from the Bay not an hour ago.'

With a rueful smile he told her he had no money.

The fat, coaxing smile disappeared into folds of malice. 'The devil rip the hide from your back, you heathen impostor!' she screamed. Then, incredibly raising her tone to make known her woes to the parading world, 'What curse is come on Holy Ireland that a poor, defenceless widow-woman can be deceived by a plamausing blackguard in the streets of Dublin town!'

Her screams followed him as he fled.

He crossed the Essex Bridge and turned right along the quays where a man gave him further directions to the Coombe. He found himself in a ravel of narrow lanes and alleys, stinking with all the vile odours which only closely packed humanity can produce. Dark figures glided by, appeared and disappeared, tentatively menaced, saw poverty and moved on with a curse at ill-luck.

At last, Fiddlers Alley – a narrow street of tall, old houses which tottered so perilously that opposite gutters almost touched. Half-way down was a sign:

MALACHY MURPHY
BESPOKE TAILOR
REPAIRS & ALTERATIONS
A SPECIALITY

He climbed a flight of sagging, garbage-strewn steps and peered through the doorless opening at blackness. He ventured cautiously in. His shuffling feet met litter, filth and broken floor-boards, but his side-stretched hand encountered a door on which he knocked.

A bed creaked, footsteps slurred and the door opened, disclosing by candlelight a dirty, raddled young woman with greasy curls, a soiled dressing gown carelessly

273

thrown over scant and smelly attire.

She quirked a horrible smile. 'Hallo, sweet man. I wasn't expecting visitors so early. Come in and play.'

Conal swallowed and blushed. The suggestion accompanied by the stench from her and her room was revolting. 'I am looking for Mr Murphy.'

'May the poxy pigs piss on you!' she spat venomously and slammed the door in his face.

For a minute or two he stood, undecided, sickened by the foul smells, longing to get away, to be rid of this terrible town and out into the clean country air.

From the darkness came a cracked, high-pitched voice, 'Who the hell are you, and what do you want?'

It took him a few seconds to recover from his fright. 'My name is Conal O'Carran and I am seeking Malachy Murphy, the tailor.'

'Is that right! And what would you be wanting with this man Murphy?'

'A friend sent me to ask is his coat ready.'

The shutter of a lantern clicked and a light, dim enough, yet blinding after the darkness, shone into Conal's eyes, then travelled down to his waist and examined both hands. A pistol appeared in the beam.

'Softly now.' It was the breath of a whisper. 'Cross your arms on your chest. Do as I say!' The pistol jerked.

Conal obeyed and the man moved silently to one side.

'Walk straight ahead into the room!'

As he did so the light followed behind. He heard the door close.

'Stop!'

The pistol rammed into his back.

'What class of a coat was it your friend wanted?'

'A green one. Green as grass.'

There was a pause.

'There was such a coat ordered by a man named Campbell. Would that be the one?'

'No!'

'Well, then what does he call himself?'

'Are you Malachy Murphy?'

There was another pause, then light bloomed from a candle.

'Sit down at the table!'

Conal did so and the man sat opposite, the candle on the table between them, the pistol still menacing.

He was a powerfully built old man with bushes of white hair on his head, cheeks, lips, chin, eyebrows and sprouting from his nose and ears, so that his eyes shone like blue glass marbles from a tangle of cotton-wool.

'Say what you came to say!'

'Are you Malachy Murphy?'

The man hesitated, then, 'I am Malachy Murphy. Say what you have to say.'

It was Conal who hesitated now. 'Put out your hands,' he said.

The man looked surprised then laughed and pushed forward his hands. The finger-ends were rough-pocked with needle marks. 'You do well to match my caution in these bad times. Tell me your news from Alexander Montgomery.'

FORTY-NINE

The position of captain of the local Yeomanry suited Mark Portis ideally and he gave increasingly of his time to it. When it took him away from the house for long periods there was welcome relief for the women; but when, as happened with increasing frequency, he returned late at night with fellow-officers to be fed, their work was increased; and as the meal was always followed by late and very noisy drinking bouts their few hours of sleep were decreased.

Georgina complained unceasingly. It became more and more difficult to make her get up in the mornings and she became adept at avoiding work. She constantly demanded that they should leave, arguing that even a life of beggary was preferable to their present slavery. But Nuala refused. Apart from the utter madness of exchanging the little they had for the certainty of starvation, she had two powerful reasons: she wanted to be where Conal could find her, and she was daily more determined that somehow she would make Mark Portis pay.

One morning, however, Georgina absolutely refused to get up. Nuala left her for half an hour, then went back again.

'You must get up now,' she said anxiously. 'He will be up soon. We must humour him until we are ready to leave.'

'I am ready to leave now.'

'But we cannot leave without money.'

'Very well; but I refuse to be a skivvy any longer. I have been very foolish, but I shall be so no longer. You may tell him so from me. I shall get up when I please; and that is the end of the matter.'

She lay down and snuggled into the bedclothes.

Mark entered the kitchen promptly at six.

'Where is your mother?'

'In bed,' Nuala replied as she went on with the work of clearing up after the men.

'Pretending sickness, I suppose.'

'No. She says she will not work for you any longer.'

'She says what!' he roared. 'By God, I'll show her who's the master.'

He snatched up a thick walking stick and marched with great, stamping footsteps out of the kitchen and up the stairs to the attic. Nuala followed and heard him yell as he flung open the door, 'Get up, you lazy bitch!'

He thundered down and met Nuala on the landing.

'She is not in the bed. Nobody has slept in that bed.'

Nuala faced him, outwardly calm, inwardly trembling.

'It was impossible to sleep there, so we moved to this

floor.'

He stared incredulously. 'You moved! Without my permission! Why, you –' He raised the stick, but was stopped by a shriek.

'Mark Portis! Don't dare threaten my daughter.'

He swung to see Georgina standing in the bedroom doorway, swathed in blankets but holding herself as imperiously as if gowned for a Viceregal reception.

'So,' he said. 'You still think you can defy me. Now listen, the pair of you –'

'I have listened long enough to your bullying,' Georgina interrupted. 'And you do not impress me any longer, because I have remembered something about you – Markie!'

'Enough of this bloody nonsense –'

'Markie, boy!' she said sweetly. 'Do you remember why papa used to spank you? Do you, Markie, boy?'

Mark's face reddened and he looked confused for a moment, then the red turned almost purple with anger. His fingers were white clenching the stick, but he said nothing.

'So you do remember!' Georgina laughed. 'Shall I tell Nuala? And your workmen? Or better still, your neighbours, your gallant fellow-officers in the Yeomanry? They would be interested, wouldn't they? Just to think, the great Mark Portis spanked by his papa for –'

'That's enough!' He was red-faced and trembling.

She laughed again. 'Well, I am now returning to bed.'

She turned with great dignity, trailing blankets, entered the bedroom and closed the door.

Mark looked from the door to Nuala and back, amazingly unsure of himself. Then he muttered, 'Pair of bitches!' and ran down the stairs.

Nuala went into the bedroom. 'What was he punished for?'

Georgina raised her head slightly and peered with one eye over the covers. 'It is far too indelicate to tell to a young girl. All I will say is that his pants and his bedding had to be washed far more frequently than is usual.'

Nuala giggled.

'Nuala!' said her mother with mock indignation. 'How dare you!'

She settled herself in the bed again.

Nuala hesitated, then said, 'Well, if you are not going to work, neither am I.'

She undressed quickly and got into bed. She had crawled out of it reluctantly at five o'clock, but now, perversely, she was wide awake. There was only the great satisfaction of defying Mark.

As she lay staring at the ceiling, her thoughts inevitably flew to Conal and she daydreamed of his coming to find her. But if he did, what prospects were there for them? The best he could hope for would be to get work as a labourer. And if he did, and they were married... She had a vison of herself as a cottier's wife – barefoot, clad in rags, washing clothes in a stream, toiling on the land, living in a hovel. The prospect was terrifying. But what alternative was there? She thought and thought but could find none.

At last hunger conquered misery and she got up and left her mother asleep. The kitchen was deserted and she could find nothing to eat. She went out and found Judy in the dairy.

'I'm hungry, Judy. Are there no potatoes left?'

Judy looked up from her scouring. Her face crumpled and large tears welled from her eyes. With a wail she flung her apron over head and wept uncontrollably.

It took much hugging and comforting to quieten her. Then, haltingly, she told that Mark had blamed her for ever admitting them to the house. He had beaten her and had flung the remaining potatoes into the pig-swill so that she had been without breakfast. Then he had dismissed Mag Kinsella. In spite of her hunger and her bruised and aching back she had been making frantic efforts to do all the work herself.

Although she realised that she was doing exactly as her uncle had intended, Nuala set to work and they slaved through the morning. Her mother had gained a victory of a sort, but *she* was worse off than ever. Yet the thought of his cruelty only increased her determination to find some way to make him pay. Later, as she was cleaning his room, she stood in front of the black oak box. It was locked. Somehow she would get the key.

The workmen had become accustomed to Nuala and they talked freely at meal-times. It was thus she heard of the happenings in the north and of the many people who had been forced to flee. She had a pang of fear for Conal's safety, but comforted herself that if harm had come to him she would have known instinctively; and she drew further comfort from the hope that he would be amongst the many who had been driven south and that he might come to her soon.

Life was a little lighter then. Her eyes were forever straying to the windows which looked towards the road. When she was in the yard she would often snatch a few seconds to run to a point from which she could see the road, looking not only for Conal but for anybody from the north who might have news of him. It was a foolish hope, she knew. The house was far from any main route. Then she heard that there were people from the north in the area and she determined to go to Mass on the next Sunday.

In Wexford, as in the rest of Ireland, the Protestant population had never been as great as it was in the north and old laws against the practice of the Catholic religion had gradually been relaxed. So, in Boolavogue, the nearest village, there was a chapel of sorts, scarcely bigger than a house, so that the bulk of the congregation had to stand outside.

The priest, Father John Murphy, was a powerfully built, red-faced man, a gentleman of some learning, having studied at Seville University as well as having had seminary training. During the Mass he left the altar and stood on a large stone at the doorway. He spoke in a deep, strong voice.

'My dear people. My dear, suffering people. I would remind you today of what you say so often in your prayers! "Forgive us our trespasses, as we forgive those who trespass against us." We pray to the good God that He will forgive us for the many times we have sinned against Him, because, we say, we forgive those who commit wrongs against us. But do we forgive others? Do we, in particular, forgive our enemies? If you cannot truthfully answer, "Yes," then you are lying to God every time you say that prayer. And if you are lying to God, how can you expect His forgiveness? What hope is there of eternal salvation?

'God knows, many wrongs have been done to the people of Ireland. Wrongs in the past, wrongs in the present. Day after terrible day wrongs are committed against us. The people of the north, some of whom are amongst us now, have suffered grievously; and, signs on it, we here will soon be called upon to suffer as terribly as they.

'I have no good word to say for those evil men who have used their power and position to rob and pillage and persecute the poor people of this unfortunate land. But let you remember that their wickedness is a much greater offence against the goodness of God than it is against man.

'I know well, and I am saddened by the knowledge, that there is a terrible spirit abroad in Ireland. Men everywhere in secret are planning rebellion. To this end, I know they are stealing, making and storing arms.

'I appeal to you. Is this the way of forgiveness?

'You must all know that the Viceroy, Lord Camden, has proclaimed that all who surrender their arms and who take the Oath of Allegiance before the end of the present month will be freely pardoned. I implore you to take advantage of that offer. Give up all rebellious ideas. Surrender your arms.

'Men! I too am a man. I too am an Irishman. I love Ireland as much as any man. I feel for Ireland in her suffering. I feel for the pain of every man, woman and child of this nation until the tears rise up to choke me. Yet I must say to you, "Forgive your enemies!"

'Brethren, let us kneel and pray for those who persecute us.'

There was a shuffling and rustling as all sank to their knees. Father Murphy began to pray. But amongst the men many sidelong looks were exchanged, and bowed heads and joined hands did not mean that they joined in the prayer. It was quite right, they thought, for the priest to say these things. But that did not alter their plight. At that very moment it was likely that the Yeos were scouring the roads, perhaps searching and burning down their cabins; and all would risk death on the road home.

After Mass the men gathered away from the woman and, after much discussion, the general decision was that, dangerous as it was to hold on to their arms, they would do so in case the French landed and rebellion started. If it did not come before the end of the month they would surrender their arms.

As Nuala was searching the crowd she was greeted by a loud shout, 'Well, and how are you at all?' It was Mag Kinsella.

'And how is Pontius Pilate Portis? There's as fine a bloody gentleman as ever robbed a starving child. God forgive me for the day that's in it!'

Nuala was delighted to see her again and asked how she had been managing without her job.

'Ah, you may be easy on that score. 'Twill take a better man than that one to beat Mag Kinsella. But, by the same token, and for all Father Murphy's holy words, God bless him, the Kinsellas will not be forgetting Mister Mark Portis when the time comes. Although when the time comes, as come it will, there's many here today who will head the rush to slit the gizzard of that hairy sinner!'

'Do you think there will be trouble?' asked Nuala anxiously.

'Ah, for God's sake, girl! Will a duck swim? But talking of your man reminded me of something he warned me I was to forget all about. It'll be a couple of weeks past, a lad came late into the yard asking for you. A groom, he was, from some doctor or other. I misremember the name. Just as he was asking me, up comes the bold Mark and asks his business. He has money, he says, for you. Money from this doctor.'

'Doctor Portland,' said Nuala.

'That's the name! God, aren't you great. Begod, if I'd half your brains I'd best the world. Anyhow, there's for you. What d'you think of that?'

'But the money? What happened to the money?'

Mag smote herself on the side of the skull. 'There I go again. Amn't I the divil's own daughter for forgetting. Well, your man hooshed me out of it and told me to wait for him in the stable. And, sure, being ever an obedient girl, for all the neighbours may say to the contrary, didn't I go into the stable and strain my eyes and ears through a big crack. I didn't hear what was said, but I did see the groom hand over a little bag and I'll swear I heard the ring of money from it as your man put it into his pocket. And when he'd hooshed the lad away, into the stable he came and threatened me with blue murder if I breathed a word of it to you.

'So now you have it. And I'd like to see him try to lay a finger on me for the telling of it.'

Her attention was suddenly distracted. 'Paddy Keogh!' she yelled. She ran a few paces, stopped, turned, waved and, 'Goodbye now!' she shouted. Then she was away after the young man. Catching up with him she gave him a staggering smack on the back.

He turned round, his face twisted with pain, one hand trying vainly to reach over his shoulder to soothe the injury.

'In the name of God, Mag Kinsella, are you for killing me or what?'

She shrieked with laughter. 'What was it, only a love tap. Come here to me till I give you a big hug!'

Paddy Keogh ran, with Mag whooping after him.

Nuala, forgetting the reason for coming to the chapel, had begun to hurry through the crowds when she heard northern accents amongst a group. She stopped and spoke to them. They could give her no news, but a woman sent her husband running after others whom she thought might know. He returned with another man.

'God forgive me for the hurt that may be in it, girl dear,' he said, 'and how much truth is in it I'm not able to tell; but I did hear that the Yeos destroyed Duncarran and murdered every soul in the place.' Seeing the horror in Nuala's face, 'Ah, forgive me, girl, forgive me!'

The woman put her arms round Nuala. 'It may not be the truth, or at the least, not the whole of it, please God.'

Nuala pulled herself away. 'I don't believe it!' she cried fiercely. 'I don't believe he is dead. He can't be dead! I would know it, if he was.' She appealed to the woman, 'Wouldn't I?'

'Of course you would, girleen. And we'll all say a prayer that he'll come to you soon.'

She found herself walking slowly along the road home with the words, 'He's not dead! He's not dead!' repeating themselves endlessly in her mind. She stopped, clenched her fists and shook them in front of her body. 'He is not dead,' she said aloud. 'And that's all about it!'

Immediately came the thought that he would come to her soon. She began walking quickly. She had to plan for when he came. She remembered her uncle's theft of her money and she was almost running.

She actually passed it. Then she stopped in the deserted road and stared fixedly ahead. Surely she had been mistaken. She turned and looked.

'Oh, my God!' Her hands flew to shield her eyes. 'But perhaps...' she thought. Slowly she lowered her hands. Protruding from the ditch was the body of a young man, his skull split by a terrible gash.

She turned away and stumbled for a few yards; but her hands clasped to her mouth could not still her heaving stomach. She vomited violently again and again, weeping with shock and with disgust at her dripping hands. At last she regained control and she stumbled on. She could not go back, could not even look back. In any case the man must be dead. There was nothing she could do for him. She must get help from the house. She had gone some distance before she realised that she was staggering along with her arms wide to keep her soiled hands away from her body. There was a small flow of water in the bottom of the ditch and there she cleansed them, scouring them repeatedly with wet sand. It was a long time before she could bring herself to use them to scoop up water to clean her face.

She flung open the kitchen door with a crash. It was empty, but Judy came running in from the hall.

'Oh, thank God you're back!' Judy cried.

'Judy! Oh, Judy!' Tears ran down her face. She had not even heard what Judy said. 'Oh, my God, Judy! It's terrible. There's a poor young man lying brutally murdered in the ditch.'

'Jesus, Mary and Joseph!' Judy whispered. Then she whirled and pointed to the hall. ''Twas them did it. They're in the dining-room now. The Yeos. He was out with them this morning hunting arms. They came in shouting and halloo-ing. Oh, delighted with themselves and boasting of the great deeds they'd done. They've been drinking ever since. And, oh, Nuala, I was near to forgetting the worst of it. They have your mother in there. They're after pouring drink into her.'

Nuala, her mind still filled with the horror, was slow to understand. Then the murder, Mark's theft of her money, his cruelty, her fears for Conal and the treatment of her mother joined with all the family misfortunes into one huge, overwhelming blow delivered by her uncle against her and produced so violent an eruption of hatred that she raced out of the kitchen under a blind, vengeance-seeking impulse.

From the dining-room came a loud burst of drunken laughter. She flung open the door so violently that it crashed back against the wall. There was immediate silence. The eyes of the crowd of men who were lolling round the table turned towards her in surprise; but her mother continued a tipsy dance on the hearth-rug, stopping only to gulp from a tumbler of brandy. The men and her uncle were in uniform and were all obviously

284

drunk. She saw her uncle, his face twisted with anger, making vain attemps to stand; but she ignored him.

'Mama!'

Georgina halted her crazy pirouetting, stumbled and turned slowly. She grinned loosely and licked her lips.

''lo, Nuala.' Then, remembering what was expected of a lady, 'Gemmen, present m'daughter, Nuala.'

All were staring with owlish appreciation, some lurched to their feet and began advancing towards her with outstretched hands. She brushed them aside as she advanced to the fireplace. She snatched the glass from her mother and flung it into the fire with a crash of glass and a whooosh! as the brandy ignited. She gripped her mother's arm.

Mark was leaning forward in his chair, an outstretched finger menacing her. 'Bitch! Bitch! Bitch!' he kept repeating.

She glared at him. 'You filthy, murderous pig! I'll talk to you when you are sober. But in the meantime remember this. You will pay, and pay dearly, for what you have done to us! Come, mama.'

She attempted to lead Georgina away, but she was reluctant and several of the Yeos were now standing round them.

In blazing anger she cried, 'If there is a single gentleman amongst you let him clear a way for us!'

Even their drunken muzziness was penetrated and they shuffled aside. Half-pulling, half-carrying her mother she made her way to the door, and managed it with surprising dignity. She turned in the doorway. 'You may now continue your celebration of murder!' she said with contempt.

She was surprised to find herself with her mother in their bedroom without any recollection of how she had dragged the flaccid body up the stairs. Georgina flopped on the bed and began chanting, 'Georgie's a naughty gel. Georgie's a naughty gel!' beating time with clapping hands and tittering between each assertion.

'Oh, be quiet, you stupid woman!'

But Georgina continued her chant.

'Be quiet, I said!' Nuala shrieked, and she rushed at her mother and slapped her face.

Then she started back in horror. Georgina stared in momentarily sane surprise, then fell back on the pillows and began to sob drunkenly.

Nuala ran and embraced her. 'Oh, I am sorry, mama. I am sorry. It was not your fault.'

But even as she spoke her mother fell asleep.

Nuala pulled the quilt over her, then stood for a long time trying to bring some clarity to the turmoil of her mind. At length, out of it all, came one word, 'Pay!' which produced an immediate idea.

She ran to her uncle's room, slipped inside and bolted the door. Mark's work-day suit lay on the black oak box. She felt in the pockets and, with a thrill of triumph, found a bunch of keys.

Swiftly she tried key after key until, delightfully, almost magically it seemed, one turned. She lifted the heavy lid. Two suits of clothes, several rapiers, a case of duelling pistols, then packets of documents – far too many for quick examination. Her fingers, thrusting down through these, felt the rough cloth of a bag, squeezed it and caressed the round hardness of coins. She felt all round the box. The floor of it was almost covered with money bags. 'Wealth!' she told herself joyfully.

Her immediate impulse was to take them all and flee from the house. But a tug at one bag disclosed the weight of it. Even if she could take a carriage and horses, even if she could get all the bags and her mother into it without being seen, where could they go? And how would Conal find her? The box held the solution of her future plans. No doubt of that. But there was nothing to be done at the moment.

She put everything back as she had found it, locked the box and replaced the keys. Then she patted, caressed the box and left the room.

FIFTY

'Wake up. Wake up, damn you!'

Conal came to consciousness to find himself being punched by Malachy Murphy. From somewhere outside sounded muffled uproar.

'Move, lad, if you value your life!'

Still half-dazed, Conal was pushed out into the dark hall. The noise came from the street, loud, hollow banging, shouting, screaming, racing of footsteps, shots and more screams.

'Up the stairs! Quietly, both of you, for God's sake,' Murphy whispered urgently.

Conal then realised that another man was with them. They had just turned on to the second floor landing when the front door burst in with a crash which shook the house, and a large body of shouting men rushed in. There was no longer any need for quietness. They raced up the next two flights, ignoring the opened doors and the bleary-eyed questioners.

Murphy led them into a small attic with ruinous floor and walls. He dragged an old trunk from a corner. 'Up there!' he said, pointing, 'The trap in the ceiling!'

He hopped on to the trunk and lifted and slid the trap aside. Shots sounded from below. He hauled himself up, disappeared, then his anxious face peered down.

'You come next, Corny. Give him a lift, Conal.'

Conal lifted the man's slight weight on to the trunk and pushed him up to Murphy's helping hands. As soon as it was clear, he began to mount the trunk.

'No!' Murphy whispered urgently, even as he hauled the other man out of sight. 'Put back the trunk in the corner and jump for it.'

Conal, acutely aware of the pounding feet on the stairs, took the trunk back to the corner, then leaped and gripped the edges of the trap. With the help of the other two he wriggled through.

'Sit on the trap,' whispered Murphy. 'And for God's sake don't either of you put your feet through the plaster.'

Even as he spoke footsteps reached their landing, hammered into their attic, paused and retreated.

'Nobody up here, sergeant!'

Foosteps descending, shouts and noise abating, then a louder shout, the wild shriek of a woman: 'No, no! Oh, God, no!' A gurgling scream of pain from a man, ending abruptly. A high-pitched wailing, wailing, wailing. Retreating footsteps, and after them a despairing scream: 'God curse you, you murdering bastards!' Then nothing but agonised sobbing.

'Thanks be to God!' Murphy breathed.

'We must go down to that poor woman,' said Conal.

'Whisht!' Murphy hissed. 'Keep your voices low. They could have left some behind to lie in wait. Anyhow, only God can help her now.'

'Are we to squat here, then, whilst people are being murdered?' Conal demanded in an angry whisper.

'Easy, lad, easy,' the stranger said, laying a hand on his arm. ''Tis hard, I know, but we're helpless against armed police and soldiers.'

'This is Corny Brady,' Murphy said. 'A member of the Executive of the United Irishmen. 'Twas he came to warn us. And, begod, we owe your lives to you, Corny.'

Corny gave a low, bitter laugh. ''Twas not alone to warn you I came, Malachy, boy. I was needing a hiding place myself and knew you were the best man to give me one.'

Conal learned then that large bodies of constables and soldiers, organised by Major Sirr, head of the Intelligence Section at Dublin Castle, had been raiding throughout Dublin during the night. Nearly all the leading members of the Executive, including Lord Edward Fitzgerald, had been arrested, as well as many ordinary members. The Newgate Prison was full of them. In addition they had uncovered large stores of arms. The informers had worked well for their Judas money.

Brady had passed by the Customs House on his way and told them that many ordinary prisoners, most arrested only on suspicion, were being held inside.

'And, begod, lads, the sounds coming out of that place were like the cries of the damned in Hell. A man told me what I didn't believe at first, that the soldiers had a new way of treating any with a cropped head. They take a canvas cap, smear it with boiling pitch and clap it down on to the man's skull!

'I tell you I disbelieved the man who told me. But not for long. We heard the most horrible screaming and a man came racing from the building, a flaming torch from head to foot. They must have poured pitch or turpentine or something over him and set him alight. The poor, tortured creature raced, blazing and screaming, across the quay and threw himself into the River Liffey.'

'And is nobody doing anything to stop this barbarism?' Conal demanded. 'There must be thousands of men with arms. Now is the time to rise!'

'Oh, there are men, true enough. And there are still arms that have not been found, true enough. But the men who have escaped will be scattered and in hiding. Who is to find them? Who is to gather them? Who is to lead them?'

'Well, we are three, for a start. And there must be some of the leaders. Where is Mr Wolfe Tone?'

'In Paris, trying to get another French fleet. If he does, itself, I'm thinking there'll be few to meet him when he lands. Make up your mind to it, lad, there'll be no rising. It's finished before ever it began. May all informers rot in hell!'

Conal squatted uncomfortably on the splintery rafters and stared into the gloom. Once again he felt that the world had collapsed around him. All his hopes and plans had been trampled by the inexorable might of his enemies. Anger rose in him.

'What of the people?' he demanded. 'Now they will be

worse off than ever. Yet there are still far more of them than there are landlords and their lackeys.'

'God help them, is all I can say,' said Murphy.

'To hell with that for a prayer! They'd be better dead than living as slaves. They must rise. Now. Before it is too late.'

'Ah, for God's sake! Here we are perched like hens in a roost, afraid to go out into the streets. What can we do?'

'We can get down from here for a start. Everything is quiet now.'

'And where will we go?'

'You find yourselves a better hiding place, if you can. I'll go back to the north. I'll find men who will fight.'

'What men? Don't you know yourself that they've been slaughtered, or captured, or driven out in their thousands! And, what's more, to get back north you'd need to cross the river. How will you do that, with every bridge guarded?'

Joyfully, Conal saw the opportunity to decide what he had secretly wanted to decide. 'Then I'll go south. I'll find men there!' Unspoken was the happy thought, 'And I'll find Nuala.'

'Why would you think to find men there?' asked Murphy.

But Brady shushed him. 'The lad cannot stay in this town, Malachy. Put him on the road to the south.'

They left their hiding place and crept down through the gloomy house. The street was deserted. No light showed anywhere. Like alley-cats they slunk along beside the tottering walls. Murphy led them by narrow, stinking ways, in darkness and stealth, until they came to the corner of an alley where he told Conal to wait whilst he took Brady to safety. But scarcely had they gone when the still darkness was shattered by the clattering of hoofs. From the black buildings around figures erupted and ran, and Conal ran with them.

Realising that he was running as one of a crowd, sure to attract attention, he branched from them, only to join another group. There was a red glow in the sky ahead and they all veered away from it; but he ran harder and gradually left them behind, all but one man.

This man gasped, 'The canal is ahead. We'll need to be careful.'

Conal did not understand until the man caught his arm and halted him. 'The bridge is just ahead. They could have militia guarding it.'

They were standing in the deep shadow of trees which hung over the roadway from the garden of a house.

'Where are you heading?' the man asked.

'South. Wexford,' said Conal, but in his mind he said 'To Nuala!'

They crept forward in the shadows until only the width of the canal bank was between them and the bridge, which was only faintly less shadowed.

'What do you think?' Conal whispered.

'Damned if I know. Whisht!'

From behind them came the sound of horses. Without thought they ran across and on to the bridge, fearing at any moment to be met with shots from the darkness. But the bridge was empty. Relief flooded them as they ran down the far side and along the road in the shadow of the trees.

'Hold up,' the man gasped. 'We're safe enough now, I'm thinking.'

He dropped into the grass at the roadside and Conal sat panting beside him.

'Be the hokey, that was close! Look back there. Do you see their torches on the bridge?'

Far down the road Conal saw the wavering torches. He remembered the night Duncarran had been destroyed and again he felt anger and shame because he was so weak against the strength of the enemy. God, for a thousand armed and obedient men to lead in a charge back into that town, to trample and slash and utterly destroy those contemptuous brutes!

'What ails you? Where the hell are you going?'

Conal found that the man was holding him and realised that, unconsciously, he had risen and started back for the bridge. He groaned with frustration.

'We'd do well to clear out of this. Those lads might well take a notion to ride along here.'

They began walking.

'Have you a place to go in the south?'

Unbidden, the answer came, 'Enniscorthy. How far is that?'

'God, I wouldn't know. A hell of a piece off, I'd say.'

They walked in silence for a long time, then the man said, 'I've to take this turning now, so I'll bid you goodbye and safe journey.'

'Oh. You're sure I'm on the right road?'

'I'm sure you're heading south, and that's the only sure I have. If you keep along this road, it will bring you into Wicklow and the County Wexford lies somewhere beyond that.'

Conal walked away. He had gone several paces before he recollected, stopped and turned. The man was staring after him.

'Thank you,' said Conal. 'Thank you for all your help. God go with you.'

FIFTY-ONE

The Orange Order arrived in County Wexford when the North Cork Militia were quartered there under Lord Kingsborough, himself an Orangeman. Although most of the privates were Catholics who, in their utter poverty, had been tempted into joining by the prospect of clothes and regular meals, the officers and NCOs were Orangemen and they swaggered about flaunting medals and ribbons of the Organisation and soon enrolled most of the Yeomanry and Protestant civilians in the Order.

Amongst the Catholics wild rumours ran that soon they would meet the same fate as the people of the north. Propagandists of the United Irishmen distributed broad-sheets displaying supposed Orange oaths. That they swore 'to destroy all Catholics and wade up to their knees in Popish blood'; 'that they would be ready at a moment's notice to burn all Catholic chapels and meeting places'; 'that the skins of Papists would make drumheads for the Yeomanry'.

Whatever the misbeliefs of the people, the North Cork Militia soon gave them real cause for fear. Every man they found with a cropped head had clapped on to it a canvas cap into which molten pitch had been poured. Often the pitch ran down into the man's eyes, blinding him; and when the pitch had cooled it was impossible to remove the cap without tearing out the hair and bringing parts of the burnt scalp with it.

One sergeant of the North Corks earned himself the nickname of 'Tom the Devil' because of his ingenuity in inventing new tortures. Tiring of the pitch-cap, he cut the victims' hair closer, in the shape of a cross, snipping off bits of the ears as he worked; then he rubbed moistened gun-powder all over the scalp and set it alight. Alternatively, he put a lighted candle to the man's head until all the hair was singed off and the scalp was a mass of blisters.

As it became obvious that the officers and the magistrates ignored the torturing, the North Corks took to slicing off ears and noses before turning the poor wretches loose. They also carried on the war against 'the wearing of the green'. Any man found wearing an article with the slightest trace of green in it was flogged unmercifully. Women, no matter what class, who were seen wearing the colour were insulted and brutally attacked and had the offending article of clothing torn from them in public. The Militia got great entertainment from examining women's undergarments in the open street.

Until that time the United Irishmen had made very slow progress in Wexford, but terror of the Orangemen drove thousands into their ranks, hoping to find the protection they could not get from the law. But they dared not keep arms in their houses from fear of the frequent searches; and, as these searches increased and terror was visited on the people whether arms were found or not, thousands deserted their homes at night and went to sleep in woods or on hillsides. Then the Yeomanry, disappointed at finding no victims during their night raids, took to patrolling the roads by day. People could not go to market without the danger of being arrested and imprisoned or deported without trial. Even when they were working on the land they were in danger of being shot. Less and less work was done, fewer and fewer people took produce to market, so the price of foodstuffs in the towns soared. But the Yeos and the Militia simply went out into the country and took what they wanted, and the owner was lucky if he escaped without hurt to himself, his family or his house.

In the towns the same system was in force. Men suspected of complicity with the United Irishmen were turned out of their homes and their furniture was burned in the street. Merchants showing the slightest opposition to, or criticism of, the Government which was ruining their trade were fined heavily and imprisoned. Writers, editors and printers of anything considered critical of the Government were imprisoned.

In spite of the efforts of the Yeos and Militia, the Government decided that arms were not being surrendered or captured in sufficient numbers or with sufficient speed. General Abercrombie was given the job of pacification. At the beginning of April 1798 he toured the southern counties, issued a proclamation that all arms must be surrendered within ten days, then returned to Dublin to report that the military were to blame for the greater part of the unrest. He was immediately relieved and on 23 April General Lake was appointed in his place.

Lake's first act was to place the whole country under

Martial Law. He then let loose the soldiers, Militia and Yeomanry to act as they pleased in their search for suspects and arms.

On 27 April an assembly of Wexford magistrates at Gorey proclaimed the county to be in a state of rebellion and empowered themselves to act as they thought fit to restore peace.

The Militia and the Yeomanry were urged to greater efforts. From then on bands of them scoured the country with portable whipping triangles and gallows. Every house found empty was burned. Every person they caught was questioned and, unless definite information was immediately obtained, they were tortured. Ingenuity produced new methods. They would hang a man, take him down before he died, question him again, then hang him again, repeating the process until he either gave information or died. 'Picketing' also became popular. A man would be hung by one arm with all his weight bearing on one bare foot on a pointed stake.

Lake's soldiers rounded up the entire population of a district and made them go down on their knees to witness sons being compelled to bear their fathers on their backs whilst they were being whipped, and then being made to change places with them. Often floggings of a thousand lashes were given. Men were burned to death in tar barrels. And all was for the edification and pacification of a helpless people.

The only possibility of safety for the people was to hide on the hillsides and in the woods. But, in spite of this, it was a daily occurrence in Wexford that already tortured men who had been condemned to deportation were carted like pigs to the market in trains of a dozen to twenty car-loads at a time.

FIFTY-TWO

All Mark Portis' workmen had vanished and only Nuala and Judy were left to do the work of the farm. Judy herself would have gone but Nuala persuaded her that she was safer in the house than anywhere else.

There were always Yeomanry in the house, shouting to be fed, bringing mounds of washing to be done, tracking mud and horse-droppings. Quite early, however, they had been taught to leave Nuala and Judy alone. Mark, constantly infuriated by the sight of his untended fields, was very conscious of his need of the women to run the house. One evening, arriving home hungry and tired, he had shouted in vain for them. Going upstairs he discovered that they had locked themselves in a room where they were being besieged by three drunken Yeos. In a white fury he drove the three downstairs and out into the yard where the rest of the troop were caring for their horses after a day's ride.

'Ah, now, Mr Portis, I mean Captain, sir.' One of the drunkards turned towards him with an ingratiating grin. 'Just a little fun, sir.'

Mark whipped out a pistol and shot the man in the face.

There was immediate silence and attention in the yard.

'All officers to me!' Mark commanded. 'Sergeant White. Put these two on their knees.'

A sergeant ran forward and thrust the two white-faced, quickly sobered men to their knees on the cobbles.

'This is my house!' Mark shouted. 'Not a peasant's cabin. You will respect my house and everybody in it. To ensure that you do, witness what happens to those who molest my women-folk!'

He plucked a pistol from the belt of each of the nearest officers, walked forward and, with great deliberation, shot the two kneeling men.

He returned to the group of officers and said, 'Thank you, gentlemen.' He turned about. 'Sergeant White!'

The sergeant sprang to attention. 'Sir!'

'Bury them.'

FIFTY-THREE

From the hiding place in Mark Portis' hay-loft, into which he had crept in the middle of the night, Conal watched the Yeomanry prepare for the day. He watched the inspection which followed and saw them mount and ride off. The hoofbeats died away. The yard lay somnolent under the warm May morning sun, the quiet clucking of the hens, the occasional grunt of a pig, the bawl of a greedy calf, the buzz of questing insects and the mellow coo of doves all insisting that the world was a place of quiet peace.

As he watched, a female figure appeared from the kitchen door – a drab-looking creature with tousled hair and wet tattered skirts flapping round her bare feet. Her head wearily bent, she carried two brimming buckets across the yard. He wondered if he could risk calling to this kitchen-maid. Then he stared, scrambled across the hay, dropped to the floor and ran to the door.

'Nuala!'

She stopped, whipped from apathy by the urgent whisper. Her eyes darted round the yard.

'Here!' He showed himself briefly.

Slowly she put down the buckets and went, careful step by careful step, peering anxiously, ready to turn and fly.

'It's me. Conal.'

'Conal!' she cried joyfully and she raced across, through the door and into his arms.

Much time had passed without any coherent speech between them when they were suddenly roused by a woman's voice anxiously calling, 'Nuala! In God's name, where are you, girl?'

Nuala sat up in the hay. 'Judy,' she whispered. She pressed her hand softly against his lips. 'Wait here, love.' She jumped up and ran out into the yard.

Conal was back in his hiding place when she returned with Judy. 'Conal, where are you? It's safe.'

He dropped down.

'Dear God!' said Judy. 'You look like a wild man.'

Nuala examined him for the first time. 'You do so, Conal,' she said anxiously. 'Whatever have you been doing to yourself?'

He told them quickly of what had happened in the north and in Dublin and of how he had travelled south through the mountains, avoiding the villages and towns, walking by night, sleeping in hiding by day and robbing hen-roosts and kitchens to eat.

He washed under the pump and Nuala brought him food as soon as he was in hiding again. She was terrified for his safety. The Yeomanry could return at any time. But he was sure that as long as he could remain hidden there was no safer place in the countryside.

'Stay in your hiding place, then,' she said. 'I must go back to help Judy. I will try to come to you later. We must talk and plan.'

The troopers returned in the middle of the afternoon in a great state of excitement. Conal could hear them quite plainly and his heart leaped at their news that rebellion had broken out in County Kildare. They ate quickly, remounted and left.

Almost immediately he saw Nuala running across the yard and he went down to meet her.

'Conal, Conal, we must leave here immediately before they return.'

'Where could we go? They would catch us on the road.'

'I have everything planned,' she said excitedly. 'There is a fine carriage and horses in the stable. We will dress in our finest clothes. You can take some of Mark's. We will drive to Wexford and take ship to England and he will never find us.'

'Wait, love, wait. Even if I wished to leave Ireland, we have no money, and I don't –'

'But that is the most important thing!' she burst in eagerly. 'I am so excited I forgot about the money. There is a great box full of money upstairs. It's all ours.'

'Ours? Where did you get it?'

Quickly she explained about Mark's black box. 'There's more than enough to take us anywhere we want to go. Perhaps we should go to the Americas. There we should be free and safe. You could study to be a lawyer as you wanted, or we could get a fine farm. Oh, Conal, my darling, hurry, hurry!' She flung her arms round his neck and kissed him excitedly.

He had to struggle to release himself. 'Nuala, it is not our money. It belongs to your uncle.'

'It does not!' she said indignantly. 'Not all of it, anyway, and probably not any of it. There's the money mama inherited from grandpapa –'

'You don't even know –'

'And there's the money Dr Portland sent, which he stole from me. And there's all that he owes us for the hard work we've had to do. And he probably stole the rest of it. He deserves to lose it all. Oh, besides, Conal, Conal, Conal,' she was eagerly kissing and caressing him, 'it is the solution to all our problems. Away from here, we'll be married and start a new life, a wonderful –'

'Nuala!' he said sharply. 'I will not start a new life on stolen money. And I will not leave Ireland. I came to Wexford to help to organise a rising.'

'No! Oh, God, no!' Her eyes were wide with fear. 'Don't even talk of it. You have seen the Yeomanry. You know what they have been doing. If they saw you, they would kill you instantly.' Again she clung to him, striving with all the force of her love. 'It is madness, Conal. It would be the end of everything.'

'It would be the beginning of everything!' His eyes

glowed with fervour. 'The beginning of peace and hope of a decent life for the people. And it has started already in Kildare. The whole country will rise now.'

She drew back and looked coldly at him. 'You don't love me,' she stated.

'Don't love you! You know well I do.'

'If you did, you would not even think of risking your life in a stupid rebellion which cannot possibly succeed. You would think of nothing but helping me to punish Mark Portis for his cruelty to mama and me. You would come away with us now.'

'Nuala, you are asking me to run away, to desert my country and my people at the time that I am most needed, to throw aside all that I have ever wanted – the chance to regain my lands. How can you ask me to sacrifice that?'

'Can you sacrifice me?' she asked coldly. 'Think on that, Conal. Perhaps it would be unwise to go today. It might be better to start tomorrow morning shortly after the Yeomanry have left. It may even be that they will be sent to Kildare. So I shall leave you to think, Conal, and to choose.'

She turned abruptly and ran back to the kitchen.

Late that night he slid down a rope at the back of the barn and quietly made his way across the fields and eventually up a scrubby hillside, softly whistling 'The Shan Van Voght' as he went.

He found men, or rather they found him and almost strangled him before he could convince them that he was a friend. But when he tried to discuss a rising in support of the men of Kildare he met opposition from them all.

The Wexford magistrates, they told him, had issued a proclamation that every man should come forward, surrender his arms and take the oath of allegiance within fourteen days. All who did so would be given a certificate guaranteeing their safety. Failing this, the military would be quartered free on the people. In some places this had already happened and the inhabitants had been forced to act as slaves to the soldiers; and many a man had died trying to save his wife or daughters from the rapacity of their guests.

Every magistrate's home was being besieged by men wishing to give up their pikes and take the oath. Hundreds had no pikes to surrender, either because they had already handed them in or because they had never had them. These too had clamoured to take the oath, but because of the numbers only those with pikes could be dealt with. So there was the amazing spectacle of men offering all they had to buy a pike so that they could surrender it and obtain the magical certificate.

It was then late on Friday night and the proclamation expired on the morrow, Saturday 25 May.

Conal argued that they could not believe the promises of the magistrates, that the certificates would be ignored by the Yeos and the military and that their only chance of ending the terror was by banding together to fight.

'For God's sake, man, fight with what?' they asked. 'There's not a single pike left to any one of us here.'

'Then we'll raid a magistrate's house and get pikes. Aye, and guns and ammunition too. If once we make a start thousands will join us.'

'In my bloody eye, they will. Every man is thinking only that his wife and children are starving and homeless. All any of us wants is to get back to the peace and shelter of our own places. Tell us this: have you a wife and family?'

'Well, I haven't, but –'

'So! Talk is easy for the likes of you. Clear to hell out of this and leave us be. At first light we'll all go down and take the oath.'

Miserably Conal crept back to his hiding place. In the morning he saw hundreds of men advance on Portis' house shouting that they had come to take the oath. Mark's answer was to set the two hounds on them; and when this was not sufficient the Yeomanry charged out with drawn sabres and scattered them over the country-side, leaving several dead behind.

Later, when the Yeomanry had ridden off, Nuala came again to the barn and called to him. When he came down she asked him, 'Well, have you decided?'

'Nuala, love,' he begged, 'have you no better greeting than that?'

'I have spent a long, sleepless night thinking and worrying. You call me "love". You expect love from me, and it is yours. But I expect from you not merely words, but action – protection, care! For the sake of our love, Conal, I beg you to take me and mama away from this, now!'

His face was contorted with indecision. 'Nuala, my love, I... Please, let me... Listen, tomorrow is Whit Sunday. After Mass I'll talk to the men and be guided by what they say. If their decision is against a rising, I'll come back and take you away.'

Her face was immediately radiant. She hugged and kissed him. 'Then we shall go tomorrow. Judy says that all the men are against a rising. You saw them yourself trying to take the oath this morning.'

'I did. And I saw how they were treated. We had better understand each other, Nuala. When I say that I will take you away, I do not mean that I will take your uncle's money. I will take you to Wicklow. We shall be safe amongst the mountains. I shall start a school there...'

He was stopped by her horrified expression.

'A school!' she shrieked. 'What kind of school? In a filthy cabin? I am not a peasant and I refuse to live like one. For months I have been treated as a slave and I have withstood it, strengthened by the certainty that you would come and rescue me, and that I would be revenged and rewarded at the same time. I mean to have that money and to live in decency. I will not go with you to live in a hovel!'

He stared at the stranger she had become, unable to think of anything to say to her, then he turned and made his way back up to the loft.

'How dare you leave me!' she shrieked. 'How dare you! Come back!'

When he showed no sign of coming down she shouted, 'You will come down quickly enough when the Yeos rout

302

you out!' And she ran out into the yard.

Judy caught up with her as she ran into the kitchen. 'Nuala, Nuala!' she exclaimed. 'God forgive you for what you said! What, in God's name, has got into you, girl?'

She fell weeping into Judy's arms. 'Oh, Judy, I love him. Truly, I would go anywhere with him, live anywhere with him. But why must he be so stupidly obstinate?'

Judy shook her. 'You little goose! Go back there now and tell him.'

Nuala looked at her and smiled, then suddenly laughed. 'Let him worry for a time. It will be good for him.'

'You are a cruel girl. Anyhow, it could be he's gone.'

'Gone!' She was alarmed. 'No. Do you really think . . . ?' She raced out of the kitchen calling, 'Conal, Conal!'

Judy followed and watched her disappear into the barn. Some moments later she walked slowly out, tears running down her face. 'Judy, oh Judy, he's gone from me.'

FIFTY-FOUR

Conal climbed back to the loft, furiously angry with Nuala and even more angered by frustration at the thought that Portis and his Yeos were at that moment ravaging the countryside unopposed. He tripped over a pitch-fork and sprawled in the hay. He struggled to his feet, cursing, grabbed the offending implement and was about to fling it off the loft when he was halted by the very feel of it in his hands. It reminded him of the pike he had carried in the north. Not as strong nor as powerful, yet it was a weapon. Without any clear idea of what he was going to do, he crawled with it to the back window and slid down a rope into the field. Shouldering the fork he marched blindly and had reached the hedge at the far side when his legs were pulled from under him and he sprawled in the ditch.

A hand was clapped over his mouth. 'Yeos, you bloody eejit! Be still!'

Only then did he hear the clopping of the horses. He lay still. The hoofbeats drew level, passed and faded down the road. The man relaxed his hold and sat up and Conal saw a big, fair-haired man.

'What, in God's name, were you doing?' the man demanded. 'Committing suicide, was it?'

Conal shook his head, still half-dazed. 'I didn't even hear them.'

'You looked like a man marching into battle.'

'I wish I were,' said Conal fervently.

'I too. Those brave heroes have just attacked Boola-vogue. They knew all the pikes had been surrendered, that we were helpless. I got out of the place along with most of the people when I heard them coming.'

He stood, thrust his head carefully through a gap in the hedge and inspected the road. 'Tis quiet now,' he said. 'I'll be going.'

'Where?'

'Back to the village. Where else? Help will be needed there.'

'I'll come with you.'

As they walked, the man introduced himself as Michael Kavanagh, a blacksmith. He had local news. On the previous day a party of Antrim Militia in Carnew had taken twenty-five prisoners into a ball-alley and shot them whilst their officers looked on. The previous night the Yeos had raided the village of Bellaghkeen. All the inhabitants had fled to the dark hillsides, except one poor wretch who had been caught, tied to a thorn-bush and flogged to death. In the south of the county, Mr Bagenal Harvey, Mr Fitzgerald and Mr John Henry Colclough, all Protestant magistrates who had been collecting arms, issuing certificates and doing everything they could to calm and comfort the people, had been arrested by their fellow-magistrates and imprisoned in Wexford gaol.

Boolavogue was a smoking, blackened ruin, reeking with the sickening odour of roasted flesh. A skulking dog and a few indifferent chickens were the only signs of life.

There were tears in Michael Kavanagh's eyes as he stood at the end of the street. He raised imploring fists skywards. 'Dear God!' he cried. 'Is there no justice in all the world?'

Conal peered into the smoking ruin of the chapel. The altar had been smashed and the broken figure of the crucified Christ lay amongst its fragments. When he turned back Michael was running from house to house in a frenzy. He came out of one door.

'Burned alive!' he screamed. 'Old people burned alive in their homes. God blast the bloody Yeos!'

Conal went to him and took his arm. 'There is nothing to be done here,' he said. 'Where are the rest of the people?'

Michael pulled away. 'How would I know?' he shouted wildly. 'Scattered.' He threw his arms wide. 'Into the woods, maybe. Anywhere to get away from those murderers.'

'Then we must find them. Surely the men will see now that they must fight.'

It was late afternoon when they found the people with Father John Murphy in the woods. They rushed to the priest, both speaking together, clamouring that something must be done. A group of men armed, like Conal, with pitch-forks pulled them away and told them that Father Murphy had already said that they must fight and had sent out messengers calling to men to arm themselves as best they could and to rally to him.

Later the priest called to them to gather round. He told them of the plan he had formed to ambush the Camolin Yeomanry, who had attacked Boolavogue, as they returned to their headquarters.

That evening, near a place called The Harrow, Father John laid his trap. Leaving a few men at a house with instructions to block the road with two carts after the last of the Yeos had passed, he took the rest a couple of hundred yards further on where they built a barricade across the road. Then he placed the men, armed only with pitch-forks, behind the hedges in the growing darkness.

At about nine o'clock the Yeos, galloping for home, food and refreshment after their bloody labours, were almost on top of the barricade before they saw it. There was an immediate confusion of cursing men and struggling horses. The men with their pitch-forks burst through and over the hedge and, in spite of the wild pistol-shots of the Yeos, they spiked them and hauled their squirming, screaming bodies out of the saddles and on to the road to be kicked, stabbed again and again and trampled under the flailing hoofs. It was over in moments. Every one of the Yeos was dead and for booty there were horses, sabres, arms and ammunition.

Conal stood on the road amidst the sprawled bodies and flourished his bloodied pitch-fork aloft, filled with the wild exultation of the moment when he had plunged its spikes into the body of a hated Yeoman. He could still see the wild fear in the man's eyes as the points had struck, still hear his screams as the blood spurted, still feel the strength which had surged through his arms as he swung the body high out of the saddle and dashed it down on to the road where the face had been immediately obliterated by the hoof of a terrified horse.

He gave a great, high-pitched yell, then shouted, 'Thank God! We have a real leader at last!'

The men around cheered and yelled in wild triumph at their victory.

But Father John shouted even louder. 'Quiet, you foolish men! This is only a beginning.'

Conal, still excited, burst in. 'But a good beginning, Father. And you planned it well and showed yourself a true leader. In the North we failed because we lacked leaders.'

The men cheered again, but Father John stilled them. 'Be quite clear in your minds. God knows, I did not seek this and I have no military knowledge. This I do know. If I am to lead you, I must have your word that you will follow my orders without question.'

'You have it, Father. You have it indeed,' said Conal; and the men echoed him.

He led them to Camolin Park, the residence of Lord Mountmorris where this particular band of Yeos had been stationed. They met no opposition and were able to collect a great number of surrendered pikes and a quantity of muskets and ammunition. Then, with men flocking from their hiding places to join them, they marched back to Boolavogue, where they settled down as best they could for the night.

Whit Sunday, 27 May 1798, was glorious summer. The sky was deep blue and cloudless. The air was fresh and sweet with the scents of early summer. Beside the roads the trees glowed golden and delicate green in the morning sunshine, the hawthorn rioted in pink and white, the chestnuts proudly displayed ten thousand candles and a myriad flowers perfumed the ditches. Birds sang the joy of life on such a morning.

All through the night men had flocked in to Boola-vogue so that there were now more than a thousand, most armed only with hastily snatched farming imple-ments, some with nothing but sticks. But all shared a fierce surging joy at the prospect of vengeance at last.

On Conal's advice, Father Murphy led them to Portis' house. They streamed along the road with no more order than is in a herd of cattle, shouting, singing, slapping each other, and after them flocked the women, the boys and the girls, all determined not to miss the excitement.

Conal led a group of men to smash down the door of the cellar and to pass out the stored arms. As their hands closed on the shafts of the pikes, the men shrieked with fierce exultation. Two strong arms and fourteen-foot pike – God for the belly of a Yeoman!

Over four hundred were armed from the cellar and they swaggered, pikes on shoulders, at the head of a rabble to the village of Oulart and the house of the

Reverend Mr Burrows. He was a harmless old man, well-liked in the neighbourhood. But besides being vicar of the parish of Kilmuckridge, he was a magistrate to whom many arms had been surrendered. His house held these arms, guarded by a body of Yeomen.

By this time the numbers had almost doubled and still men were streaming over the fields from every direction. Dusty, sweating, red-faced, fanatically eager, singing and yelling, they churned the powdery road, with Father John, grim-faced and silent, at their head. As they approached the house they could see several Yeomen's musket-barrels menacing them from upstairs windows. Undeterred, like a wave across the sand, they surged over the wide lawn, shouting for the vicar to give up the arms. There was no answer, so Father John stepped forward and called, 'You had best surrender the arms, Mr Burrows. We mean to have all in your house.'

After a moment's silence, the front door opened and Burrows emerged. 'You must understand, sir, that I must do my duty as a magistrate and guard those arms. I advise that you send these people back to their homes before there is bloodshed.'

Before the priest could reply, a musket cracked from above. A man's face was transformed to a bloody mask and he fell. With a yell of fury the man's brother leaped forward and piked the vicar. Immediately, the whole mob raced forward, fighting each other to get into the house. So loud was the shouting, so furious their eagerness, that only those beside the victims were aware of the volley from the Yeomen who then escaped through the rear.

Hundreds struggled to get into the house and those who succeeded rampaged through it, ignoring the terrified screams of the women and children who had sought shelter there. Those who found the arms were unable to carry them out against the mass trying to get in. It took Father John nearly twenty minutes to clear a space in front of the door and to organise a chain along which the pikes and firearms were passed. The pikes were immediately snatched and fought for, whilst nobody wanted a firearm. Soon all the pikes had been seized and Father John had to order men to carry the few firearms and the small quantities of bullets and powder. In the meantime, many who were unarmed stripped the house of everything which appealed to them. Two men even staggered out with a large grandfather clock and women appeared in elaborately feathered hats, silken shawls and evening dresses over their rags.

It was useless for Father John to appeal to them to put back these treasures. Persecution had been cruel and persistent. Now long-choked emotions were unleashed and had to be satisfied. He gave up and ordered that all should march to Oulart Hill. They were now almost three thousand strong, not counting the boys and women. Many scoured the countryside, raiding large houses from which the inhabitants had fled to the shelter of the garrison in Wexford. Finally, on Oulart Hill, they sat down to picnic on foods and wines which none had ever before tasted. Dressed in odd pieces of fine clothing, they lolled on soft bedding, carpets, and curtains, surrounded by their loot: clocks, mirrors, statuettes, vases, cutlery, crockery, glassware, pictures, chamber-pots, musical instruments – a great jumble of mainly useless encumbrances which they would later discard to litter the line of their march.

It was a great day, the greatest of their lives. No fair or races had ever been as gay, as carefree or as happy as this. They lolled in the warm sunshine, filled to unknown repletion with fine food and drink, surrounded by thousands of their armed fellows, secure in the belief that nobody could withstand them. Ireland would soon be theirs. The rule of the landlords was gone forever.

From the hill they could see several corps of Yeomanry keeping at a safe distance from them. The men longed to get at these persecutors, but, with so few horses, pursuit of them was hopeless. Not until a boy ran into the camp gasping the news that a large body of soldiers from Wexford was marching against them did Father John realise the position. The soldiers would come marching up a road which led right to the foot of the hill. They would attack to disperse his forces into the surrounding countryside, and there the Yeomanry would cut them down with ease. He explained his plan to his lieutenants and they quickly spread his orders. The women and children were sent to the top of the hill, the men waited half-way up, but a group armed with muskets were sent to hide in the thick summer growth of the ditches on either side of the road.

Less than an hour later the military arrived in sight – one hundred and ten men of the North Cork Militia and forty mounted Yeomen under the command of a Colonel Foote. They halted a short distance from the hill and the infantry were lined up with fixed bayonets whilst the Yeomanry dragoons were sent round the left base of the hill to cut down the rebels as they fled.

Over all was the heavy quiet of a hot summer's day, accentuated by the drowsy hum of insects. The dusty road shimmered in the heat. The Yeos lazily jogged to their positions. The militia, looking so professional and capable in their fine uniforms, stood in formation, their bayonets glittering wickedly. Completely hidden in the lush growth in the ditches lay the rebel musketeers. On the hill the great mass of pikemen waited.

At the same moment as the militia began to advance, the order was given to the pikemen and they marched down the hill. Father John led them to within two musket shots of the military, then shouted an order and the whole body turned and raced back up the hill and threw themselves behind a ditch. 'Charge!' The order rang out to the militia and, with wild yells, they stormed the hill forming into line as they did so, but slowing because of the steepness. Father John let them come to half a musket shot from his position, then, as they had been ordered, a few men at either flank and in the centre stood up. Immediately the whole line of militia fired a volley. That was the signal. Before they could reload their muskets the great mass of pikemen charged down at them. Some stood to fight with their bayonets, but were helpless against the pikes. The rest retreated precipitately to the road where a volley from the ditches ripped into them.

The colourful menace became a tatter of fallen men and a struggle of the standing remnants to extricate themselves from the shambles. Even as they struggled they saw the Yeos galloping madly away. Then the pikemen were on them to hack and trample them into the red mud.

It was all over in moments. Only Colonel Foote, a sergeant and three privates managed to escape to Wexford, to tell of the massacre and the desertion of the Yeomanry.

The rebels had suffered five dead and two wounded. They yelled and danced, clapped each other on the back and chattered in wild excitement of the thousand flashing events of the encounter. When they paused for breath there came the full realisation that they had met the cursed militia, at whose very name they had cowered in terror, and had destroyed them. The all-powerful Yeos had fled from them. What idiots they had been to suffer so long!

It took a long time for Father John and his lieutenants to restore order. When they had done so, he harangued them, striving to drive home the lesson that disciplined action had brought victory. And they all nodded their heads sagely, like the seasoned warriors they were. For Father John was a mighty leader and they were all mighty men and, begod, wait till the next time!

But he sobered them when he pointed out that even then the Yeos were rampaging through the countryside murdering and burning. It was essential that they should try to gather all the people together for their safety; and, for that reason, as well as to spread the rebellion, they would march north immediately.

He led them seven miles north to Carrigrua Hill where they made camp. They lit great fires as beacons and people crawled from their hiding places and straggled in through the night, bringing tales of how the Yeos had shot every person they met on the roads, how they had called families from their houses and slaughtered them and burned their houses. This intensified the fury of the men who swore wildly of the vengeance they would wreak on the morrow. It was late before they were persuaded to rest.

Conal made a bed in the heather and the springy comfort of it took him back to the night he had escaped from Duncarran. He recalled the misery and frustration he had suffered then, how powerless he had felt in the face of a seemingly all-powerful enemy. Now he was one of an enormous army of determined men, with a leader who had twice shown himself to be capable of planning and organising. From this beginning, with the hundreds of thousands, even millions of men throughout Ireland who would flock to join them, an omnipotent force would emerge to destroy their enemies forever.

He sank into happy sleep.

The following morning Father John told them that they still needed to collect arms of all kinds, that it was essential to rouse the whole of County Wexford before they could spread the rising to the rest of the country.

Camolin, three miles to the north, housed detachments of Yeos and militia, so he led them there, only to learn that the troops had retreated with all the arms, some north to Gorey, others south-west to Enniscorthy. Conal urged Father John that they should go north, take Gorey and so open the road into Wicklow, to rouse the men there and advance further north on Dublin itself; but Father John's greatest concerns were still with the safety of the people who had not yet been able to join them, and with the gathering of arms. Only four miles to the west, along the main road, lay Ferns and the palace of the Church of Ireland Bishop to whom large quantities of pikes had been surrendered.

At noon on that Whit Monday, four thousand men and a tangle of women and children surged into the little town of Ferns. Tied to many pike-staffs were green petticoats or pieces of green curtains, anything as long as it was green, all fluttering bravely. The whole crowd sang and whooped, skipped and danced, leaped with joy in their new-found power and freedom.

All along the line of their march they had been joined by other men and in the town itself by a large body led by Father Michael Murphy of Ballycanew. Many were still unarmed. The whole mass assaulted the palace from which the Bishop had earlier fled with his wife and children.

Smashing through doors and windows, so many crowded in that it was a violent struggle to collect the arms and pass them to the heaving multitude outside. That done, they began to wreck the place. Furniture was smashed and piled in the magnificent apartments, valuable pictures were ripped from the walls with pike-points, the library was ransacked. At last, when nothing was left to destroy, they staggered out laden with bedding, clothes, food and valuables and left the place in flames.

At the start of the disorder Conal forced his way through the mob, shouting at them to stop. He reached the steps in front of the smashed front door and grabbed at those who were struggling in.

'No, no!' he shouted. 'This is not the way. Stop! Go back!'

A big, rough-looking man glared at him. 'Who the hell are you?' he demanded.

Conal started to explain that he was one of Father John's lieutenants, but the man gave him no time. 'Some class of bloody foreigner trying to tell us what we'll do and what we'll not do. Get to hell out of this!'

He shouldered Conal aside and forced his way in. Conal could only fight his way back through the crowd and go looking for Father John.

He found him with Father Michael Murphy. Even though he could see the dismay on the faces of the priests, Conal shouted as he came up to them, 'Father, Father! This is madness. They're a rabble, a screaming mob. Stop them!'

Father John wiped his streaming face. 'You're right,

Conal,' he said. 'Now tell me how I'm to stop them. The half of them don't even know me.'

Conal looked from him to the rioting mass exulting in what they saw as a great victory and he felt a sudden chill of foreboding.

Gradually, however, the noise died down as the people settled on the street to rest and eat. Father John seized the opportunity to assemble all who could be regarded as leaders to pass out his orders. The most important thing, he told them, was to relieve the people in the west of the county. To do that they would attack Enniscorthy, which lay on the far side of the River Slaney seven miles to the south. He detailed one group under Father Michael Murphy to march down the eastern side of the river to where a bridge led directly into the town, whilst he would lead a larger group to cross the river at a place called Scarawalsh, then march down the western bank to attack from the north.

Enniscorthy was a prosperous town of four thousand inhabitants on the west bank of the Slaney, twelve miles above Wexford town which lay at the estuary. Opposite the town, on the east bank, was Vinegar Hill, four hundred feet high, its slopes patterned with gardens and small fields, its summit open grass crowned with a windmill. Above and below the town woods, thick with summer foliage, clothed both banks to the river's edge – green trees mirrored in green, sliding water. At low tide the river could be forded below the town. At high water it could be crossed only by a narrow bridge.

All day on Whit Sunday refugees and escaping Yeos and militia had fled into the town. By evening the garrison comprised eighty North Cork Militia and two hundred and twenty Yeos. These were to guard the place against six thousand pikemen.

Captain Snowe of the North Corks, who was in command, arrested all the townspeople who were thought to favour the rebels and imprisoned them in the gaol and the market house. He then set up barricades on the bridge and on the roads to the north and west. All that

314

night the soldiers lay in their positions.

Father John had given orders that all cattle should be collected along the route. A great herd ambled ahead of the horde of pikemen. An enormous dust cloud rose, hung over them and stayed in the still, hot air long after they had passed. Ahead and through the fields on either side went skirmishers with firearms. Conal marched with Father John and Michael Kavanagh, filled with confidence that the priest had once more planned well. All strode joyfully as to a carnival, secure in the certainty of their invincibility.

Within sight of the town Father John halted them to rest. They scrambled and slid down the wooded banks to the river to gulp the cool water, to sluice away the dust, many to lie fully dressed in the shallows. When at last they were all back on the road they knelt to pray for victory.

They advanced slowly, halting within sight of the first houses and just out of range of the Yeomanry crouching behind their barricades. There was a brooding silence. The sun beat down on the close-packed mass of rebels and on the barricades and glittered back from the grey-white houses from whose chimneys the smoke rose lazily. The great herd of cattle browsed in the ditches, ears flicking, tails twitching against the clouds of flies.

'Charge!'

A long, high-pitched yell. The cattle were poked, smacked with hands and shafts, pricked with pike points. They jumped, shuffled, scrambled, milled senselessly. Louder yells and fiercer pricking. Bellowing with fear and pain they broke into a run and pushed those in front into a mad, surging gallop straight at the barricades. Behind them raced a horde of shrieking pikemen.

Dust billowed up in a great blinding cloud. Cra-a-ash! A volley from the Yeomanry. A dozen cattle staggered, fell and were trampled. Another volley. More falling cattle. Then a tremendous crash as the cattle hit, broke and scattered the barricade. Terrified bawling of animals, shouts and screams of pain and fury, rattle of shots, then

315

the triumphant, blood-lusting yells of the rebels as they leaped in, pikes thrusting, ripping.

For all the confusion, the Yeomanry maintained order, re-formed their lines and backed slowly down the street, firing repeated volleys into the rebels, close-packed in the narrow street.

The rebels' own musketeers could not return fire for fear of hitting their fellows who charged with reckless fury, trampling their fallen comrades, falling and being trampled. Checking and charging they slowly advanced, forced forward always by the mass behind. As they went they set fire to the houses on either side so that soon they were fighting under an arch of flames. Dense, acrid smoke drifted down on the Yeomen, choking and blinding them, but still they maintained their slow retreat and their steady, devastating fire.

The heat of the day, the greater heat of the burning houses from whose windows long, scorching tongues of flame reached out to lick at the close-packed rebels, the swirling smoke, the maddened cattle, the irresistible pressure from behind, the murderous volleys from the front, produced wild confusion. Yet through it all women squirmed carrying jars of water and whiskey for the refreshment of their fighting men, ignoring the heat, the smoke, the bullets and the sight of so many of their sisters stretched bleeding or dead amongst the litter of rebel bodies on the cobbles.

At last, reaching the market-place, the Yeomanry raced for the shelter of the stone houses there. Rallying in this protection, they crashed out volley after volley, mowing down the exposed mass of rebels who were unable to retreat against the pressure from behind. Time and time again the rebels charged across the market-place and every time a blast of bullets drove them back, leaving dead and wounded amongst the corpses of cattle in the open square.

Conal and Michael Kavanagh had been in the forefront of the first charge, running side by side. Attempting to cross the smashed barricade Michael fell between two broken carts. Conal stretched down to help him and was immediately hit by the following horde and knocked on top of him. Both lay cursing, unable to move as more and more men trampled the timbers which held them.

For more than an hour Father Murphy struggled to curb the wild mass and eventually succeeded in getting those at the rear to retreat, thus easing the murderous pressure on those in the town, so that, gradually, they too were able to escape from the slaughterhouse of the market-place and get back over the barricades.

Some heard the shouts of Michael and Conal and released them. Bruised and sore they stood and gazed at the shambles of dead and wounded men, women and cattle littering the street and what they could see of the market-place.

Conal gripped one fist with his other hand and shook them in fury. 'Idiots!' he screamed. 'Stupid, bloody idiots!'

Michael gave a long sigh and gripped Conal's shoulder, turning him away. 'They know no better, God help them,' he said. 'All that was in their minds was revenge for their suffering.'

Conal jerked away from him and turned again, shaking his open palm with fingers spread at the street, noisy now with the buzz of myriads of flies bloating themselves on the unusual feast. 'Look at it, Michael! Look at it, for God's sake. Hundreds of them dead, not from the enemy, but from stupidity – their own stupidity and the stupidity of those who'd call themselves friends.'

Michael laughed harshly. 'I seem to remember the two of us charging at the head of them, screaming like the devils of hell,' he said.

A chill ran through Conal. It was true. He had raced at the barricade possessed by the wild lust to rip the life from the bodies of the enemy, to see their blood spurt and to revel in their screams of agony.

Michael was walking back up the road and Conal turned and followed slowly, his mind in a turmoil. The ghosts of all who had died because of his failure as a leader in the north rose to jeer at this second failure, to point the fact that he had learned nothing. A leader had to think well before acting. He had known that, had talked with Father John about the absolute necessity for careful planning, yet from the first moment of the charge all reason had left him.

A sudden thought stopped him and he turned and looked back at the town. If he had not been trapped in the barricade he could well have been lying there amongst the dead. He, Conal O'Carran, all hopes and ambitions ended, would have been just one more obscenity in that litter of fly-blown flesh. Oh, God, Nuala! He would never have seen her again. He was filled with a longing to see her, to hold her, to feel her holding him as an assurance that he was truly alive. And, to be sure that she was alive. For the first time he realised that she too was in danger, greater danger than he himself had faced – danger, perhaps from the rebels as much as from the Yeos.

'Oh, God protect her,' he prayed; yet thinking that it was he who should be with her to protect her.

He was tempted to go at once to find her, yet realised that it would solve nothing. Unless she returned to the rebels with him. She wouldn't leave her mother; and if he left now it would be desertion. The only hope was in victory; yet the difficulty of victory was proved by the butchery in the streets of Enniscorthy. They had to learn to fight like real soldiers. No more of this senseless rushing into certain death. The attack had not been properly planned. They should have ... what?

He stood in the road thinking, then suddenly ran to where the great mass of rebels, already swollen to more than their original numbers, were resting in the ditches and fields. He ran amongst them searching until he finally saw Father John.

'Father! Father!' he shouted as he ran up.

Father John glared at him. 'Here's another come to tell me that we did it all wrong,' he said. 'And before you open your mouth, Conal O'Carran, let me tell you that I know. And let me tell you again, I am not a military man. I know nothing of military matters, but God help me, I'm thrust into it.'

'Father, will you listen to me,' Conal begged. 'I know how we should have done it. We should have had a cannon. Not the cattle to hamper us in the narrow street. With a cannon we could have smashed that barricade and slaughtered those behind it.'

'Congratulations,' said the priest. 'Would you just let me point out now that we haven't a cannon, that we haven't powder or shot for a cannon. And even if we had them, would you know how to use them?'

'Well, no, but . . .' Conal stumbled to silence.

'Ah, don't mind me, lad. I'm saddened by the losses, the useless losses. But you're right. We do need cannon and powder and shot; and we must get them and find somebody who knows how to use them. We need muskets too. So, yourself and Michael Kavanagh, get a group of men together and make it your task to gather these things from now on. Will you do that?'

'I will indeed, Father,' said Conal.

'Understand me now, Conal,' said the priest. 'Leave the rest to do the fighting. Let you wait until we secure the place, then search out all we need.'

Conal stared. 'I'm to fight no more?'

Father John wagged his head sadly. 'God forgive us, Conal, all of us. We're gripped with the lust for killing.'

Conal hesitated, recognising his disappointment at the prospect of being deprived of the joy of battle. Then he rushed to justify himself. 'Weren't we driven to it, Father! We're doing what has to be done. We've no choice but to go on until we end it forever.'

The priest nodded, but his voice was full of regret as he said, 'You are right. I have taken up the sword and cannot lay it down until we are free. But, for your part, think of the lives we can save if you provide us with the arms. Will you do it, Conal?'

Conal expelled a long breath, then nodded. 'I'll do it, Father.' But there was no enthusiasm.

Meanwhile, the military had held the bridge without

difficulty. Defending a long, narrow, open stretch across which the rebels had to charge, rapid volleys had repelled every attack. The rebels, quickly running out of powder and ball, were unable to reply. Soon the bridge was choked with dead and wounded.

They tried to ford the river, both above and below the bridge, but the water was too deep and they simply lost more men.

Yet Captain Snowe, who commanded the garrison, knew that he would have to evacuate the town. The prison was crowded with rebel sympathisers with no force available to guard them, a third of the garrison had been killed and many wounded and the town was crowded with refugees.

Late in the afternoon they began the miserable, twelve-mile trudge to Wexford by the road down the west bank of the Slaney. There were few horses except those of the Yeomanry, and no carriages. Old and young, weak and strong, healthy and sick, whole and wounded – all had to walk. The strongest marched ahead, women and children straggled after with the sick, infirm and wounded. All through the night they dribbled into Wexford town.

It was some time before the rebels became aware that the only sounds from the town were the faintly heard shouts of the prisoners. A few cautiously investigated, then shouted back the news. In minutes the streets were thronged with shouting and dancing men and women, save for those who searched for husbands, wives and brothers amongst the bodies, their grieving drowned by the shouts of triumph.

The released prisoners told of their sufferings and revived blood-lust, particularly amongst those who had taken no part in the fighting, and they scoured the town. Every man identified by the prisoners as an anti-rebel was promptly piked, the bodies often being carried on pike-points for the length of several streets, the blood dripping on the exultant bearers.

With great difficulty, Father John put a stop to this and

320

ordered that all the corpses should be taken out and buried in communal graves in the fields. Then he ordered that a permanent camp should be set up on Vinegar Hill across the bridge.

In the meantime, Conal, Michael and their men searched for powder and arms; but beyond what they collected from dead yeomanry and militia, there was little to be found.

As they crossed the bridge, Conal looked up at the hill which now looked like an enormous pile of multi-coloured fabrics crowned by a windmill. Nearer, it looked like a monster fair. Tents and shelters of all shapes and sizes had been constructed from blankets, sheets, counterpanes, quilts, bed-canopies, carpets, curtains and tablecloths.

From all directions people were still flocking in; men to join the rebel army, women seeking husbands or sweethearts, liberal-minded priests and gentlemen come to offer their services, whiskey-sellers, tricksters and sharpers, the scum of the race-tracks, and a multitude of footpads, highwaymen and other criminals, all looking for free food and drink and loot.

Barrels of spirits, wine and ale were rolled up to the camp and set up for anybody to help themselves. Every house was searched for food. Cattle, sheep and pigs were driven in and kept as a vast larder in a field at the foot of the hill. When men were hungry they selected a beast, brained it with an axe and hacked great chunks from the bleeding, unflayed carcass. These were then toasted on pike-points over the huge fires and swallowed half-raw with great appreciation by people who had rarely, if ever, tasted meat.

From the large houses much finery had been looted and the peasant women, gay for once in their drab lives, fluttered, swayed and postured in vivid silks, satins, velvets and feathers, trailing clouds of perfume.

Harpsichords, pianos and harps which had lately, in gilded drawing-rooms, tinkled to the ripple of idle female fingers, were hauled out on to the open hillside where wandering musicians soon learned to strike ancient airs to warm the martial spirits, or gay dance tunes to tickle the toes.

From all the excitement, the gratification of vengeance, the wealth of loot, the endless supplies of food and drink, the finery, the comfort, the gay music, singing and dancing, the people drew more enjoyment than they had ever known. Left to themselves they would have been content to stay in the luxury of the camp and forget all about the rebellion.

The scum, however, once they had eaten and drunk their fill, were not content. Gangs of them scoured the countryside for loot and brought in prisoners to cover their activities. The prisoners were crammed first into a large barn at the foot of the hill. From there the mill on the summit was stocked. Before the mill a self-constituted tribunal of blood-hungry fanatics sat in almost permanent session. Prisoners were led from the mill to receive farcical trial. Few escaped the death sentence. The many were flung upon their knees and, in spite of the horrified protests of the priests and people, were piked and barbarously mutilated.

The constant repetition of these acts resulted in the butchery of between four and five hundred men in a few days.

Father John, desperately trying to control the immense mob, sent out parties in search of men who could act as leaders, men with military experience to discipline and direct his uncontrollable forces. In some cases men were prepared, with reservations, to follow their local leaders, but the leaders could not agree amongst themselves; and the hordes of uncommitted individuals were utterly beyond control.

Confused and noisy meetings were held at which wild plans were put forward, every man considering it his duty to support an attack on the town nearest his own home. Some wanted to return to their own districts to fight against the local Yeomanry. Others were for waiting where they were until the military came to them, when, they argued, their enormous numbers and impregnable position would assure victory. The only agreement was that, for the moment, Wexford town was too formidable to be attacked. Nobody listened to anybody else, arguments were long and loud, tempers flared at opposition and the meetings often ended in brawls.

One of the men brought in then as a possible leader was a Mr John Hay and when they learned that he had served as an officer in the French army they were ready to listen to him.

He told them that, for real success, they must spread the rebellion to the rest of Ireland. To explain how this should be done he sketched a rough map of the country.

This showed that they were hemmed in by the sea on the east and south, on the north by mountains and on the west by the river Barrow. The easiest routes out were northwards through Gorey, then by the coast road to Arklow and so to Dublin; and westward to New Ross on the river Barrow. At both Arklow and New Ross there were bridges which were heavily guarded by the military. The only other route, a difficult one, was up the valley of the River Slaney and through the mountains to County Carlow – a route guarded at the small town of Newtownbarry. If Arklow, New Ross and Newtown-barry could be taken, then they could rouse the whole country.

His explanation was listened to more or less in silence, but then there was immediate argument, some for one route, some for another, but many unable to see why they should leave Wexford County at all. This was eventually quietened when it was made clear that they had enough men to take the three routes whilst still leaving enough to defend the county.

Mr Hay, however, warned them that they were also menaced by large numbers of well-equipped troops in the fortress of Duncannon which guarded the estuary of the river Barrow. They jeered at this in their confidence that they could meet and defeat a few hundred soldiers with their thousands.

When he stated that, lacking powder, cannon and arms and completely undisciplined as they were, they could not face well-trained soldiery, he was howled down and the meeting ended in complete disorder. Many decided that they would go back to their own districts and carry on the rebellion there. In their thousands they streamed down from the hill.

Conal, hoarse from his attempts to get them to listen to reason and to stress the need for discipline under able leadership, ran frantically amongst them, pleading for them to return. But to them he was simply a nuisance to be brushed aside. In despair he stood and watched them go.

FIFTY-FIVE

All day on Whit Saturday and all through a long, sleepless night Nuala worried about Conal. Again and again she went over their quarrel, telling herself that she was trying to find where she had been wrong, and each time she was convinced that she had not been wrong. Oh, she regretted the anger-inspired foolishness which had led her to threaten him with the Yeomanry; but it had been said only because he had been so stubborn. All hope of a decent life lay in the money, her money! Conal's rejection of it was only stupid pride. Several times in the weary darkness, longing for him, realising all that he meant to her, she found herself admiring his high-principled stand, his determination to get only what rightfully belonged to him. Then she had thoughts of Mark Portis and her own determination to be revenged for his cruelty, thoughts of all that money which could provide comfort for her mother, herself and Conal, dreams of the life that could be . . .

She woke to the tumult of the mob which had come to gather the arms. She ran to the window and stared down at the heaving multitude on the lawn, heard the smashing of the windows and watched as pikes were passed out to eager hands. Realisation of what was happening was slow to come. When it did, her immediate thought was that Conal was down there somewhere.

She turned away from the window, in haste to dress, and only then became aware of her mother.

Georgina, cap awry on her disordered hair, was uttering a continuous yelping cry as she alternately ducked under the covers, then emerged to stare fearfully at the window.

'Be quiet, mother!' Nuala snapped as she hastily dressed. 'Stay where you are and you will be safe.'

'Safe! Nuala, Nuala, we are in great danger!'

'I haven't the time, mother. Stay there. Just stay there. I'll come back.'

'Don't leave me, Nuala. Oh, don't leave me. Nuala. Nuala. Come back!'

But Nuala, still only half-dressed, had rushed out.

Judy was at the foot of the stairs giving a continuous stream of orders and comments to the invaders. 'Will you, for God's sake, not be tracking all that dirt on the good carpets. Who, d'ye think will have the cleaning of them? You, there, Willie Neville, I'll have something to say to your mother when I see her. And will someone tell me how I'm to get to Mass this holy Whit Sunday?'

An older man heard this. 'You'll get no Mass this day, Judy, nor for many days to come, I'm thinking.' And he told her of the destruction of the chapel in Boolavogue.

Judy sat abruptly on the stairs. 'Oh, dear God!' she cried, then, as Nuala sat beside her and put an arm about her shoulders, she jerked up her tear-stained face and shrieked, 'Hell roast you, Mark Portis!' She gripped Nuala's hand fiercely. 'He and his murdering crew rode off to Boolavogue this morning!'

'Judy,' Nuala begged, 'will you go up to my mother? I must find Conal.'

She fought to get through the crush, asking at the same time of everybody and nobody, 'Conal O'Carran! Have you seen Conal O'Carran?' and getting no replies.

Only when men started shouting, 'That's the lot! There's not a pike left here!' did the press of bodies ease as people left the house. At last she got out on to the lawn and ran about calling Conal's name, frantically trying to make herself heard above the uproar. The crowd surging out through the gate carried her with them. She was thrust against the gate-post, worked her way round it and climbed the wall. The road was filled with a solid mass of shouting men, women and children. It was impossible to pick anybody out of that multitude. Then he appeared suddenly on top of the wall of the stable-yard, further down the road. He stood outlined against the clear, blue sky, dressed in a white shirt and dark breeches, a pike on his shoulder, a grin of sheer delight on his face. He shouted something to the crowd and they looked up at him and cheered.

'Conal!' she screamed. But he leaped from the wall and disappeared into the surging mass.

Screaming his name repeatedly, she started to scramble down. Other women were following their men, why not she? She fell into the ditch by the gate and, as she struggled to her feet, she saw Judy Doyle run out and join the mob. Furiously she followed, pushing her way through until she reached the woman.

'Judy!' she yelled. 'What about my mother? You have left my mother.'

Judy's face was contorted with excitement and with hatred. 'She's *your* mother!' she shouted. 'You take care of her!'

The venom made Nuala stop. She stood there, jostled by the crowd, chilled by the realisation that Judy and all of these people were alien to her. In their eyes she was one of the class which had persecuted them for centuries.

Conal was one of them. He had left her for them.

She stood in the road until the last straggler had disappeared, leaving the dust of their passing hanging in the sunshine, the sounds of their yelling and singing gradually fading to silence. Momentarily she felt completely alone in an empty, futureless world. Then she remembered her mother and pitied the fear she must be experiencing, yet was resentful of her dependence. She, Nuala, had nobody to depend upon. Self-pity, anger and irritation churned in her mind as she turned wearily back into the silent house.

The kitchen was empty, the fire dying, pots and pans scattered about. The hall showed wild disorder of broken furniture, torn hangings, doors ripped from their hinges, disclosing wrecked rooms and complete silence.

Suddenly anxious, she raced upstairs. 'Mama, mama, where are you?'

She hammered on the locked door.

'Mama, are you there?'

From inside, tremulously: 'Nuala! Oh, Nuala, is it safe?'

'Yes, yes. They have gone. Open the door.'

She heard the scraping of furniture being pulled from behind the door, then it was unlocked and opened cautiously and her mother's white, frightened face peered out.

'Nuala, oh, Nuala!' she wailed. 'There were thousands of wild people rampaging through the house. I was sure they had come to murder me. Where have you been? Why did you leave me alone at such a time?'

'I have been looking for the man I want to marry,' said Nuala bitterly.

Georgina, not noticing the bitterness, was all bright interest immediately. 'My chicken! Oh, how lovely. Have you found a nice young man? Is he –'

'I have found him and lost him!'

'But I don't understand, dearest.'

'Nobody understands!' She flung herself on the bed and wept.

Her tears were enough to re-start her mother's. 'Oh,

Nuala,' she sobbed. 'We must get away from here before those blood-thirsty ruffians come back and murder us.'

Nuala sat up abruptly. 'Where is Uncle Mark?'

'I don't know where anybody is. I've told you I was left alone in the house with all those murderers. Oh, what will we do? What will we do? If only your poor, dear papa . . .' Which led to a further bout of sobbing.

'Oh, stop that!' Nuala cried irritably. 'What help is that! I must think. I must think!'

She leaped from the bed and ran downstairs. Before she reached the bottom she stopped, paused, then ran up again and into her uncle's room. It was undisturbed. The black box still stood at the foot of the bed. It was locked. Had Mark taken the money? If so, why had he locked it again?'

She ran downstairs, out into the yard and across to the stables. They were empty. She went into the carriage house. The two carriages were still there. If he had not taken a carriage, then he hd not taken the money because he could never have carried that amount in saddle-bags. But where was he? Would he come back? She knew he would. The question was: how long did she have?

She searched until she found an axe. Back into the house with it, ignoring her mother's frightened calls, and into Mark's room. Then, with sudden thought, still carrying the axe, she ran back to her mother. 'Quickly. Dress yourself. There's not a moment to lose!'

Then back to the box which she attacked furiously. But, in spite of her frantic belabouring, the axe made only dents in the hard bog oak.

She flung the axe aside. 'Damn, damn, damn!' she shouted.

'Nuala!' Her mother was standing in the doorway, her face a mixture of indignation and curiosity. 'Remember you are a lady! Such language!'

'Oh, for God's sake, don't just stand there making stupid remarks. Tell me how to get this blasted box open.'

Georgina's hands flew to protect her tender ears. 'I will not listen to such . . .'

But Nuala had her by the shoulders and was shaking her. 'You stupid woman! There is a rebellion going on out there. Do you understand? A revolution. Just like France. We must do something immediately. There is money in that box. Our money. We need it. Tell me how to get it!'

Georgina was terrified. Aloysius had predicted it so often. Now she would be guillotined. But even as she opened her mouth to wail, Nuala slapped her, then dragged her to the box.

'How can I open it?' she demanded, shaking her. 'Think! How can it be opened without a key?'

'Nuala, how can...?'

Nuala slapped her again. She kicked the box and shook her mother. 'How?' she shrieked. 'How?'

'How should I know?' said her mother hysterically. 'It is the sort of thing servants do with tools.'

Tools!

Nuala ran down to the outhouses again. For the next half hour, in growing frustration, she ran backwards and forwards with a variety of tools and implements with which she attacked the stubborn box. Finally, by trial and error, a hammer and chisel forced the lock.

She plunged her hands under the clothes and heaped papers and shrieked with delight when her rooting fingers clutched a money-bag. She hauled it out, untied the string and poured a stream of coins – beautiful, golden coins – on the bed.

'Oh, Nuala! All that momey!' Georgina's eyes were riveted on the coins. Then, anxiously, 'But is it truly ours? Surely Mark –'

'It's ours now! Help me. We must find a hiding place for it, and not in the house. Now where, where, where?'

Then she knew where.

She dumped the papers and other contents of the box on to the floor. There were thirty-eight heavy bags. She was half hysterical with joy and with desperation to hide them before Mark or anybody else came. But the bags were heavy. Two made a load for each of them, and it took nearly an hour to carry them to the barn and store them in a corner of the loft where she covered them with hay. She was reluctant to leave them, but her mother's constant complaints of tiredness and hunger finally brought the realisation that she, too, was hungry. Besides, there were other things to do.

Back in the kitchen, she looked from a sack of raw potatoes to the dead fire. Then she thought, 'Why potatoes?'

She ran upstairs for the hammer and chisel and quickly broke open the cupboard in which Mark's food was kept. There was mutton, ham, bread, butter, a large jug of milk. In spite of her mother's complaints and questions, she made her help to carry them all to the loft. But before they ate Nuala forced her back to the house to collect their clothes and bedding. Finally, when they had made a nest amongst the hay, where they were completely hidden, yet were able to see into the yard, they ate.

Nuala came awake abruptly. Contentment, following the best meal they had eaten for months, had lulled them both to sleep. Something had wakened her. She crept to the peephole and looked down into the yard. A saddled horse was standing by the kitchen door, but there was no sign of its rider. The stillness was blasted by uproar as a group of fifteen or twenty mounted rebels galloped into the yard.

'Didn't I tell you 'twas Portis?' one shouted. 'Into the house, lads!'

They leaped from their horses and surged through the kitchen door.

'Oh, Nuala, what is it? Have they –'

'Quiet!' Nuala hissed.

She need not have worried. There was wild commotion in the house with crashes, shouting and yelling, then two shots accompanied by screams of pain and even fiercer yelling. She saw movement through one of the bedroom windows. Then the whole window burst outward and with it came a body, the hands still clutching the sabre which pierced it. It thudded on the cobbles and lay still. The rebels crowded in the window space and looked down, yelling with triumph.

A single voice rose above all. 'May you roast in Hell, Portis!'

Georgina clawed at Nuala. 'What is happening?' she begged.

'Hush! If we are quiet there is no need to worry.'

She led her mother back to their nest and made her lie down. Then she lay back herself in great contentment.

'Nuala,' she whispered, 'tell me what has happened. I must know.'

With great satisfaction Nuala said, 'They have killed Mark Portis!'

Then she had to clap her hand over her mother's mouth to silence the scream of horror which threatened to burst involuntarily from her. Pressing down on her mother, she demanded, 'Will you be quiet if I take away my hand?'

Georgina stared up at her, wide-eyed. Then she nodded and Nuala took away her hand.

'This solves everything for us,' Nuala whispered. 'Not only is the money ours, but his land, everything he owns. We're rich, mama!' Her eyes shone. 'Rich!'

'What are you saying? Nuala, they murdered him!'

'And well he deserved it, if only for what he did to us. As soon as everything quietens down and all this stupid fighting is over, we shall be wealthy. Now, try to sleep again, mama.'

From the house the uproar of destruction. Nuala sat up, clenching her fists. They were destroying *her* furniture, wrecking *her* house.

'Perhaps he left a will,' her mother whispered. 'It might be with the title deeds in the box.'

'Title deeds? What are title deeds?'

'I am not quite sure, but I believe they prove that a person owns the land.'

'And they're...'

Nuala rushed to the peep-hole. The men were straggling from the kitchen-door carrying their loot. From the empty window space above them smoke was pouring. Her heart leaped. The deeds would burn!

331

'Oh, dear God,' she prayed. 'Make them go. Make them go!'

She trembled with anxiety as the men, swigging from wine and brandy bottles, tied on their booty, then swung into the saddle. One leaned to untether Portis' horse, then dismounted and went to the sprawled body.

Nuala rammed her knuckles against her mouth to stifle the screams of 'Go! Go! Go!' which threatened to erupt as she saw the flames consuming *her* house.

The man pulled at the sabre, but had to press his foot down on the body before he could remove it. There was no room in her screaming mind for the horror she was witnessing as he calmly wiped the sabre on the body. He then took a rope from his saddle, looped it round the feet of the corpse and tied it to the saddle of Portis' horse.

'Go! Go! Go!'

With infuriating slowness he mounted his own horse and said something to the others at which they laughed. Then, for agonising seconds, they simply sat as if waiting for somebody to tell them what to do next. Nuala gnawed at her knuckles. 'Go! For God's sake, go!'

The man yelled, 'Yahoo!' and slapped Portis' horse with the flat of the sabre. It reared, then galloped away dragging the remains of Mark Portis bouncing over the cobbles. The men streamed after, yelling and shouting. The yard was empty and quiet.

She leaped to the ladder, almost fell down it, raced across the yard and into the kitchen where she was met by billowing smoke which threatened to choke her and drive her back. She retreated to the outer door, took a deep breath of fresh air, then plunged back through the kitchen and into the hall. The dining and drawing rooms were blazing and the greater part of the smoke was coming from them; but smoke was also rolling down the stairs and she could see a red flicker and hear crackling above. Her one breath lasted until she reached the top of the stairs, but there she was forced to gasp and at once she was coughing, her eyes streaming. To her right was the room with the broken window. It was not afire. She went in, breathed quickly and deeply, then ran across into Mark's room. The bed was a mass of flames. On a large rug near it the heap of papers were browning in the heat. She circled at a distance from the bed, took the edge of the rug and pulled it and all the papers to herself. She was then by a front window, but, although she tugged and pushed at it, it would not open. She was weeping from the smoke and with fear of the flames; yet the fear was more for the papers than for her own safety.

A chair stood by the window and she saw the solution. She threw it straight through the window and bundled the rug and papers after it. But the fire had now spread across to the door. She could not get out that way. At once she kicked away the broken glass and crawled through the window on to the broad ledge which ran round the house.

As she edged away from the window she was suddenly and happily aware of the sweetness of the soft, scented air of the beautiful summer afternoon. She looked down and saw the papers scattered below and she laughed aloud in the triumph of achievement. Even as she slowly side-stepped along the ledge, she thought, not of her danger, but that Conal could have no objections now. He had wanted land, and here it was. The house was ruined, but it was probably a good thing not to live in the place which had housed Mark Portis and so much misery. They would build another.

It was all so easy. When she came to the porch there was a thick creeper – almost as good as a ladder. She climbed down, collected the papers in her lifted skirt and went back to the barn.

They stayed in hiding for a week, Nuala being quite sure that the trouble would be quickly over, and she expected Conal daily. Several times they had visits from rebel bands searching for food, and these, to her great anger, drove off all the cattle, sheep and pigs, as well as grabbing all the poultry they could catch. But after the third day they had no more visitors.

She had been fearful that the rebels would discover

their hiding place and the money. Towards the end of the week she crept down to the stables and there decided on a new and safer hiding place for her treasure. After great labour, made all the more so as she tried to do it silently, she raised a flagstone. She hollowed out the earth under it and put the bags in the hole. The papers she wrapped in several skirts and placed on top of the bags. Then she replaced the stone and spread manure to hide all traces.

After that, the main problem was food. The hens which had escaped were still laying and she searched and found their eggs. In addition she found in the ruined kitchen the sack of well-baked potatoes.

Then came the time of endless waiting and thinking. Sometimes she heard shots in the distance, and sometimes saw smoke; but she saw nobody. Ignorance of what was happening was her greatest torture and it interfered constantly with the dream she nursed of Conal's joy when he came back to find that he now owned a large farm.

Then came the worry that he might not come back. She suffered that torment for a day and a night before deciding to go and look for him. In spite of her assurances that she might only be away for a few hours, her mother became hysterical; but ignoring tears and pleas, she told her where to collect eggs, pointed out that there were still plenty of potatoes left, and off she went.

She wore old, ragged clothes so that nobody would suspect her of being anything but a peasant girl; but she went carefully. There was an unnatural quietness everywhere. Although it was a perfect summer morning and the hedgerows were thick with flowers and blossom, their sweetness was marred by something indefinable. This puzzled her until, walking along, trailing her hand through the tall grasses at the wayside, she disturbed a cloud of flies which rose buzzing from the corruption which had been a living soul. She stumbled away in sick horror and vomited in shaking weakness until she was forced to lie down. But she lay, not in the soft grasses, but on the hard, clean road.

At last she felt strong enough to stand. Her impulse was to fly back to the safety of the barn; but that would have meant re-passing the corruption and she would have achieved nothing. She walked on, carefully in the centre of the road, looking straight ahead, but ever-conscious of the smell. Coming to a tiny humped-backed bridge, she went down beside it to the stream where she washed herself and drank and came up feeling cleaner and refreshed.

She passed cabin after cabin, smoke-blackened ruins hiding other horrors; and she learned to hold her breath when passing them. Death and desolation were every-where, incongruous in the flowery sunshine. But as she neared Enniscorthy life sprang up again. There were people everywhere in and about the town and there was all the gaiety of a fair. She questioned many until she learned eventually that the men of Boolavogue had marched north with Father John Murphy. She refused to believe at first that she had been walking in the wrong direction; but when many had told her the same thing she accepted it reluctantly.

She stayed the night and was welcomed to share a meal and a bed with the women. The following morning she was wakened early by one of them who told her that a party of men was leaving immediately to join Father Murphy. She rushed straight out and joined them; but it was two days later that they met the force retreating from Arklow.

For a long time she stood beside the road scanning the faces of all who passed. Then there was a shout, 'Glory be to God! Nuala!'

She stared at the odd creature who advanced on her, and only when she was close did she recognise Mag Kinsella. Her hair was bound up in a turban made from a length of purple silk, a violent contrast to the straggles of rust sprouting from under it. She wore a heavy brocade gown which she had kilted to her knees, and she carried a pike like the men.

They embraced and kissed each other like long-lost

335

sisters and Nuala wept with gladness.

But then she clutched her and demanded, 'Conal. Did you see Conal? Where is he?'

'Ah, sure, he's not with us at all. D'y'know what it is and meaning no hurt to yourself, but that's a queer class of a lad. There we were on Vinegar Hill having the greatest times of it. And that's where we're heading now. Oh, great entirely. Dancing and music and singing and lashings of the finest food and drink. I can't wait to get back. Come you along with us.'

She whirled Nuala along with her.

'But where is Conal?'

'Ah, God, yes, there I go forgetting again. Ah, but hold on.' She let out a roar. 'Paddy Keogh!' She charged through the marching mob, disappearing for a moment, then reappeared dragging an obviously reluctant young man.

'This is Paddy Keogh,' she said with a wide grin. 'I promised his mammy I'd take care of him.' She gave a bellow of laughter. 'But 'tis for my own sake I'm taking care of him. Isn't that the truth, Paddy?' And she cracked him on the back.

'Ah, God, Mag,' he protested plaintively. 'I'd rather the Yeos and the Militia any day than a slap from you.'

'Ah, get along with you,' she said, giving him a playful push which made him stagger. And turning to Nuala she said, 'He's mad in love with me really. 'Tis just that he's shy. Isn't that the truth of it, now, Paddy?'

'Oh, God!' Paddy moaned.

'Mag, please,' Nuala begged. 'You were telling me about Conal.'

'Sure, didn't I tell you?' She smacked her forehead. 'This bloody head of mine! God forgive me for the bad language. Well, the way I was telling you. There we were having the time of our lives. But your man, Conal, would have none of it. He was forever prating about discipline and leaders and obeying orders. Sure he was out with everybody. Then Father John sent him off to New Ross with some fellow named Harvey. But, sure, he's maybe back in Enniscorthy by now.'

Nuala accompanied them for most of the way back, but as they drew nearer she became more and more convinced that Conal had gone back to the house in her absence, so she cut off the main road and went back to the barn.

Her mother was still alone and, she assured, 'Doing quite well, thank you; although I must say it was not the conduct I expected from any daughter of mine to go off and leave me at a time like this.'

Nuala was too weary and disappointed to reply. For the next two or three days she did little but rest. Then she returned to waiting and hoping and worrying through the slow hours.

FIFTY-SIX

Conal sat on a boulder at the foot of Vinegar Hill, utterly disconsolate. Vast numbers of men had left and others were straggling down past him, dragging their pikes. He heard their loud complaints, blaming, he thought, everything and everybody except their own unwilling- ness to be led. The rebellion was over before it had really begun. What was left for him?

Nuala! He could go to her now, be with her in a matter of hours. But then what? He had absolutely nothing to offer her – no money, no lands, no position, no hopes except the possibility of a cabin in the Wicklow Mountains and a life of poverty as the wife of a hedge- schoolmaster.

He suddenly became aware of great clamour up on the hill behind him, then a swelling chorus of cheers which grew so loud that it reached out into the countryside to the ears of the deserting thousands. These hesitated, looked back, then curiosity brought first ones and twos to return and finally all were hurrying back.

The news spread rapidly. One party, retreating down the Wexford road, had met two gentlemen, friendly magistrates, Mr Fitzgerald and Mr Colclough. They had been released from the prison and sent as messengers to the rebels with a plea to spare the town and its inhabitants.

There was the amazing, wonderful fact! Wexford, which they had thought too strong for them, was actually afraid of them. There was immediate and complete agreement. They would take Wexford at once.

Leaving ten thousand men on Vinegar Hill, Father Murphy, riding a white horse, set out at the head of his army. Behind the throng Conal and Michael Kavanagh and their men drove carts laden with their precious arms and powder, to which they slowly added from houses raided along the way.

They halted and made camp at a place called Three Rocks, four miles from Wexford on the road which led westwards to the fortress of Duncannon which commanded the estuary of the River Barrow.

All, save the scouts that Father John sent out, were settling down for the night when the scouts brought the news that a military force was approaching from Duncannon. Father John immediately set an ambush.

The military knew nothing until the flash and crash of five hundred muskets described a circle around them. Then the pikemen charged. The half-trained militia turned to fly and were butchered.

Conal, who had learned from the scouts that the military were equipped with two cannon, deliberately held his men back from the first charge of the pikemen, then raced in to capture the precious cannon. They had secured them and the carts which carried the powder and ball when there was a tremendous explosion from the camp. When they got back with the cannon and carts they found that their hard-won supply of powder and arms was completely destroyed. Conal ran about the camp like a madman demanding to know what had caused the explosion, raging at the stupid destruction, but unable to discover how it had happened.

Michael grabbed and held him. 'Take a hold of yourself, man!' he shouted. 'Conal, will you listen to me! Take a hold of yourself!'

'Fools, fools, fools!' Conal yelled. 'We have an army of fools.'

'Right,' said Michael, shaking him. 'You're right. Fools. Them and us.'

'Why us? Didn't we collect all that stuff?'

'Oh, we did, surely. And then what? We went charging off like the rest. We should have left a guard on it.'

Conal stood rigid and stared at him and again he felt a foreboding chill. From the moment he had heard of the cannon his determination to get them had driven all other thoughts from his mind. And once again he had failed in leadership.

Michael clapped him on the shoulder. 'Ach, who knows what caused it? Maybe a thousand men could not have stopped it happening. Come on. We'd do well to sleep.'

But there was to be little sleep, because at that moment there were shouts from the men who were watching the Wexford road and three horsemen galloped into the camp. They were led to where Father John was trying to settle down, and Conal and Michael followed.

The men, who had been released from gaol, brought a message that the town would surrender to the rebels on condition that the lives of the inhabitants were spared. To emphasise this, they also brought a letter from Mr Bagenal Harvey, one of the friendly magistrates who had been imprisoned.

I have been treated in prison with all possible humanity and am now at liberty. I have procured the liberty of all the prisoners. If you pretend to Christian Charity, do not massacre, or burn the property of the inhabitants and spare

your prisoners' lives.
                              B.B. Harvey
                              Wednesday, 30th May, 1798

There was wild excitement amongst the crowd
thronging round Father John, with everyone asking
questions or shouting suggestions. The messengers told
them that the majority of the townspeople were on the
side of the rebels. The merchants, concerned only that
their property should not be destroyed, had begged the
commander, Colonel Maxwell, not to defend the town.
But, although he had at first rejected their plea, many of
the troops had deserted and Maxwell was preparing to
evacuate the remainder.

Conal, after much effort, reached Father John's side.

'We must have all the stores of arms and powder,
Father. Tell them that.'

So the messengers were sent back to say that they
would agree to the terms on condition that the arms,
ammunition and powder of the garrison were surrendered.

Conal lay all night beside the cannon; but he slept little.
All rose early for the advance on Wexford. He wanted to
take the cannon, but was forced to give way to Michael's
argument that, until they found somebody skilled with
artillery, the cannon were useless; and that, further, they
needed the carts empty to carry the arms of the garrison.
Reluctantly, he left them with men detailed to guard
them.

When they arrived near the outskirts of the town they
were halted by the sight of a barricade ahead of them.
Everything was quiet and they could not see if there were
men behind the obstruction.

'Didn't I tell you we needed the cannon?' said Conal.
'Two good shots would have blasted that to hell.'

'If we knew how to use the yoke,' said Michael.

'Dammit, man, we could have tried it. There cannot be
much to learn.'

He ran to Father John. 'Will I go back for the cannon,

340

Father?'

Even as he asked, there was a shout from a man who had climbed a tree, 'They're gone. There's ne'er a one of them behind that thing!'

There was an instant's silence, then a triumphal yell and the whole horde raced down the road, across the barricade and into the town. Conal sped with them, calling for Michael and the other men to get to the barracks before some fool destroyed the ammunition. He raced on, calling to ask where the barracks was, then, turning a corner, he saw it with men racing through the open archway. These men, however, were only concerned to haul down the Union Jack and to hoist a green flag in its place.

Conal and his men ran about searching for the armoury. They found it, its door wide open displaying the empty interior. He could not believe it. He had been certain that they would have a great store of munitions which would, at last, put them on equal terms with the enemy. But they searched the entire place and found nothing.

In the meantime, the rest of Father John's force had discovered that not only had the military left at midnight on the previous night, retreating by the sea road to Duncannon, but another body of rebels, who had come down the eastern bank of the Slaney, were already in the town, having crossed by the bridge. They had gone first to the prison and had released Bagenal Harvey, who had not been freed as the magistrates had promised, and had insisted that he should become their commander.

Father John's men, furious at the manner in which they had been deceived, were restrained only with difficulty from setting fire to the town. But they were boisterously welcomed by the townspeople who had decorated their houses with green boughs and makeshift green flags and who now gave out all that they had to eat and drink. And the loudest in their welcome were those who had deserted from the Yeomanry, burnt their uniforms and put on civilian dress.

341

There were still gangs of men who scavenged for loot, attacking any house which refused them entrance. Yet, for the most part, they were quieter than had been feared.

Conal and his men frantically searched the entire place but found only three barrels and some odd casks of gunpowder – not one hundredth part of what was needed.

Outside the harbour lay a number of ships crowded with gentry who had fled. Many belonged to a man named Dixon, a tavern and billiards-room owner on the quay. He had extorted large sums in payment for supposed passages to England, but had deliberately delayed the sailing. When the fugitives saw the green flag hoisted over the barracks, they begged the captains to set sail; but, to their horror, the green flag was hoisted to every masthead and parties of rebels went out in boats and brought ashore every man and all the arms and ammunition.

Conal and his men immediately carried off these latter to add to their small store in the barracks. The prisoners, in the meantime, were examined by the horde of rebels on the quay. Many, recognised as their earlier persecutors, were killed immediately. Those who were known to be sympathetic were given the opportunity to join them, and many did. The rest were crowded into the prison or on to a rotting hulk in the harbour.

After three days the rebels were persuaded to move out of the town, some to the permanent camp which had been established at Three Rocks, others to a new camp on the Windmill Hills. Conal, Michael and an increased number of men were left in the town to supply the armies with food, whiskey, leather and, hopefully, arms and ammunition. They found a valuable source of supplies by sending out four oyster boats, each holding twenty-five armed men, to waylay ships bound for Dublin. But, although they obtained large supplies of provisions, they brought back only a few unmounted ships' cannon and a little ammunition.

In the camps some degree of order was gradually established, and there was complete agreement that they should carry the rebellion to the rest of Ireland.

One group, led by a Father Kearns, was ordered to march on Newtownbarry, sweep all opposition from the north of the county and rouse the counties of Carlow and Kildare so as to threaten Dublin from the west. Another, under Father John, was to march through Gorey and Arklow to attack Dublin from the south. The third, under Harvey, was to take New Ross, cross into Kilkenny and rouse the southern and western counties. At Father John's request, but reluctantly, Conal went with this group to collect the contents of the New Ross armoury.

So three large groups of men set out. They could not be called armies. They were simply huge assemblies of individuals with pikes on their shoulders, with scarcely one firearm between every hundred and even then with only enough powder and ball for a few shots. But they marched joyfully, singing, with heads high, every man determined to be in the forefront when they met their persecutors. And the only unifying factors were a desire for revenge and the certainty that they would bring freedom to Ireland at long last.

Unknown to them, outbreaks had taken place in other parts of Ireland, although on a smaller and less successful scale. Camden, the Viceroy, sent a plea to England for reinforcements. In the meantime, however, he enrolled fresh regiments of militia from amongst the Dublin loyalists and gave them the task of defending the city, thus releasing a part of the garrison troops. These he sent in three groups to deal with the Wexford insurgents. One group was sent to Arklow, one to Newtownbarry and the other to Carnew, which lies between those two places. Their orders were that, having reached these towns, they were to advance towards Wexford, hopefully driving the rebels before them.

The soldiers arrived in Newtownbarry only a few hours before a large force of rebels arrived from the south. The commanding officer ordered his troops to retreat northwards but halted them after about a mile on hearing the sounds of gunfire from the town. The rebels, thinking the town was theirs, had poured into it, cramming the main street; but, in the stone houses, loyalists, well-equipped with guns and ammunition and safe from attack by the pikemen, fired continuously into the dense crowds causing appalling slaughter. Hampered once again by their very numbers and by the bodies of their fallen companions, their pikes useless, there was complete confusion amongst the rebels. Whilst many tried to force their way back against the pressure of the still larger number trying to force their way into the town, others tried to advance through the town, only to be met by the soldiery who had been reformed and who now advanced steadily, pouring volley after volley into the solid mass of bodies. At last the rebels outside gave way and those inside turned and fled. The Yeomanry dragoons were then loosed on them to cut them down with their sabres as they streamed out over the countryside in their flight back to Vinegar Hill.

The other two military forces reached Arklow and Carnew at the same time, and the first then advanced to Gorey.

In London, Mr Pitt, the Prime Minister, having decided that the state of Ireland was now such that he could claim that the Irish Parliament was incapable of governing, and so should be abolished, despatched to Ireland an army consisting mainly of German mercenaries from Hesse.

In the meantime, Father John Murphy, with twenty thousand men and the cannon and ammunition which Conal had collected, but without Conal himself, had encamped on Carrigrua Hill between Gorey and Ferns. There he had learned of the arrival of the military at Gorey and that this force had split and was now advancing on him by two separate routes. He immediately sent a large body of men, equipped with all the firearms he could muster, to ambush the soldiers who were advancing by the main road from Gorey to Ferns.

The narrow road, bordered by hedges and wooded enclosures thick with foliage, was filled with a solid mass of marching soldiers. Suddenly, at a narrow pass, they found the road blocked and at once intense musket-fire was poured into their packed ranks from both sides. The soldiers, unable to advance or to penetrate the thick hedge, struggled to retreat, only to meet another barricade and a hail of bullets. After three-quarters of an hour of desperate struggle, during which more than half their number was killed, the remnants managed to force their way into the fields. Back to Gorey they raced, pursued by the rebels who were highly amused to see their enemies trying, in mid-flight, to turn their highly coloured uniform coats inside out.

Even when they reached Gorey the soldiers were still not safe but had to run the gauntlet of other rebels who had entered the town and who now fired on them from the houses. The few survivors managed finally to struggle back to Arklow.

The other half of the Government forces was commanded by General Loftus. From across the fields he heard the sounds of the battle at the ambush, but, as he was unable to take his artillery across country, he continued by a long, circuitous route only to find the narrow pass filled with dead soldiers. He then retreated to Gorey. A large rebel force, however, had positioned themselves with their artillery on Gorey Hill overlooking the town and from where they fired down on Loftus. Only the inexperience of the rebel gunners saved the military. They retreated to Carnew, joining the forces there, and then, although twelve hundred strong, they retreated through the mountains to County Carlow, leaving Father John's force with a clear road to Arklow and so, hopefully, to Dublin.

At the same time the third force, under Bagenal Harvey, marched westward towards New Ross and encamped on Carrickbyrne Hill about nine miles from the town. From there foraging parties sent out into the

345

surrounding countryside brought back a variety of supplies, some prisoners, but very little powder. The prisoners were placed in a barn at a place called Scullabogue at the foot of the hill and men were left to guard them.

On 3 June, Harvey's army marched to Corbet Hill which overlooked New Ross and the broad River Barrow. The town was surrounded by a wall which had once defied Cromwell's cannon and in the wall were four gates – two facing the river and two at the top end of the town.

Conal's disappointment at being separated from Father John's force and his cannon had been forgotten in his confidence in Bagenal Harvey. The same confidence had been inspired in the whole army. As he looked down on the little town a mile away, Conal was certain that this time everything would go right. They would attack the gate which he could see, whilst at the same time two other sections of their forces would attack from two different directions.

At three o'clock on the morning of 4 June, with a faint misty light in the sky behind them and swathes of fog curling round the town below, the rebels rose and prepared to attack. The soldiers lined up before the gate could not see the hill through the mist, but eerily out of the nothingness the high-pitched battle-cry floated down to them in welling waves of sound. Then, ghostlike at first, but gradually solidifying, they saw the enormous mass of men steadily advancing. They marched slowly – barony by barony, parish by parish under their local leaders. At a musket-shot from the military they halted and vested priests carrying crucifixes moved up and down the lines. Every man knelt and at the head of every column Mass was said.

For half an hour the astonished and worried soldiers watched the vast multitude, heard the thin, high voices of the priests and the tremendous rumble of the responses.

Harvey had counted on the impression which his numbers would make. When Mass was over, the stamping of feet, clearing of throats and clattering of arms as thousands of men rose to their feet so suddenly shattered the silence that the soldiers involuntarily started back. Again there was silence. Harvey kept it so for agonising minutes. Then out from the rebel ranks cantered a rider carrying a flag of truce and a demand that the town should be surrendered to avoid bloodshed and destruction.

He had barely covered half the distance when a musket cracked. The rider lurched and fell from the saddle still clutching his white flag.

The rebels, whom Harvey had so assiduously disciplined, stood aghast for an eternal second. A man roared in agonised anger. Thousands of voices echoed him and the whole mass torrented down the hill. Mounted officers galloped amongst them, shouting orders to halt, but all in vain. Nothing could stop that mad rush.

Harvey's other two divisions had not yet reached their positions when they heard yells and firing and all the tumult of conflict. They stopped irresolute for a moment, then broke and fled back carrying news of a great defeat at New Ross.

Neither the solid blasts of musketry nor the devastating slash of grape-shot could halt the surge of the frantic rebels of the main force. They yelled and struggled against each other in their mad lust to thrust their pikes into the bodies of the soldiers. The military were swept back through the gate and retreated down the main street. A regiment of Dragoons charged the rebels, who greeted them with delight, hooking them from their saddles, piking them before they reached the ground. Before their fury the Dragoons broke and fled. The rebels captured the gun before the gate, but, lacking artillerymen, were unable to use it.

Another gun had been set up further down the street and the soldiers, firing steadily, retreated behind it. Immediately it belched grape-shot. Hundreds fell. An entire column was annihilated.

This checked the onrush and gave the soldiers a moment to rally. Then the rebels charged again, setting fire to the houses on either side. Through the smoke and flame they surged, over the dead bodies and the blood-slimed cobbles, meeting the blasts of shot and falling as those before them had fallen. And still those behind them pressed onward between the roaring flames which singed the hair and blistered the arms and cheeks. A looter, trapped on the upper floor of a blazing house, appeared momentarily at the window, a screaming torch, then disappeared as the floor collapsed beneath him.

Nearer and nearer they fought towards that murderous gun, until at last one wild, ragged fellow leaped forward and thrust his hat into the smoking mouth of it.

'Come on, boys!' he yelled jubilantly. 'Her mouth is stopped!'

The next instant he was spattered in the faces of his followers. But the next wave swept over the gun, ripping the gun-crew to tatters.

Back to a third gun the soldiers retreated and the carnage was renewed. But eventually, when, at terrible cost, the rebels had captured four guns, the soldiers were driven part down to the river and over the bridge, part into the market-place where the stone buildings became a fortress which the rebels could neither burn nor penetrate. But it was also a prison in which the soldiers could be starved into submission.

New Ross was won!

The cheers of the victorious could be heard ringing out for miles. Then victory had to be celebrated. Houses and taverns were looted of whiskey, wine and ale. The forces were hopelessly jumbled. The officers ran frantically about seeking their own men, for the rest would not obey their orders. The revellers laughed at their anxiety. Ross was won and the way lay open into the whole of the south. It was a time to rest and rejoice and celebrate. In a very short time the rebel army was a horde of drunken roisterers who staggered singing through the town or flopped in corners to sleep off their excess.

All this could be seen by the soldiers. Those who had been driven over the bridge re-formed, waited for the

348

drink to take full effect, then charged with fixed bayonets back into the town, where they were joined by their comrades from the market place. Through the streets they ran, sticking every drunken rebel as well as many townspeople who had ventured out. All who could still run did so. The guns were recaptured and were soon slaughtering the fleeing drunkards. In wild disorder they scrambled out through the gate. In the open some officers tried to rally them, and a few tried to make a stand where they had first stood that morning, but the soldiers charged and broke them and they fled up the hill.

The battle had lasted eleven hours from four o'clock in the morning until three in the afternoon. By that time more than two thousand rebel bodies sprawled in the streets or before the town; and the sweet smell of blood rose into the hot air of the afternoon.

In the moonlight the walled town of New Ross was a fairy citadel of ebony and silver with the shimmering river gliding by. Silence and peace lay over it and over the surrounding hills. Most silent and peaceful were the scattered huddles, black against the dew-glittering grass, on the open ground before the gate.

Conal moaned and opened his eyes. His face was crushed against the wet grass by some weight which lay on him. He struggled free and sat up. He explored his body with fearful fingers and, first with surprise, then relief discovered that his only injury was a large lump on the back of his head. Turning he saw that the weight which had lain on him was the body of a young man. He realised that the eyes were open, that they were pleading and that the lips were moving. He bent over him. He was a boy no more than fifteen years old.

'My leg,' he whispered.

Conal saw a leg lying some yards away.

'What do you want?' he asked.

'My leg.'

Conal stood unsteadily, crossed to the leg and picked it up, surprised to find it so heavy. He placed it beside the boy and received such a smile of gratitude that pity for the boy squeezed his heart with actual, physical pain.

'Will I get better?' the lad pleaded.

'Sure, why not? You're a fine, healthy lad.'

The boy smiled gratefully. His eyes closed and his face settled into youthful roundness. Conal brushed back a lock of hair. There was no flicker from the face. He stared into it, then felt for the heartbeat. The boy was dead. For him the deaths of all were in the death of this unknown boy, and the grief he felt was for all he had seen die in these few days of rebellion. He could not bury them all, but he buried them symbolically in the grave he scraped with the head of a broken pike and into which he carefully laid the young body with the leg precisely in place.

Then he knelt and prayed for the lad and for all who had died. Suddenly he realised that he had been kneeling for a long time, that his prayers had strayed to thoughts of himself and his own position, to Nuala and his longing for her, and to the question of their future together. Their quarrel seemed so stupid now. He found it impossible to understand why he had insulted her when she had thought only of how to solve their problems. But his greatest regret was that he had left without trying to see her, to apologise, to say goodbye and to promise to return to her. Astonishingly, he realised, when he had led the rebels to get the arms he had not even thought of her. She would have been in danger from soldiery and rebels alike. She might not even be there now. She could be dead.

His anxiety brought him to his feet. He set out to find the rebel army on Carrickbyrne.

It was nearly three hours later that he arrived at Scullabogue. In the quiet moonlight he passed the barn in which many people had been imprisoned. Some vague peculiarity about it drew him closer. A sickening smell, mingled with the smell of burnt timber, puzzled him until, under the tangle of charred wood, he saw the roasted bodies of men, women and children, so closely packed that even in death they were still standing.

Into the barn, thirty-four feet long and fifteen feet wide, had been crammed one hundred and eighty-four persons, whilst there were thirty or forty others in the nearby house. Some of those who had deserted at the beginning of the attack on Ross had raced back shouting of a great defeat and that they brought orders for all the prisoners to be killed as they might be dangerous. The men were brought from the house and shot. But whilst this was being done a group of deserters barred the door of the barn and thrust burning faggots into the thatch. Mercifully, the majority of the prisoners must have quickly suffocated.

Conal staggered away from the horror as he had done from the horror in Paris and, as then, he was physically sick. He cleansed himself in a stream, then lay for the remainder of the night in thick grass. But not to sleep. Until now he had welcomed every fight. He had killed, thrusting home his pike joyfully, revelling in the screams of his enemies, feeling that he was repaying some of the injustice and that he was helping to bring justice and peace nearer. Now he recognised sickeningly that cruelty and horror were not confined to the enemy, but lay dormant in every man, himself included, waiting only the opportunity to leap out in ravening bestiality. True, the enemy had set the example, but what kind of victory was won when the victors practised the very cruelties against which they had fought! Injustice and cruelty bred injustice and cruelty as surely as lice bred lice.

He determined then that he would take no further part, that he would go back, find Nuala and somehow salvage what they could to build a life for themselves amidst the wreckage.

But when, at dawn, he went into the rebel camp on the hill he found he could not leave. Sickened by the desertion of part of his forces and by the sheer stupidity of the rest, Harvey had returned to Carrickbyrne to be confronted by the horror of Scullabogue. He now saw that his efforts to discipline the force had been far too gentle. In fierce anger he determined to enforce discipline. He issued a proclamation promising death to all deserters, to anybody killing prisoners, to any officers who left their corps, to any man refusing to obey orders, to any man leaving quarters without permission and to all who plundered or burned houses.

He then moved his forces to the hill of Slievecoilte, where they had to remain inactive because of the acute shortage of powder.

A short time later they received news that Father John Kearns with a force of four thousand had been defeated at Newtownbarry, and that Father John Murphy himself had been defeated with heavy losses at Arklow and had been forced to retreat to Vinegar Hill.

This bad news, coupled with their inactivity and the new, galling discipline further excited the unrest in the camp. The grumbling grew louder. Harvey was blamed for all their misfortunes, including the defeat at Ross. So widespread did the discontent become that Harvey, realising that his command was purely nominal, resigned and went back to Wexford.

His departure was the signal for rejoicing throughout the camp. They cheered his successor, Father Phillip Roche, not only then but for days later whenever they saw him. He was a great, boisterous man, much more to their taste. Now, they told each other, they would get on with the rebellion. They were slow to learn that they had lost a leader and gained nothing.

Simply to give them something to do, Father Roche moved camp to Lacken Hill, overlooking Ross, and the men concluded that they were preparing for a new assault which they would win. But Father Roche knew that without powder any assault would be suicidal; and he did not know where to get powder.

Meanwhile the military were content to wait for reinforcements.

One morning the camp was wakened with the alarm that a large enemy force had issued from New Ross and, thanks to their unwatchful sentries, had almost surrounded them. Father Roche ordered the pikemen to

352

march to Wexford. To guard their rear, he gathered all his horsemen, equipped them with banners and scattered them to give the impression to the distant soldiers that they were a huge force and so deter attack.

But the soldiers had no intention of attacking. Their orders were to drive the rebels in towards Wexford, just as was being done in other parts of the county. The military, reinforced by nearly thirty thousand regular troops, were beginning to tighten the circle.

Father Roche, well pleased with the apparent success of his plan, followed after the footmen and camped with them at Three Rocks, only to learn that armies were advancing on them from all directions: from New Ross, from Duncannon, down both sides of the River Slaney, from Carnew and southwards by the coast road. There was only one chance – to stop the Duncannon force, sweep round behind the body from New Ross and seize the town in their absence.

In frantic haste he galloped to Wexford and demanded supplies from the commissars who had taken over from Conal's men, ordering them to be brought to Three Rocks by the following morning. But the commissars, now mainly the scum who had joined the rebels for the pickings, had no supplies and they disappeared with the loot they had accumulated.

So, on the morning of 20 June, Father Roche marched to meet and fight the Duncannon force with pikes. They met near Foulkesmill and, after a long and bloody battle, the rebels were forced to retreat to Vinegar Hill, where Father John was with all his forces and which now became the centre of the military's tightening circle.

At dawn on 21 June the soldiers advanced on Vinegar Hill. They approached from the north, the west and the east and formed up round it. Only the road to Wexford lay open. Beyond that the way was blocked by armies and by the sea.

General Johnstone attacked Enniscorthy at five o'clock in the morning. In spite of their lack of powder and the tremendous fire from the cannon and muskets of their enemies, the rebels gave the fiercest resistance. But slaughter and pressure drove them steadily back until, by seven o'clock, they had been driven out of the town, over the bridge and on to the slopes of Vinegar Hill where the main mass of the rebels were assembled.

Sixteen thousand of them stood on the open brow of the hill. They had thirteen cannon of various types, but only two charges for each. About a third were equipped with firearms, but with scarcely enough powder to give them two shots each. The rest stood with their pikes and waited to be butchered.

The soldiers were in no hurry. They set up their cannon and systematically pounded the exposed mass of men with balls and bombshells. On and on went the carnage. Those who remained alive and unhurt stood helpless amongst the mutilated dead and the moaning, screaming and squirming wounded, gripping their pikes, cursing their impotence, lusting for the chance to come to close quarters with their enemies.

At last the bombardment ended. For long moments there was unbelievable quiet. Then, through the dispersing smoke, the soldiers could be seen marching to the foot of the hill – line upon line of them, like the waves of the rising tide. A long shout of relief, fury and delight rose from the standing rebels. Down the hill they charged, ignoring the flesh on which they slipped and stumbled, ravening for vengeance. For three hours the hand-to-hand battle raged up and down the hill until there was scarcely a place that was not covered by a fallen man. But every fallen soldier was replaced and at last the exhausted rebels were driven up and over the top of the hill until they broke and fled down the southern slope towards Wexford, to be pursued and cut down by the cavalry.

FIFTY-SEVEN

Away off the main routes, as they were, Nuala and her mother knew nothing of the armies advancing on Enniscorthy. One day, however, she heard a low thudding and rumbling coming from the direction of the town. At first she took it for thunder, but the summer skies were clear. With shock came the realisation that it must be artillery. Anxiety flared. There had been nothing like this before. It could only mean a great battle – a battle in which Conal was engaged – and every thud was a menace to his life.

It lasted many hours, then abruptly ceased. For an endless time she waited for it to recommence, becoming paradoxically more anxious when it did not. When she could bear the suspense no longer, she simply said to her mother, 'I am going to find out what has happened.' Ignoring all Georgina's protests, she set out for Enniscorthy.

It was evening when she started, but she walked on through the night, losing her way more than once, and straying much too far east; but it was thus she missed the pickets. In the early dawn she approached the hill from the south-east and she heard a peculiar high-pitched sound, a blood-chilling sound, the sound of a multitude of women wailing for their dead.

As she began to climb the easy, southern slope the sky to her right showed pale, flowed imperceptibly into faintest green, deepened and spread, strengthened to bars of yellow which tinged to orange, then rioted in slashes of pinks and reds. The whole eastern sky blazed with colour and every bird burst forth in song to welcome the new-born sun as it leaped from the sea and flung wide arms to embrace the dew-starred morning.

And to reveal a sight, commonplace in Ireland: Irish

women, keening their sorrow, as they searched the battlefield for their butchered men.

She reached the summit near the windmill and looked down. A carpet of horror clothed the slope. Trampled fields and gardens were almost obliterated by tattered flesh.

'There now. She's opening her eyes.'

Nuala stared dazedly at the woman who held her, then up at the concerned faces around.

'Rest, quiet for a minute girl, dear.'

'Conal!' she sat up abruptly. 'I must find Conal!'

She struggled to her feet, swaying for a moment and hanging on to the woman. She turned her head slowly and looked at her – a girl no older than herself, her face streaked with tears. She looked her anguish and the girl looked back in silent pity and gestured helplessly at all their grieving sisters.

'No!' Nuala shouted. 'No! Dear God, no! Conal!'

She ran, but for no more than three steps, for it was impossible to run where there was no space for her feet. She stopped, closed her eyes tightly and clenched her fists, fighting for calmness. Then she followed the example of the others and began a methodical search. She threaded through bloody bodies and limbs, through heaps of unrecognisable meat, striving not to walk on mangled flesh, waving her hands constantly to clear away the clouds of bloated flies. Dead faces, hundreds of dead faces, and more and more hundreds until it seemed as if the whole world was populated by dead faces. Hour after hour she searched, back and forth across the hill, gradually working her way down, then returning and finally reaching the top, convinced that she had looked at every face and, thankfully, that Conal's was not amongst them.

She had learned unconsciously from the talk of the other searching women that many had fled to Wexford. Curiously calm, she sat on a rock on the southern slope and rested in numbness, staring blindly at the beauty of the river as it slid, green and glassy under the lovely trees. Then she trudged down with many other women examining the corpses on the hillside and the more numerous wounded and dead in the ditches of the road. On and on, hour after hour in the dust and heat and lazy buzzing of the satiated flies, unconscious of the many soldiers, not realising the protective ugliness of her grief, until at last Wexford was reached. And her search went on through streets and lanes for days.

But she did not find him – ever.